When Tigers Attack

Copyright © 2012 Nicola A Hare, All Rights Reserved

Published by
Impressions Publishing
Tel: 01487 843311
www.printandpublish.co.uk

All rights reserved.

No part of this book may be reproduced in any form by photocopying or any electronic or mechanical means, including information storage or retrieval systems, without permissions in writing from both the copyright owner and the publisher of the book.

First Edition published 2012
© Nicola A Hare 2012

Printed and bound in Great Britain
Impressions Print And Publish

A catalogue record for this book
is available from The British Library
ISBN 978-1-908374-29-5

Nicola A Hare

For Erin, Evie, and Josie

PROLOGUE

I never used to believe in fate. Fate was a romantic's favourite word. Romantics thanked fate when they fell in love, claiming '*it was meant to be*'. Then they used it to justify why it all went wrong with, '*it wasn't meant to be*'. Fate was a scapegoat for those evading responsibility, a convenient reason for one's failures in life.
Advocates of 'everything happens for a reason' were usually those sitting on the sidelines watching opportunity pass them by. Everything happens for a reason? Everything happens for a reason alright, it happens because of something you have done or because of something you haven't. That's what I used to say.
I was wrong.
As I sit overlooking the silhouetted shore waiting for the sun to rise, I look back and I know.
Everything does happen for a reason.
Fate plays a part in everybody's life.

Chapter 1

Colombo, Sri Lanka

"**Miss Davies,** you may go, you have bill here, and medication, and taxi is waiting," the tiny dark nurse said in broken English. She handed me four or five paper bags all containing different tablets I should take for my various ailments. As I left the ward the nurse added, "You are lucky, very lucky."
I had been working in Colombo when I contracted pyelonephritis followed consecutively by gastroenteritis or, in layman's terms, a kidney infection followed by perpetual vomiting and diarrhoea. I had been in hospital for what seemed like an eternity and now I was finally free to rejoin the big, wide world outside. I would have been bouncing off the walls with excitement at leaving if I had the energy. Before I fell ill out here my bosses back home had taken it upon themselves, without consulting me, to book me on a flight back to England. Being none too happy about this, you could say I was lucky to have been hospitalised and deemed medically unfit to fly. It certainly put an end to their plans to bring me home. I desperately wanted to finish the work assignment I'd been sweating blood over and I also strongly disagreed with their logic. There had been a terrorist attack, it happened just before I got ill. The American Embassy advised all their citizens to leave Sri Lanka due to 'present circumstances'. 'Present circumstances' were that terrorists had bombed the airport turning threat into reality. England followed America's lead soon after.
Now if they had told me to leave *before* the raid because an attack was imminent then, yes, I would have been one of the first in line to buy a ticket out of here. But why leave now? It's happened, if anything now is the safest time to be here.
My cynical head surmised my boss's boss, Leon, was worried my family would sue him if anything should happen to me. My

friends and family were worried sick and wanted me home, yet apart from an increase in media attention nothing had really changed here. I could understand their anxieties completely after watching some of the coverage. The media had portrayed the entire country as a war zone. I tried to imagine sitting in my living room watching the six o'clock news, dinner on lap, seeing the real-time video footage of shootings, bombings and aeroplane wrecks. I would be worried too if I had a family member out there. It is different though when you are actually there. You gain a better sense of perspective. You see people carry on with their every day lives just as you get on with yours, all relatively unaffected. I knew that the whole time the media regurgitated one-off scenes of death and destruction there was no chance of getting my way in this battle. Panic-stricken tourists made their fretful calls home and all consoled one another throughout their ordeal. It sounds callous now but I really could not fathom at the time what their 'ordeal' was. None of them had been affected directly. None of them had been anywhere near it. Finding sympathy for people who had to leave their luxury hotel to be shipped out to the Maldives was difficult when I'd seen families' lives destroyed then watched them pick up the pieces with the kind of inner strength I hope I never have to find. Perhaps if I had been a holidaymaker and not researching for an awareness campaign to improve people's lives I would have better understood.

America downsized their travel warnings to 'essential business travel only' and England followed suit, giving me a loophole to get my own way with my bosses and remain in Colombo.

Knowing I had an uphill struggle and lots of convincing to do, I waited until I was a little stronger before calling my friend and immediate boss, Victor. It was time to test the powers of my persuasion.

"Victor," I said in a pseudo-strong assertive manner when actually I was shaking on the end of the phone. "I am halfway through something here. If you call me home now you will ruin everything I have worked for, making the whole damn project worthless. It'll

be a waste of my time and of Leon's money. I'm sure neither of us wants to waste Leon's money, do we Victor? I'm following a family at the moment; they have agreed to be interviewed on film if we end up sending a team here. We are getting on really well, well we were until I was..."
Steer clear of the word hospital Rachael, it will only invoke emotion about your well-being.
"...interrupted. They are very open with me and, Soma, the daughter, is due to give birth any day now and I think that it would be a good idea, you know, to err, follow and err..."
My big impressive speech lost momentum and I was rapidly losing the ability to string a sentence together. "Err, well the stress of having a baby anyway is, and out here, well..."
"Running out of steam are we Rachael?" Victor interrupted, triumph oozing through his tone. I realised he knew I would hang myself having been given enough rope. "Look Rachael, the advice was..."
"Exactly Victor, the advice *was* to leave and now it isn't. Besides I could fly home tomorrow and get hit by a bus on the way to work. Nowhere is a hundred per cent safe you know, in fact statistically speaking I am safer here than in my own home. Did you know most accidents actually occur...?"
"Yes, yes, in the home, I know, but when you are at home you still use an element of common sense do you not? You wouldn't stick a knife in the toaster would you?"
"Not without unplugging it."
"Similarly, you wouldn't stay in a country that is at war with itself."
Victor always sounded like a children's storyteller when he spoke in his kind, soft voice full of the wisdom he had collated over the years yet still patient and unpatronising – most of the time. He emphasised his main words well, which made him both interesting to listen to and passively intimidating to argue with.
"Victor, please? The country has been at war with itself for over twenty years. The threat was here before I came. The attacks have happened, past tense, the uselessly late warnings have been

retracted. I reckon it's probably the safest time to be here. Lightning doesn't strike twice now does it?"

"Icarus was not aware he was flying too close to the sun until he fell back down to earth."

Oh, I did not mean to start that game. It was the game of using wise adages to win an argument. A safe verbal war Victor and I often ended up in. Needless to say, Victor knew more than me and usually came out the winner. Poor Victor, he had no idea what he was taking on when he took me under his wing. Or maybe he did, he deals with me very well.

"The mind is like a parachute, it only functions when it's open."

"Rachael, as true as that may be, it hardly counter argues my proverb now does it?"

"I'm talking about *you* Victor! Open your mind up to the possibility of me staying just for a second. I'm well. I'm happy to remain here. I can really do some good if you let me. Just trust me to make this judgement call. Please?"

"Rachael, the advice…"

"The advice is too late in coming. The horse has well and truly bolted on this one Vic. You know if I felt at all unsafe I would have put my arse on a plane before you could say… um… 'Rachael get your ass on a plane'."

There was a long pause. I tried to remember if staying meant that much to me or if I just wanted to win the argument. Either way I knew I had tapped into the part of Victor that wished he was as spontaneous as me and most young people today.

Victor sighed in defeat.

"Don't make me regret this Rachael."

"Phew, and to think I nearly went with 'nothing ventured nothing gained'. Seriously though, thank you, thank you so much! You won't regret it Victor, I promise. You're not angry with me are you?"

"No, I'm not angry. Just go away and prove to me I have made the right decision. Don't make me have to go out there and search for a missing employee, you know how I hate to fly these days."

"Well, if you do have to at least you'll get pensioner rates," I joked, testing the water.

"Watch out you, I can always change my mind."

The water was fine.

Victor and I had many, many discussions or debates, however you want to look at it. This may give the impression we were argumentative or that we clashed somehow. It was actually quite the opposite. I trusted Victor's opinion so implicitly that I could test my boundaries through him. I could push and push with an idea that I was unsure of knowing that Victor would not back down from his point of view if he really didn't approve. This gave me free reign with my imagination to explore what I thought, how I felt, what was grandiose and what was achievable. Victor had permeable lines that I could penetrate if I tried but he also had a solid line that no matter how hard I tried I could not break through. It is because of this line that I trusted his advice and accepted it as truth, after a damn good attempt at changing it that is. He has become so important to me that I can barely remember life before him.

"Look, thank you Victor. Not just for this but for helping me to get here despite the bad feeling towards me from the rest of the office."

"Rachael, it was not the whole office, it is just those who share your poise and ambition. You are not the only one who strives to get what they want. There may be one or two who are more finely attuned to the politics game than you perhaps."

"You mean they don't care who they stab in the back to get what they want more like. They make allies of the rest of the office by bad mouthing me. It's like I said, I have a lot to thank you for."

"You should be thanking yourself, not me."

"Yeah, but it's true. I wouldn't be doing this at all if it wasn't for you."

"You are right. You would most probably be a qualified OT if it wasn't for me and would, therefore, not be here at all."

"That's all in the past now Victor and it was hardly your fault. You could have believed Doctor Clifton like the rest of the world did but you believed me."

I paused as I pictured his great-niece in my mind's eye.
"I still think about Maria you know. She could be quite funny at times, in her own way."
"That she could, she had her moments. You did a tremendously brave thing there, standing up to all those bigwigs."
"Hmm," I sighed, not wishing to think about that experience, not even for a minute.
"I had faith in you then and I have faith in you now. But I do not like this Rachael."
"I won't let you down Victor, I give you my word."
We spoke until Leon called Victor on his other line. We covered everything from what it was like to be in a foreign hospital to his wife's up and coming ingrown toenail operation, at which point we were interrupted. As far as timing goes, that was spot on. I was so grateful to have spoken to Victor, to the point of being desperate. I hadn't spoken to a soul from back home for over two weeks and was beginning to feel isolated. I could talk to him more openly than I could to my friends and parents in times like these. My friends wanted to hear about beaches, bars and men, all of which I had nothing much to comment on. My mum and step-dad were still uncomfortable with the places I was going to, so anything more than a quick hello, how are you, I'm still alive, became an uncomfortable medley of small talk and silence. My mum worked as a nurse in A&E before they moved away. I think her job made her panic over my safety more than your average mother and as a result, I kept my fears, problems and imminent challenges from her. The last thing I needed was her worries to rub off on me while I was trying to be strong. Paradoxically, my biological father didn't even know I worked in developing countries. The contact we kept was sporadic to say the least. I could tell Victor how things really were, how I really felt.
Victor looked out for me on home turf as well as on the away pitch. He tried to look after my love life too once, although not to much avail. The second I split from my on- off -ex Derren, I was invited for dinner with Victor and his wife. There was nothing unusual there, or so I thought. He failed to tell me about the other

guests attending that night. They were Mick and Jane, friends of Victor's wife from the over-50 keep fit club, and their twenty-eight-year-old son, complete with a law degree. Did I mention he was single? Well Victor did, more than once. I don't know who was more embarrassed, me or Mr Law-Degree, or Matthew as he would prefer to be called. After a few glasses of wine the atmosphere was more or less forgotten and we had a good time. Matthew was very pleasant and so were the phone calls that followed but I didn't once honour any dates we arranged on the phone.

My friend Laura was quick to pick up on the 'waste not, want not' philosophy there and a date between her and Matthew was arranged. The end result was disastrous. Laura said he would make a great husband – for her mother and Matthew said he thought he had strolled unwittingly into a shampoo advert, the way she swished her hair about and ruffled it every seven minutes. He joked that all that was missing was the camera crew. I apologised to both and remained friends with both. The only person to get their nose out of joint was Victor. He found out about Matthew's date with my friend and told me I was ungrateful, that I was no better than those people who give away their unwanted Christmas presents. I told him to stop sending me gift-wrapped men.

The truth was I was far from ready to meet anybody new at that point in my life. I was still moping about over Derren Sediki. Derren was half Italian, from his father's side, but was actually as English as they came. He had never met his father and I think this is why he despised his Italian roots. I guess the absent father was something we both had in common. Our relationship was always on again, off again, right from day dot. We finally ground to a halt soon after Derren got too friendly with our friend's new girlfriend's friend Tanya. I took him back after that and it turned out to be my job that finally broke us. It took me away from home and Derren couldn't handle it. It was so silly, he had no cause to be jealous. He resented the new love in my life, my job. And for me, there was no reviving the belief I could have a peaceful life with him so I ended it and I ended it for good.

Perhaps I should explain what my job entailed. In short, I researched potential families that could be used in documentaries to raise awareness of mental health issues. It was cheaper to send the likes of me out first before sending out an entire camera crew. My research was also used to help place volunteer doctors. The stigma of mental illness in Sri Lanka was so great that people would generally suffer in silence and this usually had disastrous consequences. You might think the hardest part about going to these countries for this reason is acclimatising to the new and sometimes upsetting surroundings. But after spending time with happy, beautiful children who had no material possessions I found the hardest part was reacclimatising to life back home. Materialism lost all appeal after my trips to Cambodia and Thailand. Coming home made me feel distant and empty. A noticeable chasm formed between my friends and me. Before I knew what I was doing, I was turning to drink to fill the void, which only served to make the void bigger. Maybe that was the driving force, the reason I was so desperate to stay in Sri Lanka. Or maybe it was because I'd had to fight so hard to get put on this task. My boss's boss, Leon, wanted to send Jonathon Jackson, a guy who was far less qualified for the job than I was. He was a kiss-arse. He was referred to by some as Leon's bitch. Apart from my lack of skills in the work politics game, the other problem was that I didn't shave my face every other day, change my socks even less frequently or get more emotional over a football match than my own granny's funeral; I wasn't a man. Well, five o'clock shadow or no five o'clock shadow I was going on this assignment and team Jonathon would have to accept it. I was going to make a difference, no matter how small, to a country with the highest suicide rate in the world. I put every ounce of effort into that goal but my work had become an obsession that seemed to push everybody away.

Chapter 2

***I'm not** going to be sick. I'm not going to be sick. Oh my god, I'm going to be sick.*
I ran to the bathroom for the umpteenth time that night to stand over a sink, where ants crawled out of the tap that no longer worked, and retched. My stomach was empty bar a quarter of a cracker, some tablets and a few sips of water. I would eat a piece of cracker before taking a tablet in an attempt to keep it down but it wasn't working. My stomach muscles pained as they squeezed up the miniscule contents of my stomach beyond my control.
It was my third night out of hospital and I still felt just as ill as the first. I examined all my packets of tablets and began to wish I had paid more attention when the nurse told me what each paper packet was for. I was too excited about leaving to take in her instructions at the time. The instructions on the packets are all written in Sinhala. One of the packets contains anti-sickness tablets. If I knew which ones they were I could take those first then maybe all the others would stay down. I would lie in bed sweating in the oppressing heat with only warm bottled water to sip. My sole job was to ignore the queasy feeling stirring inside me. I became grateful for every minute that went by after swallowing the meds. Then, an intense heat would engulf my body and I knew what was coming. Mouth salivating and heart thumping in stereo, I knew it was time to race under the net and into the bathroom again. How I managed to sound sprightly on the phone to Victor is a mystery to me. Nothing I did seemed to bring any relief from the discomfort I was in.
My room in the guesthouse was, well, let's just say I'd seen better. Everything was covered in a thick layer of old dust. The first time I stood barefoot on the hard floor I gave myself a shock as the grime I stood on lifted away with my foot, sticking to the sole as I tore it off the floor with a *crrrk* sound. Right there on the

floor was a perfectly formed footprint of the true colour of the floor - a deep, rich, maroon. The mosquito net above my bed was musty, moth bitten and full of tiny dead insects that never quite made it all the way through from one side to the other. I spent hours taping up the little holes and removing dead bugs before meticulously tucking the net in after every visit to the bathroom. I had to be organised and make sure I had everything I might need in bed with me because forgetting something meant exerting more energy than I had to give. Sagging corners of the net made me feel claustrophobic and grotty as the dirty net threatened to graze my skin. As I eeny-meeny-miny-moed the packets of tablets from the hospital, looking for the anti-sickness pills, I decided there was no point in starting my anti-malarial meds from home again while I was puking for England. I put those ones aside and tried to get some sleep, as sleeping was the ultimate highlight of my day at that time.

One small mercy in my solitary confinement was Gertie – the little gecko who lived in my room. Second to the fact that his diet consisted of insects, I liked him for his company, in the way you might like a pet. Sometimes I even found myself talking to him, just little comments like 'here we go again' as I ran under the net and into the bathroom to double up over the sink. I figured it was better than talking to myself. To my knowledge, the name 'Gertie' is not usually synonymous with small brownish-green lizards. I, however, named all the geckos I found myself cohabiting with by this name. Gertie was welcome in my room, especially seeing as he liked to snack on mosquitoes.

I laid there on that third night wishing for sleep and cursing the monotone click, click, click, click, click of the fan on the ceiling. If it would only stop, I was sure I would be able to get to sleep.

"I will bring you a banquette of flies if you make that noise stop," I said to Gertie as he snaked a little further up the wall. I fidgeted and stuffed a pillow over my ears but I could still hear that fan. Day and night had merged to become a twenty-four hour cycle of napping and lying awake, feeling like I had not slept at all. To my surprise, the clicking that had been slowly driving me insane simply stopped. I reappeared from under my pillow and glanced perplexedly to Gertie as if he had just answered my prayers. The silence was so blissful I gave a satisfied sigh and closed my eyes, vaguely remembering something about the power being turned off for two hours each day for a while. I was told this was because the monsoon rains that produced their electricity were late coming.

Very soon after the clicking stopped, the room filled with a stifling heat. It was like my whole room had been put into a preheated oven. The hot air festered around my nose as I breathed in – which did not help my cause. I watched the spinning blades of the fan slow to a stop and became aware I was better off with the clicking after all. Sweat caused my face to slip off my arm where it had been resting and I decided there and then. Enough was enough. The next morning I would check into the luxurious and pricey Gaulle Face hotel. At some point that night I managed to fall asleep, dreaming of clean sheets and air con.

"Morning madam, breakfast for you? Coffee, king coconut, good for you!" asked my guesthouse owner, all smiles.

"Not today thank you Ravi," I replied weakly using gestures to help communicate my point. Ravi's English was limited so we did this often. He was a little, thin man in his early thirties. He had short yet bushy black hair and a wonky set of teeth.

Before I went into hospital we would sit and chat for hours about anything and we could, given the language barrier. We spoke a lot about the problems between the Tamils and the Sinhalese and how the war between them first began in the 1980s whenever his friends were there to translate. On one of these occasions he said some of the terrorists wore pendants of cyanide around their necks so they could take their own lives if need be. Some were children who were made to blow themselves up in crowded places. Ravi feared the war that had claimed over 30,000 lives already would never end as it brought too much money to the terrorists in the country.

When I turned down breakfast and checked out without much in the way of an explanation, Ravi looked hurt even though I promised I'd be back the minute I was feeling better. I always preferred to stay in the cheapest accommodation on my assignments. It brought you away from the false tourist life and allowed you to mix with the locals.

Despite all that, until I was better, I needed to swap the creatures for the creature comforts.

My tuk-tuk journey to my luxury seafront hotel – The Gualle Face – completely drained me. I found myself eternally grateful to have bellboys and staff to do everything for me upon arrival. The hotel was palatial. I felt guilty checking in after spending time with people who had huts for houses and bought cigarettes one at a time because a whole packet was too expensive. Bread was often bought in halve loaves too for the same reason, yet here I was, about to live like a queen.

While checking in, I participated in the usual first meetings' dialogue that never seemed to alter no matter who you met. I have lost count how many times I had this conversation:

"Hello!"

"Hello."

"Where you from?"

"England."

"You studying?"

"No, travelling."

"Ah, you backpack yes?"

"Yes."

There was no point or need to explain the reason I was here during first meetings. I would explain that at just the right time. It had to be before you got too close or you ran the risk of letting people feel betrayed.

"Married?"

"No."

"Children?"

"No."

"Ah, how long you here?"

"Three months."

I gave this answer regardless how long I had been there. It seemed to stop people trying to take advantage or acting as though you

were born yesterday.
"Oh. OK, where you go after?"
"Don't know yet."
"You need restaurant, taxi, place to stay after here?"
"No, thank you."
When I first arrived in Sri Lanka I thought it was an amazing coincidence that everybody had a relative in the very next place I was on my way to. It took me a little longer than I would like to admit to realise they wanted to take me to these places so they could claim the commission.

After check-in, I fell swiftly into the beautiful, king-sized bed in my clean pre-cooled room. I felt better already. I crashed out in front of the television; television, what a novelty! Half a trashy midday movie later, I was asleep.

I spent the next few days lazing by the pool in the early evening when the sun was a deep, burnt orange colour and it hung large and low in the sky. The warmth it gave off at this time of day was gentle. The slight breeze mixed in to give the perfect temperature for convalescing. When the sun was high, bright and white I slept in my cool room. In between this busy schedule I sipped ice water and ate basic Western food such as toast and jam or sandwiches. My medication stayed down and each day I was noticeably better than the last. My thoughts turned to the outside world. It felt like I had been out of it for an eternity and I had an urge to get back into it. While lying on my bed, bored with this constant state of inertia, a thought shot through my head so fast it made me jump.

"*Victor!*" I exclaimed, sitting up abruptly. I promised Victor I would keep in regular contact while the country was – in his words – in a state of unrest and while I was – in my words – utterly shagged. I picked up the phone by my bed and dialled the operator. They asked for the number and put me through.

"Good afternoon, Leon Cassidy," the voice said on the other end of the phone. There was a slight echo – very annoying.

Ever since Victor warned me Leon was likely to turn us into a profit-making organisation I have found it hard to humour the man.

"Oh, hello Mr Cassidy, it is Rachael Davies speaking, I was actually after…"
I started in my posh telephone manner before I was drowned out.
"Miss Davies, what a pleasant surprise. How is life in Columbia?"
"Colombo," I corrected.
"Oh yes, so you are. I trust you have been liaising with Victor while stuck out there in a war?"
I could hear his overly shiny black shoes tapping on the floor as he paced up and down. I could picture his huge nose that was made all the more prominent by his lack of lips.
"Of course I have, and I'm making great progress."
"Oh marvellous, marvellous, I'll just put you through to Victor, hang on..."
I listened as Jonathon helped him transfer me then apologised profusely to Victor for not staying in touch.
"Rachael, we had a deal. Have you seen the news lately?" Victor sounded more disappointed than angry.
"No, nothing else has happened has it? I am so sorry, I have been really ill, I am much better now though."
"No, nothing new has happened and quite frankly Rachael if you are too ill to pick up the phone, you are too ill to continue the assignment."
"No, I feel better now, I thought I was OK last time I spoke to you but it got worse, but I'm fit as a fiddle now!"
"Rachael, the previous attack was the worst in thirteen years. The Tigers used weapons that country has never seen before. The terrorist who blew up the aeroplane then blew himself up. The army were lucky to save the terminal building, which was also under attack. Twenty-seven people were killed…"
"They also targeted the military base killing more people and destroying military resources. I know Victor, I'm here. I hear what people say, I read English newspapers. I know what happened that day."
"The point is, young lady, you need to report back to me so I know your plans and you know what is going on."
"I know I should have called you. That's why I am trying to say

sorry. I know I'm always having to apologise lately but I am genuinely really, really sorry."

"Ok, just call in future, as you promised."

"I will I promise, again."

Victor hung up after talking shop, no small talk today but I didn't take it personally. That just meant Leon was around. The background office banter reminded me that any form of banter would be really good right now so, armed with a bottle of water, I strolled down town to Indica's stall in the market. Indica was the father-to-be in the family I had been following. He was married to Soma and living in a tiny basic house with Soma's mother, father and brother. They all started off as people I wanted to research before becoming good friends who I always looked forward to seeing. Especially Indica, he spoke good English and always had a huge smile on his face. He was so animated and full of vigour that it was easy to see why people, including myself, found him such a pleasure to be around.

Knowing the sun would be strong that this time of day I wore a big floppy sun hat, a white cotton top and beige drawstring trousers. The decline of my fitness levels became more than apparent as I huffed and puffed up the smallest gradients. Many tuk-tuks pulled up to me and asked, "Hey lady! Where you go?" Needing the exercise I declined them all and struggled on. It was stifling heat, the kind that makes you appreciate every small breeze that dances around you once in a while. Sweat trickled between my shoulder blades and sopped down back as locals walked passed me in full office attire without breaking a single bead of sweat. They seemed completely untouched by the powerful rays of the sun. *Spot the tourist*, I thought to myself. I rarely set eyes on other tourists in Colombo because it was July which is out of season, the very best time for people like me to come out to work.

"Good morning!" I exclaimed as I approached Indica's fruit stall. He turned around, recognising my voice.

"Ah! Rachael! Where have you been?" he asked, all smiles. Indica's smile beamed across his whole face making his eyes smile too. His smiling eyes were infectious. You felt warm inside when Indica smiled at you and you couldn't help but smile right back. Indica had straight black hair that flopped over his head in the curtain fashion. His jaw was square and chiselled, giving him a Western appearance. His skin was clear and his teeth were near perfect. Indica's wife and her family had fairer skin and looked much more Eastern in their features, dress and in the way they carried themselves.

"I haven't been well Indica. I had a, a tummy bug but I'm fine now," I said, opting to play it down rather than drag it up. I wanted to talk about something else, anything else!

"We thought maybe you had gone home after the Tiger attack. It is good that you stayed. Many have gone home."

"Ah thanks, I am glad to be here. Besides, I would never leave without saying goodbye, you know that."

"That is good to know. We have all missed you. Will you come to dinner tonight? We can surprise Soma and Komari."

"Um, I would love to, I really would but I've only just started eating proper food again. I'm sticking to Western food only for now."

Indica glanced down for a moment, his thinking pose.

"Then come over for some tea, yes?"

Who could resist that smile?

"OK, no food though, just tea. OK?"

"Just tea. Come by later yes?"

"Yeah, I'll see you later."

As there seemed to be no such thing as time here I knew just to turn up later and not ask. Later soon came and there I was at Indica's house seated around a table with his family and at least eight different curry dishes sprawled out in front of me. The rest of his family only spoke a small amount of English but their faces said it all. They were all looking at me in anticipation, waiting for me to start filling my plate so they could begin. I scooped some plain rice onto my plate, some plantain and finally a tiny helping of one of the curries Indica told me was mild. I glared at Indica who smiled and said,

"It is mild, for you."
"Thank you. Istuti," I mumbled, trying hard to appear grateful. I tried the curry. Mild to Indica seemed to be the equivalent of a vindaloo and I never ventured past a dansak myself.

I gulped down a glass of water without giving a thought to whether it was boiled first or not. As I finished my glass Soma got up gracefully and without saying a word. With one hand on her nine-month bump she brought a jug of water over to me and refilled my glass. It surprised me that Soma took on the role of hostess despite being heavily pregnant. She got up again minutes later to light the candles ready for the planned power cut. My first instinct was to help her but I knew they would never let me so I stayed where I was. During our candlelit dinner I was much quieter than usual. This was partly because I hadn't seen them for a little while and partly because it took a lot of energy communicating the simplest of comments and I was already tired.

Soma intrigued me. Naturally shy by nature she took the longest of her family to warm to me and she rarely spoke unless it was to answer to her father or Indica. Her hair was always tied loosely at the nape of her neck and draped over her left shoulder, over the shiny bright colours she donned. Her father, Johan, was a stern character who had full influence over the mood of the household. If he was happy his family were happy too. If he wasn't, the household fell silent. Soma had a younger brother who was also called Johan. When I was introduced to him I jokingly called him baby Johan to differentiate between the two but baby Johan was far from amused. Like most fifteen year olds, he did not like to be teased.

As I pushed food around my plate, it was mentioned that Soma's brother was getting married. I turned to him, hesitantly.

"Congratulations, Johan," I said in full animation so as to be understood. There was silence before everybody at the table fell about laughing.

"What?" I asked, searching faces for clues to explain their amusement.

"What have I said?" I smiled at their uncontrollable laughter.

"Indica?"
"Not baby Johan!" he laughed.
Baby Johan spoke excitedly in Sinhala as if making a joke until his father gave him a warning in the form of a cold glare.
"My other son, Nishantha." Soma's mother Komari whispered slowly to me as she put her hand on my arm. The gentle way she did this almost pacified me. All the women in this family had a way of sending me into some sort of trance. They all shared the same aura of serenity that made you feel calm just by being in their company. They made me very aware of how restless and fidgety I looked and how busy my mind always was. They made me consider the way I spoke too; impatient and quick compared to them and not nearly as considered. The carefully chosen words they used made what they had to say all the more significant. But the effect they had on me never lasted long after I left their company, much to my frustration.
After some more talk about the wedding, I reluctantly returned my attention back to my plate of food and discovered that pushing it around with a fork didn't make it magically disappear after all.
"You no like?" Johan asked. I hesitated as I tried to answer without offending the man of the house. Indica spoke to Johan in his mother tongue while the rest of the family turned to look at me.
"Ah, OK," Johan said. Baby Johan sniggered under his breath. I knew exactly what Indica had told them and began to feel embarrassed that they all knew the state of my digestive tract. Johan lost his patience with baby Johan and gave him what appeared to be a harsh verbal warning then turned to speak to Indica. Indica told me Johan suggested black coffee for a loose stomach. Johan spoke to Indica again, for longer this time. The whole family joined in but I couldn't work out what they were talking about at all. All I knew was that it involved me because they kept gesturing subtly towards me with their hands as they spoke. I heard the words 'Esala Perahera' repeatedly but this was not a phrase I understood at the time. Finally, Indica turned to me to fill me in.

"Next week, Johan, baby Johan and me, we all going to Kandy. The Esala Perahera start then. You are invited, will you come?"
"I'm sorry, the what?"
"The Tooth Temple parada!"
"Oh yes! I have heard about this. It happens every year doesn't it?"
Now I was the one being studied for clues to what I was saying. "I would love to go!"
"Good, you will stay at a guesthouse we know well. We will stay with Nishantha, not far from where you will stay."
"Thank you, istuti, I've heard a lot about this. I never would have gone on my own."
"It will be something for you to enjoy Rachael."
"And Soma?"
"Komari will stay with Soma while we are there. She cannot travel at this time."
"Oh, I see."
I felt bad for her but she didn't appear to mind being left behind. Soon after dinner I made my excuses and left for it had been a long and tiring day. Indica insisted on walking me home and explained to me on the way that Soma's brother was yet to meet his bride and that he would be coming to Colombo soon to meet her for the first time. This led to a debate on the pros and cons of arranged marriages as I struggled to imagine marrying a stranger of my parent's choosing. I'd be Mrs Law Degree by now, no doubt. Not wanting to end our debate, Indica and I sat drinking smuggled arrack by the hotel pool until the bottle ran dry. We sat looking up at the moon, it was almost full. Indica told me that tomorrow would be the national holiday they called Poya and that the people would spend it at leisure or pray. He told me it would be illegal to sell alcohol and the banks and many shops would be closed.

People would also be patrolling the beaches looking for freshly laid turtle eggs so they could take them to the hatcheries where they would be safe poachers. When I laughed at the pun, I knew I was drunk. What a lightweight I'd become. Making my excuses and heading up to my room I thought about how amazing the significance of a full moon was here. I was in awe. Head spinning I stumbled into bed. Completely unaware my world was about to take another deadly turn, I fell into a deep, drunken slumber.

Chapter 3

"**Rachael, Rachael**. Come! Come!" Indica exclaimed as he paced up and down like an excitable puppy in front of his stall. If he'd had a tail it would be a-wagging now.

"What is it?" I asked, hurrying toward him. It was the day after Poya.

"Soma, she had the baby, yesterday, on Poya! We had a, a baby boy. Daniel! We have named him Daniel!"

"Oh Indica, I am so happy for you!" I said, giving him a heart-felt hug. "Congratulations! How are they?"

"Well, they are well! You come and see them soon yes?" Indica's voice was breaking as though he were a teenager.

"Of course I will," I laughed. The more excited Indica became, the less able he was to string a sentence together.

"I can-not go to the parada now. We all go on the last day instead, will you come?"

I tried to work out the dates in my head. I knew the festivities lasted for ten days and that I had many interviews lined up for around that time.

"Shit Indica, I can't come."

"Oh Rachael, you must see the Tooth Temple, it is one of the most celebrated festivals of the year."

"I know, I really want to go but I'm here to work, remember? I'm not free like you lot."

"Don't worry Rachael, I go find you the address to the guesthouse, you still go tomorrow. Leave it to me," he said as he walked away, leaving his fruit stall seemingly unattended.

"You don't have to go now!" I called out after him as he waved me off and broke into a jog. Needless to say, he ignored me.

I soon forgot about Indica's hasty getaway when I reached a market stall full of summer skirts. Most of mine now sat precariously below my hip bones after the illness and I was fed up with living in drawstring trousers. Three skirts and a new top later, I returned to my hotel, checked out, and moved back to Ravi's where I requested a fresh room for a fresh start. Pleased to see me he obliged and he set a table up for me in the dining area so I could work where it was light and breezy. I spent the evening writing up my research on suicide and death certificates. It was commonplace for doctors to only write suicide as the cause of death if absolutely pushed. Even then the reason would be logged as something like a 'break down of marital relations' to avoid using words such as 'stress' and 'depression'.

I spent the power cut portion of the evening talking to Ravi and his friend in his empty restaurant. While I sipped my banana lassi by candlelight, I told Ravi I was going to Kandy for the parade but would keep renting my room while I was away to store my belongings. His friend and interpreter spoke what I might see there, there'd be elephants dressed in embroidered silks fringed with fairy lights, fire dancers back flipping through the air and drummers drumming beats that you hear with your body, not with your ears. He told me that every year, just before the parade begins, it would rain heavily for a few moments to wash the roads clean for the Gods. I smiled politely while instantly dismissing the idea that rain could be predicted to the very minute on an annual basis.

The next morning I waited outside the guesthouse for a tuk-tuk to take me to Indica's where I would pick up the address he had for me. As I waited, a man idling his time away a few doors down took to staring at me. Staring at strangers was quite the norm here but I found it intrusive and impossible to get used to. Right, I thought, this time I am going to stare right back at him because I was tired of having to avoid looking in an entire direction because people were smiling and staring at me. This time I was going to face the problem head on and stop the staring once and for all by giving him the best evil-eyed stare I could muster. It didn't work. He winked at me. I looked away, defeated and decided to keep my eyes down as his eyes burned into the side of my head. When a tuk-tuk finally pulled up to take me away, I was relieved to escape the staring man until I realised I'd jump out of the frying pan and into the fire. The driver glared at me like I had just landed here on earth in a spaceship for an eternity before we drove off. He seemed to take an instant dislike to me and became very agitated when I asked him to wait for me outside Indica's house.

"Sorry for the inconvenience," I mumbled under my breath. People here seemed to love you or hate you. It was clear where this man stood.

Indica's little newborn baby was beautiful. His squirmy little movements and his newborn cry were so pure and innocent I nearly shed a tear. And he had so much hair for a newborn. It was a pleasure to see the magic a newborn could bring to a family as Soma and Indica brimmed with pride. Indica saw me out and closed his front door before handing me the address of where I would be staying.

"The institute? What is this?" I said as I read the address.

"The Kandy Institute of Education, where you will go to meet Nishantha, Soma's brother. He teach art there. He will show you the guesthouse and he will take you to the parada. If you go alone to parada, they charge you many, many rupee for seat. With Nishantha you only pay five maybe ten rupee."

"OK..." I said, sounding unsure.

"Don't worry, he is expecting you."

The tuk-tuk driver beeped angrily so I said goodbye to Indica and hopped into the tuk-tuk full of apprehension. We dodged everything from buses to cows to clapped-out cars as the driver attempted to overtake vehicles when there was no chance we could make it. As if asking for a head-on collision, he swerved back into the line of traffic at the last possible second.

Trying to make a point methinks.

At least there was no need to learn a highway code here, the rules were quite simple: if it was bigger than you, it had right of way; a rule that had slipped this driver's mind. He swerved in and out of the traffic like a maniac as I sat in the back, my feet cemented in each corner and my face wincing at every near miss. Everybody beeped frantically at each other with their attention-grabbing horns. The tuk-tuks joined in too but sounded more like quacking ducks compared to their rival foghorns.

As we pulled into the station I realised I had just broken the unwritten law in the unwritten book of how not to get conned in Sri Lanka. I had forgotten to negotiate a price with the driver before getting in and now an argument was inevitable – rookie mistake. So by way of damage control I asked for the cost in Sinhala. If he thought I had been here for a while he might give a 'very good price' for me instead of a 'very good price' for him.

"Kiyadha?" I asked.

He stared at me for a moment. Ha! Weren't expecting that now were we? I thought to myself, believing I held the better hand. But proving he held the aces, he answered me in Sinhala, both calling my bluff and discovering my minute vocabulary didn't extend to understanding the answer. His face grew smug with a smile as rupee signs flashed up in his eyes.

"In English please," I said, folding.

"Eight hundred rupees."

"What? That's too expensive, *garnha redhee, garnha redhee*!"

"Eight hundred rupees," he repeated.

"No way buddy, *three hundred rupees*, this should only have cost *three hundred rupees*!"

Then just like that the driver could no longer understand English. I had nothing smaller on me than a one thousand rupee note and I knew I would miss my train if I carried on arguing so I gave in and paid the extortionate fare. As it so happened, I missed the train anyway. It pulled away as I flew past the beggars on the bridge. Assuming there would be another train shortly I bought a ticket to Kandy in the ticket office, and took a seat on the platform. A few moments later the ticket men came out of their office and started laughing at me, and I thought staring was rude.

"What?" I asked.

"You crazy lady! No train come for hours. Then mail train come. Slow, slow!"

"Oh," I sighed, scanning my surroundings. The place was deserted. "Well, how many hours?"

"Huh?" they asked at the same time.
"Three hours?" I held up three fingers.
"Oh, yes, yes," one of them said with a head waggle.
Getting the feeling they would have said 'yes' no matter what number I said, I asked again.
"OK, the next train to Kandy is in eight hours time right?"
"Yes," they answered in comical unison, both still smiling.
Too fed up to see the funny side I walked away from the ticket men and decided to use the unknown quantity of time to sunbathe. I lay down on a grass verge and pulled a couple of postcards out of my bag that I had picked up along the way. I pondered for a while over who to write to. My parents? My friends? Derren? No, definitely not Derren. He would either take it as some sort of insult or take it to mean more than it did. Derren was probably seeing Tanya again anyway, now that she had fully integrated into our social group because her friend Alana was seeing our friend Ben. Derren was Ben's wingman when Ben met Alana and that is how the fling with Tanya started. She was the sort of girl who was up for anything if it got her the attention she was after. Alana was so different to Tanya it was hard to see how they were friends. She was very quiet and down to earth. She had blondish curly hair, a little like mine but much longer. She was athletic looking because she was a personal trainer and she was taller than me. If Derren had picked Alana over me back when they all met it would have seriously dented my ego. Alana was good for Ben though and he doted on her. I think she is the one who has finally ended his philandering ways.

I could write to my mum? No, I couldn't. She was still unhappy about me taking this trip so a 'wish you were here' greeting through the mail was probably a little insensitive. My flatmate Jenny came to mind but we really were not that close. She was wrapped up in yoga, tofu and her boyfriend Hardy. She had pigeonholed me as a boring mainstreamer who was happy to plod along with whatever the government and/or media fed us. She was wrong. I just wasn't as hard core as her. Neither was Hardy. He played along with her from what I could see. Another friend to come to mind was Jacky, a friend I'd made while waitressing to get myself through college. She was ten years my senior but that didn't stop us having a good time. We'd lost touch of late though, so a postcard might seem a little out of the blue. The other person I wished I could write too was Jaycee. Jaycee was the supervisor in the office I temped in before coming to work for Victor. She was also the reason I embraced the travel element of my job because she opened my mind to the idea right before Victor offered me the role. I'd have loved to have told her about my job and all the places it was taking me, but I didn't take her contact details when I left. Such a shame. In the end I decided to write to my oldest friend, Laura. With that decision made I studied the picture on the postcard. It was of a typical tropical beach scene with crystal clear waters, pristine white sand, the sky a brilliant cloudless blue and palm trees lining the beach with sporadic bars and beach. It was also from Bentota, a holiday destination south of Colombo I had never been to. Laura didn't need to know that though. Let's face it, the main reason for sending a postcard is to invoke envy anyway.

Dear Laura,

How are you? And who are you seeing now? The ex, the ex-ex or someone new? How is everyone? Say hi for me, please-thanks. Mate, u'd just love it here, the white sands and palm trees stretch for miles along the beaches, the little tuk-tuks on the roads are really funny! Weather is beautiful, even though it's meant to be monsoon season. The rains are late which means power cuts every evening. (That's how they get their power.) It's surprisingly easy to get used to though. I'm much better after being in hospital with a kidney infection, I'm sure I'll end up telling you all about that when I get back. You can ring Victor for the low-down like last time if you like, he loves it! Right now I'm toasting away quite nicely in the sun, wish you were here. I keep thinking about all our times away together, so funny, wish you could share some of this with me. Well take care matey, see you when I get back.

All my Love Rach xx

Then, in tiny letters all squished up next to where I had written 'England' in capitals, I wrote; Ps, people here are lovely and no I haven't met any men!

Well, I knew she would be wondering.

As I gazed at the heat-hazy tracks I noticed the beggars sitting on the bridge. The sight of them left me feeling a little abashed at moaning about paying premium Western rates in the tuk-tuk and getting annoyed over missing my train. At least I was waiting to board one. For most of the people on the bridge, this station was their final destination. They had nowhere else to go.

By the time the train pulled up, three hours later, the station was heaving with men, women and children. It was hard to believe just a short while ago I was the only one here. It then occurred to me that nobody else was stupid enough to wait three hours for a train. I squeezed onto the train and peered through the masses of arms to see out the window. There were still floods of people waiting to board and I had no idea how they were all going to fit. *This cannot be possible,* I thought to myself, as the carriage was already crammed with people doing their best contortionist impressions in order to fit around each other. Being first on, I had managed to get a seat but many were standing and all I could see were arms everywhere, holding on to anything and everything to keep anchored ready for departure. I thought about the trains and buses back home and laughed to myself as I pictured the sign behind the driver's seat on the buses. 'This bus is licensed to hold 18 persons seated and 16 standing.' If this train had one it would read, 'this carriage is licensed to hold 30 persons seated and three times as many as you thought humanly possible standing.' Health and Safety would have a field day.

Clutching my bag close to my chest to take up as little room as possible, I decided to make conversation with the man next to me. It was either that or ignore the stare he was giving me, and I wasn't exactly spoilt for choice for places to rest my gaze.

"Hi. So, when does this train get to Kandy?"

"What?" he said, smiling.

"Um, what time, do we, get to Kandy," I said slowly, gesturing to

my watch and then to the train.
"Oh no. This train not go to Kandy!"
"Huh?"
"No lady, this train go to Galle. That train go Kandy!"
He pointed to the train that had pulled up next to ours. I could just about make it out through the gaps in the sea of arms. Jumping up, I threw my bag on my back and barged through the crowd. I had to get off that train. As I made my way clumsily to an exit I could hear the doors shutting along the train as the last of the passengers alighted.
"Excuse me, sorry, thank you, istuti, sorry! Excuse me, sorry, thank you, oops, sorry!" I chanted continuously as I trod on feet and invaded personal space. I kept squeezing through gaps only for my backpack to get stuck. Panicked and flustered I tried to make my way to the platform. All eyes were on me, the silly blonde haired, blue eyed foreigner who managed to board the wrong train. Finally I was near the door, only a young man stood in the way of it.
"You want Kandy train, you go that way," the young man said to me in broken English. He pointed to the door on the other side of the train. The surrounding people tried to stand back to create a clear path to let me through. I stood and looked at him in disbelief. Funnily enough I didn't think to use that door, considering the lack of a platform the other side of it. What did he want me to do, hop from one train to the other? Another young man who had been standing near the door that everybody was encouraging me to use, was now pulling hard on the top of my backpack. I just sort of flew effortlessly after my backpack across to the other side of the train. Somebody else opened the door and suddenly I was faced with a sheer drop down to the tracks and a narrow gap between the trains. Everybody wanted me to jump but as I peered down to the tracks my stomach tied itself in a knot and leapt up into my throat. *Do they really expect me to do this? What if the train starts moving?* I looked around at all the faces smiling at me. They were clearly waiting for me to jump. I guess my bravery came from their approval because without a seconds

thought I wriggled free from my backpack and jumped down between the trains.

"Here, you ready? Catch!" the guy who dragged me from one side of the train to another said as he threw my bag down to me. "Now run, go quickly! Train is leaving, train is leaving!"

I peered up to see two trainloads of people smiling at me, waiting to see if I would make it or not. *Right Rachael, keep it together, find a door, where is there a door? There doesn't appear to be a door. Nope, there is definitely a distinct lack of door where I am standing.*

Even if there was a door, it would be too high for me to jump to anyway. The audience from both trains pointed a way up the train to where the nearest door was and shouted at me excitedly, although what they shouted I have no idea. This was nothing short of a nightmare. A little way up the train a door swung open and three or four people hung out to call me to them. I ran like an awkward hermit crab up the train to them while other passengers cheered me on. When I reached the door I found a group of teenage lads were ready and waiting to help me up.

"How do I get up?" I shouted, red-faced. There was no way I could jump that high.

"Pass me your bag," one of the lads asked as he reached down with an extended arm. The train I had just leapt off rolled forward a few feet and came to a stop again. For one awful moment I thought the Kandy bound train was leaving as I knew it would at any moment. I threw my bag up to the willing lad. He passed it behind him and came back to me. I still had an intrigued audience watching the silly English girl making a scene. Two of the lads reached down to me while two more held on to them. I jumped up into their arms knowing I would never make it all the way up to the doorway. With ease, the lads pulled me up the rest of the way. The next thing I knew there was a chorus of cheers as, just like in a movie, both trains departed.

Everybody on the other train waved as they went by. I made it.

As I caught my breath I shook my head in amazement at what had just happened. I had waited hours on the wrong side of the station for the wrong train and the ticket men didn't think to let me know. There wasn't even a platform on the other side. Crazy. It warmed my heart to think about how so many people had helped me on this day and from the day I stepped off the plane. On my second night in the country I managed to leave my evening purse at a tiny, basic restaurant after eating a meal there. I assumed I had lost it for good and forgot all about it. All it had inside was three hundred rupees or so and some lip gloss. On day three I walked past the same place and a man called out to me. I was surprised to hear my name called out in a place where nobody knew me but it was also pleasing. He gave me back my purse and walked off. I looked inside to find about three hundred rupees and some lip gloss, nothing had been taken. I called the man back to thank him and offered him some money to show my gratitude. His name was Ravi, he owned a guesthouse and that is how I came to stay there.

The journey to Kandy was long; it was also interesting. Once the lads who helped me got off at the next stop, I sat and gazed mindlessly out of the window at the staggering mountainous views. The sheer beauty of the landscape blew me away. Across the aisle another group of boys were tapping out a beat on the side of the train, singing and tapping their feet to the tune. They sang everything from Celine Dion's *Titanic* hit 'The heart goes on' to Sinhalese songs (at a guess) I had never heard before. There was a small cafe in front of me. Passengers were buying rice and curry and various soft drinks that they would discreetly spike with arrack under the table while they played cards and gambled. It seemed to me that the loser had to by the singular cigarettes on sale at the counter. One thing that struck me was that wherever I looked people were having a good time. I shuddered at the thought of the dismal, monotonous train journeys back home. All those nine-till-five faces coming home from their office jobs, avoiding eye contact at all costs, apart from the people watchers. Even people watchers who meet the eyes of fellow people watchers break eye contact as soon as they mistakenly make it. Most people on this train were on for one stop only so I found myself answering the usual set of questions over and over, but I

didn't mind, they were all so sweet and almost shy with their questions to me. When there was nobody to talk to, I passed the time by taking in more of the lush view of the vast mountainous landscape. The peaks rose up high, disappearing into the mists. The lush green valleys and tea plantations squiggled into the distance until they were just fine black lines between the mountains. Sporadic waterfalls trickled down the hills. As I gazed in awe I secretly ached for somebody to share it with, even an exchange of glances that showed we were both thinking the same thing. As I gazed, and ached, the face of a teenage boy suddenly appeared right in front of me, blocking my view and making me refocus. Inches away from me he said, "Hey lady, you got fire?" (A lighter.)
"No! What are you doing?"
"Having fun!" another voice replied. I peered out of the window to find the owner of the second voice and found three lads all holding on to the side of the train, the *outside* of the train. The boys were smoking, and not cigarettes either.
"You're crazy!" I shouted out to them collectively. My words caught in my mouth as the air forced itself into my lungs.
"What is your name lady?" the first one asked.
 "Rachael. What is your name?"
"I am Tharindu. Lady, go to the door."
"What about my bag?"
"No problem, leave it there."
I had picked up a *when in Rome* attitude and had ignored every other piece of sound travel advice so I thought little of leaving my bag while I went to meet the daredevils hanging off the train. I wasn't brave enough to join them out there but by the time we arrived in Kandy I was feeling very, very relaxed.

Chapter 4

For sale: One backpack complete with one lost English lady owner. Please claim before the masses hack chunks off it. Standing outside Kandy train station looking bewildered made me perfect prey for the average con artist and I knew it; knowing it was my only advantage. I had no idea where I was going and everybody was willing to help, for a fee. Taxi and tuk-tuk drivers abandoned their vehicles and rushed to me, all with one question on their lips.
"Hello! Where you go? I have good price!"
Yeah, good price for you, I thought as I showed the drivers the address Indica had given to me. It was snatched and passed around as they made price offers to me. Some of the drivers walked off as soon as they saw the address, which made me immediately suspicious. If this fare wasn't worth their time the odds were the journey was a short one.
"Come in my taxi. Seven hundred, good price!"
"No, I take you in tuk-tuk and show you sights, same price!"
Six or seven men still surrounded me, battling for my fare. I'd acclimatised to being mobbed and no longer found it daunting. Calmly reclaiming my piece of paper, I made my way over to a little shop I'd passed at the station. The drivers followed me all the way to the shop door then waited just outside. In the shop I picked up a bottle of water and a packet of digestives before slipping the address to the shop assistant at the till.
"Is this far? How much should I pay to get here?" I asked.
The man behind the counter studied the address, then me, then the address again before finally resting his gaze back on me. Clocking the mob outside, he tried to stifle a smile as the corners of his mouth turned up. He was trying to figure out whether to tell me the truth or to put the drivers first.
"Look," I stated, in my 'don't even try that' voice. "I have been in

Sri Lanka for months," I lied. "Just be honest with me. How much?" The shop assistant looked over at the drivers then at me as though his loyalties were torn. I gave him my best vulnerable look to nudge them my way and it worked, he broke.

"OK, OK, this is not far. You can walk this. Here," he took a pen and proceeded to draw me a little map on a napkin while he drivers circled outside, waiting for their prey.

"Here," the shop assistant said as he passed me his map-on-a-napkin.

"Thank you, istuti, that's so great," I said as I backed out of the shop.

I was instantly pounced upon by the pride outside as if I was a youngster separated from its herd until a young and very pale looking white couple appeared from the train station. They came complete with backpacks, a huge map and a look of utter confusion painted all over their faces. Disorientated and worried, this couple made for a far easier target than me and all the men dashed off toward the fresh meat leaving me standing alone. Looking into the shop, I could see the assistant laughing as he watched.

"The lions move off to find easier prey and the youngster is saved, this time," I said to myself in my best Attenborough voice.

It was late afternoon yet the sweltering Sri Lankan sun still had a ferocious feel to it and to make matters worse, the walk was an uphill trek so once I reached the cool interior of the institute it was as if I had found heaven. Offloading my backpack and enjoying the AC, I failed to notice the receptionist smiling at me from behind her desk. Upon noticing her I felt a little foolish, after all, what was I really doing here? I couldn't even remember Indica's brother-in-law's name so what was I supposed to say to the girl at reception?

"You must be Rachael. Hello," she said softly – and much to my surprise. How did she know who I was? She struck me instantly as a very attractive young lady.

"Hello," I replied hesitantly, walking over to her. "Yes... I am Rachael."

"Nishantha is expecting you. Go to the third floor madam. First turning on the left, second room on the right. Oh, you can leave your bag with me," she added. Thanking the lady I made my way up the stairs.

As I climbed the stairs, I noted how modern, light and well cared for the building looked. I also noted how far outside my comfort zone I was. How was I to know what Nish– whatever his name was, was? I also wished I had paid more attention to the directions from the lady downstairs because when I reached the third floor, all the other directions escaped me. I peered into a couple of rooms to see if anyone could help me. All the rooms were full but only one looked arty, full of easels all facing in towards an empty platform where perhaps a still life model might pose. There only appeared to be two men in the room. One of them looked in his late teens and had a very cheeky-looking face. He spotted me peering in and gave me a typically laddish grin complete with a wink. I could see him speak to the other man in the room. This man was mostly hidden by his easel but seemed older and calmer than his friend Jack-the-lad.

"Nishantha, Rachael is here," he said suggestively, raising his eyebrows. Who *didn't* know I was coming? Indica had apparently forewarned the whole institute I was making a visit. A pair of eyes peered over the easel at me, then the man they belonged to walked over to me as I let myself in. A wave of foolishness came over me again. What was I doing here?

"Hello Rachael, I am Soma's brother, Nishantha, and this is Paul."

He spoke slowly and deliberately, just like his sister Soma. He gestured over to Paul.

"Hello Paul, Nishantha. You already know who I am?" I enquired politely, extending my arm out to shake Nishantha's hand.

"No. I am dirty from paint," Nishantha said, showing me his hands.

"Oh, OK," I looked at Paul and offered to shake his hand. He took my hand and bent down to kiss it while looking into my eyes with his cheeky smile.

"It is good to meet you too, Rachael,"
I tried to ignore Paul's attempts to flirt.
"Well, can I see?" I said to Paul, gesturing to his easel.
"I am only sketching an outline. You should see Nishantha's, go take a look."
"OK," I looked towards Nishantha.
"Do you mind?" I asked.
"Please…" he said, stepping aside. Nobody had answered my question on how they knew who I was, which I was glad about as the answer was obvious. Indica had told them I was coming and the place was not exactly overrun with blondes this time of year.
"Wow," I managed, completely awestruck. What a beautiful sight. I was staring at a painting so real and so moving it was hard to believe it was the creation of somebody's imagination. The painting was of a night view out of a car window of a bombing in the street. The scenes of destruction were alive and full of terror, a complete contrast to the reflection of the passenger in the car. You couldn't see their actual face, just hints of their reflection in the window as they looked out onto the streets. The shadows that carved out the essence of the face portrayed perfectly the sorrow he was feeling. Still entranced by the magnificent piece of art before me I thought I should say something profound.
"Wow," I repeated. It may not have been profound but it was fitting.
"This causes me great sadness," Nishantha said, looking deep into the painting and moving his fingers slowly over the scenes of terror he had captured so superbly.
"It's a masterpiece," I said, finally.
"It is not finished."
"Oh," I was nearly as entranced by the artist's voice as I was by the artist's work. It wasn't so much the husky broken English, it was more the careful, deliberate way he spoke. Clearly a family trait, I thought to myself, thinking about Soma and Komari. His mannerisms matched theirs too, composed, calm, soothing.
"You get here OK?" Nishantha said, breaking the silence that had crept in unnoticed.

"Yes, thank you, the journey was...was interesting."
"Oh, you come by train, yes?" Nishantha smiled as if he knew what the train journeys could be like. I smiled and nodded as I became more relaxed. It began to feel less like I was encroaching as we all exchanged friendly banter, during which I noticed Nishantha looked different from the rest of his family. They all had a slight build and very fine, flat hair with a slight wave. Nishantha was tall and well built. His hair was thick and curly.
 I glanced back at the painting and the penny dropped.
"That's you!" I exclaimed. It was like finding the image in a magic eye picture.
"That is me. Many can-not see, you have a good, err..." he pointed to his eyes. Paul and I both finished his sentence simultaneously, 'eye'.
"Thank you," I said as I studied his eyes again. They were large, deep and soulful, like the painting. And as with Soma and Komari, they had the power to subdue me with one look. Snapping out of my trance I tried to divert attention away from the fact that I had just stared into this man's eyes.
"So, um, what's happening later then with the parade, where do I need to go?" I said quickly, struggling to stay composed. I was sure they had noticed and to make things worse I could feel myself blush. Paul threw Nishantha a cheeky sideways glance. He had noticed. At this point my whole face was hot to the touch. I think I could actually feel the blood pulse through my temples and there was no chance in hell of hiding it. The words ground, open and swallow came to mind as I blushed profusely beyond my control. Nishantha clocked the sideways glance from Paul then tactfully ignored him. Paul followed his lead and stopped grinning.
"Go to the Suisse View. It is at the bottom of this, err... hill. My mother has friend there. She will be good for you, I mean, she will be good *to* you. There is map, in my pocket. If you don't mind..." he said, turning around. He couldn't get it himself, not with his hands all covered in paint.
As I pulled it out of his back pocket Paul fell about laughing.

Once again, he was ignored, by both of us this time.

"OK, that's great," I said looking at the map. I wanted to take the map and run but Nishantha insisted upon talking me through it – like I was going to be able to take directions in, now of all times.

I gave off over-theatrical signs of concentration as he spoke. Frowning and nodding in all the right places until finally he finished explaining his map.

"OK, thanks for that, I'll find it. Well it was nice to meet you both," I said with my composure still far from restored, despite Nishantha's tact.

"Goodbye."

I walked out the door and started down the corridor. A few strides in, I realised I'd headed off the wrong way; how I'd made it this far in Sri Lanka on my own was a mystery. As I turned to head the right way I smacked straight into Nishantha who had come out to tell me I was going the wrong way. My nose came off pretty bad on his chest and I winced, holding my hands up to my face.

"Rachael! Are you OK? I am so sorry! How, um..." he said something in Sinhala as I stood there with my hands cupped over my throbbing nose.

"It's OK," I said nasally. "I'm fine."

My eyes were glossy and bloodshot and all my words ended in d's or b's so I obviously wasn't fine. Nishantha took me back into the room and sat me down on the platform in the middle. Paul was on the verge of hysteria as he said something to Nishantha in his mother tongue. I sat there for just a few moments until the pain dulled to an ache. When Nishantha was convinced I was 'fine...d' he led me out and pointed me in the right direction.

On my way down the hill, which was over a mile long I might add, I bounced perpetually back and forth from wincing in pain to cringing from sheer embarrassment. Great, now they think I fancy Nishantha, just because he had the same lovely manner about him as his family. It was a good job Paul didn't see me at the dinner table back in Colombo. He might have thought I fancied the whole family. I was angry with Paul for being immature and making me uncomfortable. At the same time I couldn't help smiling at how cheeky he was and how colourful the 'meeting' had been.

Tired from a long day's journey, I was pleased to finally check into a room at the Suisse View guesthouse where I could shut everybody out, and close my eyes. And this is exactly what I did after falling onto the bed in my new room that was both bigger and cleaner than my room at Ravi's.
 The weed from the train made my head swim as I gave in to the heavy, weary sensation behind my eyes. Somewhere between wake and sleep, I fell into an unintelligible dream world full of random pictures and abstract dream fragments. That is when it happened. It was like it crept in while I wasn't looking and hid, ready to pounce at the right moment. A disturbing scene filled my head for just a split second. It left as quickly as it entered yet that did not make it any less unnerving. I jumped bolt upright. My head swam heavily as I sat up too quickly. The vision was of me holding the rigid body of a dead baby. I could feel the stiffness through the soft blanket it was wrapped in. The clothes and baby blue blanket were covered in old blood. The sickly sweet, pungent stench of decaying flesh accompanied the image. I had never seen a dead body let alone smelt one, yet there it was. I felt sick and dizzy. After that little incident I decided to get up and shower, rather than lay there with the feeling the image had left me with. The anxiety from the dream – if that's what it was – followed me around while I got myself ready for the parade so I started looking forward to getting away from my own company so I could forget about it. A knock at my bedroom door made my heart race. I opened it to find the guesthouse lady on the other side. She was bouncing a toddler lovingly in her arms and I wondered if he belonged to her. The lady looked old before her time and somewhat dishevelled. Her greying, wiry hair was matted, her clothes were ragged and stained and her teeth were a dark yellow colour as if tarnished by years of neglect. Her two top front teeth were missing. I found it hard to imagine Komari having a friend

like this. Nishantha had said his mother's friend ran this place and would look after me. Was this really the lady he was talking about?

"Man here, for you," she informed me with her dry manly voice.

"OK, one minute," I said loudly and slowly, the way you might speak to the hard of hearing.

"Yeah, yeah, yeah, I tell him…. I tell him," the lady flashed another gummy smile at me, revealing her rotting teeth stumps before shuffling off down the corridor, toddler on hip. The child looked large and cumbersome in the stick thin arms of the frail woman. I watched for a moment before realising I should be gathering my things to leave. I checked out my new calf-length, pink skirt, white spaghetti-strapped vest and cotton cardigan in the part of the mirror that hadn't turned green then walked along the corridor, down the stairs and into the living room area. Nishantha was standing there waiting with his back to me. I looked at him for a moment before saying anything, safe in the knowledge that Paul wasn't around to catch me this time. Nishantha looked fresh and smart. He wore jeans and a relatively tight-fitting T-shirt, tight enough to show how broad and muscular his shoulders were but not so tight you might question which team he bats for. He was a picture of strength and health, a complete contrast to the guesthouse lady.

"Hi there," I said, finally. Nishantha turned around at my voice.

"Hello, Rachael. How are you?"

"I'm fine, thank you. You?"

"Fine? That is good, yes?"

"Yes, 'fine' is good."

"Then I am fine also. Was the map OK?"

"Oh yes, your map was perfect, I found this place with no problems, thank you."

"I am glad. And, um, how is your…" he pointed to his nose.

"My nose is better now, thank you, how is your chest?" I asked, placing a hand on mine.

"I am in a lot of pain actually."

"Really?" I gave a concerned glance then realised I was being had and smiled.

"No, your nose did not hurt my...chest."

"Good. That is good to know."

"Are you ready to go to parada?"

"I am indeed. I can't wait!"

"I am sorry, Rachael, please speak slowly for me. I can understand when you speak slowly."

"Oh, sorry, I am ready, shall we go?"

"Let's go," Nishantha said agreeably. With that we said goodbye to the guesthouse lady and her toddler and made our way to the Tooth Temple. The awkward silence, broken only by the slight crunch of our footsteps on the dusty gravel surface, made me feel nervous again. I wanted to start a conversation but couldn't settle on a subject that was worth bringing up. It was a bit rude to comment on the appearance of the guesthouse lady and small talk was not coming easy to me either. What was I going to say? *Nice weather we are having today isn't it Nishantha? Yes, Rachael, just it was for the last six months, the weather is great!*

Our footsteps began to sound very loud – crunch, crunch, crunch – until Nishantha finally broke the silence.

"I am sorry for Paul today. He can be, how do you say, excitable."

"I noticed. Don't worry. I am sure he is a lot of fun to have around."

"He is. He make me think of my brother, Johan. You have met him, yes?"

"Yes, I have and now you come to mention it they are both very cheeky chappies."

"Cheeky...chappies? I will have to remember that one."

Then there was another long pause – crunch, crunch, crunch...

"Rachael, my mother and my father would think this is...not so good, you and me to-night."

"Well, I won't say anything if you don't. Can I ask why?"

"It is not allowed, for mans and womans to be alone together. Do you understand?"

"I've spent time with lots of men alone here," I stated clumsily.

"Not *lots* of men, I mean, not *alone*, well not like that, I just

mean... Indica! I spend time with Indica and your family knows and they don't seem to mind."
"That is because he is married."
"You see, at home it is the other way around. It would be more inappropriate for a woman to spend time with a married man than a single man. Except, you're not really single, are you? You're getting married?"
"That is correct."
"Congratulations on your engagement."
"Thank you," he said with a polite smile rather than a sincere one. He then looked down at the ground before him and put both his hands in his pockets. His body language wasn't exactly screaming, "Way-hey, I'm getting married!"
"You don't look very happy? I'm sorry. It is none of my business..."
"It is OK. Maybe I am not. My mother and my father, um, how do you say, when somebody is...too much in your life?"
"They...interfere?"
"Yes, that is right. My mother and my father interfere," he said, pronouncing 'interfere' as 'inter-fare'. "That is why I come to Kandy, to get away. Things are different here, more modern."
His openness surprised me. He had taken us beyond mere small talk between two strangers and, lonely as I was, I really appreciated that.
"I'm sorry," I said reassuringly.
"Do not be," he said more cheerfully. "To-night we see the parada."
"Yes, I cannot wait to see it. I have heard so many great things about it."
"I think you will like it. If you have any questions to-night, I will be happy to answer them for you, as much as I can."
"There is one thing puzzling me already actually. That lady at the guesthouse, is she your mum's friend?"
"My mum's friend?" he said, absorbing the question.
"The lady back there," I pointed to the direction we had come from, then at my two front teeth. "The one with the teeth." I said,

speaking through mine. Nishantha smiled at me for my inventive, goofy means of communication.

"You mean Imanie. Imanie is not my mother's friend. She live and work at the Suisse View *for* my mother's friend who owns two guesthouses. My mother's friend, she work in the other one. That one is...better...but is now full because of the parada."

"Oh, I see."

"I lived there, when I first come to Kandy, when I had no money for a place of my own."

"Did you like it?"

"I liked the guesthouse , but my mother's friend, she became my mother's eyes. And her husband, he is a police guard."

"And that was a problem was it?" I said mock accusingly.

Nishantha looked up to see I was joking and he smiled back. It was the first inkling that he too may have a cheeky side to him.

"It might have been!"

As we neared the temple, both sides of the road started to fill with people. The volume of onlookers grew rapidly and there were police, army and bomb squad men on every corner. Various temporary stations in the form of tents were placed at a stop point in the road. Each onlooker was searched individually. Men were farmed to the right and women to the left. The Tooth Temple parade was a huge Sinhalese event and, although not as religious as the festival in Hambantota according to Ravi, there was still a very real risk of attack from the Tamil Tiger terrorists. Nishantha and I were separated and duly searched. I entered one end of the tent, was frisked, and moved quickly out the other end where I took a moment to look for Nishantha. I couldn't see him as I was shoved along in the throng of the merging crowd. Men scanned the crowds with urgency for their women and vice versa.

"Rachael! Here, come over here!" Nishantha shouted. I followed the voice to see him by the curb, out of the swell of the crowd. I muddled through the sea of people all trying to make their way in different directions.

"Are you OK?" he asked. His attentive concern touched me more than it perhaps should have. I'd had nobody to care for me when I was ill and I had never been without the support of friends or family for this long before. I was well aware he was just being polite, but it touched me all the same.

"Yes I am. You?"

"I am always OK. Come on, let us go, I know where is the best place to be."

"Let's do it!" I was nervous about the threat of attack and excited by the atmosphere all at the same time.

As we found our places amongst the thousands of others finding theirs, a few men came along selling sheets of plastic to the crowd. The crowd reacted by eagerly holding out their money; they seemed to really want their sheet of plastic. Nishantha pulled ten rupees from his jeans pocket to buy one. I watched on in puzzlement. My first thought was that we would be sitting on these but I then surmised there would not have been enough room for everybody to sit down.

"What's it for?" I asked Nishantha.

"The Gods send rain to wash the way for the holy men. Every year, before the parada it rain."

I paused for a moment. Ravi had told me about this and I had simply dismissed it. Was this a universal joke to play on the unsuspecting westerner? I was just trying to think how to phrase my doubts on this politely when the heavens opened right before my eyes.

"Right on cue!" I shouted over the din of the golf-ball-sized rain drops rebounding off the hundreds of sheets of plastic. We took shelter under ours, arms up stretched with a hand at each corner. We both stood facing in, the length of the oblong sheet between us. Less effective than an umbrella, I was still grateful for any cover I could get from the torrential downpour. Under the pillar-box-red plastic sheet Nishantha looked like a drowned rat as corkscrews of his curly hair stuck to his forehead. Rainwater dripped from my nose and strands of my hair had stuck to my face so I guessed I looked about the same. I laughed at the state of him, at the state of us, and he laughed back. Surrounded by thousands of people yet stood under a sheet of plastic, it felt intimate. We only had each other to look at and it was hard to speak over the din of the rainfall. Again, I was aware it only appeared intimate to me because I had spent so much time alone. I knew it wasn't the same for him. After just a few minutes my arms began to ache as I held plastic above my head. My smile faded as the ache grew into a pain.

"What is it? You do not like the weather?"

"No, the weather is great, it makes me feel right at home. Being warm and dry is highly overrated anyhow!"

"Here, you look like you could use some help," Nishantha offered, concerned as my side of the plastic began to droop considerably. Water was now gushing off and pouring down my back.

"Come close to me and turn around."

Please don't make me do that! I thought. The last thing I needed was to position myself more intimately with him. With little choice, I did as he asked and he held the sheet up over the both of us. I wrapped my arms tightly around myself and tried to ignore and resist the sense of security forming within me as he towered above me keeping us both dry. It didn't help that he was wearing a hint of aftershave and smelt absolutely amazing. I told myself it was only natural to like this feeling of being taken care of and regained my grip on the situation.

"The rains, they will stop now."

"Pardon?" I said, turning into him to hear him better.

"You see, the rains, they are stopping now." Slightly distracted by how muscular his arms were I thought, enough is enough and stepped away from him. The rain was light enough now.

Mini rivers and pools had formed in the uneven surface of the road and they trickled down the slope of the road.

"I'm glad that's over," I stated as the rains disappeared completely. "The elephants would be swimming by if it went on much longer."

"That would make an interesting change."

"Do you really believe the rains are from your Gods?"

"Yes. They come for a short time every year just before the

parade."

I opened my mouth to talk but then noticed that Nishantha was distracted by something behind me. I turned to see to see two policemen standing behind me. One of them was talking to Nishantha, he sounded angry. Both were looking at me. Nishantha spoke back just as testily. His usual soft, husky voice now sounded deep and harsh, which suited the frown on his face. They maintained an uneasy eye contact before one of them pulled Nishantha away.

"Nishantha?" I said shakily.

"Rachael, do not worry. They just want to speak to me. Do not go anywhere, stay here OK? I will be only over here," he said as the policeman pulled on his arm impatiently. I wanted to keep watch of them in case they disappeared but the policeman who stayed with me stood directly in my line of vision.

"You English?" he asked sternly.

"Yes."

Seriously, this line of questioning again right now?

"What is your business with him?"

Ooh, a variation.

"We are friends."

He looked me up and down in the 'must be a whore' manner. It was an unusual concept to a number of the locals that a woman should be so far from home on her own and that was sometimes the conclusion they drew from it. A lot of the women I met appeared to fear the world unless they were standing beside their man. I remember sitting on a bumpy bus journey when I first arrived here. Every time the bus jolted, the man opposite me squeezed his wife's hand reassuringly. She looked up at him with such love and admiration. It confused me. Was I watching a beautiful thing or was I watching years of oppression at play?

"You here alone?"

"No. I'm with him," I said sarcastically to avoid having to tell him I was in fact alone. He looked over his shoulder at his colleague, as did I. The other policeman gave him a nod.

"OK. Enjoy the Esala Perahera."

Both policemen left as Nishantha strolled back over to me.
"What was that about?"
"Rachael, do not worry. They wanted to know what I was doing in the company of a for-eign girl on her own."
"Why?"
"I do not know. He wanted to know about you. A woman on her own."
"A woman on her own."
Now that little fact keeps coming up and upsetting everybody.
"I thought for a moment it had something to do with the bombings and terrorists. After all, that is why they are all here isn't it?"
"That is why they are here but they just want to know why you are here. They are happy now I have told them."
Six or seven men from the bomb squad marched passed us with a military air, their dusty blue uniforms were dark around the tops of their shoulders where they'd become rain-soaked. We stopped talking about the police incident and watched the bomb squad walk by.
"Are you worried?" I asked, assuming he knew I was referring to the threat of attack from the Tigers.
"Now? Yes."
"Oh."
"I am sorry, that was not very reassuring to you. Indica tell me you stay here after the attack in Colombo. Were you not scared?"
"I am now!"
"Oh, I am sorry. Look, I am no more worried right now than at any other time."
"I guess it's a threat you learn to live with."
"You are right. This war has gone on for many years and will go on. It brings many moneys into the country for the Tamil Tigers so I fear it will not end. It has changed the parada. The Tooth Relic is no longer brought out for fear that it will be stolen or...damaged by the Tamil Tigers."
"Why are the Tamils fighting you?"
"It is not all Tamils. It is the Tamil Tigers, the Jaffna secessionists. I think Prabhakaran, he want the peoples to um,

believe he fight for all Tamils. He make money from other countries."

"I don't really know much about it. They are suicide bombers aren't they?"

"The terrorist who fired the rockets at Bandaranaike, he blew himself up and there are many more man, woman and children training to do the same as we speak."

"Bandaran…Was that the attack at the airport?"

"Yes, this is true. But don't worry now, we are here for the parada. And I have prayed to Buddha to keep us safe."

A single beat of a drum silenced both us and the crowd and all heads turned to the road. The clouds began to subside and the moonlight flickered mysteriously in the glimpses of night sky as an entourage of drummers proceeded down the rain-washed road. The front drummer hit his drum again producing another penetrating beat. Then another, and another, then other drummers joined in. The magic of the parade was beginning and I was quickly covered in goose bumps. Fireworks filled the sky and music filled the air. Huge, immense bull elephants carried holy men in decorated glass carts on their backs. The elephants stepped in time to the slow beat of the main drum. Nature's gentle giants passively obeyed their commanders while looking proud and glamorous in their elegant attire. They were dressed in colourful silks and velvets skilfully covered in delicate embroidery and tiny fairy lights; deep purples and blood reds, emerald greens, warm burnt umbers. Their mammoth ivory tusks jutted out in a powerful contrast to the colours adorned by the beasts. Large golden teardrops were embroidered around the holes made for their eyes making them look even more magical and powerful than they already were. Fire dancers and gymnasts impressively somersaulted in mid-air while dodging fire balls with precision timing in carefully choreographed routines. Men walked either side of the parade lighting the way with lanterns attached to long poles towering many feet above their heads as they carried them over their shoulders. The lanterns were fuelled with dried coconuts that, once lit, burned for hours. Embers from the lanterns fell to the ground as they burned out. A piece of burning coconut fell from a lantern above my head. Instinctively I flinched back. Instinctively Nishantha pulled me into him. He let go as quickly as I pulled away. I thought back to the woman on the bus and confused myself all over again with the beautiful thing versus oppression debate that couple had stirred in me.

The parade took about an hour to pass and it was so fantastic I was left feeling drunk with amazement. Excited and full of life we made our way through the dispersing crowds. Confidence came to me as a side effect of the endorphin rush and I forgot all about feeling self-conscious in Nishantha's company. To top it all off, the heavy rains had given the air the sweet, dusky aroma of tarmac and grass.

"Wow! I was looking forward to tonight but I had no *idea* it would be this good!"

"Slow down, slow down!"

"Oh, I'm sorry. I've never seen anything like this! You didn't tell me how magnificent this would be!"

Nishantha smiled at me knowingly as though he was glad to have shared the magic with somebody who had never experienced it before.

"Have you eaten yet, to-night?" he asked.

"No, you?"

It occurred to me that all I had eaten since breakfast was a half a packet of biscuits.

"No. Would you like to come with me for something to eat? I know a good place."

"Yeah, I am starving."

When we found ourselves away from the crowds I bounced along the road excitedly, buzzing on my natural high. Nishantha walked along side me as calm and collected as when he came to pick me up. He had what I can only describe as a contained contentment about him.

"You enjoy the parada very much," Nishantha said, half in question, half in statement and still in contemplation.

"It was amazing. I really did enjoy it. Did you?"

"I love to watch this every year. It means a lot to me but I am...used...to these sights and these sounds. Watching it with you, it remind me how wonderful the parada really is. You have reminded me of the first time I saw it."
I *knew* he had been thinking about what I had said, I knew it.
"You're seeing it anew."
"A what?"
"You're seeing it *anew,* as if for the first time."
"Oh, anew! I find your accent very...different."
"What accents are you used to?"
"Um, well, I am used to English accents, just not yours. The people I have met, they sound different to you."
"Oh, do day soun' like this?" I said in an appalling Liverpudlian accent.
"No."
"Then how about this wee laddy?" I said in an equally abysmal Scottish accent.
"Um, no, I do not think so."
"Loik this then maybe?" I said in a better – but still not great – Brummie accent.
Nishantha threw me a look. "I will pray to Buddha for you."
"Why?"
"Because you are crazy!" he said playfully.
"Uh! There is nothing wrong with being excited!"
"OK, OK, I was joking," he put his hands up in surrender.
"Don't you ever just, I don't know, let go?"
"What do you mean?" he frowned in confusion.
"Well, do you ever get overexcited, mess about, fool around?"
"Not like you!"
"Is that so? What if I do...this!" I said as I poked a finger into his side. He didn't flinch. Not one bit.
"That will not work on me. I am not, how do you say..."
"Ticklish?"
"Yes. Tick-lish."
"Is that right?"
Not believing him I put both hands around his defined waist and

tickled him with my fingers.

"No, stop it!" he laughed, trying to pry away my hands.

"Ah, so you are ticklish!"

"I am not!" he said as we ran around in circles.

"Then why are you running away?"

"Because, it tickles!" he said, laughing.

"Ah-ha! Your inner child has emerged!"

"Maybe we should see a little more of yours!"

Nishantha pulled my hands away and turned on me. I ran away screaming as he chased me down the street then scooped me up with one arm while tickling me with the other.

"Get off, stop it, please!" I screamed.

"I am not holding you tight, Rachael, you can get away!"

But I was stuck. I was laughing so much I lost all my strength so I just sort of involuntarily slumped down to the ground.

"OK, OK! I will stop, I will stop."

We both sat on the path, out of breath and laughing at our playful outburst. Looking into each other's eyes as we smiled, we enjoyed a silence that seemed natural rather than awkward.

That moment right there was perfect. Sometimes I wonder what would have happened next if we had been left alone to enjoy it. Like a freeze-frame picture in my mind, I can still smell the dusty sweet grass and aromatic tarmac in the air. I can still remember how happy and carefree I felt, still giddy from the parade and from the pull I felt towards Nishantha. That moment was one of the happiest moments of my life, and I stand by that to this day, despite the fact that it was also to become one of the worst.

Chapter 5

Bang, bang, bang, bang, bang, bang, bang, bang, bang.
The din ricocheted across the vast night sky that now looked eerie, instead of beautiful as I had always seen it. Nishantha's body tensed and I knew we were not listening to fireworks. We sat still with our ears poised, but the deathly silence provided little in the way of clues as to what was going on, or where.
Bang, bang, bang, bang, bang, bang, bang, bang, bang.
Another round of gunshots was fired into the air only this time they were followed by harrowing screams of fear like none I'd heard before. As the colour drained from Nishantha's face, we looked up and around us, trying to determine the direction of the shots. But as more shots echoed around the sky, I just became disorientated. The sky fell silent after that third round and adrenaline burst through my chest with such force it felt like my heart was bleeding hot, thick blood. I wanted to run but had no idea which way. Like a petrified rabbit I froze on the spot.
"We need to get off the road. This way!" Nishantha ordered as he snatched my hand. We picked ourselves up and ran at speed through the streets that led back to the Suisse View. More rounds of infrequent gunshots fired creating a taunting cocktail of silence and harrowing screams followed by more gunfire. The soundlessness in the pitch-black was the most frightening of all because each round after grew louder and closer and I wondered if the next round would be at us.
We kept running. We ran until my legs burned and then we ran some more until finally I skidded on the scratchy gravel path and faltered as I tried to keep pace with Nishantha. He pulled me up before I hit the ground and urged me on by telling me we were nearly there. Reaching the guesthouse, we ran up the stairs to my door where a stuffy heat had lingered on the landing. I tried to catch my breath and steady my hands enough to slot the key into

the bedroom door but my palms were sweaty and my vision was blurred. The lack of food, the heat, and the post-adrenaline slump made me feel faint so I crouched down to the floor and handed Nishantha the key.

He opened the door in an instant and we slammed it shut behind us. With our backs to the wall we caught our breaths and listened as the gunfire continued to grow louder. I thought I would feel better in the safety of my room but instead I was overcome with an almost hysterical need to keep running.

"Nishantha, what's going on, why is it growing louder, are we safe? What the fuck is going on, why does it sound so close and...?"

Poor Nishantha had no hope of understanding my whimpering, which was steadily becoming inaudible. He drew his hands up to his frowning forehead as if to regroup then grabbed my arms and pushed me back up against the wall to shut me up. It worked. I was still breathing heavy and finding it hard to calm down but at least he had silenced my rambling hysteria.

"Look at me. Listen to me," he said remarkably calmly. My nostrils flared as I tried to breathe through my nose.

"I do not know why they are so close. All I know is you are safe. They are after the Sinhalese only. They would not shoot a foreigner and risk bringing the West into this war," his voice wavered. I understood he, too, was scared and I needed to get a grip to be of any use to us both. He swallowed hard, frowned to compose himself then started again.

"They will not come here. They have no reason to. And even if they did, they would see you are white and leave you alone. Do you understand?"

His eyes began to glisten and he swallowed hard again like he was only just managing to stay in control of his voice. His dilated pupils in their dark brown spheres flitted rapidly in the whites of his eyes as he blinked. I nodded, completely unaware what he was getting at.

"So we just wait here?" I asked, still standing rigidly against the wall in his grip, wearing my shoulders for earrings. Nishantha

fixed his eyes on the floor and said something in Sinhala followed by,
"I am a danger, to you, Rachael," he said, letting his statement hang in the air. The penny dropped, he wanted to leave me on my own.
"No Nishantha," I said, shaking my head.
"I am going Rachael. I am going because you are safer alone than with me. I also need to make sure Imanie and her son are OK. They will be scared. OK?"
I was on the verge of panic at the idea of being left on my own and deep in my gut the idea seemed wrong, or was that the fear talking? How could I tell the difference? Either way, who was I to keep him here with me?
Another short round of gunfire went off, this time it sounded like it was outside and was accompanied by the sound of engines and shouting. Nishantha walked over to the window and I watched his face for answers.
"Rachael. They are outside."
"What? Why?"
"I don't know why!" he snapped.
"What about Imanie?"
"There's no time."
"Then stay here. Surely you are safer here with me, a white girl?"
Nishantha ran his fingers through his hair.
"No, it does not work that way around. I am more a danger to you than you are a safe place for me."
We both froze as we heard cacophony of uneasy noises beneath us, the sound of scuffling boots, metal clanging and more screaming and shouting. They were inside. Time had run out, we could hear clear voices now. We could also hear a baby crying.
"Imanie's baby?" I whimpered in a whisper that caught at the back of my throat.
"I'll take the baby; he'll be safer with me." I said as I made for the door. The need to keep the baby safe had somehow superseded the fear I'd felt for my own life.
"No! I will go..." Nishantha said, putting a hand on the door to

keep me from opening it. But it was too late. We heard boots mount the stairs as the baby cried louder.
"Rachael, I am going out the window."
"What? We are too high up, you'll kill yourself!"
"If I stay here I will get you killed. If they come in do not hide, let them see the colour of your skin."
Nishantha opened the window and looked down. I went over too and saw the empty LTTE trucks abandoned outside.
"Nishantha, no."
"It's OK. I will down from the ledge."
Shouting and stomping sounded from out on the landing.
"If they find me, you tell me you did not know I was there. Do you understand?"
I nodded yes.
I closed the window behind Nishantha and said goodbye to him silently in my head. He would never be able to support his weight by hanging off that ledge and even if he could, the odds of them spotting him were high.
With legs made of jelly I shuffled over to the bed and sat down. I could hear doors being forced open and machine gun fire some way up the corridor. The baby cried out long, low notes. I sat on the bed trying to defy the need to run or to hide. Fight or flight beckoned me as adrenaline filled my body, filling my chest with its hot, oozy pain. *I'll go away if you move*, it told me. My heart pounded violently, moving my entire torso visibly with every beat. Terrified, my lip trembled and for some reason I latched on to the sound of the baby crying as if it was a song playing on the radio. I let it distract me from my reality as I absorbed every sob and whine, every pitch and tone, just to stop myself from panicking. My heart thumped. The baby cried. That is all there was.
A woman screamed; I blanked her out. Three shots fired; I listened harder to the baby crying, and then there was silence. My song on the radio had stopped playing. A single tear rolled down my cheek. I knew what the silence meant. I rocked nervously and my lip quivered again as a cold sweat consumed me. The door to

my room swung open and hit the wall with such force that the top hinge came loose. I closed my eyes tightly to brace myself for my own execution. Nothing happened. I opened my eyes to see two terrorists stood before me. I refer to them as terrorists not for effect but because I cannot bring myself to call them men. They both wore military uniforms complete with pendants around their necks filled with white powder – so Ravi's stories were true. The rage in their crazed eyes made them look inhuman. One stood by the door as if looking out while the other stepped further into the room. He was holding a machine gun in his arms. The one by the door didn't. He had blood spatter on his face interrupted by channels of sweat running from his forehead down to his neck. He looked high and out of control. As he ripped the door clean off the hinges I noticed he had a machete in his hand. The sight of it chilled my bones and scared me witless. I could not bring myself to look at the knife at all. If my eyes couldn't see it, it didn't exist; out of sight, out of mind. This may have been bullshit but it was effective bullshit. I even stared at the gun as if willing it to shoot me just to save me from that blade. They stood there looking at me in disbelief. I expect a tourist was the last thing they thought they would find out here this time of year. The one in front pointed his gun at me. He was older than the lookout. In some twisted messed up way, the anticipation of having to face these terrorists had been far worse than the actual situation. I found that I was a little calmer than I had been in that awful moment before they burst in. I could think more clearly now I no longer had to fight the compulsion to run. Now I could see what I was dealing with I felt alert and a little more in control than before. Fuck Red Bull, fear gives you wings.
"Wo kommst du her?" the armed one said, pulling his chin up and looking down his nose at me. He revealed his rotten teeth, twisted, black and yellow. His dark skin was covered in pits and craters and the whites of his eyes were yellow with brown flecks. He was grotesque.
"I am English," I replied. He had assumed I was German.
"Where you from?" he asked, more angrily this time.

"E…" my voice failed on me.
Come on Rachael, you know this drill well.
"England." I found my voice.
He spoke to his lookout while keeping his eyes on me. Scared of angering or antagonising him further, I kept my eyes down and stared at his boots. They seemed like the safest place to look. The lookout marched over to me, still hosting that crazed look in his eyes. The veins in his hand bulged out through his skin as he tightly clasped his machete. I looked away, back down at the boots. A noise from outside prompted both the terrorists and myself to look toward the window. I held my breath and prayed. The responsibility I felt at that point was unbearable. All I wanted to do was run up to them to divert their attention away from Nishantha's hiding place. I struggled once again to stop myself reacting. The night sky on other side of that window was noticeably calm and serene. The indigo sky was strewn with masses of champagne pinpricks. The depth of the stars' layering lent a sense of infinity to the vast expanse above that is not always apparent. The peace and beauty behind the glass pane seemed so unobtainable now. I thought I'd never be able to stand underneath it again. It was a staggering contrast to the evil that had come upon this guesthouse. Apparently satisfied there was nothing out there, their attention fell back on me. The lookout sat down close to me, invading my personal space. His breath was so vile I retched. Not wanting to anger him, I closed my eyes and tried once again to transport myself out of the situation. I felt a hand run up my thigh so instinctively, I opened my eyes. The man was smiling at me, his face just a couple of inches away from mine.
"No!" I whimpered almost inaudibly. I did not want Nishantha to hear me for fear he might try to play hero and get us both killed. He showed me his knife and smiled as though showing it off to a friend. My throat closed in and my eyes welled up with tears. I was trembling.
"You give me joy!" he snapped impatiently.
"No." I closed my eyes and cried. He pulled my head back by my hair to bare my throat and forced me to look at the knife again.

The other man came close and gestured for the knife to be moved. The lookout moved it away from me and moved a few inches away.

"You here alone?" the armed one asked.

I wanted to say no to save myself.

"Yes."

"What is your business?"

"I'm travelling."

"You have friends here?"

"No."

More men from outside poured in and shouted at the two men in my room. They then saw me and held their guns up like a firing squad.

The armed man spoke to them and they lowered their weapons. After much shouting in what appeared to be a disagreement they all left the room and trundled noisily down the stairs.

I ran straight over to the window and forced it open. Nishantha was still there, hanging on. His knuckles were deathly white and blood seeped from under his fingers. We had only seconds to pull him up before he became visible to the terrorists who were heading outside. With one last surge of energy I helped pull him up. He scrambled the rest of the way on his own and fell to the floor. I stood over him to close the window again. We sat in silence as we listened to the trucks disappear back down the road.

Chapter 6

Four days passed. I was back in Colombo, back into the Gaulle Face Hotel and was reading my morning newspaper, delivered to me by room service. There had been so little reported in the papers before that fourth day that I started to wonder if I had dreamt the whole thing up. I had nobody to talk to who could understand and the whole world around me was carrying on as if nothing had happened. I was glad of this; I just couldn't figure out how to join it. Desperate for answers I couldn't find, I was unable to think about anything else. It took four long days for any substantial facts to hit the Sri Lankan press. In *Sri Lanka Today*. The headlines read, 'LTTE Suicide Killings in Kandy'. Another page was entitled, 'Tigers Kill in Tooth Temple Attack'. On reading the latter I learned that the intended targets had been guards, bomb squad and policemen. Some were targeted after the parade and some were targeted in their own homes surrounded by their families. The report said the killing spree started in the eating haunts near the parade where Sinhalese servicemen were known to eat. This is where eight uniformed men and seven civilians were found DOA. Another seven service men and a further eleven civvies were found dead in at a number of homes including the Suisse View guesthouse. Seeing it in print made it real and it made the death of that baby and his mother hit me on a whole new level. As unhealthy as it was, I had been playing out scenarios in my mind where Nishantha and I held the baby close, stopped him feeling afraid and more importantly, saved his little life. He should still be alive and so should his mother but all the fantasising in the world could not bring them back now.

The reporter was unclear as to why the Suisse View was a target but to me it made perfect sense. Nishantha had told me the owner was a policeman who lived with his wife in their other guesthouse. The Tigers must have thought this policeman lived at the Suisse View. As I read on I learned that three trucks were found just outside Kandy. Inside were the bodies of the Tamil Tigers. They had all ingested cyanide. If they were already dead, what was I to do with all the anger that was still so raw and fresh inside me?

The paper went on to talk about how the suicide killers came from a culture of martyrdom, a culture willing to die for their cause. The newspaper reports acted as a remedy, lifting me out of my catatonic state. It was time to face reality and it was time to face Victor. I should have contacted him and I knew I was going to be in the shit, I just couldn't deal with it on top of everything else. The threat to my own life had affected me too. I was anxious, jumpy and scared of my own shadow. You might wonder why I didn't just go home and get some help but leaving was the last thing I wanted to do. Nobody would understand at home and also, I would have to contend with reacclimatising as well coping with the raid at Kandy. I considered telling the police here my story; it seemed like the right thing to do. But I couldn't. I couldn't speak to anybody. If I told Victor, my friends or my family I'd be sent back on the first flight home. For my own sanity I knew I had to remain in control of that decision by keeping it all to myself. Sitting on my bed I planned what I was going to say to Victor. I felt like I was about to 'pull a sickie' only in reverse. I begrudged having to lie again but this was the lesser of two evils. I had to stay, every ounce of my being screamed out at me to stay.

During the overdue and difficult conversation with Victor I held back the awful truth and told him I had been in Colombo at the time. I told him I had considered going to the Tooth Temple but in the end I decided against it. I said I only heard about it properly that morning and had called as soon as I could. Given how long it took for the facts to come out, that was a feasible statement to make.

I used to tell Derren that lies acted as barriers between people. Now I was the one building barriers. I came away from our phone call knowing Victor hadn't swallowed my story fully. He didn't outright accuse me of lying, as that wasn't his style. I knew he would go away and mull over it until he had something concrete to come back at me with. He was like Columbo that way, except with proverbs and quotes instead of the one-liners.

Indica insisted we keep his family in the dark about my whereabouts that night and of my unorthodox rendezvous with their bachelor son. I was only glad that Soma's baby came along when it did, keeping them all out of harm's way.
I spent the next few days working, sitting with Indica or moping. I stayed away from his family because I knew I was incapable of putting on a plausible mask of normality. I thought a lot about the immense difference in how this was handled here compared to how it would have been handled in England. In England help would have arrived that night and a detailed account would have been extracted from all potential witnesses. Even when the authorities came the next morning, nobody asked for a formal statement from us. When I pressed the matter they told Nishantha I should go to the police station to do that, which of course I chose not to do. At home I would have been grilled, fried and roasted in case I could give a valuable clue that perhaps I didn't even realise was relevant. I would have been offered counselling, compensation, a medical assessment, transport home and ongoing support. I had taken for granted the security our laws provided for us at home. I had been oblivious for a long time to how bubble wrapped our lifestyle was. This opened my eyes up well and truly.
Another thing to play on my mind was Nishantha. After I pulled him up into the room Nishantha went straight out to see if he could help Imanie and her baby. He also searched the building for more people. He was distraught when he came back to my room, telling me Imanie and her baby were both dead and there was an old man lying dead by the back entrance. If there were any other guests they would have still been out which was a blessing. We washed the cuts on Nishantha's hands and laid down together on top of the covers on my bed. He wanted to know what happened when the terrorists were in my room. I kept the details to a minimum. There was no point in making him feel worse than he

already did. He felt bad for leading me to the very place some of the terrorists were headed and he felt that he had abandoned me even though he left me for my own safety. Nobody could have known we were running to their next target. Not one ounce of me blamed him for what happened. In my mind he saved me. He kept me calm and I survived. If I had been on my own the outcome of that night could not have been guaranteed. Perhaps I would have still gone back to my guest house and hidden, which could have been fatal. He looked guilt-ridden when I left and I didn't even say anything back to make him feel better. This played on my mind more than any other single point, perhaps because it was the only thing I had any control over. I replayed conversations in my mind where I put Nishantha's mind at ease. The truth is, we fell asleep on my bed without any memory of doing so then woke up in each other's arms. I was so taken aback by this that I'd shied away from him even though he looked like he wanted to talk. I also had an intense headache and the shakes from low blood sugar so we finished the rest of my biscuits before leaving with the police.

"Are you going to eat that?" Indica asked, eyeing up the remains of my Bittarai Kirihodi.
"No, you have it."
I swapped our plates so he could finish my curry. We were sitting in the outside dining area in my hotel. Although it was expensive to eat there, I didn't much feel like venturing out so I paid for Indica's meals when he ate with me. My appetite was volatile. I would get really hungry and look forward to eating only to find I couldn't stomach more than a few mouthfuls.
"Istuti," he said, receiving my plate.
"No, thank you Indica."
"For what?"
"For being here. For spending so much time with me even though my company is poor. I don't know what I would have done without you." I looked at him with gratitude.
"I promised somebody I would," he smiled softly.

My ears pricked up and my eyes widened.
"Who?" I asked, far too keenly.
"You know who."
"Nishantha? You didn't tell me he said that!"
"He tell me to look after you."
"When?"
"When you come back to Colombo."
"How is he, have you spoken to him?"
"You seem to have woken up, since the subject turned to Nishantha," Indica said, throwing me a disapproving frown that made his eyebrows go all crazy.
"I'm just concerned, Indica," I said defensively.
"Rachael. I want to say something to you."
"What?"
"I would be sad to see you go but I think you need to go back home, to England."
"No. Uh-uh," I argued, shaking my head in immediate protest. "If I leave now, this will hang over me forever. I need to deal with this my way. The upheaval of going back is the last thing I need."
And I want to see Nishantha again. I added silently. Well I did. I wanted to say sorry, thank you. I wanted to ask how people were coping with the aftermath.
Indica held his gaze on me as if deciding whether to speak or not.
"What is it Indica?"
"Nothing."
"No, if you want to say something to me just say it."
"OK. You have to stop thinking about Nishantha. This is not healthy."
"What? I'm not."
"You have to move on."
I sighed in frustration.
"The trouble with puddles is you don't know how deep they are until you jump right into…"
"Rachael, what are you talking about?"
"Nothing. I don't even know."
Indica left soon after dinner, it was the only way to disperse the

slight atmosphere between us.
"Go see Ravi. He is asking where you are. Spend some time with him."
That was his parting statement. He was washing his hands of me.
I stayed out of his way for the next few days and threw myself into my work as if desperate to do some good to make up for the bad I had witnessed. As the days went by, the need to see Nishantha grew. I needed to speak to somebody who knew what I was going through. I needed some closure. The night I decided to do something about it was the night I couldn't get to sleep. I'd been tossing and turning for hours when I decided to give in and see what the time was. My clock read 2.07 a.m. I'd been trying to get to sleep for over three hours. Checking the time made me anxious, I shouldn't have done it. Annoyed by my own emotions I decided to get up and take a practical look at my options. What was it going to take to put me back on the road to recovery? I pictured myself at home and the idea scared me. I pictured myself staying here and became worried nothing would change; after all, it hadn't so far. I then pictured myself back in Kandy, seeing for myself some proof that this did happen, seeing for myself that the people of Kandy had moved on and were living their lives after the attack. I pictured myself talking things through with Nishantha. And I knew, instinctively, that was what I had to do.
I glanced at my clock again as I climbed back into bed. 2.22 a.m. Jesus, and there was me thinking hours had passed. Content in the knowledge I was going to head back to Kandy, I fell asleep with ease and with a renewed hope of finding some peace of mind.
The next day, after working well into the afternoon, I nervously made my way to Indica's stall to tell him I was going back to Kandy. His approval would have given me the confidence I needed to look forward to the trip instead of worrying about it. His approval would have somehow meant Nishantha would be pleased to see me. There was no sign of Indica at his stall. My big declaration would have to wait. I walked eagerly to Indica's house. The weight I had put on Indica's approval was unhealthy. I knew that if I didn't get it I would never have the nerve to turn up

unannounced to see Nishantha.

Feeling desperate and disempowered, I power-walked over to Indica's house, praying all the way he would be there. When I got there I knocked on the door and waited nervously for an answer. I could hear a lot of chatter inside so the chances were he was just spending some time with Soma and baby Daniel.

When the door opened I was relieved to be greeted by Indica.

"Hey, how are you?" he asked enthusiastically.

"I'm doing good thanks. How come you're not at the stall?" I tried to sound casual.

"I spend some time with the family."

"Ah, good. How are they all?" I said, surprised to still be on the other side of the door, considering that on every previous occasion I had been welcomed in, in a whirlwind.

"They are good. Would you like to go for a walk?"

"Yeah, that would be good."

"Let's go."

Indica and I ended up back at the beach outside the Gaulle Face. We sat on sun lounges, facing the roaring Indian Ocean. An ocean I hadn't set foot near due to the constant danger warnings out this time of year. The falling sun took with it the overpowering heat of the day, which left a sense of warmth and calm in its place. The once brilliant blue sky now looked like a soothing oil painting made up of burnt orange, creamy pink and fading purple. The canvas of colour reflected onto the ocean and shimmied across the water all the way to the shore from the horizon. Magnificent. The cool wispy breeze fanned my warm skin that was now deeply tanned.

"You look happy Rachael."

"Well, I am. I have made a decision."

"Oh, you are going home, no?"

"Nope. I'm going to Kandy!"

"OK," Indica took a moment to digest what I had said. I waited with baited breath. He sighed. "Why?" Indica was struggling with my statement.

"I need to make peace there. I need to see life goes on there and

replace the last picture I have in my head of that place. I also want to talk about it with somebody who will understand what I went through."
Indica looked at me, then looked down as if he was disappointed.
"You want to see Nishantha?"
"Yes, Indica. Why can't you understand that?" I asked, pulling out my cigarettes from my day bag. For an ex-casual smoker, the stress of this time had brought the habit back.
He looked at me like he was holding something back. I took two cigarettes out. Indica took them both, lit them and handed one back to me.
"Just put me out my misery, Indica. What is your problem? Do you know something I don't? Does Nishantha hate the idea of seeing me so much he wouldn't want to help me? Did you ever think that seeing me might help him as well as me? What is it Indica? You need to tell me because I'm hurting here." Two escapee tears of frustration ran down my face. I wiped them away defiantly, showing Indica I was not after his pity.
Indica looked stunned. He then pulled hard on his cigarette and exaggerated the exhalation as if he needed the hit of nicotine to help him think. He then looked out toward the ocean. I followed his gaze. He was watching two young children splat in and out of the small pools of water left behind by the receding shore line as it ebbed away.
"You never know how deep they are until you jump into them. Do you Rachael?"
I looked at him, amazed he had understood me the other day when I came out with my puddle analogy.
"This is not a puddle."
Indica raised his eyebrows, a visual instruction telling me to think again.
"OK then. In what way is this a puddle?"
"Because you think you can see Nishantha once and everything will be OK again. Like a magic pill. You cannot see beyond past seeing him again. You cannot see how wrong you are."
"OK, maybe I do think seeing him will help. But I don't think it is

a magic cure."
"You still cannot see it, can you?"
"See what!?"
"What if you...fall for him? Then where would you be? You would be crying over a man you cannot have is where you would be. Now that is a puddle, Rachael."
"What makes you think I will fall for Nishantha, Indica?"
"The way you talk about him. The look in your eye."
"You're wrong. I don't fall for people easily, Indica, and I certainly do not fall for people quickly."
"No, I don't think you do. But I do think that you have a romantic view on life that has no place here."
Put out by Indica's insight, my cheeks flushed. Indica noted my reaction, softened his tone and carried on.
"He is getting married. Nothing will change that. I just don't want to see you more hurt than you are now."
"I just want to talk to someone about what happened, to try to get over it. I want to go to Kandy."
"You don't need to Kandy," Indica sighed in capitulation. I could tell by his tone what he was going to say next.
"Nishantha is in Colombo, at our house."
I sat back, buying some time so as not to seem overly interested in this piece of information.
My eyes widened and I bit down on the insides of my lips to suppress a nervous smile.
"Well, do you think he would want to see me?"
"I think he would. If you meet him, that has to be it, OK? No more meetings."
"That is all I want, I promise. This is about closure, I swear."
"We will be in the Roof Top Bar opposite the Cricket Club later tonight. Can you meet us there?"
"I'll meet you there."

By the time I was ready to make my way to the Roof Top Bar the sun and all the colours it brought with it had disappeared from the sky completely and the oil painting was now a paint chart of varying navy blues. The sky had changed and so had my mind. Since the minute I left Kandy I had longed to see Nishantha again yet now the opportunity was here I was overcome with nerves. I am surprised I wasn't able to fly to the bar with all the butterflies in my tummy. It was absurd, I was fourteen again. I blamed Indica for all his talk of me falling for Nishantha. Whatever the reason was, I was nervous.

As I walked there, I started to wonder if Indica had told Nishantha of our conversation. I so hoped not.

I saw the Cricket Club on my right and looked to the other side of the road. There it was, the electric blue neon writing: Roof Top Bar. It was time to put on an air of elegance and confidence. One must play the part to become the part. The street was busy at this time of night. I walked past people gathered together in little clusters and over to the stairwell. As soon as I made it to the top I saw the two men I had come to see. They were sitting at a little table set away from the bar. The bar was heaving. Western tunes were playing. Nishantha clocked me straight away, eyes wide. Indica looked at him and then followed his gaze to me. I gave a polite smile and a casual wave to both of them. The atmosphere was perfect for our meeting. There were small groups of people everywhere and the music, as funky as it was, was at just the right volume so you neither had to raise your voice to be heard, nor had to strain your ears to listen. I walked over, gave them both a greeting kiss on the cheek and sat down on the chair they had saved for me. A waiter took our drinks order and produced three bottles of beer within a couple of minutes. And oh how I needed that beer. The dynamics between the three of us were peculiar. I had spent a lot of time with Indica on my own and some time, both amazing and frightening, with Nishantha, on his own. I had not been in the company of both of them at the same time and it was strange. I tried to cover it up with smiles and niceties. We all made small talk but I was inherently aware I couldn't say what I really wanted to say to Indica in front of Nishantha or, even more so, vice versa. I daren't even think about what they had said to each other or what they wanted to say. I didn't mention Kandy. It was an inappropriate time to do so. I asked about his journey here and spoke about how beautiful Daniel was and sunk my first beer before either of them were halfway through theirs.

"Rachael, we are thirsty today?" Indica said, flashing his trademark smile at me.

"Well, I'm two rounds behind you two, so I should really catch up."

Nishantha was very quiet. He smiled as Indica and I bantered.

"I'm going to call the waiter over. Do either of you want another?" I enquired.

Nishantha examined his bottle.

"No, thank you, I am still full."

"OK. Indica?"

He said something to Nishantha in his mother tongue then turned to me.

"Rachael. I am going to go home. I have to be home for Soma and Daniel. I am sure you two have a lot to talk about."

He said something else to Nishantha before saying goodbye to me and leaving. He sent the waiter over on his way and I ordered another beer.

Indica's departure unnerved me. I was not expecting the dynamics to change again so soon.

Having already covered all the obvious topics of small talk, we found ourselves in awkward silence territory.

"So...," we both started in unison. He looked fresh and neat again but he also looked tired. Maybe that is how I appeared to him, tired.

"Go on," he said. As I didn't really know what I was going to say I insisted that he spoke first.

"You look good to-night, well, you look well."

"Thank you, so do you."

We took a prolonged gulp from our beer bottles, laid them back down on the table and looked at each other.

"Rachael. How are you?"

"I'm fine, like I said earlier. I'm doing really well now. I'm..."

I started talking to him about my work, in the way I would talk to

Victor, trying to persuade him I was coping. My spiel was going well yet, as I ranted off the autocue in my mind, I saw something in Nishantha's eyes that made me stumble. It wasn't judgement or impatience for me to stop talking so he could start. It was far more unsettling. He could see right through me. I had no place to hide. My lies caught in my throat.

"I mean, how are you, really?" he asked.

Dormant needs saw their opportunity and tried to bubble up against my will. Part of me longed for somebody to listen and care in the way he was offering now yet a bigger part was still guarding such emotions. I used to wish Derren would really hear me, really see me instead of putting himself first and only hearing what suited him best. Somewhere along the line I had learnt it was easier to cut off from my own needs rather than be left wanting. Somewhere along the line my true feelings had become the centre of a set of Matroyshka dolls. Was I going to drop my guard for the first person to show me some sincerity? I looked down at my beer as I tried to ward off inner conflict.

"I'm sorry."

"Hey, it is OK, Rachael. I know. I know you are not OK."

"No I am. I am OK."

My tried and trusted walls won the battle and I suppressed anything that remotely resembled a true feeling. If I opened up now who knew what might come out. But then, wasn't this what I was after? To talk about feelings? It had sounded good in theory.

"Please do not be...angry...with Indica. He tell me you are not coping all so well."

"Oh. He said that? I'm not angry. What did he say?"

"Not a lot, just enough."

"I see.' *Full marks on your ability to be evasive there Nishantha.* 'And how have you been?" I asked, concerned.

Nishantha sat back in his chair and took some time to think about his answer. I admired that, was envious even. He always paused for thought before he spoke instead of opening his mouth mindlessly. It was refreshing.

"Hurt. All my life I see innocent peoples murdered for this war. I

try to believe that one day it will all stop. Now I do not think it ever will and it makes me hurt."
"Is this why your paintings are so sad?"
"Yes, it is like a...release."
His soft husky voice spoke slowly and with much feeling. I could learn a lot from this man. As I watched and listened I knew I had been right. A warm blanket of peace swept over me. I was exactly where I needed to be. His openness made me wish I had at least tried to be more honest. The conversation naturally curved away from that night and we engaged in a lot more small talk. We both made attempts at humour that didn't work out well for either of us. Our failed attempts made us laugh anyway. The atmosphere in the bar grew louder and more rowdy as the evening went on and the chance to really talk about what happened past. I was disappointed. I'd ruined my only chance to clear the air between us.
Reading me perfectly, Nishantha asked, "Would you like to leave?"
"Huh?" I said, straining to hear.
"Do you want to go?"
"Oh, yes, I think I would." I wanted to leave the bar, not his company. I only hoped he felt the same.
"Rachael. Do you want to go down to the beach?"
Yes, yes, yes, yes, yes, yes, yes!
"Could do I guess."
"I think a walk would be good."
The beach was strewn with couples and cosy groups of couples who wanted some privacy. We took off our shoes to walk more easily on the sand.
"I wonder if their parents know what they are all up to," I said smiling.
"I can tell you now, they do not."
The waves of the ocean roared up the beach wildly as if warning you to stay away. One body a week was pulled out of there during monsoon season. It was easy to see why. Nishantha appeared to be heading down to it all the same.

"Rachael, take my hand."
"I can't hear you!" I shouted over the roaring waves.
"Take my hand. I want to show you something," he repeated, raising his voice.
I looked around; we were the only people anywhere near the waves.
"OK.'
He took my hand and we edged into the crashing waves.
"Oh, Nishantha I don't like it, I really don't like it," I said nervously as a retreating wave sucked back into the ocean almost taking me with it. At the same time a monster wave was busy, swelling to full capacity, ready to steamroll towards us. Though still far away, it clearly towered above me and I tried to pull out of Nishantha's grip to run away.
"Trust me," he said, turning to give me a pleading look and tightening his grip on my hand.
I ignored the urge to run and stopped trying to pull away. As the wave hurtled towards me I grimaced and waited. By the time it got to us it wasn't towering above our heads anymore. In fact, it only came up to Nishantha's calves and my thighs. We stood there as it raged past us. I had to push my feet into the sand and stand strong to stay upright. As the ocean reclaimed its wave, it sucked even stronger and took me about a foot inwards. Nishantha gripped my arm with both of his hands and pulled me back in.
"Whoa!" I screamed as I held on to Nishantha. When the wave had passed we both ran back onto the beach.
"How did you like that?"
"It's so strong. I'm shocked, I'm exhilarated!"
"Were you scared?"
"I was shit-scared Nishantha, you know I was!"
"I am sorry, Rachael. I just wanted you to feel its strength."
"That's OK. I seem to be scared a lot when I'm with you!"
Nishantha stopped smiling and ran his fingers through his hair. My statement had killed the mood.
"I, I'm sorry, Nishantha, I didn't mean to bring it up again," I said

as we both walked back up the beach to drier sand.
"I think you did. I think you want to talk about it."
"Well, don't you?"
"You saved my life, Rachael. I can-not stop thinking about you."
My comment turned out to be the much needed icebreaker we were both waiting for.
"Yes, I can't stop thinking about it all either. It is only natural, after what we both went through."
He concentrated fully on me as I spoke to understand what I was saying. Then sat down on the sand, propping himself up on his elbows. I took a seat opposite him and sat cross-legged.
"Yes. Yes that is what I meant."
"So, what do you think about?" I asked.
He pondered for a moment. "I wonder if I did the right thing by you. I feel shame that I did not help you when they came into the room. I wonder if I could have saved Imanie and..." It was Nishantha's turn to choke up. "I wonder what you must think of me for not trying to save them."
"Nishantha, that isn't how I see it. If you had tried to help me or Imanie and her son, they would have shot you, for sure."
"I tried to protect you and I led to you straight to them."
"Nishantha, stop! Listen to me. I do not blame you for anything. Not for taking me to the guest house and not for hiding from them. You were brave when I was hysterical. You made me stay in sight when I wanted so badly to hide. We are both alive because of you."
By now my eyes had welled up and my voice was trembling.
"That means a lot to me, Rachael. Maybe one day I will believe it in here," he put his hand to his chest.
"Don't beat yourself up. I mean, do not blame yourself any more, it's not worth it if you are the only one doing it."
"I am only glad you had Indica to help you. I called him every day to see how you were."
"You did? He didn't tell me."
"I know."
"How have you been dealing with it back in Kandy?"

"I have been helping with the clean-up. I have tried to help people so I have been, how you say, 'fine'."
"Your family don't know by the way. I guess Indica told you that?"
"Yes, thank you for not telling them."
"That's OK."
"You know, I haven't told Indica this, or anybody come to that, but something happened to me before the parada. Before I met you I was laying on my bed, falling asleep when an image came into my head. It made me jump. I could even smell what I was seeing. I dreamt of a dead baby. It unnerved me. It was like a premonition. Does that sound crazy?"
"No, that does not sound crazy. I believe in premonitions. They are common here. Those who meditate seem to get them a lot."
"Oh. I thought you might laugh at me."
"Not at all."
We sat in silence for a while, watching the sporadic clusters of youths. The silence was natural and comfortable again, the way it is between two old friends. I was quietly pleased with myself for having finally opened up a little. We sat and talked for hours until, eventually, Nishantha offered to walk me back to my hotel. He showed me an unusual short cut I never would have thought to take: the train track. Nishantha strolled along side it while I walked on it, carefully stepping between the wooden slats. Never having walked along railway tracks before, this appealed hugely to my inner child. I'd always wanted to do this, ever since seeing it on *The Railway Children*. Nishantha laughed at me again for acting childishly.
The slats were spaced quite far apart so I had to take long strides and lots of care not to trip over. I couldn't divert my attention away from my feet in case I misplaced them.
"I used to walk along here every day when I was a child."
"Yeah?" It only occurred to me then that this was where he spent his childhood.
"Yes. I used to think it was magical. I have not seen it in that way for years."

"Until now? I have that affect on you a lot, me and my fresh eyes!"
"Yes, you do."
"There is nothing wrong with revisiting your childhood. Come on, walk with me."
I stopped walking so I could look up to gauge his reaction. He was strolling along on the dry grass verge with his hands in his jeans' pockets.
"No, thank you."
"Oh, come on."
"No, really, I am good here."
"Suit yourself."
"You see how the track curves around the, edge here?"
"Yes."
It followed the shore line beautifully, leading all the way to two skyscrapers at the end.
"I painted this view."
"Was there a sunset in the background?"
"Yes, that is right. There is a train on the tracks, there are many people looking out of the window, laughing and waving."
My embarrassing train boarding fiasco flashed before my eyes.
"Yes, I can imagine that well. What made you decide to teach art, Nishantha?"
"I love to paint, it is my first love."
"Do you ever sell any?"
"Some. Not many. I also make, um, with wood, how do you say?"
"Oh, carpentry, like your father?"
"Yes, my father teach me. So I teach art and I sell things I make from wood."
"That's good, not all your eggs are in one basket."
"Eggs?"
"Oh, sorry, it is a saying back home."
Usually I adapted to talking in ways people with limited English could understand but I kept forgetting to extend this courtesy to Nishantha.
Losing my balance and nearly falling over, I joined Nishantha on

the verge. Concentrating on two things at once in the dark was tricky after all that beer.

I explained what it meant but he still thought it was a strange analogy. Once we reached my hotel I realised I wished we hadn't. I'd have walked those tracks all the way to Wadduwa if I could have. Knowing goodbye was imminent we shared a lingering moment where we were just looking at each other knowingly, with intimate eyes. I surprised myself by enjoying it rather than pulling away.

"I had a good time to-night, Rachael. It was good to see you, to see you are OK after, after everything."

A lady walked by in a hurry. She was clutching a tiny baby. We both followed her with our eyes. She took me right back to that night at the guesthouse and my heart sank. The look on Nishantha's face told me he was thinking about it too. Not wanting to end the night on a downer I tried to revive the situation.

"They are in heaven now. Angels in heaven."

"Heaven? Tell me, Rachael, what does this heaven look like to you?" Nishantha asked.

"Well, everything there is calm, safe and tranquil, I guess. And somehow everybody you lost along the way is waiting for you there. Do you believe in heaven?"

"You hear people talk about heaven, heaven where every-thing is perfect. If you ask me, we are already there. We have two eyes to see the blue sky, to see somebody smile. Some will never see these, these beautiful sights. Some will never hear the voices of the peoples they love, or hear the sound of the sea breaking. Some will never walk on the sand at night or use their arms to hold a baby. We can. If there is a heaven, I think we are already in it, we just need to know it. Some will never know it. What more is there to ask for than what we already have?"

For the second time since I met Nishantha, I was rendered speechless. I thought his painting was profound but this was something else.

"If only we all saw things your way. We would be spared a lot of unnecessary pain I'm sure."

We looked at each other longingly again, as if neither of us wanted this to be goodbye.

"I, I better go up now."

"Thank you, Rachael."

"For what?"

"For forgiving me and for to-night."

"You don't have to thank me, Nishantha. The real truth of the matter is that I pushed Indica into letting me see you. I needed to talk to you about Kandy."

"I came here to see Daniel, yet, in my mind I hoped I would see you. I asked Indica if he would ask you."

"He didn't tell me that either."

"I know. I tell him not to."

"Oh. Well, then it worked out pretty well for the both of us, hey?"

"Yes I would say it did."

"Goodnight, Rachael."

"Goodbye, Nishantha."

And with that, he disappeared down the street.

Chapter 7

I was aware I had been smiling incessantly since my evening with Nishantha but I was not aware that Indica had clocked it too. After working hard all morning I had gone over to his stall to keep him company or, more accurately, to do some digging. If Nishantha had talked at all about our evening, Indica was keeping quiet. Refraining from talking about Nishantha to Indica was like leaving a child alone with a sweet and telling them not to eat it – it was torturous. After thirty minutes of squirming I finally cracked. Unwrapping the proverbial sweet, ready to revel in all its sugary goodness.
"Last night was...," *can't say lovely, can't say perfect, need a safe adjective...* "It was great. Thank you for arranging it."
"Ah, good! So you are better now, about that night?"
"Yes, I am."
I realised that for the first time since it happened, the attack hadn't even crossed my mind.
"Then it served a good purpose," Indica stated, closing the book on the subject. He was going to make this hard work. He was my only link and I was peeved that he wouldn't play ball.
"Is he still here?" I said, trying to sound only mildly interested.
"He left this morning."
Sticking with the sweeties theme, I can tell you my smile disappeared faster than the purple sweets in a box of Roses at Christmas.
"Oh."
"Rachael, you said to me you wanted to..." he broke off to sell a bunch of mini bananas and a few small, green oranges to a young girl.
"You say to me you want to see Nishantha to help you with Kandy."
"Yeah, and?"

"I say to you it is not a good idea."
"Oh god, this is the puddle thing again isn't it?"
"You say to me there is no puddle. So let it be now," he was frowning. "You make trouble for you and my family."
"I just want to know if seeing me has helped him, too," I said, pouring water on the fire.
"You say you only see him as a friend?" Indica asked accusingly.
"I do. Oh come on Indica just tell me, please!"
He laughed at me and shook his head.
"I do not believe you. He say nothing – like you. He does not have to say anything – like you. It is all in your eyes. Both of you."
"What's in his eyes?" I blurted out far too eagerly. Those pesky butterflies rose in my stomach again.
Indica threw me a glare that told me to drop it and that is what I did. So near yet so far. Goodbye little sweet.
Having left Indica to it, I decided to walk to Ravi's. Every time I suffered a trauma I seemed to neglect him, finding the language barrier and his accommodation too hard to contend with. The walk alone was bliss. The alone time enabled me to be able to smile to myself without risk of accusation. Knowing I should refrain, I indulged in Nishantha's words and let the memories of our evening replay in my mind. Yet despite all this, I still stubbornly held on to the belief Indica was wrong.

Ravi was entertaining his family when I arrived. They were visiting from Kalutara, just south of Colombo. They mentioned the attacks, as most people did, and I kept my experience to myself, as mostly I did. I was about to leave them all to it when they started talking about a subject I had recently found myself fascinated with. They were recalling the story of how Ravi's brother, Pryantha, had come to meet his wife, Nahindra. I tried to ask questions without appearing too nosey.
Nahindra only spoke Sinhala so Pryantha relayed their story.
"When we meet, we meet with tea."
I frowned, trying to understand what he meant. He had a high,

soft and husky voice that reminded me of one of the doctors I had interviewed here. Both Pryantha and the doctor did the confusing head waggle that looks like they are saying 'no' but actually means 'yes'. He did it more in habit when they spoke rather than to convey a 'yes'. I was often confused by the waggle so it made me wonder if we listen more with our eyes than with our ears. Pryantha also rolled his r's in the way of the doctor I had met too.
"She bring tea to her family and to my family. She pour the tea and then she leave us all to talk about the dowry."
"Oh. And that the very first time you met your wife?"
'Yes', he said, shaking his head.
"Did she get to talk to you, or anybody?"
"The woman, she can talk if she want to. Most woman are shy, they are shy. They do not want to talk."
"Is this how most men meet their wives?"
"Actually, yes, this is the way."
"How do people know they will love their spouse, or like them even?"
"You start with respect and then this grow into more. You trust your mother and your father choice for you."
"Wow. I'm sorry, it is a very new idea for me. From where I come from we choose our own husbands and wives. Did you ever want to have the choice for yourself?"
"No, not for me. More people do today actually. This bring nothing good. People make bad choices."
If my parents or Victor had chosen a husband for me I would be Mrs Law-Degree by now.
On leaving Ravi's I still felt like I was betraying him by staying in a hotel that was about five-hundred per cent more expensive than his place. I knew it was almost time to move back to his. As I walked back to my rented mansion I rummaged through my day bag for my sunglasses. The sun had settled at a level where it was right in the eyes of anybody who walked in a westerly direction. As I rummaged, I came across the postcards I had written on my way to Kandy. I hadn't given them a second thought since the train journey. I read the words on the card intended for Laura. The

handwriting was mine but the words belonged to somebody else, somebody who sounded enthused about discovering tuk-tuks and late monsoon rains. I knew this person once. I felt a distant familiarity with them. Now all that was there, was a sense of loss of one's self. As I read the part where I wished Laura was here, too, I thought, no, I do not wish you were here. In fact, I'm glad you are not.

Thinking about home had become a chore. All those people who were never satisfied with what they had, who only concerned themselves with what else they wanted, or what else they had to have next. I had been the same before my career change. Now here I was with practically nothing of any monetary value to my name and I was happier and more grateful than ever before. Not only did I *like* being around people who thought being happy was more important than worrying, or wanting, I *needed* it. My chest panged at the regret of not keeping in touch with the person back home who might have known how I felt; Jaycee, from my days as a temp. Her parents lived in India and, in the time I knew her, she made the decision to join them so she could travel the East. If I could turn the clock back, I'd have kept in contact with her. After all, she sort of put me on this path of exploration by opening my mind to the idea right before Victor offered this job to me.

I posted the postcards only because I happened to be passing a post depot, then pushed all thoughts of home aside.

As I lay on my bed trying to reread my work notes, the phone rang. *Please be Nishantha, please be Nishantha*, I thought, knowing it couldn't possibly be him. I guess some things never change no matter where you are.

"Hello?"

"Rachael, it's Victor…"

"Oh… Hi."

"Don't sound too disappointed. Who were you expecting, Brad Pitt?"

"No, Brad and I left it that I'd call him. Look, I'm sorry. I am pleased to hear from you. How is everything your end?"

"Everything is good. Martha is just getting over her ingrown toenail operation, she is glad to have finally 'nailed' that problem! Do you get it?"
"Oh, Victor, how long have you been waiting for an opportunity to say that?"
"Oh. Not funny then."
"No."
"Yes. Nobody else laughed either. You were my last hope."
"So that's why you've called me, to see if I'll laugh at your jokes, huh?"
"No no, I have been asked by Leon for feedback on the victims in Kandy."
I hadn't even thought to do that even though it was blindingly obvious that is what I should have done.
"Since when did we produce the finished article while still out in the field?"
"I know, Rachael. The latest attacks have really caused a stir and he wants to push this through as soon as possible."
"What? Without me?"
"He has suggested you forget the doctors and families and roll with the more topical victims in Kandy."
"That's so typical. Does he know anything about what I am doing? No. So why does he get to bully me, no, undermine me like this?"
"I have suggested more subtle changes. But as you know it must seem like all these suggestions are his."
"I'm not dropping the doctors, or the hospitals, or the real people this affects. It's the mixture together that paints the picture."
"Keep doing what you are doing. Just make sure you cover the civil war victims. Have you been to Kandy yet to see the aftermath?"
"I was waiting to see if it was safe."
"Really? That doesn't sound like you."
"What can I say? I'm a changed woman."
"You must be because the Rachael I know would be on the first plane, train or...flying carpet over there before the dust had a

chance to settle."

I hadn't seen that one coming. He was right. I would have been over there in a flash.

"Don't sweat it Victor. I'm on my way."

Awesome, an excuse to go to Kandy. I got on with the preparations right away, to head there the next day and as I busied myself the phone rang again.

Please be Nishantha, please be Nishantha.

"Hello?"

"Rachael, it's me again."

"Oh hey, Victor. What's up?"

"A couple of things actually. I'm a bit confused. You told me last time we spoke you nearly went to a parade in Kandy but decided not to go."

"That's right."

Liar.

"When were you planning on going?"

"I didn't get as far as a specific date."

"So you didn't go?"

"No, what is this Victor? You sound like you don't believe me?"

"I was expecting to hear how lucky you thought you were to have narrowly escaped being present at a terrorist attack."

"If my plan was to go *that night* I might have said something like that. But it wasn't, so no coincidence there for me to mull over."

There was a long pause. I held my breath and bit my lip on the end of the phone.

"What's going on Rachael? You would have at least called to beg for permission to go to Kandy after the attack."

"Nothing is going on Victor. I had things going on here that I could not just leave," I said, adding substance to my lie.

"Are you alright Rachael?"

He knew I was lying and I wasn't going to share. The change in the tone of his voice told me he just wanted to know if I was OK.

"I am good, Victor, honestly."

"Right. Well, when you get to Kandy let me have your new contact details as soon as you have them. Oh, and the other thing.

I have just been speaking with Leon. I should warn you he has your leaving date in mind."

"Right, any ideas when?" I asked, after a delay while I processed.

"A week, at a guess. Then again it could be in a few days for all I know."

"Oh, OK. Well thanks for the heads up. Please let me know as soon as you hear."

"I will. You take care of yourself, Rachael. Stay in contact."

"Yes, of course I will. You take care too. Oh, and send my love to Martha."

"OK, speak soon."

I hung up and tried to remember details of the lies I had told. Perhaps I had already tripped myself up. Either way Victor knew I was lying. I had to. Staying superseded truth, of that I was sure. I felt so guilty lying to that man. He was the only person who stood up for me when the rest of the world thought I was a liar. Before I worked for Victor I was training to work as an occupational therapist in the mental health sector. I loved the job. I looked after people in a residential care home who would never be able to look after themselves. The day after our Christmas work do it all changed. I wasn't supposed to be on shift that day but one of the girls was too hung-over to come in so I took her shift as a favour. While at work, I walked in on one of the doctors with his hands on one of the female residents. He was touching her breasts. The shock of what I had seen caused me to walk straight back out again. I was shocked because we all liked and trusted the doctor in question, Dr Clifton. He was sickeningly nice to me for the remainder of the day. He reeked of guilt. It wasn't until two days later, when her family came in to give her a birthday present, that I decided to go to the manager. Seeing Maria with her family made me realise she is a human being, with people who love her. If she couldn't stand up for herself, I'd have to do it for her.

My manager thought I was lying. She refused to believe a word of it. Despite this, she was duty-bound to put him on immediate suspension. The matter ended up in court and the whole thing was a sham, an unfair battleground. The young lady in question was

Maria. She had the mental capacity of a four year old and was not allowed to give evidence. So that left just me. Dr Clifton denied any wrongdoing and his defence trashed my character. He had all my colleagues on his side, too. He concocted a story that I was seeking revenge on him because he rejected my advances at the work do. I made no such advances yet he had everyone believing him. I guess they believed what they most wanted to believe. At the work do a picture had been taken of me doing a shot of vodka while sitting on his lap. It sounds worse than it was. A few people sat on his lap that night, men and women, while he acted as Santa and gave out all our secret Santa presents. Despite this, the picture was used against me. It showed I was drunk and that alcohol would still have been in my system when I saw the doctor in Maria's room. It also added plausibility to the rumours that I had a crush on the accused. Even my on-off relationship with Derren was dragged into it. They made it sound like the absence of my father, and my unstable relationship, drove me to think I could find stability in Dr Clifton. They mentioned Derren was in a band called N-Trails, just to hammer the final nail in the coffin. It was really bad timing because he had only just joined. The court ruled in Dr Clifton's favour and I had to leave my job and training. Employers in that sector avoided me. Despite the ruling, Maria was moved to another home by her family. She died shortly afterwards of a stroke. She was always having strokes. She outlived her predicted life expectancy but it was still very sad to think I'd caused upheaval in her life so close to her death. I carried that guilt around with me until her family invited me to the funeral and there I learnt they had all believed me. Her great-uncle believed me. He even offered me a job. His name was Victor.

Life in Kandy was going on much the same as it had the first time I arrived there. I made a taxi driver's day and let him take me to a hotel of his choosing. Looking around the streets from inside the taxi, it was hard to believe this city had been under attack at all. Kandy had moved on. Children played, people worked (or stood about socialising somewhere near their place of work) and the conmen still loved me. Most people I met could not do enough for me – for free, I might add. After checking into a hotel owned by the taxi man's 'brother' I took a leisurely stroll around town. There was something soothing about being there. My only regret was that I had left things with Indica on a low note before leaving. I'd told him my boss wanted me to go to Kandy. He didn't even ask whether I would try to catch up with Nishantha or not. He just looked disappointed. By the same token I chose not to ask Indica if he was going to tell Nishantha I was going. As I ambled along the dusty roads lined with stalls I saw everything from clothes to utensils to fruit for sale. The market along the road stretched on as far as the eye could see. A group of twenty-something guys at a fruit stall singled me out and called me over. They reminded me of Indica, making me wish he was here. One guy seemed to be working the stall while all the others were drinking around it. They offered me the chance to try anything I liked from their stall free of charge. Straight arrack was included but I disappointed them by pointing to a fruit I'd never tried before. It was deep purple in colour and was about the shape and size of an orange. They broke one open for me. The purple skin was at least half an inch thick. Inside the segmented flesh was pure white. I took a piece from the guy, Raj, who handed it to me. He told me what it was but I forgot straight away. It tasted like a mixture of strawberries and grapes. It was delicious. We all chatted and joked for a while until I felt comfortable enough to bring up the dreaded topic of the Tamil Tiger attacks. Nobody there had been involved directly yet they all knew somebody who knew somebody who had lost their life that night. One guy, really skinny and adolescent looking, told me he knew a couple who had lost their son in the raid. He told me they lived in the house next door to his friend. He was almost completely deaf so I was really pleased with how well we communicated. His name was Daniel. He was very young, much younger than the other boys working at this Kandy market. I wondered if he was born with impaired hearing or if he had lost it somehow. I guessed he had lost it somehow because he spoke English so maybe he'd learnt that before losing it. Either way, I decided to steer clear of the subject. He possessed such a strong, charismatic charm it seemed so unjust that he was deaf.

I told him my friend in Colombo had just had a baby boy and named him Daniel. He was pleased and made out like all the best people were called Daniel. It was becoming a popular name amongst the younger generation. I told him I would like to talk to the parents of the boy who died and before I knew it I was in a tuk-tuk with Daniel and a driver, and on my way to Daniel's friend's neighbour's house. Halfway there we found ourselves stuck in traffic due to a roadblock. Roadblocks were commonplace. They were all over Colombo as well as Kandy. Daniel hopped out of the tuk-tuk and ran into a shop. When he came back he handed me a hand-drawn map on a piece of scrap paper. The driver explained it would take too long for us to go there today and asked me where I would like to be taken to instead. I knew where I'd *like* to be taken but could I? Sod it, yes I could.

"To the art institute please."

Chapter 8

As I stood outside the institute I smiled and breathed in a big sigh of ultimate contentment. Kandy made me feel so content and fulfilled that everything I had back in England now seemed futile in comparison. I felt good here, at peace.
The sun shining down on me, the kind and loving people who actually had time for each other, and the draw of discovering more and more that Sri Lanka had to offer had me locked under a spell. Kandy might just be a place but for me it was a place that gave me a sense of equilibrium. Strange, when you consider all it had given me so far were strong emotions at both ends of the spectrum. I'd experienced excitement and wonderment and fear and deep sadness, both to extents I'd never known before. Far too busy feeling glad to be back in Kandy, I wasn't nervous about surprising Nishantha (be it pleasantly or otherwise) at all. As it turned out, I was the one who was pleasantly surprised. Nishantha was standing at reception when I entered the building. He was with a dumpy girl, oriental in appearance, perhaps Thai. They were leaning over the desk and reading something. The pretty receptionist from before was there too. She was leaning over from her side of the desk. I crept up on him. Nobody noticed me standing right behind Nishantha and the oriental girl.
"We have to stop meeting up like this!" I said playfully. They all startled at the sudden interruption and looked up at me. Nishantha turned around, his eyes flitting up and down my person. He did it in an innocent way, not in a sleazy way that is often followed by 'ello darling' back home. Nishantha blushed, his eyes quickly returning back to mine as he caught himself. I blushed in turn. It was more subtle though this time – unlike the last time I was there when I looked like I was concealing the red planet under the skin of my cheeks.
"Rachael, you...you look, good."

"Thank you, so do you." The two girls looked like they were watching tennis as their eyes, and only their eyes, moved from Nishantha to me in turn.
"I have come back for work purposes and I thought, maybe you could help me with that?"
"Of course, if I can, I will."
Silence.
"Perfect. Err, have you had lunch? Are you hungry?" I said, fearing an awkward situation.
"I have already had lunch."
"Oh," I said, finding myself in an awkward situation.
"Nishantha, you have one hour until your next class. I can cover if anybody asks for you," The pretty girl at reception announced as a quick solution. Her eyes were cartoon like, large, doe-brown and framed with long, curling lashes. She wore large twenty-four carat gold earrings, purple eye shadow and glossy pink lipstick. If I wore all that I would look like a clown; she looked sensational, a Walt Disney beauty.
"Istuti. I will not be late."
She nodded to Nishantha while wearing a cheeky grin, much like Paul's I noticed.
We left the two girls at reception, buried in whatever it was they were all reading before I interrupted, and made our way into town. A late onset of nervousness almost paralysed me as we walked together. After all I was in his company uninvited and he hadn't been that forthcoming about spending the rest of his lunch hour with me. I found myself explaining again that work had brought me to Kandy; I was trying too hard to prove I wasn't stalking him. He had seemed genuinely pleased to see me at first but now he was back to his usual composed self and was giving nothing away in the form of much needed reassurance. I rambled on about this guy Daniel who had given me Irshaad's address and Nishantha nodded in all the right places. I told him how they had ended up bringing me here and had refused to accept payment and how the driver had given Daniel a driving lesson on the way here, which was a bit hairy in places. He basically received a step-by-

step account of my journey. On reaching a Western-style cafe he held the door open and gestured for me to walk in. I asked him if this was the sort of place he would usually come to .When he didn't understand I rephrased.

"Do you come here often?" I asked.

"Oh, no, only with people who are not from here."

I smiled, thinking about the chat up line I had just inadvertently used.

"Why are you smiling?" he asked as we slid into a booth. I forgot I was in the company of somebody who noticed these things. Too much time ignored by Derren had made me forget people can actually see the expressions on my face when they appear.

By the time he understood that I had just used the world's cheesiest chat-up line, our drinks had been ordered and were sitting in front of us. The humour in it had been lost in translation by then. I felt awkward again. We were not feeling comfortable together, as we had the other times we'd met. Then, with one look and with one question Nishantha put it all right.

"Rachael, how have you been?"

Hundreds of people ask that question every day as they engage in small talk and more often than not you give a polite *yeah, good thanks, you?* It was different when Nishantha asked it. It was as if he put the whole world on hold and looked into my soul. I could feel my outer Matroyshka dolls cracking open. I was flattered by the intimate attention but, sadly, it was still a concept I found uncomfortable.

"Yeah, good thanks, you?" I said, hiding behind what I knew best.

Nishantha looked into my eyes a moment longer as if trying to see what I was hiding behind my standardized answer before sitting back in his chair.

"I think I am moving on from what happened more, more, slowly than other peoples seem to be but, ah, I am still moving on, all the same."

It was pathetic. Now that somebody was actually interested in how I felt, I didn't even know myself. His truthful, open answer made me long to be able to open up so much I felt a pain in my chest.

"Maybe it just seems that way you know? Other people might look at you and think you have moved on faster than them. Maybe they think they are the ones who are struggling. We all make out like we are doing better than perhaps we really are."

"Is that what you are doing now?"

My cheeks burned.

"No. I don't know. Maybe I am. I mean, yes, yes I am and I don't know why. I can tell you one thing for sure, I love being here, this place, it agrees with me. I'm so happy to be here."

He smiled as if satisfied I had told him something real and drank his coke through the straws in his old-fashioned American-milkshake-style glass. I, too, was happy that I had accessed and divulged a little snippet of truth from inside. I sucked on the straws in my banana fruit shake and drew up a lump of banana that had escaped the blades of the blender. The banana interrupted the flow of my drink so I swirled my straws around the top of my fruit-shake, making shapes where it was still thick and frothy.

"So, what do you do for fun around here?" I asked, changing the conversation.

"Well, I might start making pictures in your shake. It seems to be working for you," he teased.

"Look, it kinda' looks like a bee."

"Let me see," Nishantha said, leaning forwards. "That does not look like a bee, it looks like a, how do you say? Like a squiggle."

"A squiggle! How do you even know that word? It does not look like a squiggle, it looks like a bee!" I said, laughing and tilting my glass for a better angle.

"Just like a child."

"Hey! Quit with the childish theme would you?"

"You sound like one now as-well," he laughed.

"I like it when you laugh."

Did I really just say that out loud?

"And why do you like it when I laugh?"

"Because it means I am funny!"

Nice save.

"You can be funny too. Mostly I laugh *at* you."
"I'm going to ignore you now and make another bee-friend for my little bee to play with."
"So you do not want to know?"
"Know what?"
"What we do for fun?"
"Go on…" I said, setting my drink to one side.
"We go to *The Ivory*, in the evenings."
"What is *The Ivory*? Is it a club?"
"No, for a club you need Colombo. *The Ivory* is more like, err, like a bar, people meet there, drink, and there is dancing too, and poker, sometimes."
"Yep, that sounds like a good place to go to have fun, all the right ingredients."
"It is. You should go, while you are here," Nishantha said smiling slightly smugly at me. The corners of my mouth turned up involuntarily as I realised he was playing a little game called 'I know she is fishing for an invite so I'm going to make her work for it'. If anybody had the inclination and enough patience to open me up it was this guy. Not having anything clever to say at hand I just smiled and shook my head.
"What? Is there something you would like to ask?" he said with mild sarcasm.
"No. Like what?"
He was wasting his time. As much as I would love to go there with him, I was never going to ask him to take me. Not in a million years would I have enough balls to do that.
"So you only wanted to know where we go to have fun, you did not want to go have fun yourself?"
"I…well, I'm not about to invite myself out with you if that is what you are getting at!"
"Why not?"
"That would be rude."
"But you want to go right?"
"I would consider going should I be invited, if not, it's no big deal."

"Rachael?"

"Yes?" I was huffy by this point, displeased at being plucked out of my comfort zone. Nishantha lightened up.

"Remember how you felt at the beach. When you were scared by the waves? You faced the waves, and after, you were glad you did."

It was time to grow some balls.

"Well, would it be so terrible if you maybe took me there, one day, perhaps?" My cheeks began to glow.

"Yes," he paused. "Yes, it would be terrible."

I believed him for all of a second but that was long enough for him to see the expression on my face.

"No, I am joking! It would not be terrible. I would love for you to come with us. With me and my friends, I mean."

"You're mean!" I said, throwing a napkin at him. "Making fun of me all the time."

"I am not making fun of you," he said reassuringly. "Although you do make it easy!" he added.

"I do not!"

And so the banter flowed. In a matter of minutes we were laughing and joking around in a way that made me forget my hang-ups. I forgot more than just my hang-ups. As cheesy as it sounds, I lost all awareness of the rest of the world as I immersed myself in our bubble. I wondered if we had a special chemistry or if he was just a great guy who made everybody he met feel this important, this great. I wondered what Laura would say if she knew I liked Nishantha, a Sinhalese guy. I didn't care. Anyway I was just getting carried away in the moment. This was all purely platonic.

After our drink Nishantha and I stood by the side of the road waiting for a tuk-tuk to take me back to my hotel.

Not wanting to make him late for his class I assured him I could wait on my own so that he could head back to the institute.

"I have time," Nishantha said. I started to wonder if Nishantha was going to ask for a contact number or something, to honour our pending night out. He said nothing about meeting again before a tuk-tuk pulled up beside us.

Nishantha negotiated a fair price for me and gave me the money, despite my efforts to decline it.

"I hope you didn't mind me turning up unannounced today."

"No, I liked you coming."

"OK then, well enjoy your class, and thanks for the drink," I said, trying to hide my disappointment that he didn't suggest a way we might meet up again. I thought about mentioning *The Ivory* but my nerves were holding my voice captive so I climbed into the tuk-tuk and waved goodbye.

"Wait," Nishantha said, putting a hand on the roof as the tuk-tuk made to pull away. The driver stopped while Nishantha spoke to him in Sinhala.

"Rachael, I meant to ask you, do you need me to come to this Irshaad's place with you? I can help you if they do not speak English."

"Oh, yeah, that would be great, if you want to?"

"Can you meet me here, to-morrow?"

"Yes, what time?"

"At, err, at one past thirty?"

"I think you mean thirty minutes past one!"

"Oh, yes, I always get that confused."

"OK then, I'll see you tomorrow, at one."

"See you, at 1p.m," he said as if trying to bank the correct phrase in his long-term memory.

With that, the driver put his foot down and we were soon overtaking everything on the road all the way to my hotel.

I spent the evening preparing questions for the interview in case the parents of the murdered boy agreed to talk to me. I knew I would have to tread carefully where such raw emotions were concerned but that was hardly a problem, I empathised greatly with them already and I was still to meet them. When I'd had enough of working, I sprawled out on my bed like a starfish and tried to sleep. It had been such a long day and I was so tired. Once again my busy mind refused to give me the peace required for sleep. Something about the room was bugging me. It lacked character; it seemed lifeless and lonely and was quite aptly numbered room 101, which is exactly where I would put it should that old show be revived. I started thinking about what else I would put into room 101 and figured those little half-seats you find at bus stops would have to go in. I can't understand why you would bother making half a seat that you can only lean on awkwardly and that you couldn't actually sit on. If you are going to make a seat, why not just make one big enough to sit on? Full of random thoughts, my mind refused to quieten to let me sleep and I found myself tossing and turning at all hours of the night.

The next day I took a tuk-tuk to meet Nishantha outside the cafe as planned. The driver had never heard of this place so I had to give him the name of the road and walk up and down until I found it. Despite the slightly stressful search for the place, I was still there just before Nishantha. We sat at the same table as before and ordered the same drinks. This time I ordered chicken salad to munch on while I went through my notes one more time. I was starting to feel tired already from a poor night's sleep and nervous at going to this house.

"Have you got time for all this?" I asked Nishantha, taking a break from stressing and taking a minute to consider the poor man being ignored opposite me.

"I am finished now, I have time. Later I have to go to lebadu, I mean, furniture shop," Nishantha gave a cute little frown at his mistake of speaking to me in Sinhala and I had to stifle a smile.

"Can I see your map?"

"Yes, of course," I said, hoping he hadn't noticed I'd been staring.

"This is far Rachael. This is out of town."

"Oh. Do you want me to go on my own?"

"No, I am coming with you. This is a like a... a shantytown, you know? Like a slum."

"Oh. Is it safe?"

"You should not go alone."

Half a plate of chicken later (the salad aspect of the chicken salad never arrived) we took yet another tuk-tuk to Irshaad's house. The compound was *exactly* like a shantytown. There were goats and chickens roaming around the yellow dusty paths and all the makeshift huts were roofed with ill-fitting corrugated iron. The huts were on par with your average garden shed in diameter and consisted only of one room. There were many people around and they all stared at us, especially the children who would usually have raced up to me by now to beg for school pens or small change. Nishantha asked around, trying to locate my contact. The people he spoke to were very reluctant to speak to him, brushing him off and avoiding eye contact as they walked away from him mid-sentence. Nishantha had to tell the story of who we were there to see many times before we were finally pointed in the right direction. What was I thinking trying to come here alone? I would have been completely out of my depth. We were led off the main path and deep into a maze of ramshackle homes, the smell and humidity intensifying as we walked further in. Although I trusted people in Sri Lanka on the whole, I was acutely aware we were completely at their mercy here.

Irshaad only spoke Sinhala so Nishantha translated for us. Mosquitoes were whining and buzzing around me in great numbers so I pulled out my industrial strength chemical lemon repellent and coated myself in it while they conversed. The children all looked on in amazement then covered their little noses to escape the chemical smell that was so alien to them.

Irshaad walked off in his tablecloth sarong while Nishantha tentatively sat me down on a small stack of hessian bags. It was looking like bad news.

"Rachael, the boy shot at the parada, he was a young police-man. He lived in Kandy town and he make monies for his family who stay here so they could eat."

"Right," I said, taking in every detail so I could later create an accurate account.

"The mother and the father have more children, small children, and no monies other than what their son brings them. The father, Sunil, has been missing since yesterday morning."

"Because his son died?"

"Because he can-not feed his family, so Irshaad believes."
"Well, he can't feed them now can he? Not if he has left them completely on their own?"
"Rachael, nobody knows what happened to Sunil. Irshaad has gone to see if Sunil's wife will talk to you."
Irshaad came back alone holding a banana leaf package. He took out what looked like a nut, started chewing on it and offered some to Nishantha who politely declined. I had seen men chewing this before so I prepared myself for all the spitting of the dark red liquid that was surely to come.
He spoke to Nishantha again who then translated for me.
"Rachael, Sunil's wife will not speak to you without her husband, I am sorry. Irshaad has said you should come back another time. He tell me many people are out looking for this man."
Irshaad spat out a blob of blood-red spit on to the ground, which made me wince. I just could not get used to it.
"That's fine. Can we go?"
"You want to go now?" he sounded surprised.
"Yes. I am so hot in this sun, it's making me feel sick."
"Istuti," I said to Mr Spit. And to Nishantha, "Please give these rupee notes to Irshaad. One is for him, for his time, and the other is to go to Sunil's wife. Tell him please, please let it get to her."
Nishantha nodded to me. "Bohoma istuti," he said to Irshaad as he handed him the money. They spoke a little longer while I stood waiting in the heat. The kids all ran up to me now that I was on my own. Some of them hid their arms up their sleeves to appear disabled. I shook my head and ignored them until they went away. I didn't have any more small money to give. I felt so uncomfortable in that place and was annoyed that this Sunil had left his family alone to cope with the loss of their son and brother. My reaction surprised me. It's not like I knew this family. It was as though I could sense their abandonment. This place was shocking.
Nishantha and I were escorted back to the main path where we parted from their company and made our own way out. When we made it to the main road we both sat under the shade of a tree to

cool off. The shade took the edge off the sticky heat and my nausea passed.

"Rachael, what are you angry about?" my new mind-reader friend asked.

"I wouldn't say I'm angry, as such. I just think if he has run away, that's selfish. I don't know the situation so I shouldn't even be judging."

"He may have gone away to find work."

"No, he would have told his wife. I just think it's selfish to leave somebody who loves you wondering if you are dead or alive."

"You have a gentle nature Rachael. Just remember it is not you and it may all be OK in the end, for all you know. You have walked in halfway through a story that is not over."

"Well I wish I knew the ending."

"Then we will come back."

I looked at him and smiled a grateful smile at him.

"Thank you, Nishantha. This is really kind of you."

"I have a confession to make," he said.

"Go on?"

"I wanted to come help you today because there is something I want to ask you."

"OK?"

"Would you like to go back to the Suisse View with me?"

"Oh."

"Say no if you do not want to."

"Have you been back at all, since?"

"Once, soon after, but I was still in shock then. I would like to go again, with you."

"When do you want to go?"

"Right now, if you want to?"

"Let's do it."

When we arrived at the guesthouse, Nishantha explained to the new manager that we would like to take a look around and he let us in. My first impression was that very little of the damage had been restored; a money issue I imagined. Walking around the place invoked a mixed bag of memories. The smell of the place flooded my senses and took me right back to that night. I hadn't even been aware this place had its own smell, or that it had imbedded itself in my memory. After convincing my reptilian brain I was safe here this time, I remembered other things from that night. I remembered feeling tired and stoned on arrival and excited about seeing Nishantha and going to the parade. I remembered being terrified as we bounded up the stairs to my room, and the disturbing vision of the dead baby that, with hindsight, may well have been a premonition. Nishantha and I both looked around slowly and wide-eyed like a cat exploring its new surroundings. The slightest noise in that building made me jump. Once we reached the room we'd run to that night we both drifted into our own little world, separately internally processing our own experiences of that night. No key had been needed to enter the room because the door was still hanging off its hinges. Nishantha stared at the window. I stared at the bed. I don't know what was going through Nishantha's mind but I was trying to remember sitting on the bed, dealing with the terrorists. Oddly, I was remembering it all like it had been a movie, or had happened to somebody else. The emotional side of it was absent no matter how hard I tried to feel it. I had hoped it would be more like a funeral where you feel the pain and let it out in order to move on but I felt nothing.

"Rachael?"
"Jesus!" I jumped right out of my skin.
"I am sorry. I did not mean to scare you. Are you OK?"
"Yes, yes I am. This is also your first time in this room isn't it?"
"In this room, yes."
"How are you doing?"
Nishantha took in a deep breath. "I still hurt for the peoples I found and for bringing you right here," Nishantha had tears in his eyes. "Rachael, if I could go back, I would never have led you here."
It was sad that the one thing giving Nishantha the most trouble was the only thing getting me through all this. I needed him that

night, no matter how it turned out, but he couldn't see it.

"If you only knew how much I needed you that night. You would know I don't blame you for anything."

"I left you with them. I could not protect you."

"If you had tried, we wouldn't be standing here having this conversation right now, would we? You would have gotten yourself, or maybe both of us killed. Please, stop beating yourself up and start admiring yourself as much as I do. For what you did I mean, I admire what you did, that night," I corrected.

"I will try to believe you are right."

"That's a good start. Now, let's get the hell out of here."

We both thanked the new manager for letting us in and Nishantha dropped some change into the makeshift donation pot in the form of an old rusty tin. I still had no small money so Nishantha donated on my behalf too.

"You would never see a charity box like that in England. It would be sealed and chained to something very, very heavy."

"Do you miss England?" he asked as we walked along a familiar road where the gravel crunched softly underfoot.

"I miss my family and friends sometimes," I thought hard to find something else I missed. "...And baked beans. I miss baked beans on thick doorstep bread, lightly toasted, with loads of butter and just a touch of black pepper, yummy. It's odd though, I only eat beans on toast once every few months – if that – I just really miss it now I can't have it."

"Do you miss the country?"

"Not at all."

"When will you have to return?"

"Soon I think. It depends on my boss. I prefer not to think about it to be honest. I don't really want to go."

We turned into a little alley off the main road that that ultimately led to the shop selling Nishantha's furniture. We walked in and the customers stopped inspecting their potential purchases to turn and stare at us. Their stares made me feel proud to be in Nishantha's company and I wondered if they thought we were together. I'd be lying if I said I didn't hope that's what they thought. It's funny, I never once thought in that way when I was out with Indica.

Everything in the shop was made from wood and wicker. Every join looked perfect and there appeared to be no screws or nails holding them together. The workmanship was immaculate – to my knowledge. I was left to admire Nishantha's work while he spoke to a man behind the counter in his mother tongue.

"Nishantha, you are truly gifted," I said once he'd finished talking.

"Istuti, I mean, thank you. My father, Johan, taught me this trade and now I can give him some of the money I make from selling my work."

"That's good of you. You have a lovely family."

"They seem to think a lot of you."

"Do you miss them now you live in Kandy?"

"Sometimes. I see them often enough and it stops them trying to make all my decisions for me."

"Like your marriage?" I asked, looking up at him and bracing myself as I ascertained whether or not I'd crossed a line.

He looked at me and took a moment to gather himself.

"Like the marriage."

"I'm sorry. It is none of my business."

"It is OK. I guess I just do not think about it, like you with going home."

So they were. The two inarguable reasons that any budding feelings I may have had for Nishantha should stop right there. I was going home and Nishantha was getting married. So why then, was my heart racing at the thought that maybe, just maybe, Nishantha liked me too?

Chapter 9

Every time I see you I get high
I'm on it, I want it
I've flirted with your mind and now it's time to give your body a try
Do-do-do. La-la-la

I was dancing and singing around the hotel and I had every reason to. After Nishantha and I left the furniture shop yesterday, he asked me if I would like to join him and his friends at a bar and then onto *The Ivory* the next day. I managed to remain composed when he asked me, but the minute I was behind closed doors in my hotel room I jumped up and down on my bed in a shameless victory dance. He was so lovely to be around, and he made me feel good about myself. He made me feel calm and it was as if the rest of the world didn't matter. And every time I pictured those big soulful eyes looking at me I just wanted to be back in his company again. Indica would be so mad with me. But Indica was still wrong. I may have liked Nishantha a little more than planned but so what? People have little crushes all the time. In a week I would be out the way and Nishantha would become a fond memory to look back on. So what was the harm? Also, Nishantha was an attractive man with muscles and a waist that formed a chiselled 'V'. Who wouldn't fancy him?
If I'd had a friend with me, Laura, Indica, or anybody, they would have brought me down with that dreaded voice of reason. For this reason I was happy I was on my own; that and the fact that I wasn't hitting the high notes of my song with any degree of decorum.

Every time I.... See you I...
Struggle to remember my name

To miss this opportunity would be a shame...

The cool, inviting evening persuaded me to walk into town for my night out. I wore a slinky short – but not too short – spaghetti-strapped cream dress that clung and swung in all the right places. I slipped on my high – but not too high – cream sandals and I applied some subtle make-up, well, we were going out on the town. The intricate chain of my delicate white-gold necklace slunk into the contours of my collarbones and back out again and the small curved cross pendant rested between just a hint of modest cleavage that was covered by my cotton-soft dress. I sprayed on a light misting of Light Blue, which, like my make-up and my dress, was subtly feminine in scent.
Nervously I waited outside the bar for Nishantha. He had chosen a bar near the cafe we had been to so I would know where to go. The longer I waited the time I had to get myself together and talk myself out of any romantic notions I may have been having. Nishantha and I were meeting as friends and that was that.
When Nishantha arrived, it has to be said that he looked amazing and smelt even better. A small covering of gel tamed his dark curls making him look smart. He was wearing dark jeans with a light pink T-shirt, and he smelt shower-fresh with just a hint of masculine cologne. It was just enough to make me want to lean in to take in more of the scent; in fact, I had to make a concerted effort not to. Instead I stepped back and watched Nishantha drink me in with those large dark eyes of his. He'd never seen me dulled up for a night out before and his told me he'd noticed the effort I'd made. When we finally tore our eyes away from each other, we walked into the bar to meet his friends. Even before we met them we seemed to be on an exciting new wavelength, one where we both knew the only reason we were in each other's company now was because we wanted to be, not because circumstance had thrown us together. We were like kids who had spent all day in a classroom together and had finally been let out into the playground.
Inside the bar Nishantha introduced me to his friends with pride,

smiling right into my eyes knowingly as he told me their names. First there was Paul, who I had met in their art room. He dipped his head and gave me a wink as he greeted me. Then there was Shikandra, he had a number one haircut with two short, thin, parallel lines shaved out completely at the left side of his head. He looked like he followed fashion a lot more closely than I did. And he had the face of a model; very classically good looking.

The last two introductions were to J.T and Ranil. J.T came across very extrovert like Shikandra and Paul while Ranil was very reserved, more so than Nishantha, and was also largely overweight making him look almost round in shape.

Despite the mix-bag of personalities, we all hit it off instantly. It felt instantly like we had known each other for years. I got on exceptionally well with Paul and J.T. They were totally on my wavelength, chilled and a little bit nuts. Shikandra"s aura of trend put me off a little at first. He came across slightly pretentious and I wasn't sure how to fit in with him. I asked Nishantha about him and he told me Shikandra was indeed a model but that he was a 'good guy'. As the night drew on I found that out for myself. He was more down to earth than I had first given him credit for. Nishantha and Ranil took a back seat as the rest of us encouraged each other's mischievous sides to come out to play. We were like a bunch of kids, which was already Nishantha's view of me anyway so I nothing to hide there. In an attempt to bond I told Nishantha's friends about his 'one past thirty' comment from the time we were arranging to meet to go to Irshaad's place. They fell about laughing and took the mickey out of him for it. Apparently Nishantha's inability to say the time correctly in English was a known trait to his friends and they were only too happy to have some new ammunition to throw his way. After that revelation we all took to telling stories about Nishantha and making fun of him, light-heartedly of course. Poor Nishantha, he obviously didn't realise that being the common denominator between his two sets of friends made him the target of our amusement.

"Don't worry Nishantha, you are helping us bond!" I said to him, holding up my arrack and coke to say 'cheers'.

He took it on the chin and thanked me, sarcastically, for my input while everybody clinked glasses. Paul and Shikandra jumped on the bandwagon then and both put an arm around me while looking at Nishantha for a reaction.

"Do not worry Nishantha, we are just *bonding*!" Paul said while Ranil and J.T. looked worriedly to Nishantha for his reaction too.

"I think you do not need me here now. You are all getting on so well without me."

Nishantha stood up, about to walk off. He had spoken in such a serious tone and with such a straight face that I almost believed him. My face gave me away and his friends, who all knew he was playing, laughed at me for falling for it.

"We probably should head to *The Ivory* now anyway," Nishantha pointed out. So we all drank up and left the bar.

On our way to *The Ivory*, Paul and Shikandra put their arms around my shoulders again and called Nishantha to look at us 'bonding'. We all laughed as they teased him while I got busy thinking that I liked what this inferred. They must have thought Nishantha liked me. I had to fight the beaming smile trying to appear on my face as I wondered what he'd said to them about me. As we laughed, I decided we must be cursed because once again our innocent fun was cut short as we passed a rowdy ex-pats pub. There were hordes of English and Irish drinking bottled beer outside. I hadn't even noticed them until a familiar, yet out of place, accent shouted out at me from the crowd. The voice grabbed my attention and I looked over to see a couple of English guys who had spotted us all messing around. At first I was excited to hear a familiar accent. That was soon to change.

"Hey! Goldilocks! Come over 'ere."

They were Londoners.

"Yeah, what you doing with them? They'll stab ya' they will, the locals are savages."

We ignored them and walked on in silence as Nishantha fell back to walk by my side.

"They should be at home cleaning our toilets with their tongues!"

"Yeah, while we clean you with ours," they cackled at their own pathetic gag.

"Ah, come on darling, at least show us your tits before you go!"

I'd spent so long away from a-cerebral drunken trolls that their behaviour shocked me more than it would have if I'd heard it at home and I was ashamed in front of my new friends. Their comments about Nishantha and his friends offended me even more so than their comments to me and I felt somehow responsible for the English louts.

"I'm so sorry guys. I don't know what to say."

"Hey! Do not apologise for them."

"But they are English!"

"You must be a busy girl, Rachael, if you are responsible for everybody in your country," J.T. said to me profoundly. His undertones secured him the attention of the rest of his friends.

Nishantha looked at me, awaiting a reaction. I wanted to come across cool, calm and collect, how Nishantha always did, but I lacked the discipline to be anything other than myself.

"It just makes me so angry..." I vented.

"Do not be. Their problem is not our problem," Nishantha squeezed my shoulder reassuringly and I melted there and then. That was the first time I realised saying goodbye to this man might be harder than I thought.

By the time we reached *The Ivory* our efforts to forget the ex-pat incident had paid off and we were back to messing around. *A club is a club is a club,* I thought as I looked around. It was dark, loud and full of hotties looking for some attention – exactly the same formula as back home. The night went on to become a whirl of boozy fun and I was in my element. The only negative, if I was going to be picky, was that a couple of girls took to giving me dirty looks when they saw me surrounded by my new Sri Lankan friends. But I didn't care because whenever nobody was looking, Nishantha would silently mouth the question 'are you OK?' to me. I would smile and give a little nod, while inside I was bouncing up and down in my victory dance. As much as I was enjoying the club, there came a point when I just wanted to have Nishantha to myself again. I needed more of the alone time we'd grown accustomed to sharing.

Nishantha and his friends knew a lot of people. Nearly everyone in *The Ivory* nodded hello to them or came over for a chat yet they never left on my own. Where ever I was rushed off to, to meet someone new, I always looked out to see where Nishantha was and sometimes I caught him looking out for me too. I always had a drink in my hand and was never allowed to buy a round with my own money. Considering I was rich compared to these guys, their hospitality was extraordinarily touching.
"Hello Rachael!" A voice boomed out over the music. It was Raj and Daniel from the fruit market. They'd spotted me and had come to say hello.
"Oh hey! I mean ayubowan! Come and meet my friends!"
I was excited to know people independently of Nishantha. When I was making introductions I noticed they were all going through the motions mockingly. As it transpired, they already knew each other, I should have guessed. Later in the night, the girls who had previously been throwing evil looks my way approached me. By Western standards there was nothing inappropriate about their attire yet here their short skirts and low-cut tops looked out of place. Most of the other girls in the club were more modestly dressed.
"Are you Nishantha's new girlfriend?" one of the two girls asked, their hunger for gossip glimmering in their eyes.
"Err, no, I'm not his... We are just friends."
"Would you like another drink?" Nishantha asked, coming up behind me putting a hand on my waist.
"No, no I'm fine with this one thanks," I said in response, then to the two girls, "I think his friends are trying to get me drunk."
They looked at each other and walked off.
"How odd, do you know them?"
"That is Dayani and Vidu. Everybody knows them. They like to get into everybody's life, they are 'nosey' as you would say."
"Oh," I said, wanting to ask more but opting not to. I was a little upset that they had implied I one of many Western girls Nishantha

kept company with. I kept on smiling regardless, savvy now to Nishantha's attentiveness. The change in pace of music distracted me soon enough anyhow. It slowed from Dance music to Culture Club and couples wasted no time in getting together to sway to *I Just Want To Be Loved*.
I ached for Nishantha to ask me to dance as we stood by the edge of the dance floor. It would be the only opportunity we would ever have to be physically close and I didn't want that moment to go by.
"Madame, would you do me the honour?" J.T. jumped in and asked me, bowing and holding his hand out for me to take. It seemed rude to turn him down after such a grand gesture so I let him whisk me onto the dance floor to groove to Boy George. Nishantha stood with Ranil on the sidelines but I tried not to look at him. There was no hiding the disappointment on my face.
"Do not worry about those girls," J.T. advised. "They like to know everything before it happens. We do not talk to them anymore as they have made up stories in the past."
"Do they... do they like Nishantha?"
"Everybody like Nishantha! Now, are you ready to dance?" he asked, twirling and sweeping me around gracefully as my dress swished and swayed with every move. The dance floor was full of men leading their ladies, dipping and spinning them around. It was so romantic, I felt like I had stepped into the era of my grandparent's youth as I had only ever seen people dance this way on old films. In my experience men were too-cool-for-school nowadays when it came to dancing.
While we danced, the music phased out of the eighties reggae/soul mix and into the slow, sensual vibe of the nineties. Out of the blue, the atmosphere in *The Ivory* changed from vibrant to intimate. Hands moved south, bodies moved closer and lips touched as Eric Clapton's *Tears in Heaven* set the scene. While I danced, I looked out for Nishantha. I was aching to dance with him as the emotive words of Eric Clapton tugged on my heartstrings.
"Oh, I have to give you back now, thank you for the dance," J.T.

said to me. Give me back to whom? I thought, not realising Nishantha was standing right behind me. J.T. made his way back to the bar where a group of girls stood. He picked one to dance with and she smiled as she followed him to a little space between the other couples. Nishantha and I saw her turn to her friends looking pleased with herself while J.T. led her. We both smiled.

"I, I hope you do not mind?" Nishantha asked me after we had finished watching J.T. and his new dancing partner.

"Not at all," I said, wanting to say a whole lot more. Nishantha slid his strong arms around my waist and interlocked his fingers. He held me so gently. My heart raced. Every fraction of an inch we pulled closer made me drunk with desire. Adrenaline made my breathing heavy, my eyes wide and my palms hot. He still smelt so good and this time I was able to take it all in. I closed my eyes and phased out the rest of the club. My hands were spread out unnaturally on his back as I fought the overwhelming urge to squeeze him tightly and I found myself swallowing hard to suppress the desire growing inside me. Nishantha pulled me in tighter and moved his hands down to the small of my back. Lust soared right through me and I lost control of my disciplined hands. My fingers sank into his skin as I moved my hands down to the small of his back in response. I rested my head on his chest, the highest point of him I could reach, and he momentarily rested his chin on my head. We had inched and nudged into each other and were as close as we could get. With my eyes closed, I savoured the moment, knowing it would soon pass. I was finally exactly where I wanted to be and I wanted to hold on to it as long as I could. Near to the end of the song Nishantha pulled out of our lock just enough to look at me. My gaze settled on his lips. I wanted to kiss him so much it hurt. He leaned in, not to kiss me, but to whisper in my ear.

"I saw a different side to you today," he whispered to me with his soft husky voice. This was better than a kiss. This was the alone time I had been pining for half the night.

"Oh?"

"When you were working, in the cafe. You were so focused, so

full of thought. And to-night, you look so beautiful."
Not knowing how to take the compliment, I rested my head back on his chest and gave him a tight squeeze to compensate for not knowing what to say. My consistent shortfall in knowing what to say to his honesty made me screw my face up in annoyance. I wished I could be as open as he was.
Our song came to an end and I hoped for another but off went the music and on went the lights. My insides churned as the chance to be close to Nishantha disappeared.
"Thank you for the dance," he whispered in my ear, so close his lips lightly brushed my skin, sending me wild with the urge to kiss him.
"Thank you," I replied robotically.
Nishantha and his friends spent a long time saying goodbye to all the people they knew as the crowds poured outdoors. I thought we might leave then but instead we took up residence at the bar. It seemed we were all staying for a lock-in. Sweet. I was accustomed to having lots of lock-ins with Pav at the Tav back home because of Derren, Nick and Ben's band. One of the barmen pushed two tables together and placed a full bottle of arrack on both. He brought a deck of cards to the table and poured our drinks. Apparently we were drinking it neat, and as I had already had more than enough to drink, I left mine alone. A different barman dealt the cards for a game of poker. They all played and I tried to pick it up by watching Nishantha's hand. Ranil, the gentle giant, won the first game and the barman won the next two. I could see that for Ranil this was the most important part of the night. The focus had switched from socialising to playing poker. Most of the conversation was in Sinhala so I quickly grew bored. Poker is not the most interesting of spectator sports at the best of times, let alone in a different language. I thought I would end up sitting there all night. Too many nights like that with Derren caused me to underestimate how sensitive Nishantha's nature was in comparison. Although I said nothing to Nishantha about wanting to go home, he could see for himself I was tiring.

"Shall we get out of here?" he whispered.

"I'd love to!" I said as we shared a secret smile.

"After this game, we can make our excuses and leave, OK?" he said reassuringly. When I was with Derren, firstly, he would probably not have noticed if I was tired and wanted to leave. Secondly, he wouldn't have cared enough to do anything about it even if he had and, thirdly, he would have accused me of trying to ruin his night if I said anything. By the end of their game Ranil had won all his money back from the barman. Although their battle was far from over Nishantha and I got up to say our goodbyes. As I hugged everybody goodbye, the barman stood and pointed to my drink.

"Too strong, eh?" he challenged. The rest of the table looked at me, awaiting a reaction. They were right, it was too strong for me but I was not one to shy away from a challenge. To their surprise, I walked back to the wooden table, picked up my glass and downed the whole lot in one, slamming the glass down on the table to accentuate my point.

"Good night gentlemen," I said as I sashayed across the bar to the door. Nishantha looked simultaneously shocked and amused as he followed me out.

The second we got outside my face screwed up from the drink and my eyes watered.

"God that was horrible," I rasped.

"Are you ok?" Nishantha asked in disbelief.

"I will be," I announced hoarsely, still unable to iron out my face.

"You are crazy! But my friends, they like you."

"Even though I didn't play poker?"

"Even though you did not play poker."

"You know…" I said as I laughed, "you are horrible at poker!"

"Is this based on to-night? Because I win, sometimes I win."

"Sure you do. Sure you do!"

"I do!"

I hiccupped, a loud one-off hiccup.

"I think your so-called coconut drink has gone to my head."

"Come on, I will take you home."

"Arrack is so bitter. It so does not taste like coconut."
I had developed an acute case of verbal diarrhoea now that I had my voice back. The cool night air and the neat arrack had knocked me sideways. "A real coconut drink is Malibu, the real Jamaican rum. Jamaican rum? Ja'maican-me drunk!" I said in a relatively decent Jamaican accent. I laughed at my own little joke and at the way Nishantha half-laughed at me like I was insane. He looked like a parent who was trying to tell their child off but could not stop themselves from laughing.

Embarrassingly, I rambled on mindlessly for most of the walk home. Too much drink had eroded the already precarious filter between mind and mouth. When we reached my hotel we stood by the old rickety gate that led to the front entrance. Before opening the gate I turned to Nishantha as if I was going to say something. Nothing came out. Now my filter was on overdrive. I could not articulate my feelings at all.

"So, what do you think about what we do for fun around here?"
"I think I am very glad you made me ask you to show me. You have a great circle of friends there, you really do."
"Thank you, they like you."
I didn't reply. We were talking but neither of us was saying what we really wanted to. Then Nishantha shook his head and squinted his eyes shut before opening them to say,
"Rachael..." He moved in closer to me.
I don't know what he wanted to say because we were interrupted – again – by an all too familiar sound. I jumped back in fear as gunshots filled the air. It was as though they had ricocheted through my chest.
"Rachael, it is only fireworks. Come here, come here."
Petrified, I stayed rooted to the spot. I looked up and behind me to see the colourful explosions cascading and dispersing in the sky, then looked back at Nishantha.
"See, it is just fireworks."
The shock of hearing what I thought was gunfire brought a flood of tears to my eyes.
"I'm sorry," I blubbered, considerably more sober now. "I don't

know why I'm crying, I feel like such an idiot."
"It is OK, Rachael. It was so...the same... as last time, us coming back from an evening, the noise in the air. It made me jump also, only I could see the fireworks in the sky."
He took me in his arms again and stroked my hair reassuringly.
"Shh, it is OK, Rachael."
"I know," I said, half laughing this time. "I know. I'm such an idiot." I pulled away.
"This is better, you are smiling."
"Oh, no, I'm really sorry!" I gasped, seeing the mascara marks I had left on his light pink T-shirt. He followed my eyes down to the black eyelash shapes and said seriously,
"Oh no, what have you done?"
"I am really sorry. I'll buy you another shirt," I said, trying not to laugh, it did look funny.
"Hey, I do not care about the shirt."
I shook my head at my irrational response to those damn fireworks and bit my bottom lip, trying to stave off a laugh as I looked at Nishantha's T-shirt again.
"You have Racha-fied my shirt."
"I'm sorry to laugh, it's not funny, it just looks...funny."
"Oh, so it is not funny, it is just funny? That makes a lot of sense! Is that another of your strange English sayings like your eggs in your baskets?"
"No, I'm just not making any sense this time, even in my mother tongue!" I giggled.
"Maybe I keep my shirt this way. It is a different look, for sure."
Nishantha pulled his top and looked down to see the new artwork.
I stopped laughing as Nishantha looked into my eyes in that deep all-consuming way he had. Large and deep, they glistened. As I looked back into his I felt scared, good scared. He took a step towards me and reached down by my side to squeeze my hand with his. I squeezed his hand back. I was so nervous. We interlocked our fingers tightly, with a tension only passion could create. I now knew for sure these feelings were not one-sided. He looked at my lips like he was longing to kiss me then pulled me in

for a hug instead. As we lingered in this electrically charged embrace, I knew it was in place of the kiss we were not going to have.

"Thank you again, for to-night," he whispered. "I should go now. Will you be OK?"

"I'll be fine," I said stepping back again.

"Good night, Rachael."

"Good night."

He walked off without any word of seeing me again and for the first time since coming here I wish I had my mobile with me and I wished Nishantha owned one. I used to watch old films where it took ages for guys and girls to get together without the aid of bars and mobile phones. I thought it was romantic but this night proved differently. It wasn't romantic, it was frustrating.

As I lay on my bed and closed my eyes it was clear that I was still rather drunk and that the shock hadn't sobered me up as much as I'd previously thought. Either that or my room really was spinning. I was doing my own head in, wondering if Nishantha wanted to see me again, or if I would ever see him again. To hush the incessant thoughts in my head I put the little TV on. It took two attempts to press the 'on' button as my finger missed it the first time. I couldn't be bothered to channel surf so ended up watching some cheesy shopping channel. They were selling a pen that claimed to be indestructible. It came with another ten free pens and appeared to double as a dart. As my eyes grew as heavy as my heart felt, I slowly drifted off to sleep watching them throw the amazing – must have – indestructible fountain pen at a dartboard and puncture a coke can with the nib. I fell asleep wondering why you would ever need a pen you could throw at a dartboard.

Knowing I had very little time left, I worked through my hangover and spoke to a reporter who gave me substantial and frank information on the suicidal side of life in Sri Lanka that was kept so hush-hush. She talked about why it happened, how it happened and why it was such a taboo subject. She agreed that there was plenty of scope for help that could be given to prevent it

– funds and the right attitude allowing. She spoke about how children were still expected to keep their feelings hidden and provided some startling statistics that more than backed up those I already had. I knew Sri Lanka had the highest suicide rate in the world but the sub-group information she provided made it real to me.

All day a little part of me hoped that Nishantha would stop by my hotel, maybe leave a note or something. The bigger part of me tried not to, to save myself from the likely disappointment.

I smiled to myself as I replayed the night in *The Ivory* in my mind. It was impossible not to and it also kept me sprightly during my self-induced mother of a hangover. When I returned to room 101 later that day, there were no signs Nishantha had been. There were no messages on the phone, or at reception, or on the door. I had to check, I couldn't help myself. My heart sank into my stomach after exhausting all possible means of communication. I was now paying a heavy emotional price for my "enjoy it while you can" attitude from the day before. My room had a depressing feel to it on a good day so I opted to get the hell out of there and sit by the pool outside instead.

This hotel was much smaller than that of the grand Gaulle Face Hotel and was a little unkempt in comparison. I found a spot to park myself then went back inside to ask if they would bend the rules and allow me to eat by the pool. As there were no other guests around and I looked desperate to be granted one little comfort, they agreed and ordered me a pizza from the kitchen. It was like they could sense my heartache. As I lay back on the sun lounger I decided to study the sky. As pretty as the star-studded sky looked, it failed to raise my spirits. It somehow made me think of all the advice I decided not to follow from Indica, probably because Indica and I had spent time lounging by the pool at night together back in Colombo. I only had myself to blame for feeling this low. The magnetic pull towards Nishantha had been so strong it had dragged me blindly into denial. This was a puddle and I didn't know how deep it was until I jumped right in. I'd allowed myself to develop feelings for a man I could never have. A waiter brought the pizza I ordered out to me and I managed two slices before giving up. Jaycee from my temp job once told me to imagine I was somewhere far away, somewhere new and exciting while dealing with Derren going off with Tanya. I did and it worked. Now I am somewhere new and exciting so, what do I do now?

As the sun disappeared behind the horizon I watched day gradually turn to night. It put me in a profound mood, making me think about time; how only yesterday the sun had set on such a different day to this. How tomorrow's will bring another and how, no matter how much you want to, you cannot stop time. You cannot bend it or pause it or prevent it from bringing new days as it leaves the old ones behind.

Taking a break from watching the sky, I looked at the inviting water in the pool. The underwater lighting made me want to jump right in. *Jump right in.* Why did I always have to jump right in? My philosophical mood was being fuelled by a hangover, heartache and lack of sufficient distraction. I stared back up at the clusters of stars layered out in the indigo-sapphire sky. Some individual stars sparkled brightly like a skilfully cut diamond, with every ounce of its brilliance and fire gleaming in its perfectionist's cut. Others, further away, looked smaller and closer together, dull in comparison yet their sheer mass gave them an awe that was hard to rival. Back on earth, the crickets chorused on and off creating a white noise you were only aware of once it ceased. When they were quiet the night fell eerily silent. The moon was so thin I wondered where the rest of it had gone and if it had taken all my good times with it. I despised the fact that I wanted to be with Nishantha so much. It didn't make any sense. Only a day ago I was under the illusion I was in control of all this.

"Rachael," a familiar, husky voice spoke out. I had been so transfixed on the night sky that I hadn't noticed anybody come out to the pool.

"I am sorry about last night I..." Nishantha started before I interrupted him. My heart raced but I kept my eyes on the sky. They had stared into the stars for so long that they were comfortable there, fixed there even.

"Shh, come here," I ordered.

"What is wrong?" Nishantha asked as he sat on the sun lounger next to me.

"Isn't it amazing?"

"Oh. You are stargazing. I see. Yes, it is very beautiful," he said as he humoured me by laying back and looking up too.

We both lay in silence for a moment while I enjoyed blocking out reality and not worrying about a thing. Not work, not Nishantha and not home. The beauty of the sky was keeping it all at bay. The crickets started chorusing again. This time I hadn't even noticed they'd stopped. As I switched off from all worry and thought, all of life's little mysteries poured in, in their place. I wondered if it was true that if you looked down to earth from the nearest star you would see dinosaurs roaming. I'd read that in a museum somewhere. If it *was* true how does anyone know that for sure? And isn't the sun the nearest star? Did they mean the sun? Or did they mean the next nearest star after? And if there is no up and down in the universe because the universe is infinite, why do we view the world the way up that we do? I was sure there was an obvious answer, I had just never thought about it before. Another question that came to mind was, if there was no moon, would there still be life on earth? Or would it change the delicate balance too much? If life on earth could exist without the moon would it be very different from the life forms we have now? Would humans have evolved? And if we are such a tiny part of this infinite set-up, why do we only believe the things we can prove ourselves? And how does stripy toothpaste come out the tube stripy? OK, that might not have been one of life's little mysteries but it sure was one of mine.

"If we had no moon, would there be any tides in our oceans?" I asked, not really expecting an answer.

"There would be some because the sun also creates tides. The spring tide is a result of the sun and moon together."

I looked at him, eyebrows raised. In his face there was no sign that he was showing off with his knowledge. He was just giving me the answer. I should have asked him about the stripy toothpaste. I wished I hadn't looked at him at that moment because seeing his face ended my worry-free moment. By looking at him, I was looking at something I wanted desperately yet couldn't have. I looked back to the sky and swallowed hard as if to try to keep my feelings from escaping, again.

"Look Rachael! Did you see it?"

"What?"

"A shooting star, look there's another one!"

"I missed it, I missed both of them!"

We sat in silence again, until I broke it.

"If the universe goes on forever, why do most people think aliens are something out of a science fiction movie when, really, the odds are that they must exist? Forever is so vast that there must be another mass of rock somewhere at a suitable distance from a star, where it is possible for life to evolve. If you think of it that way, people who believe in aliens are the more logical thinkers than those who don't."

"I can-not answer that. Maybe you have a point there."

"OK, well here is one you will know. What is that fruit called you have here, the one with a thick purple skin, with white segments inside?"

"Oh, you are talking about mangosteen. That is my favourite fruit of all."

"Mine too now I've tried it."

"You have them in England."

"No, no we don't."

"You do, I have asked somebody before. You have them imported."

"Oh. I'll have to pay more attention to the exotic fruits section in Tesco next time I go," I said, more to myself than to him.

"I have a question for you."

"Go on?"

"How can something so far a-way, be so beautiful?"

"Yeah," I sighed, not tiring of the vast mass of stars above. Then I

sensed Nishantha's eyes were not looking at the sky. I turned to look at him. He was looking at me. I felt an instant desire so strong there was no point in bothering to fight it. My face flushed with desire as we both simultaneously left our sun loungers at lightning speed and found ourselves pawing each other without any hesitation. Nishantha kissed me wildly and while it was the release I'd longed for, I still couldn't get enough. His hands moved rampantly all over me, squeezing and touching me in all the right places. He then changed pace, teasing me with soft light kisses, kissing my top lip then my bottom lip until the tension built and we couldn't help but storm back into full on, heated pashing. After his hands had grabbed and felt every inch of my body, he slid them underneath my clothes like he was desperate to be even closer to me. He grabbed my waist underneath my vest top causing me to dig my finger nails lustfully down his toned back in an involuntary reaction. I could feel his excitement as he writhed against me. A surge of giddy desire soared through my entire body. I had to have him there and then. What was the point in holding back now? I was already hurting so I may as well postpone my misery another day. I wanted him in every possible way you could ever want another person. My skin tingled and shivered with arousal as he kissed my neck softly, his breath teased me warmly as he nuzzled my ear. My breath became heavy, my chest rising and falling, deep and fast. We writhed together eagerly as he ran his fingers through my hair, away from my face, and held my head in front of his. His eyes, wide and wild, flitted all over my face, and mine all over his.
"Let's go upstairs?" I whispered, through a laborious breath.
"Come on."
We dodged the hotel staff, went through the lobby like naughty little children playing hide-and-seek, and ran up the stairs holding hands. Unable to control ourselves, we stopped halfway up the stairs to kiss again. At the door I looked for my key as Nishantha kissed the back of my neck tenderly. He withdrew me from the task at hand, turned me around to face him and pressed me forcefully up against my door. With my thighs wrapped around

his toned waist and the back of my head pressed up against the door, he kissed me all the way down the neckline of my vest top. His teasing was so intense it was torture. I pulled free and rummaged again for my key, successfully this time. We both became nervous because behind the locked door of my bedroom, there was nothing to stop us from doing what we both wanted to do. It had all become very real. All too suddenly the situation acquired a serious feel to it. Both doubt and guilt showed itself on Nishantha's face. Now this is where I know room 101 was not doing me any favours. He stood in front of the door somewhat standoffishly, still breathing deeply in the way that only desire can manifest.

"I am sorry about the mess. I wasn't expecting any visitors," I said, trying to break the tension. My room looked like a bomb had hit it, but that was really not a good analogy to use, considering.

"That is OK," he said, looking round at the mess I had left since my night out in Kandy. I moved closer to him, took his hand in mine and kissed him softly, reassuringly. I thought maybe I could soothe his away his doubts but I could tell from the kiss his doubts had already won out. The mood was now more sensual than sexual. He finally reacted and squeezed my hand back then led me over to the bed where we kissed again in the same slow, loving way. Nishantha pulled back and positioned himself away from me. It didn't take a body language expert to work out this was not going to be good. Remaining true to form, Nishantha ran his fingers through his hair in the way he did when he was contemplating.

"What is wrong Nishantha?" I asked, bracing myself for rejection.

"I am sorry, Rachael."

I walked around the bed, knelt down on the floor in front of him and put my hands around his. His giant hands dwarfed my small fingers and, despite everything that was happening, I was pleased to have had the chance to learn that little fact. I waited for him to look at me and say something.

"Rachael, I am getting married and you, you are leaving soon."

What could I say? They were the two teeny-tiny facts I had been putting to the back of my mind all this time, but they were the facts.

"I know. That doesn't stop me wanting you."

"That is how it is for me. I like, so much, to be around you," he said, smiling genuinely and entwining his fingers playfully with mine. I smiled back. The thought of him walking out of room 101, never to be seen again, scared me so I laid my cards on the table while I had the chance.

"If you don't want to see me again, Nishantha, I will understand. Just so you know, I would spend every day with you until I have to go home if I could."

I was down to my central Matroyska doll, finally. Nishantha's face gave nothing away as to what he was thinking.

"Nothing has to happen you know? We could just enjoy each other's company as we did before tonight," I added.

"That is easy to say, not so easy to do. You made me feel, something, that first day you came in to my classroom. I did not know what it was."

"Really?"

"You did not know? I thought you knew? Paul was laughing at me because he could see how, how unnerved I became when you walked into the room that day."

"I thought Paul was teasing *me* because he thought I liked *you*."

"He was. He was teasing us both because he thought you liked me, but, I didn't believe a woman like you would like a man like me."

"Oh come on. I've seen you out remember? You are not short of admirers. Those Sri Lankan girls in *The Ivory* were like your adoring fans."

"I do not like it. Those two girls who spoke to you, they try so hard to get a man, like having a man comes before what they think of themselves."

I took a more relaxed seat on the bed and he turned towards me so we could speak. We had now re-entered our more familiar comfort zone.

"They giggle and agree with everything you say."

"Have you... have you had many girlfriends?"
"When I was younger I had only Sinhalese girlfriends."
"And when you were older?"
"There was one girl who was special to me. She was German."
I knew it. I knew I wasn't the first Western girl to be the object of Nishantha's affections.
"What happened?"
"Let us say, she was not as beautiful on the inside as she was on the outside. We were together for three, maybe four months, but we saw each other a lot."
"And what happened?"
She had a boyfriend, back home, in Germany. When I found out she did not even say sorry. She said she thought I knew we were just having fun. She looked at me so coldly even though I had given her my heart. It was hard when I realised, at that moment, she had not cared for me at all, the whole time."
"I'm sorry."
"Do not be."
"And your wife-to-be?"
"That is different, Rachael. Sinhalese girls are different. It is not fair for me to compare Somana to Western girls."
"Her name is Somana?" I said feeling upset. Hearing her name made it real. His future wife was a real person, a real person who was going to spend the rest of her life with this man.
"Do you want to marry her?" In for a penny, in for a pound...
"I have to. I came to Kandy to have some freedom before I married. I have had that now."
My tantrum-producing epicentre wanted to shout 'what, so I was part of your last bid for freedom? Thanks!' But I got a grip and reigned myself in.
"If you don't want to marry her, Nishantha, why do you have to? Why can't you refuse? It's your life you know, you only get one."
Nishantha looked at me intently for a moment.
"This, coming from the girl who wants to stay here yet is going home?"
Touché.

"Point taken."

"Maybe we should be forgetting about marriage and England tonight."

"I think I've been doing that since I met you."

Nishantha looked into the distance as if fondly picturing something in his mind's eye then smiled and gave out a half laugh.

"What is it?"

"It is nothing."

"No, what is it? Tell me!" I said throwing a pillow at him.

"I am just thinking about my friends' faces when you downed your arrack last night. And how drunk you were after."

"Oh, I know, I am so sorry. I chewed your ear off..."

"You did what?"

"I mean, I talked a lot!"

"You sure did," his smile waned as the reality of our situation crept into the forefront of his mind. I think it was then we both realised. No matter how much fun we had, no matter how great our time together was, it was always going to be there, looming over us. Any good times we could have had from then on were already tainted.

"When do you have to go?" he whispered.

"I have less than a week. A few days probably."

Nishantha looked sad.

"So in a week I will be able to paint again."

"What do you mean?"

He laid back on my bed and I nestled my head into his chest. I could see his sculptured muscular body through his top. He traced a finger up my arm.

"Since I met you, my paintings, they have changed."

"Changed how?"

"I would not like to say."

"Tell me!"

"Maybe you will see for yourself, before you go."

"That would mean seeing you again?"

Nishantha got up and walked to the window leaving me on the

bed. He leant on the window ledge and looked outside.

"We have been through a lot in very little time," I shared.

Nishantha carried on looking out the window. I could see his reflection perfectly in the glass. His eyes looked sad and glossy, like in his painting.

"You are made up of...of opposites. You are so caring and soft yet you are adventurous and brave. You are focused in your work yet carefree when you are out. I have never met anybody like you. It is like a dream that you feel the same." Nishantha turned to look at me. I was taken aback by his words. I had no idea he'd looked at me in so much detail *and* had liked what he had seen.

"I love how I feel around you, Nishantha. I have never met somebody as gentle and caring as you. I've never met a man like you," I broke off, a little overwhelmed with emotion.

Nishantha turned, walked back over to me and pulled me up. As he put his arms around me again I sensed it would be for the last time. A lump formed in my throat.

"This is it, isn't it?"

"Don't be sad. This is just the middle of your story that you do not know the end to yet."

He looked at me for a moment, his eyes glistening.

"I am never going to see you again, am I?" I asked, still looking for closure. But he couldn't bring himself to say it.

"Good night, Rachael."

"Goodbye, Nishantha."

Then he closed the door behind him as he left.

Chapter 10

Two days. That was how long I had been back in Colombo and that was how long I had left. It seemed that every time I returned to Colombo from Kandy I had to pick myself back up off the floor. Kandy and Nishantha were both like drugs you could never get enough of. Without them, life was flat. And now that I wouldn't be seeing either of them again I just wanted to get going home over with.

I studied the departure times on my Emirates tickets. They made it so real, so final. CMB to DXB then DXB to LGW. Hoping Nishantha would be saying goodbye to me at the airport after spending every possible minute with me was now nothing but a fantasy. I carried on studying my ticket. Gate 6, Class "Y" – whatever that meant. My thoughts drifted into analytical territory. I analogised that each day I had spent with Nishantha had been like a petal torn from a daisy in the schoolyard game – he loves me, he loves me not. It had ended with the petal I had hoped for, *he loves me.* It just wasn't accompanied by the "happy ever after" that should have come with it.

On my last day in Kandy I went back to Irshaad's with Daniel and his tuk-tuk driver friend. Being there without Nishantha made me miss him tremendously. Knowing we were both there together just days before made me long for him all the more but I had to focus. Irshaad and Daniel were quite clearly good friends and I got my interview with Sunil's wife. It took a long, confusing and sweltering time to find a decent translator because everybody wanted to help even though their English was poor. The frustration of the day distracted me from my own problems, which were nothing in comparison to theirs. Despite this, the emptiness looming behind the concentration of my work still cut deep. Especially as before then, the heady, intoxicating hope of spending more time with Nishantha had been my white noise behind it all.

Sunil's wife still had no idea where her husband was. Her son, the main breadwinner, had been shot dead in the terrorist attack and her three remaining children were all under six years of age. She was eating the parts left over from vegetables that her neighbours threw away and continued to breastfeed all three of her children, despite their ages. Watching a six-year old boy run up to his mother, lift her top and feed from his her sagging bosom was certainly a new experience. The last question I asked Sunil's wife was where she thought her husband was. She shrugged. She didn't know. Knowing it would go a long way for her and her children, I gave the lady five hundred rupees for her time and then I left.

When Daniel and the tuk-tuk driver dropped me back to the market that day, I gave them some money for petrol and said goodbye to them too. I walked home from there with my reticular sensor set on Nishantha watch. My radar homed in on any human being who remotely resembled him, but my hopes were dashed as they all turned out to be strangers.

By the time my train arrived in Colombo I had to suffer a new disappointment: that my reticular sensor was null and void from here on in. There was more chance of Leon giving me a pay rise than of bumping into Nishantha now.

After checking back into Ravi's and spending some time with him I took myself off to Indica's stall. Given the time of day, I guessed that's where he'd be.

The moment Indica clapped eyes on me his face dropped. I should have heeded his advice - if I was trying to do the right thing, but neither logic nor thought played any part in the way I had acted.

"You probably know I met Nishantha," I said sheepishly.

"I think we should go for a walk." Indica replied sternly.

Indica left a friend in charge of his stall and we walked off along the beach road.

"I do know I should have listened to you Indica. But I wouldn't change any of it. He is really special."

"He think the same of you... as I knew he would."
I noted how Indica spoke so much more quickly than Nishantha. "I knew from the morning after the parade you both like one another. And I was the only one to see that it could only end badly."
Indica put a friendly arm around my shoulder.
"But I am sorry," he said warmly. The genuine compassion in his eyes brought me close to tears but I choked them back.
"Thank you. Thank you for not being angry with me."
"I am sad for you, not angry. When do you go home?"
"The day after tomorrow. How's Soma? And Daniel?"
"We have moved out of Johan and Komari's. We are now a few houses down the same road. They are both doing well."
"Oh, that's good."
Despite Indica's kind words, we were struggling to find the comfy slipper rapport that had come so naturally to us before.
"What time is your flight?"
"9.20 in the morning."
Nishantha would have said 'nine-past-twenty'. Every little thing made me think of him.
"Then tomorrow evening you must come here for one last meal with us. I will invite our family and you can bring your friend Ravi, if you like. It will be a, a send-off party for you."
"Really? That would be lovely." This time his kindness touched me and I couldn't stifle my tears at this emotional time. "Look at me welling up already, don't let me have too much arrack tomorrow, I'll be a nightmare!"
"You know you will have too much arrack. I cannot believe you are going, Rachael. I will miss you. We all will."
"Don't say things like that, it means I really am leaving. No, no, it is time. I am ready now." I said, swallowing hard as I tried to turn my words into truth.
"So, how was Kandy?" Indica asked in a cheery tone more akin to his true nature. Then, to my relief, we slipped back into our comfy slippers.
The road we walked along, adjacent to the beach, was a road I

had walked down many times. It had become so familiar to me that I had stopped noticing the dusty smell, the large, modern buildings that stood out amongst the others, the unyielding traffic and the tuk-tuk drivers with their little 'quack-quack' horns. I was seeing it all anew today, as if it was the first time I'd set eyes on it all. Of course the opposite was true. I was taking it all in because I would soon be seeing it for the last time.
"You know, with a little bit of time, I know I will be able to look at the bright side of all this." I said with a positivity that surprised even me.
"Oh?"
"Well, I can't be with Nishantha, this is true, but it's not because he didn't like me. Neither of us need come away from this feeling any sense of rejection. It's almost.... romantic. Yeah, romantic. I think I can go home now with a little bit of peace of mind, just knowing Nishantha liked me too."
Indica fell silent and I looked up to see he was frowning, clearly deep in thought.
"Is Nishantha ok, do you know?"
"I tell Nishantha what he tell everybody else. I tell him this is only part of his story and yours, and that you should not be sad because there is more to come for you."
"Yes, he said that to me!"
"It is one of Nishantha's sayings. It means if you are upset now, do not worry about it, it is only temporary. It will pass and you will be happy again. Sadness is part of life and it leads to happiness, if you accept it and let it pass."
Advice only the strong will follow. I thought as we parted ways.

Finding myself once again alone I set about shopping for presents for friends and loved ones back home. For Laura I bought a hideous laughing elephant ornament that said 'I LOVE COLOMBO' on its belly. It was perfect for mine and Laura's strange holiday gift pact. When we went abroad we had to come back with a present that had 'I love...' on it. This also leaked into Christmas presents where we often ended up with all sorts of tacky mugs, teddies and pens from each other. Most of my presents from Laura read 'I LOVE NEW YORK' as this was one place you could be sure she would visit at least once a year.

For the office I bought a bottle of arrack to share and for Victor and Martha I bought a handmade silk tablecloth. I picked up two of these in case I decided my parents could handle a gift without seeing it as an insult to their wishes for me to stay away from developing countries.

I tried to find something for my flatmate, Jenny, then decided we were not close enough to partake in gift exchanges. We were definitely more pass-in-the-hallway housemates than proper roomies. Anyway, I was sure she would find something morally wrong with whatever I bought. I'd be supporting the corrupt corporate world or encouraging child slavery or, if I bought her an ornamental elephant, I'd be held accountable for elephant exploitation. Don't get me wrong, I am all for responsible purchasing, it's just that that girl could find a problem with anything you could stick a price tag on.

My thoughts turned to Derren. Should I get him something too? We were not really in a present buying place either. I opted for no present for Derren either although I did wonder what headspace Derren would be in when I got home. He would either be seeing Tanya or wanting to get us back together. I didn't know. All I knew was that there was no way back for us, not now I'd seen how I wanted to be treated. I felt sorry for him. He still thinks I will take him back, after years of having him mistreat me. And we have the same group of friends so it isn't like we can avoid each other.

If I could wish that just one thing would change when I get home, it would be Derren's unhealthy obsession with me and Nick. Nick is a grunger with dreads from Brighton who plays guitar in Derren and Ben's band. When Derren and I were together, he had this crazy, unfounded notion that there was something going on between us. It was as true then as it now yet Derren still makes it awkward when we are all together in a group. On top of everything else I would have to deal with on my return home, I really hope the pettiness of that isn't one of them.

After shopping I packed up most of my things, for the last time, and ate dinner with Ravi in his little restaurant area. It was empty again so he put on one light and one fan just for our table. He brought out vegetables in spicy rice and two banana lassis. While I waited for him to come back from the kitchen I looked around the room, silently saying my goodbyes to the high off-white walls, the empty tables and the cobwebby fans overhead.
"You leave in...?" Ravi said.
"Deka," I said, holding up two fingers to show I leave in two days time.
"Where you go?"
"Home. England."
"Oh. Home."
"Yes. Here," I passed Ravi Indica and Soma's address. "Tomorrow evening, I say, err, aayu-bowan to all my friends here. This is where Indica lives. Will you come?"
"Owu, owu. And my wife, me children?"
"I will ask Indica tomorrow then I tell you."
"OK, OK."
"Thank you for dinner Ravi, istuti. I see you tomorrow, aayu-bowan."
I got up early on my last full day to make the most of using the pool at the Gaulle Face Hotel. I'd spent so long there I doubted the staff would care. I'd gone to bed the night before very early to read my book in bed but ended up mulling over Nishantha's saying. It made sense. I knew one day I would get over this, the problem was, I didn't really want to. I'd found a place and a man that made everything fit. I didn't want to let go of what I'd found. At least I could take comfort in the fact that he liked me too, and we got to say goodbye to each other, and we didn't cheapen our time together despite coming close in Kandy.
I tried again to read by the pool and succeeded this time. Nishantha's manner and adages had comforted me and I felt calm, something I hadn't expected to feel at all, especially with only one

night until it was time to go home. Thirty pages of *The Body Packer* later I walked over to Indica's stall. I had to ask him if Ravi's wife and children could come to my goodbye soirée.

He wasn't there so I bought a mangosteen to eat and took a tuk-tuk over to Komari's house. I was just too tired to embark on another long walk. I was hoping Komari would be able to tell me which house Indica had moved to but it was he who opened the door.

"Oh! Here you are! I've been looking for you!"

The colour drained from Indica's face.

"I thought you said you were busy today?"

"Oh, don't worry if you're busy, I only came to ask you something about tonight."

"Rachael, ah..." Before he could finish – or even start – Johan junior pushed passed him and gave me an excited hug. It was the first time he had shown any real affection towards me.

"You made it!" he said excitedly. "Indica said you could not come, yet here you are!" he shouted back into the house in his mother tongue, mentioning my name. Indica still looked terrified.

"What is it?" I mouthed to Indica silently.

"He shook his head lowly as Johan senior and Komari came to greet me at the door. They hugged me too and ushered me into their living room.

"I know how interested you were in this, I am so glad you could come!" Komari said as clocked a room full of faces. The room was at full capacity with guests sitting on chairs or on rugs on the living room floor. I stood in the doorway trying to take in all the strangers' faces smiling at me. Indica stood behind me as Komari looked for a space for me on the floor. I still had no idea who all these people were or what I had walked in on.

"Rachael! Meet my brother!" baby Johan said excitedly as he gestured to the far end of the living room. Before I had time to connect the dots I found myself looking at a man dressed exquisitely in fine copper-coloured garb, and he was sitting next to a beautiful woman adorned in gems and brightly coloured silks. *Nishantha.*

Somana.
I had walked in on their dowry.

Chapter 11

"**This is** Nishantha, my brother, we tell you about him before the Esala Perahera, yes?" baby Johan said as Nishantha stood to greet me. Nishantha's hair had been scraped back with what seemed like half a tub of hair gel. It looked wrong.
"And Nishantha, this is the English girl we tell you about, Rachael!" Nishantha could barely look at me, and his face was as wan as the smile on my face.
"Hello Rachael. It is... a pleasure... to... meet you."
"Likewise," I managed to say through the lump in my throat. "Congratulations, both of you."
"Istuti," they both replied.
Komari said something to Nishantha in Sinhala, then he took Somana's hand to help her up.
"Rachael, this is Somana, my bride."
Somana was slight of build, had long tumbling hair cascading in layers down her back and was naturally very striking. She had kind, bashful eyes and she held herself demurely. I could tell she was a sweet person just by looking at her, albeit a little more reticent than I thought Nishantha would have liked. But then he did tell me it was unfair to compare.
"Hello Somana, it is a pleasure to meet you," I said as my head spun. Hiding such strong emotions while under such close scrutiny was causing an implosion inside. Historically, this was not something I was well practised at, at the best of times.
"And you, Rachael," Somana said softly while her smile brimmed with pride and happiness.
After Nishantha and his bride sat back down on their shared sofa, Johan junior took me around the living room to introduce me to both his extended family members and to the family they were soon to unite with. On some sort of greeting autopilot I made my way through the introductions but had no memory of who was

who by the time I took my seat on the floor on an old threadbare rug. Nishantha and Somana were directly behind me so luckily, I could avoid eye contact with them as the families bonded.

I wondered if he was looking at me. I wondered if he was hurting anywhere near as much as I was. All I wanted to do was run away and cry, not sit there on display while trying to engage in polite conversation. By way of distraction I began to play nervously with the long fibres of the rug and that's when it dawned on me that any peace I'd managed to find about leaving Nishantha had just flown out the window. Across the room by the door, beyond the mass of relatives, Indica stood looking at me. His face was so full of sympathy I had to avoid eye contact with him at all costs. One look of sympathy from him would have melted the glue holding me together.

Soma and Komari handed out cups of tea to everybody, including me. I decided I would stay until I'd finished mine then make my excuses to leave. Once all the tea had been poured Soma came over to me holding a very sleepy looking Daniel in her arms. She passed him over my head to his uncle, Nishantha. At this point, I did look around. The whole room was looking at Daniel so it would have been strange if I didn't. Somana and I both ogled the baby in Nishantha's arms and she smiled at me knowingly, like she couldn't wait to have one of her own, one day. I caught Nishantha's eye momentarily as we watched the baby staring up at him then whipped around quickly to tell Soma how beautiful her son was. I had told her that many a-time; it was the only appropriate comment I could think of to say to avoid eye contact with Nishantha. In a way I guess I was the paramour, yet, sitting there, it was me who felt deceived. Deception was quite normal coming from Derren, but from Nishantha, I wasn't expecting that. I felt deceived because all this time both Nishantha and Indica knew this was taking place today yet neither of them told me.

Although my tea was too hot to drink, I sipped at it anyway. I figured I could leave once I had finished without insulting their hospitality so wanted it gone as soon as possible. Between sips I continued to finger the frays in the rug beneath me. My fingers traced the bald base where the red fibres had completely worn away. I must have appeared so rude. People were making the effort to speak English for me yet I couldn't take any of it in and I barely said anything back. I took to nodding and smiling. An overzealous gulp of tea scolded my tongue. Now that *did* bring a tear to my eye. Komari asked me what was wrong and the entire room waited to hear my answer. They looked on at me with concern. The unwanted attention and hidden raw emotion caused my cheeks to redden as my tongue smarted. I quickly explained to the room that I had burnt my tongue on my tea and inadvertently caught Indica's eye in the process. Guilt made Indica's usually light and smiley face look heavy and sullen. Soma looked at him, then at me, as I glowered at him inadvertently, caught her eye, and then looked away. She knew something was up.

"Poor Rachael," baby Johan said as he pushed in to make a space next to me. He gave me a 'feel better' hug then smiled at me.

"I don't want you to go," he whispered to me.

"Tell her to stay Nishantha. Tell her she must stay to see your wedding!"

Baby Johan and I looked around at Nishantha.

"She has to go Johan. She has a home to go to."

"You can make a home here, can't you, Rachael?"

"Your brother is right, Johan. I have to go."

He accepted my explanation and stayed by my side. I sat there for about twenty minutes before I plucked up the courage to say I was leaving. I told everybody I had to pack and promised to come back later for my leaving gathering. Baby Johan told me excitedly he would be allowed a small glass of arrack then if he was good now. His father corrected him and told me he would not be having any arrack. Baby Johan then gave me a nod when his father wasn't looking as if to say he would be.

"Well, it was good to meet you all. Congratulations Nishantha, Somana. What a lovely memory you have left me with to take back to England," undertones entirely intended.

"Thank you, Rachael, good...to...meet...you," Somana said politely, still wearing her prom queen smile.

"Yes, good to meet you," Nishantha mumbled, still barely able to look at me. I wanted him to look at me, to take in how bad he'd made me feel. I wanted him to see the pain I was feeling. But even at that moment I was seduced by his husky voice and soulful eyes. I still wanted him with my all my being. I was angry that I would be leaving on this note, left to deal with this on my own. It was cruel and unfair.

Somana took Nishantha's arm proudly as I left the room. I knew how good she felt. I knew because that had been me a few days ago. I felt sick. A small committee saw me off at the front door as I stormed down the street, my blood boiling from an anger I knew had only risen to protect me from the hurt I was feeling deeper down. My face felt red and puffy even before any tears were shed. That whole 'jumping feet first into a stinking puddle' analogy proved itself to be correct. I was only now just finding out how deep it really was. Indica had been right from the get-go. As I walked, it was as though my legs had given up on me. They felt so weak and wobbly I had to sit myself down on a neighbour's garden wall. Once there, I broke down and sobbed. I felt jealous, angry, devastated, rejected, deceived and outright desperate. As I hid my bawling face in my hands, an arm appeared from nowhere and placed itself around my shoulder. I looked up to see it belonged to Indica.

"Don't even think about mentioning puddles, Indica," I whined through involuntary sobbing.

"Shh, Rachael, come here. Nishantha is hurting too. I can see it in his eyes."

I pushed Indica away from me and stood up to face him.

"Yeah, sure he is. Or maybe he is thinking 'oh well, we're only halfway through the story, and look at the beautiful woman I get to spend my life with!'"

"That is not fair."

"Why didn't you tell me?"

"That she is beautiful?"

"That today was their dowry!"

"I only found out yesterday and I thought I would not need to.

This was all supposed to happen tomorrow. I thought you would be gone and would not have to deal with it."

His point made it difficult for me to carry on being irrational.

"I thought she was supposed to serve her precious tea at her house."

Indica didn't even warrant my comment with a response. Fair enough.

"Rachael. You always knew he was to be married."

"I know, I know, I know," I said, looking up at the sky with both my hands on the back of my head. "But I didn't expect to have it rubbed in my face. I feel...I feel stupid. I thought I was special to Nishantha, how he is to me. The reality is, he has been thinking about her, about today."

"Nishantha cried for you when he left you in Kandy. He told me on the telephone."

I started pacing slowly up and down the pavement. "So he does like me?"

"Yes. But what can he do? He cannot let Somana and their families down. And you are going home. Do you think he wants to marry a stranger?"

"Well, she is beautiful."

"Many women are beautiful, Rachael. That does not mean he wants to spend the rest of his life with them all. If you know Nishantha as well as you say you do, you would know he has never wanted to marry a Sinhalese girl. He refused the first two suitors Johan and Komari found him. He cannot keep refusing." Indica was frowning as he spoke and once again I thought how unsuited he was to such expressions.

I sat back on the wall and slumped down in defeat. Nishantha had done nothing wrong. In fact, he had gone all out to do the right thing by me and by Somana and by his family. Indica stepped forward and put a reassuring hand on my shoulder. I put my hand on his and lent my head towards him. From behind Indica I saw a figure rapidly approaching.

"Nishantha? Oh shit! Indica, he's coming, what do I do? What do I say?"

Indica looked as surprised as I was when he turned to see Nishantha walking towards us.

"No, don't look! He will know I am sitting here saying I don't know what to say!"

"What? Rachael, you are human, we all know it. Maybe if you knew it too you wouldn't make yourself so unhappy."

"Really, Indica? You're choosing right now to get all judgemental on me?"

"I am sorry Rachael, but it is true. You need to be told. You put on this mask, but we all see through it. You pretend nothing gets in. You pretend even to yourself. It is time to, to start being honest with yourself."

"Stop lecturing me and tell me what I should do. Quick! He is coming!"

"I just have," Indica said as the frown disappeared from his face.

Before I could respond, Nishantha was standing just behind Indica.

"Rachael. Can we talk?" Nishantha asked, swallowing hard. He looked stressed. My stomach lurched into my throat. He stirred a reaction in me far beyond my control. Just his mere presence rocked me at my inner core. It had been that way from the very first day I saw him. Indica spoke angrily to him in Sinhala. Nishantha spoke back, their arms flailing in frustration. Indica pushed Nishantha's shoulders with his hands. I stood up, concerned as to where this was going. Nishantha held his hands up in surrender thus diffusing the growing animosity. Indica held his hands up in surrender too, gave me one last look, then set off back toward the house. Nishantha stood in front of me. Fear, love, desire and more fear coursed through my body, making me giddy. I just wanted him to go, to not be something I had to deal with anymore. These emotions were bigger than me and I was all out of fight. The bottom line was I couldn't go through another goodbye. Not like this. I cried into my hands again.

"Rachael, please, I am so sorry," he said sincerely. Whatever he said, however much he comforted me, I had to keep in the forefront of my mind that it was all over and I was never going to see him again.

"Rachael?" he said, bringing a hand up to meet mine. I brushed him off. His smart attire looked wrong, false.

"What is the point, Nishantha? Nothing you can say can fix this. And don't tell me this is only part of my story. I don't want to hear it right now."

Nishantha looked shocked. He attempted to run his fingers through his hair before realising it had been gelled rigid.

I looked into his eyes and he looked into mine. It was like two wild animals trying to work out if they had met with friend or foe. I was angry because Nishantha couldn't do the one thing I needed him to. He couldn't tell me we could be together. I was acting like a spoilt brat, cutting off my nose to spite my face because if I left things between us like this I would regret my behaviour for a long time to come. I had to calm down. His look of uncertainty turned into one of hurt. It was only when tears welled in his eyes that my anger subsided.

"I'm sorry, Nishantha. This is not your fault, none of this is, I just…"

"Shh," he said softly as he pulled me into his arms, his reassuring hands firmly holding the back of my head. It was bittersweet.

"You shouldn't hold me like this. Anybody could come out and see you."

"It does not matter now. When you walked in today, Rachael, I was, I do not know how to say... In my heart I knew, I know, I can-not marry Somana. I *should* marry her just as you *should* go home but that is not what I want. And I think it is not what you want," his voice trembled the way it had the night of the parada when we realised we were trapped in the guesthouse. "I could not let that, back there, be how we say goodbye, Rachael. I do not want to say goodbye at all."

"Nishantha, don't," I said trying not to let myself get carried away by his words. The tease was too much.

"Rachael, stay. Do not go home," he said, holding my arms and looking me square in the face.

"I have to."

"Then let me spend to-night with you."
He had a crazy, spontaneous look in his eye that I'd never seen before in him.
"What? What about Somana?"
"I have just walked out on her, on her and both our families, with no explanation. I will be asked why and I shall say I cannot marry a woman I do not love. Rachael, even if you walk away now, I will not marry Somana. I will not marry any of my parents' suitors."
Nishantha wasn't in the habit of saying things he didn't mean but still, the one-hundred-and-eighty degree U-turn was way too fast for me.
"This doesn't make sense, Nishantha. How can you just walk away from all that, from all them?" I asked, pointing back toward the house. "You will disgrace Somana in front of her family. You will disgrace your family. You may even lose them, Nishantha."
"I know. I know. I will have to go back now. I will have to go back now and talk to them, before they come out here, before I start thinking about everybody else before what I want."
"No, Nishantha, this isn't you. You don't make important decisions like these on a whim, you think, and assess, you do the right thing."
"Why are you talking me out of this? Is this not what you wanted for me? For me to live my own life how I see fit?"
"I'm just scared you will do something you regret because of an impulsive response to seeing me. My life is dictated by my emotions – to hell with the consequences – but you, you are different."
"I already tell Indica to tell Soma. It is too late. I already have decided to do this."
"Do you know how crazy this sounds?"
"Ou, I mean, yes. But that is how being with you makes me feel. Crazy, alive, and like I am really me."
"Do you know I am leaving tomorrow morning?"
"Are you telling me your plane is the last plane ever to fly between here and England?"

Sarcasm? We really had role reversed. Nishantha had thrown caution to the wind and I had snatched it back.

I gave out a little nervous laugh born from both shock and disbelief. This was starting to sound believable. My dreams were back in my reach. But I had to be sure.

"So you are going to walk in there, break her heart, and let everybody down?"

"I do not want to hurt anyone. I feel bad for what I am going to do. But I *am* going to do it. Meet me on the beach in front of the Gaulle Face, soon."

"What if I wait and you don't come back. I don't think I could handle that."

"Rachael, I will come back. I know it is hard but you have to trust me. OK?"

"OK," I said against my better judgment. I was annoyed at putting myself back at his mercy, back out of control.

I walked off, shaken and unsure. Something told me there would be no leaving party for me now. Poor Ravi, I didn't even go back to let him know the party was off.

Time on the beach passed both slowly and far too quickly at the same time. I was burning to see Nishantha yet I did not want my last night to pass. Since I got here, I had enjoyed watching the waves crash onto the shore so much it was like I was already missing them. For the last time, I sat and watched them roar in and suck back out again in their own rhythmical continuum. The power and the beauty humbled me.

How could I say goodbye to Nishantha if I couldn't even say goodbye to the ocean? I sank my feet into the sand and tried to stay positive. I had no way of knowing how Nishantha's confession was going. Part of me wondered if he had said all that to me in fantasy. Maybe he was avoiding having to say goodbye to me again as he had back in Kandy. Was that was the last time I would see him? Was I being foolish waiting for a man who was never going to come?

To my left, a familiar figure strolled over to me, diminishing my spirits. It was Indica – not a good sign. I could only think he was here to tell me 'sorry Rachael, Nishantha is not coming'. I put on a brave face for him and held my breath until he spoke.

"Rachael, do not worry, Nishantha is talking to his father. He is still coming. I just wanted to say goodbye to you." He had read me well and he quickly put my mind at rest.

"Oh, Indica, I'm so glad I met you. I'm really going to miss that big smile you wear so well."

"That's me," he said, dipping his head in jest. "You will be coming back so do not be sad. All this will be waiting for you when you come." He looked out across the ocean. Either he was a mind-reader or I really was transparent. I think I can guess which was true.

"I hope so," I said, giving him a huge hug. "I am sorry for coming along and complicating…"

"What is done, it is done. Did I say that right?"

"Yeah, close enough. So you don't hate me for all this?" I asked, amazed at how he was able forgive me for not listening to him *and* for turning his family upside down.

"No, Rachael. I believe now this is what was meant to happen, for both of you."

I frowned, not a big believer in the whole fate spiel. "So how did it go, Nishantha's confession?" I asked.

"Not well. But do not worry. Soon they will see Nishantha has done what is right for him. I told Soma about you and him. She was not surprised when I tell her. She could see her brother was not happy with the marriage. She just want him to be happy."

"Do Johan and Komari know? Oh my god, they are going to hate me."

"His father say nothing. His mother, she blame Kandy, not you. Kandy is a modern place. She say it changed him, that it had taken him away from his…beginnings."

"But they must feel betrayed by me. They trusted me and I lied to them."

"They are in shock. Komari is more concerned with her son than with you. I will not lie, I do not know what they will think of you when they have had a chance to think it through. I know

Nishantha will defend you. As will Soma. As will I."
I smiled thankfully at my good friend.
"And Somana?"
"Somana is beautiful and her family, they have money. She will not be short of suitors."
"Wow, I can't believe he's gone through with it."
"He cares for you, Rachael. And even if he cannot have you, he knows how he wants to feel about the woman he marry. It is not the way he feels about Somana."
"Do you really think he'll come?"
"I know he will. I will stay with you until he come. I keep you company in your puddle!" he mused, lightening the atmosphere. I threw him a glance that jokingly said 'don't go there'.
Indica stayed true to his word and waited with me. He even made a special effort to keep my mind off the situation by asking me to teach him cockney rhyming slang, and had me laughing as he tried to say 'up the old apples and pears' in a London cockney accent.
When Nishantha came, Indica got up and gave Nishantha a friendly pat on the back.
"Goodbye me...old...china."
"Perfect! Bye, Indica. You take care of that beautiful family of yours."
Indica saluted me as I watched him leave footprints across the sand for the last time.

All the games were over and our cards were on the table. I felt conspicuous now that the veil of excuses had been lifted. We were only in one another's company because we wanted to be again. The air between us grew serious, as it had back in Kandy, in room 101.
Nishantha stood before me. I remained seated trying to suppress nerves which were only comparable with those of a first date.
"So, are you a free man now?"
Nishantha sat down next to me. "No, Rachael, I am not."
"Oh," I said disappointedly.

"I am yours if you will have me?" he said, smiling.
Oh.
"Come here!" I pulled him into me and kissed him gently on the lips. He reciprocated and we shared our first morally appropriate kiss. With no shards of guilt tainting this kiss, we became fully absorbed within it.

"So how was it? Really?" I asked, once our immediate thirst for each other had been quenched. Sat between his legs, we both faced the ocean and interlocked our hands. Nishantha sighed.

"Somana was crying when I got there because Indica had told them. I wanted to talk to her alone, to save her from embarrassment, but Somana's family, they would not let me take her out of the room. And they would not leave."

I turned myself to face Nishantha. He was looking into the distance as if he could see it all unravelling before him. He was clearly upset by the distress he had caused this woman and the two families.

"Her father tell me the marriage is still to go ahead, despite what I have done. I told them I am sorry, from my heart, but I can-not marry Somana. My mother, she send my brother up the stairs saying he was too young to see my mistakes. Somana's mother start to shout and cry hysterically. Then Somana stand up, she ask me why and the room, it fell silent. Even our mothers stopped to hear what I had to say. There were so many faces watching me. I froze. Then I pictured you leaving and I knew what I had to say. I walk up to Somana and tell her I did not mean for any of this but in my heart I want another woman. She ask, 'the white girl?' like I was crazy to think you would want to be with me. I said nothing. I did not need to. My mother looked at me with tears in her eyes. Somana run out and her family go after her. Her father, he give my father words as he left. My mother was crying. She said she did not understand. She blame Kandy and she say I do not know what I want."

"What did she say about me?"

"She could not understand it, Rachael. She think I want all woman, that I do not want just one so she does not blame you.

She say Kandy take my values away from me."

"So, in her eyes, if it wasn't me, it would be someone else?"

"In her eyes, yes. But it is not true. I am not as she thinks I am."

"And what did your father say?"

"He say nothing. I do not know what he will do," Nishantha paused in thought for a moment. "Will you come back?"

"I will. I can use my holiday to come back but what then?"

"I don't know. I guess we spend more time together and see what happens then."

I knew I would move to Kandy in a heartbeat if I could still work there. I knew our situation was difficult but right then I truly believed if we wanted to we could make it work, one way or another. The only thing that mattered was that I was going to come back to spend time with Nishantha.

We spent the rest of the evening sitting in each other's arms people-watching young couples on the beach. It was clear the beach belonged to carefree lovers. We watched couples stroll along together who had the freedom to choose to be together. Or maybe they didn't; it didn't matter either way here. Maybe they were meeting in secret to watch nature's evening show together.

As we watched a young couple see how close they could get to the waves before running away from them I asked, "Do you regret walking out on Somana, now that you have seen their reactions?"

"I am watching the sunset with the woman I want to be with. I do not regret anything."

"Even though I am leaving?"

"Even if I never see you again. This is perfect, this moment right now."

As we watched the low-set sun in the sky I tried so hard to savour every moment but time was slipping by so quickly. All the will in the world would not slow time down so I clung on hopelessly to the little we had. Before we knew it, the night was upon us and we were safely snug on my bed at Ravi's. I snuck him in because I was scared Ravi would think badly of me. I'd be lying if I said that I didn't enjoy the thrill of the sneak. We were both feeling close rather than carnal. Actually, that is a lie but it seemed inappropriate to go down that road so I ignored all improper thoughts and enjoyed the closeness all the same. We were both content to talk about absolute rubbish until the sun came up, at which point we snatched a couple of hours sleep before I had to leave. As I left Nishantha on my bed to shower, a little girlie voice in my head chanted, 'Nishantha's on your bed, Nishantha's on your bed!' I was smiling incessantly again, amazed at how events had swung my way.

When I came out of the bathroom I noticed Nishantha had put my day bag on said bed. He appeared to be studying it.

"What are you up to?" I asked.

"This little bag here, I like it very much."

"OK…Any particular reason why?"

"You are always searching in it, always, for something, every time I have seen you."

"Are you making fun of me, again?"

"Yes. No, no I think it is, um, cute, the way you look through it. It seems whatever you need is always in the last place you look."

"Well, that's because," I pulled the mosquito net up into a knot out of the way then climbed on the bed and nuzzled at Nishantha's neck and ear. "When I have found it, I don't need to look anymore!"

"Oh come on! You know what I mean," he turned to kiss me and nudged me away from his sensitive neck. "You need to stop doing that or you will not be getting on any plane today."

"Don't tempt me!" I lay back down with Nishantha in my flight clothes – combats and vest top – with ringing wet hair.

Nishantha returned his attention back to my bag.

"It reminds me of all the places we have been together, from when you came to the institute, to the Esala Perahera, the Roof Top Bar, Kandy, *The Ivory* and all the way to right now," he said, looking at my now dishevelled day bag with a sense of nostalgia. It was soothing to hear positive connotations about the parada instead of wincing in pain at the thought of what happened after.

"You know, I am going home because I have to, not because I

want to," I announced as if an explanation had been asked of me. He caressed my face with his fingers and looked deeply into my eyes.

"I know. I am still sad to see you go. Will you be OK in England?"

"I will. I have a lovely group of friends at home. We have all grown up together from school, since we were just young teenagers."

"What are their names?"

As I thought about my friends back home I wished again that I'd kept in touch with Jacky, my friend from my days as a waitress. As I thought of her and her two little girls I realised they wouldn't be so little anymore and I'd missed them growing up. Putting thoughts of who I hadn't kept in touch with aside I concentrated on who I had.

"There's Laura. We are very different from each other but she is my best friend. Then there is Neal, he is like the daddy of the group. He organises us and makes himself available in a crisis. There's Ben and Michael, they are brothers, and there's Derren. He is," there seemed no point in worrying Nishantha with details. "A bit of a mess really. Very up and down, very angry with the world."

"So these are the people who will look out for you at home? Not your parents?"

"Yeah, I guess they are, along with my boss, oddly. We get on really well. My parents live a long way away and they don't agree with my chosen career, travelling to Eastern countries they believe are unsafe."

"I can see why they would worry. Do they know what happened to you?"

"No. I will be OK though. You don't need to worry. Will you do me a favour?"

"Sure, what do you need?"

"For you to say goodbye to your sister for me? I'm not sure what she thinks of me but I really admire her. I never got to say goodbye."

"Soma wishes she could be more like you. Soma and I, we are not traditional in the way our mother and our father would like. The difference is that I am a man. I have the freedom to decide for myself how I will live. Soma does not have this choice. She like you."

"She doesn't bear ill feeling toward you, then, for having freedom where she doesn't?"

"No. She has a big heart, like you. She wants me to be happy as though her own happiness depends on it."

A little wash of shame came over me as I realised I would not have been so graceful if I were in Soma's shoes.

"She is happy though, right? With Indica and her baby?"

"She is. Indica has always been a great friend to us both and they are in love. She is lucky our mother and father allowed the marriage. He only sells fruit at the market, it is not a good living."

"So, if they thought they could find a better suitor, why did they let her marry Indica?"

"They allowed it in return for her promise to stay close. She took the offer gladly."

"Do you think they will forgive you?"

"Maybe in time. It is too, um, new, at the moment, like open wound," he looked at me again as though taking me in. "How much time do we have?"

The answer was none. It was time to leave. I jotted my email address down on a piece of my notepaper. Nishantha slid it into his jeans pocket. As an afterthought I also gave him my parent's address in Ulverston as I could not guarantee mine at the flat would stay the same, so it seemed like a good idea at the time.

Sneaking back out of Ravi's was not so easy. He caught us as we reached the restaurant area. The sight of us stopped him dead in his tracks yet he was good enough not to mention it. I said goodbye to Ravi then waited outside for one last tuk-tuk ride.

When it arrived I said goodbye to the man I felt inexplicably close to; the man who had opened my eyes, my mind and my heart in a way that would change me forever.

He loves me.

Chapter 12

West Sussex, England

A confusion of dizzy snowflakes darted frantically to-and-fro inside the glass sphere of my snow globe. Inside the globe there was a little stone cottage. Children played in the garden outside as their rosy-cheeked mother stood there looking on. A look of glee had been painted on her face. A little deer watched them nervously as he peered into the garden from afar.
I'd begged my mum to buy the snow globe for me at a fete when I was five and it had survived every clearout from then on. It had even managed to find its way here to my flat.
Each frenetic little snowflake in the blizzard raced and swirled past each other aimlessly, panic stricken. Then slowly, slowly, slowly, each one found its place and settled on the bottom allowing the water to be still, clear, and calm once more.
It took a long time for my blizzard of emotions to settle, for my head to be still and calm. After an initial gathering to say hello to all my friends, I kept myself to myself for a long while, for too long really. The only person I spoke to was Laura and that was only because she badgered me relentlessly. Laura kept calling me to fill me in on the group's gossip and soon enough I started to look forward to the next instalments of their lives according to Laura. Did Neal get the job he went for? Was Ben still with Alana? Had Derren mentioned me? The answer to all these questions was yes. Neal got his job in recruitment in London, Ben was still with Alana and Derren had mentioned me. Laura told me he knew I was no longer interested in pursuing our relationship and, in her opinion, was putting on a front to hide his feelings on the matter. Laura also told me Tanya had moved to Kingston and was still coming out with them, just not as much.
At first, fitting back into the Western way of life was hard. I

coped by knowing I had something better to look forward to. Nishantha. Kandy. Sri Lanka.

Every evening I excitedly logged on to Jenny's PC to check my emails and every day I was disappointed. The count of new, unread emails would set my heart racing but there was never one from him. The more time that passed the more disheartened I became. I had no idea if Nishantha was dead or alive, married or missing me, or just plain uninterested. At first, Jenny was supportive, offering me explanations as to why Nishantha hadn't been in contact. One of which was maybe he was giving me time to settle in, another was maybe he had misplaced my email address. All were great attempts to make me feel better. All were bullshit. After a few weeks, Jenny turned her efforts to encouraging me to move on. For flatmates who used to just pass in the hallway or discuss bills, we had come a long way. Jenny had become a valuable and unlikely friend. No matter how much I tried to explain that this was more than just a holiday romance, I sounded just like somebody who had just had a holiday romance. I could hear myself saying all the fluffy clichéd rubbish I'd heard so many times before.

After a month or so I gave up talking about him to other people. Instead, I would think about it all at night when I was going to sleep. Why hadn't he been in touch?

My mum was relieved when she learned he hadn't been in touch as she had already made up her mind that this man would take three wives and only wanted me for a visa. My mum and my stepdad John could not be convinced that Nishantha was one of the good guys, even after I took a trip up north to see them. They were convinced I had been suckered in by a professional con artist who knew all the right things to say to a 'vulnerable young woman'. The atmosphere around their dinner table was strained whenever I mentioned Sri Lanka in case it led to conversation about my sordid affair with a man of different ethnicity. For this reason, I stayed off the one subject I most wanted to talk about. Consequently, I just wanted to get back to my own flat again as quickly as possible, where I was free to brood and share my

thoughts with Jenny. During dinner at my parents' house, while I picked at a crunchy roast potato, I commented on how beautiful their garden looked. John had always had green fingers and up there he had the time and space to make use of his talents. I thought I was on to good thing, talking about the garden, but my mum wasn't listening as John and I talked bushes.
"You didn't give him your address did you?" she asked accusingly. And before I could answer, "He'll turn up on your doorstep expecting a place to live. Oh please tell me you didn't, Rachael?"
No mum. I gave him your address.
"No mum. I gave him my email address. So the yellow flowered bush is hypericum?" I said, carrying on my mini lesson in horticulture and ignoring my fretting mother.
"Yes, it's St John's Wort."
"Really? It's the stuff you buy in the shops?"
"Yeah, they use it to treat depression or something," John said before devouring a buttery new potato from his plate. My mum always cooked two types of potato at dinner because John liked new tats and everybody else liked roasted.
"You didn't sleep with him did you, Rachael? Maybe we should get you checked out. My god! You could have AIDS!"
"Mum! Jesus, what is wrong with you?" I slammed my knife and fork down on the plate. "No I didn't sleep with him but I wanted to!" I announced, standing up from the dinner table. I was met with a deafening silence.
"Sit down love, ay, your chicken is getting cold," said John the peacekeeper. Watching him sitting there at the table, it dawned on me for the first time that he was a calm, good-hearted, and outdoorsy man. Was I drawn to Nishantha because he had the same traits as the man who brought me up? I sat back down and carried on my conversation calmly instead of ranting hysterically.
"I wanted to but it wasn't appropriate." I sighed because I knew the truth was going to cause another shit-storm. "It wasn't appropriate because other people were involved."
"How do you mean?" mum asked quickly and in monotone.

"He was supposed to be getting married."
"Oh this just keeps on getting better and better this does!"
"It was an arranged marriage, mum. He didn't love her, he barely knew her! You know what? I'm sick of your attitude to my life," I was back to hysterical ranting. "I work hard, I don't do drugs, I don't sleep around, I have respect and compassion for other people, most other people anyway. My job is in helping other people. You should be proud of me, mum. Not putting me down at every opportunity."
She looked hurt.
"Is that what you think?"
"Yes. When do you ever praise me for what I do? You are so scared of the world, you can't accept that I want to go out and live in it. You would rather cut me off than hear from me when I'm away because *you* can't handle it," John put his head down into his hand and rubbed his forehead. "How do you think that makes me feel? You want me to live out the picture you have painted for me in your head but I won't. I want to be with a Sinhalese man, mum. He made me feel loved and at peace, he was funny and he hasn't been in touch so I'm hurting. And all you can do is breathe a sigh of relief.
And while I am setting the record straight, I won't stop going to developing countries. You need to deal with that or you'll miss out on my life. *You'll* miss out mum, not me."
After a long spell of silence, my mum finally spoke.
"Would you like more gravy Rachael?" This may seem like she was ignoring me but she wasn't. I knew my mum well and this was a good thing. This meant she thought I had a point and she needed time to digest it. Everybody was on their best behaviour for the remainder of my visit and my mum kept her doubts to herself.
Back down south I became like a lost soul. Dissatisfied with my life in the UK I felt rejected by the place I wanted to be: Kandy with Nishantha. Jenny took full advantage of my vulnerable state, cooking me her sort of food because I couldn't be bothered to make any for myself. She enjoyed moulding me into a little mini

Jen. She had me drinking dandelion coffee instead of caffeine-loaded Robusta, rice milk instead of cow juice and all sorts of weird and wonderful fake meats instead of the real deal. She also had me on the floor doing pose-of-a-cow during her yoga sessions and performed Reiki on me whenever the mood took hold. For the most part we were good for each other. She loved to promote the way she lived and I was way too impressionable to object.

At work, Victor knew I was unhappy and I could see he was worried about me, yet he never once gave me a lecture or pushed me into confession. He just gave me knowing looks to let me know he was there if I needed him.

After two months had passed without word from Sri Lanka, I knew everybody else had been right. I knew I had to get over Nishantha.

Chapter 13

"**So Rach,** you around for dinner tonight?" Jenny asked as she walked into the lounge. She was wearing nothing but a towel around her body and hair removal cream above her top lip. She looked wired and excited. Something was up.
"Actually, no, I am going out tonight," I said proudly, knowing that would surprise her.
Jenny raised her eyebrows at me. "Well, good. Hardy is coming over tonight and I think he has something important to ask me, if you know what I mean?" she gave me a wink and a nudge as she parked herself on the couch next to me to moisturise her skinny, dry legs.
"What, you mean, the big question?"
Jenny nodded with a smile.
"No way. Oh my god! How do you know?"
"Well, we have been together for like, forever and we had a convo about it the other week."
"The other week? So why is tonight the night?"
"Because Friday was payday and he has been in town all day today, ah!"
"Picking out the perfect ring I guess."
"Abso-fucking-lutely. So, I am making spicy quinoa and tofu risotto and bringing in the beer. I'll leave him to bring the champagne. Where are you off to tonight anyway? Since when did you leave the flat except for when you go to work?"
"Hey, that's not fair. I also take out the rubbish and…" I struggled to think of any non-work-related outings out. I hadn't even been out to do the shopping since coming home. "...well I went to my parents that time."
"Ooh, you diva. How do you manage such a hectic schedule?" Jenny said in her true sarcastic style. She was now busy combing her damp, dark hair with her bony nail-less fingers. For the

amount of vegan chocolate and vegetarian beer this girl packed away it was just plain wrong that she was so thin.

"I'm actually going out with Laura and Ben."

"And..."

"And Neal."

"And..."

"Well Alana will be there, Ben's girlfriend, but I doubt Tanya will be around. She lives in Kingston now and Laura says she doesn't come out all the time anymore."

Bing! A little egg-shaped timer sounded from the kitchen.

"Right, time to take this 'tash cream off, we'll talk in a mo cause I know Derren will be there and I know you are purposely avoiding telling me he will be there, *and* I know he will try it on and that you will be at it with him tonight!" she chorused from halfway down the hallway.

"Hell no, J. Lo, I don't think so!" I shouted back in some lame Southern American accent I always used when I came out with that phrase. I had taken to rhyming something with 'J. Lo' if she was getting the better of me because she hated being likened to a pop princess. This fact made 'Lowe' an unfortunate surname for such an anti-mainstream girl like Jenny. She poked her head out the bathroom door with a half-naked top lip and 'baaed' at me. That was always her comeback, because of my curly blonde hair. I would usually straighten my curls before going out on a Saturday night but not tonight, I hadn't even looked at my straightening irons since I'd stepped off the plane from Sri Lanka.

That night I made a mediocre effort with my appearance and wished Jenny all the luck in the world, before leaving for my local, The Tavern.

When approaching The Tavern, I noticed Derren's baby parked outside, his beloved and immaculate MX5. Seeing it there, all pristine and perfect, it made me a little nervous, awkward nervous not good nervous. I had always danced to Derren's tune. He dictated when we got together, when we split up and when we could see other people. I'd let him get away with it for years. Now I was the one in charge and I was choosing to keep a distance between us. After all the times he kicked me to the curb I should have been pleased with the role reversal but that was not the case. His feelings had always mattered, no matter how he had treated me. Walking into the pub I noticed I was well and truly back in a world where looks meant everything, and everything else hung a distant second. It showed in the way everybody held themselves as I made my way through the bar to find my friends. It also showed in the topics of conversation and in the way people spoke. Thank god I lived with Jenny. I used to think she was a bit off the wall. Now she was my anchor of normality. My group of friends raised their glasses to me as I walked in and Neal got up to buy me a drink. Derren and I did not speak directly to each other, we just exchanged a few uneasy glances. I was glad Tanya wasn't there. She was always so sickeningly nice to me and it was tiresome keeping up with the act. To me she was just a groupie fling who had stuck around too long. To everybody else in my circle of friends, she was a well received new recruit. Laura told me that Tanya always knew she would come in second to me, in Derren's eyes, so I should cut the poor girl some slack. Maybe my views were outdated. Maybe I needed to change.

Neal, the daddy of the group, came back from the bar with a glass of wine for me and a pint for himself. Everybody else already had a full glass of their chosen poison in their hand. Neal was very down to earth. He was career driven, which is why he opted to get into one of the bigger companies in London. He was stocky and muscular from lifting weights in the gym three times a week and he had very pale blue eyes. His auburn hair and face full of freckles made eyes stand out, not necessarily in a good way. His pale eyes against his darker hair and freckles made him look cold in appearance and he had to smile to inject warmth into his appearance.

"Thanks, Neal."

"That's alright, gal. So tell me. Are you still a MIF or did they finally teach you how to make a decent cup of tea on your travels?"

"Well actually, they don't drink their tea with milk so the correct milk/water order didn't come up. I will never change the way I make my tea, Neal, so quit asking!"

Neal and I had this joke between us about the very controversial subject of making a cup of tea. I was in the minority and liked to put the milk in first which made me a MIF as opposed to a WIF (water in first). The whole group and I had a huge debate about it one day when Neal thought Laura had made his tea and proceeded to tell me he could tell it had been made properly. He went on about how it was 'all in the flavour' and if I'd made it, he would be able to tell. Little did he know I *had* made it – milk in first. When Neal and I have not seen each other for a while, he brings it up again like some kind of re-bonding aid. It always worked and we always slumped back into our cosy armchair of friendship with ease. Neal was the organiser of the group. He was the one everybody turned to when we had a problem or when something needed sorting. He always kept his head about him. He was the alpha male, a natural leader. Derren wasn't but wanted to be and sometimes this caused ructions between the two. It didn't help that Neal was better with the ladies, beefier, and oozed self-confidence. Strange when you consider Derren was the one with looks on his side – dark hair, olive skin and tall genes. Derren also had issues with Nick. I think he used to see all his short falls come good in other men and it made him insecure. He never thought to look at what he had and make the most of that instead.

"Just joking with ya, Rach. It's great to have you back out in the land of the living. Cheers bird."

"Cheers!" we all chorused as we clinked glasses over our usual table. Looking around the pub, it was like nothing had changed at all since I'd been away. A strange sensation washed over me as I realised how much life I'd experienced while everybody in the pub had been doing the same things, in the same routine. The old man with the grey hat still sat at his table for one, drinking real ale and reading the paper. The tubby couple with the northern accents still sat in their little booth, ordering fish and chips followed by apple crumble or, occasionally, sticky toffee pudding. They both looked more interested in their food than in each other. Yep, life

had just been ticking over while I'd been away.
"Well it's good to be here, it's good to see you all."
"Come to think of it," Ben said, still stuck on the previous conversation. He did that a lot, adding in his comments after we had all moved on. Although we all laughed at him for it, his comments were usually interesting and I loved the quirky perspective he brought to the table. "Tanya makes tea the same way as you," Alana nodded along in agreement as Ben spoke. Her hair was back to blonde. When she started getting closer to Ben she dyed it brown. She suited blonde much better.
"Mm, yeah, she does put the milk in first," she said.
"Derren, is this part of your dating criteria? Number three, must be Miffy!" Ben said, ticking off the imaginary list on his palm.
"It's better than being Wiffy!" Laura whispered to me while Neal asked, "So what are the first two items on the list, Ben?"
"T n A my friend, T n A."
"What's 'T n A'?" Laura asked. The men at the table chorused 'tits and arse' and all the women groaned 'men' back at them.
"Ooh, Rach did not like being compared to Tanya. Did you see that look?" Ben mused. OK, so I didn't always appreciate Ben's quirky perspective. It was true though.
"No, I've got nothing against the girl. She's not the brightest little bulb in the box but I've got no problem with her."
"That's a bit harsh Rach," Laura said, forever in her defence of late.
"Well, she believed Ben when he told her his surname was Nevis!"
The whole table fell about laughing until they noticed an unimpressed Alana. She was sitting with folded arms, sending dagger eyes to Ben who was laughing without permission.

Neal and Ben were really interested in my stories of Sri Lanka and asked me all sorts of questions about it, which was really lovely of them. My two worlds always seemed so separate it was as if one of them didn't exist. Their interest in my time in Colombo helped bridge the gap. Ben and Neal shared a genuine interest in other people and could talk to anybody they met from any walk of life. I used to imagine them talking to Nishantha, making an effort to make him feel comfortable if I were to bring him back here. Laura and I got to talk a little and I gave her the elephant present. She was touched by the present and made me promise we'd meet up again soon, just the two of us for a proper catch up. I apologised for being such a hermit; she just seemed happy to have her friend back. Just before closing time Derren and I found ourselves alone at the table – awkward. Neal and Ben were playing pool and Laura and Alana were dancing on the improvised dance floor. It was odd to see them looking as though they'd been friends for years. When last I saw Laura, she was still a little wary of the two new arrivals.

"So, how's the band, how's Nick?" I regretted mentioning Nick the moment I said his name. I'd forgotten it was necessary to check and double-check the conversation choice after Derren had been drinking in order to prevent an argument. I was out of the habit of policing every word I spoke before I spoke it. I don't know how I did it now, or why I entertained it for so long. Nick was the guy from Brighton who made up the third member of N-Trails. He was in it before Derren, when Ben's brother Michael was still a member. I asked after Nick because I was unlikely to bump into him and, in the land of the normal people, it would have been a perfectly acceptable means of small talk.

"We're gigging next Friday. You should come. I'm sure you and Nick will have a lot to catch up on." Derren's undertones were embarrassingly overstated.

"Derren, this is the first time I have seen you in ages. Why are you being like this? You always thought I had a thing for him and I never did."

"Yes you did. Why else would he sit and talk to you about his childhood dreams and about how his guitar is the only love of his life. He was flirting with you."

"You're insane. He used to talk to me to make me feel better when you were off flirting. You dealt with your own guilt about that by telling yourself there was something between Nick and I."

Nick used to sit and talk with me about his childhood dream of becoming a marine biologist. We both loved the sea so it was common ground more than anything else.

"So what are you, the resident psychologist now?"

"There's nothing between me and Nick and I am sick of having to explain myself to you."

"Oh, that's right, you've moved on. How is your fella', Rachael?"

I scowled at Laura who had arrived back at the table with the guys and a double vodka lemonade. Laura may have been my friend since day dot, but boy did she have a gob like the Dartford Tunnel.

"You know you really should stay away from married men, you'll get hurt," Derren said with a smug look on his face.

"Rachael, just ignore him, he is being a jealous prick," Ben said, looking disapprovingly at Derren.

"Shut up, Ben. What is there to be jealous of anyway? A phantom boyfriend all made up in Rachael's head? I don't think so. I'm going to the bar."

"Thanks, Laura."

"Rachael, what's the big deal? I thought he would get in contact with you the way you went on about it. You wouldn't have minded me telling people then would you?"

"Forget it, Laura. I wouldn't expect you to understand something as complicated as keeping your mouth shut."

This is where Laura and I brought out the worst in each other. She could never just say sorry and it wound me up. Derren got up and walked off smiling smugly to himself, pleased with the drama he had created. Neal watched him then turned to Laura and me.

"Come on girls, don't argue. Derren's the one with the problem. None of us are laughing at you Rachael. I, for one, am really sorry to hear he hasn't been in touch. I think it's really cool you had a boyfriend from, where was he from, Sri Lanka right?"

"Yeah, he was."

"You should be well happy, Rach. None of us have done all this stuff and met all these people. Seriously, don't listen to Derren. Look, don't tell him I said anything but he was really looking forward to you coming home. He wanted to make a go of it with you this time, like properly, no more messing about. I'm telling you, he has been a nightmare lately."

"You didn't tell me this!" Laura said, astounded that gossip existed without her knowledge. Maybe I just had to accept my little gossip queen the way she was.

"Really?" I said, watching Derren standing at the bar looking sorry for himself.

"It's true," Ben said, nodding his head in a drunken, enthusiastic, manner.

"Has he not been with Tanya?"

"No, well, not as far as I know. Tanya was only a bit of fun ages ago, Rachael. He wasn't even that pleased when she started hanging out with us but, you know, she's Alana's friend, and she's cool. I think you should wait 'til he's sober and talk to him, sort things out."

"He is pretty wasted," I observed as I watched him sway at the bar. "You won't let him drive like that, will you?"

"No, Rachael, he's staying at Neal's. Stop worrying about him. He is not your responsibility anymore."

"Sorry, old habits and all that," I said as Pav, the barman, shouted at us in his usual quirky way. His friendly northern accent allowed him to say pretty much anything he wanted and he still came across as charming. That was yet another thought I was too scared to share with Derren in case he took it the wrong way. I can't believe it took meeting Nishantha to realise how hard Derren made everything.

"Time at the bar ladies and shit-heads please! You have fifteen minutes to drink up and fuck-off, thank you and good night!"

I returned to a dark and quiet flat so I tried to tiptoe through it without waking anybody up. As I passed the lounge, a silhouetted figure made me jump out my skin. I gasped aloud.

"Rachael?"

"Jenny! What're you doing? I thought you were an imposter or something."

She moved over to the windowsill and sat down on it. I turned on the side lamp and walked over to her. She opened the window and lit a joint, despite the fact that it was raining outside. Coal-coloured eye shadow had smudged around her eyes and mascara ran down her cheeks in the channels made by her tears. I didn't know what to do first, grab the make-up remover or ask what was wrong.
"Jenny, what's happened?"
"There is an envelope in the kitchen for you, I picked it up with my mail by mistake, sorry. There is also some spicy quinoa in there if you're hungry."
"Forget that, what happened? Is it Hardy?"
Rain started to spatter onto Jenny and the windowsill so she took a long drag on her joint, put the rest out and pulled the window shut.
"I was wrong, Rachael, so wrong. He doesn't want to get engaged. He wants to break up with me."
"What? Why?"
"He wants to go travelling," said Jenny as she slid down onto the couch.
"Well, that could be good. Can't you go with him?"
"He wants to do it alone. He said he *has* to do it alone."
"Oh, Jenny," I said, passing her a tissue. "I'm sorry."
"What can you do?" she asked, shrugging dejectedly.
"Well, for one, you can look at the bright side. He hasn't stopped loving you. He hasn't found a new model. He just wants to do something for him, to feel fulfilled."
Jenny looked at me with a perplexed expression on her face.
"You seem to know an awful lot?"
"I'm only guessing, Jenny. I know the pull of the travel bug, remember? Going off into the world alone to find out who he is, I can understand that."
"Why now? What made you decide to do it?"
"I don't know. Because of Jaycee and Victor I guess. Jaycee worked where I was temping for three months, remember?"
"Oh yeah, Lourdes Components, right?"

"Yeah, that's the one. She told me I was the type – whatever that means. She made me see it as an option right before Victor put the job offer to me."
"So what made Hardy want to go now?"
"Did you ask him?"
"He said it just feels like the right time. He said he wants to split up now to get used to being without me before he goes – or something like that."
"No, Jenny, it's not "something like that," it *is* that. He needs to gain confidence on his own before tackling the world. I totally get that, too. Anyway, just think of all the fun you will have meeting new guys, hey?"
"Seriously, is that the best you can do? I've been saying that to you for weeks to get you over Nishantha and you're hitting me with it the *day* I get dumped?"
"You're right, Jenny. I'm sorry. I don't know what to say. Except that, someone once told me, no matter how hard things seem right now, you don't need to worry, this is just one chapter in your life's story and your story isn't over."
My words got Jenny's attention. She looked like she was going to let them give her comfort then changed her mind and cried again. I changed tact.
"OK. What would make you feel better, right this minute?"
"I don't know. For Hardy to call and say he made a big mistake?"
"No, no, no, that's looking back. You're not allowed to do that. Try again."
"I don't know. When I was little, my mum used to put *My Little Pony* the movie on when I was feeling down. God, how simple things were back then, right?"
"Have you still got it?"
"Yeah, I still have the video version."
"Right, go and get it. I'll set up the old VCR and heat up some of that dinner in the kitchen; it smells delicious. We are watching *My Little Pony* on the couch until you fall asleep."
Jenny smiled, wiped away a couple of escapee tears and went off to find her childhood feel-good movie. I sat with her until she fell

asleep then took myself off to my own empty bed.

What with Jenny's late night dinner and the milk thistle she made me take before I went to sleep, I escaped the dreaded hangover I thought I would face the next day. So when I woke up the next morning I decided to take my friend's advice and go clear the air with Derren. I wanted the friction between us to cease for the sake of our friends.
I pulled up outside Derren's little townhouse wondering if this was such a good idea after all. For all I knew he was out anyway. It was difficult to tell if he was in or not as he always parked his baby at the back of the house.
I knocked, waited, and was halfway back to my car before Derren rocked up wearing nothing but a towel.
"Hi, Derren. Is this a bad time?"
"No, babe, I was just showering. Come in, I'll just throw some clothes on and I'll be back down."
I couldn't help but notice the dividing line around Derren's middle. His skin from there down was red as if he had been sitting in a hot bath. It stood out to me as odd because Derren hated baths. He only ever took one when we were together and that was only because he joined me in it in a spontaneous attempt to be passionate.
I sat down at the breakfast bar in his kitchen and looked around at all the familiar fittings and trimmings I had spent years surrounded by. When I looked out the window I noticed his car. It was parked on the skew and the windscreen was grubby. It didn't look like that the night before. By the state of the parking I worried that he had driven home drunk the night before.
Derren walked in a few moments later, half dressed in a pair of tracksuit bottoms that I had bought him years ago when we were going through our gym stage. He looked sweet with his blackish brown hair all fluffy, not yet styled or gelled.
He sat opposite me at the breakfast bar and asked me if I had a good night. Sober Derren was far easier to be around than drunken Derren.

"Yes, I did. It was great to see everyone again."

"I'm sorry, Rachael, I was out of order. It's just weird, you know, we"ve always been... close before. I'm sorry."

"I know. And I appreciate that. I just hoped we would be able to sit around our table in the pub, or in my living room, and all get on without any...weirdness between us."

"It's not easy, babe. All I could think about was you coming home. Then when you did I find out you won't come out because you're moping over some bloke you met."

"It wasn't just him. I always find it hard to come home. You know that. Derren, you and me, we are in the past now. And, as horribly clichéd as it sounds, I still want us to be friends."

Derren looked at me like I had just delivered the death sentence.

"I'll just have to get used to a different way of being us now, I guess."

I felt guilty yet slightly annoyed that he couldn't see our relationship was neither happy nor stable.

"But you must be able to see that we were not good together? You hated me going away, I wasn't prepared to stop, you liked to stay out all night, I liked to be home by the time the sun came up. And the arguments, Derren, they were not normal. Normal people do not have that amount of stress in their relationships."

"It was all my fault. I can see that now. I should have just let you go, but I was so jealous. Rachael, we can still make it work. I know it's a cliché but it really would be different this time."

He often did that when he wanted me to see his point of view, repeated words I had just used. I'm sure he read in a book somewhere that it helps you win the other person over.

"Derren, it shouldn't have taken for me to move on for you to come to this conclusion. If you had realised all this when we were together it might have been different but…"

"What if we take things slow?"

"Look, Derren, I…I came here to see how you are, generally, I mean. And to make sure there are no hard feelings between us."

"This is about that guy you met isn't it?"

I sighed. "Partly, I guess."

"But he hasn't even bothered getting in touch with you. The reason he seems so perfect is because he was a holiday romance; it wasn't real, it was fantasy. Everyone seems perfect when you have a quick fling, you told me that."

I did tell him that, right around the time he met Tanya. Derren really knew how to press my buttons.

"You say all this but if we got back together we both know you would never be able to get over that fact that..." I trailed off, realising how insensitive I was about to be.

"Get over what, Rachael? Did you sleep with Nick?"

"What?"

Where did that come from? I was talking about my having feelings for Nishantha!

"Come on, Rach. I know you had a thing for him."

"No, Derren. I didn't have a thing for him. You are *way* off the mark."

"Well, what then? What were you going to say?"

"OK then, if you really want to know," he had rubbed me up the wrong way so now he was going to get the truth. "I was going to say, if we got together, you would never get over the fact that if I could be with Nishantha I would be. I'd choose him over you any day."

I wanted to take it back as soon as I'd say it because I didn't want hurt Derren, but his reaction was to laugh as though I was being ludicrous.

"Rachael, trust me, I am not going to be jealous of a Pa..."

"Of a what? A Paki?"

"That's not what I was going to say, Rachael."

"Oh save it, Derren. That's exactly what you were going to say."

I rolled my eyes in frustration from Derren's innate instinct to lie. A familiar feeling of exasperation bubbled up inside me until I remembered I was free from that world now. My eyes fell beyond Derren and to the kitchen worktop where I noticed something there that made all the other little insignificant oddities come together from when I arrived. A subconscious mini detective had been at work inside my mind and now he was letting me in on the secret. I stared at the two little, used teabags on the mottled grey and white worktop. One was darker than the other. One had been made MIF style, the other WIF. I knew then that Derren had driven to Kingston to pick up Tanya this morning, hence the dirty state of his car and hence his uncharacteristically haphazard parking. I knew they were in the bath together when I had knocked on the door, and I knew he was going to try and weasel his way out of this.

"I thought you said you were in the shower when I knocked on the door?"

"I was, why?" he frowned, feigning confusion.

"It's just, the bottom half of you was red when you opened the door, as if you had been in a hot bath. You had a line, a hot water line across your middle."

"Well, bath then, same thing, sorry."

"But you hate baths."

"People change, Rachy. More so when you disappear for long periods of time. So I like baths now, what is this all about?"

He was trying to manipulate me by calling me 'Rachy', an old pet name, and also by suggesting I should feel guilty for not being around. His mind games were not going to work on me this time. Tanya was there, I knew it. It was time to see if Derren had it in him be honest with me.

"OK, sorry. It's a shame you took so long to come round to the idea," I said, giving him a friendly wink. Derren just shrugged and busied himself by cleaning his worktops with a cloth. He faltered when he reached the offending teabags and quickly picked them up to take them to the bin.

"So how was your hangover this morning? Have you managed to leave the flat yet today?" I asked underhandedly.

The bin lid snapped shut and he looked up at me. I could see the cogs turning. He knew I would have noticed his car and answered accordingly.

"My hangover was *bad* man, my head hurt so much so I went down the shops this morning for some painkillers."

I guess the answer to my question was no, he had no intention of being honest.

"Oh, really. You couldn't give us a couple could you? I'm not feeling too great either, totally out of practice."

"Yeah, they're upstairs, in the drawer. I'll get them in a minute."

"Ah, don't worry, I'll go. It's not like I don't know my way around."

"No, I'll go. I don't know if they are in the drawer or under all my dirty washing, so I'll go look for them. Then do you fancy going out for some late breakfast or something?"

"And leave Tanya here all by herself?" I said in a pitch an octane higher than intended.

"What the hell are you talking about, Rachael? I knew you were interrogating me."

"Interrogating you? I asked you some simple questions that would be easy to answer, had you nothing to hide."

"I do have nothing to hide, Rachael. You just make me feel guilty by the way you talk to me, in your psycho way, like you're reading into everything I say. You talk to me like you have already decided I am guilty of whatever you are accusing me of, then wonder why I look uneasy. You try being interrogated and let's see how guilty you look."

"Err, have all those Operation Nick interrogations just completely gone from your mind?"

"Then you should know what I'm talking about."

I took a moment to pull myself back out of the confusion he was pulling me into.

"So you are telling me your car got that dirty from driving to your local shops that are all of two minutes away?"

"Neal used it actually. It was parked at the pub last night remember? Neal used it this morning before bringing me home. Call him, call him and ask him," Derren said, flipping up his flip-top mobile. I considered it for a moment.

"No, I'm not calling him. I'm going upstairs to see for myself."

"I hope you are sure of yourself, Rachael, because if you search my house for some girl who isn't there you are going to know it is all in your head. You are going to feel like the psycho you are and we…we are never going to even be friends again. I will tell everyone what you did here."

Looking back I should have told him he was going to great lengths to stop me looking, for a person who had nothing to hide that is. It was none of my business if Tanya was there or not, I just wanted Derren to be honest.

"I know she is here, Derren, I could tell by those teabags you just freaked out over and hurried off to the bin. We were only saying last night that Tanya makes tea like me. Remember? Point three? After tits and arse?"

"You are losing it, Rachael, fucking losing it," he said, throwing his hands from his temples. "I wish you could hear yourself."

I could hear myself and I did sound like I was losing it. I was talking about bloody teabags for goodness sakes. Derren had raised his voice and was all up in my face to the point where I had to lean back in my seat. He made me doubt myself and I started to feel about two inches tall.

Derren looked away, and in a quiet, submissive voice he said, "OK, I'll be honest with you. When we were talking about the way you make tea last night it made me think of the way you'd always make your cup your way and mine my way. It reminded me of old times. That is why… That is why I made it like that this morning, when I woke up. I did it because it reminded me of you, babe."

I thought about what Neal had told me in confidence, about how Derren had been looking forward to me coming back and how he hadn't been seeing much of Tanya. Oh dear, I had made a big mistake.

"Well," Derren said, half laughing. "It was mostly that and partly to see which one really does taste better."

I smiled at him but said nothing. Although I had been wrongly mistrusting, I had become that way because of how Derren had treated me in the past. I couldn't let this mistake cloud that fact.

"I feel really stupid for doing it but I miss you, Rachy. I miss what we had. Nobody knows me like you do."

Derren had stood back a little now, allowing me to straighten up.

He was looking into my eyes but he couldn't see into my soul the way Nishantha had. When I looked back into Derren's eyes I realised I couldn't see into his either. He was a closed book. Looking into his eyes only made me feel uneasy.

"Look," he continued. "I won't tell anyone about you accusing me of hiding Tanya upstairs if you don't tell anyone I've missed you so much I turned into a MIF man?"

I merely smiled wider in response.

"Shall we go and get that breakfast? I'm starving," he said.

"Come on, then," I sighed. "I'm sorry I accused you of lying."

"Come here," Derren said, giving me a side-hug and kissing the top of my head.

He pulled a hoodie on over his head as we walked out the door and was gibbering on enthusiastically about how the new guy at his work was called Rob Christmas. He told me that when Rob took a while to get things done people would say "what are we waiting for, Christmas?" He started recalling some other joke related to his name as we got in the car but I wasn't listening. Instead I was wondering why the windscreen wipers came on automatically when he turned on the engine. It had been raining last night, not this morning. He was lying. He had driven last night to pick Tanya up. That car had not been used since the rains last night.

"Oh no, Derren, I left my wallet in the kitchen. Gimme your keys."

He paused then handed them over.

"Be quick though or I'll be forced to eat my own arm."

I let myself back into his house. Heart racing, I peered back outside to the car. Derren was fiddling with the radio. He couldn't see me so I crept up the stairs and peered into the bedroom. And, sure enough, there was a person-shaped mound under the scrunched up duvet.

"Get up, Tanya. I know you are there."

Nothing happened.

"Don't make me pull the covers back," I said, hoping I wasn't now talking to a bunched up duvet. Talking to a gecko is one

thing but this was quite another.
"Tanya!" I shouted with conviction. The duvet moved and out she came.

Chapter 14

Tanya was naked under the duvet and her hair was wet. She looked so scared I thought she might burst into tears.
"Rachael, I'm so sorry," she said, bursting into dramatic sobs. It was such a pitiful sight.
"Sorry for what, Tanya? I'm not with Derren anymore so why are you hiding?"
"He thinks you might work things out."
"And you're OK with that are you? Playing second fiddle and doing whatever he asks of you until he can have what he really wants? You let him come and get you last night knowing he was hammered. If you want him to respect you, you need to stop coming running whenever he clicks his fingers. Jesus."
"So, you don't want him back then?"
"No Tanya, surprisingly, I don't want him back."
"But, people are saying you're guy abroad was just a holiday romance."
I sighed. "Well, if he is, or if he isn't, it makes no difference to me and Derren. That ship sailed a long time ago."
"Oh."
"Now, excuse me. I have to go and see a man about a dog."
I left Tanya wondering how to take that comment and ran down the stairs, my hands shaking. Derren was standing in the kitchen with his hands in his hoodie pockets and a look of shame slapped across his face. I stood looking at him, waiting for a reaction.
"Why?" I asked.
"Because it's company, that's all!"
"No, Derren," I said exasperatedly. He was never going to get it.
"Why couldn't you have just been honest?"
"Because I knew you would react like this!"
"And how am I reacting?" I said calmly.
The formidable Derren was lost for words.

"Well, you were interrogating me. How did you want me to react?"

"Derren! You only felt interrogated because you had something to hide! You just made me doubt myself and feel like a fool, and not for the first time either. You'd rather do that to me than tell me the truth. You're just...incorrigible!"

"Why? Because I'm damaged goods? That's what you have always thought of me, isn't it?"

"If this about your dad again, Derren, I'm bored with that excuse now. In fact, you know what? If it affects you that much go and find him or get some help. Just get over it. Don't use it as a guilt trip weapon on me."

"Oh, you're bored with my problems. You know who your dad is, Rachael. You can *never* understand what it's like for me."

"What, you mean how abandoned you feel? How all the other kids had a dad around and you didn't? As sorry as I am about your dad leaving before you were born, your dad left before he knew you. My dad *knew* me and he still cut me out of his life. The dad I ran up to at the front door to give him a hug when he'd come home from work, the dad I loved and looked up to, he walked away from me without so much as a goodbye. I waited for months for him to call my mum to arrange when to see me. Months! Then every birthday I waited for a call from him. 'Today will be the day!' I thought. And every Christmas I was convinced, *convinced* he would knock on that door with a big smile on his face and his arms wide open. And every time I got my hopes up, my mum had to pick up the pieces and stroke my hair as I cried myself to sleep. My mum had to hear me ask 'why, mum? Why hasn't dad some back to see me? What's wrong with me mum?' Do you know what *that's* like? *Do you?* I'd do anything to trade places with you, to not have to take it so personally. I'd do anything to go back in time and tell that little girl to stop staring out the window, looking for his car; to tell her to stop living in empty hope because her daddy is never coming back. But I'll tell you one thing for sure; I will never, *ever* use that as a reason to treat other people the way you do." Tears welled up in my eyes as

I spoke the words that I held closest to my heart. Words that until Nishantha showed me how, were inaccessible to me. And what was Derren's response?

"Well at least you knew where you came from..."

His words hung in the room as I looked at him blankly. I think he realised then, at that moment, that he had lost me.

"I can't help you anymore. I can't watch you play victim, not when there are true victims out there with more balls than you. I'm sorry about your dad, I really am, but you need to get help if it's ruining your life. Good luck with that."

I stormed off towards the door just as Tanya appeared wearing one of Derren's shirt.

"Rachael, you are right. I'm sorry. Rachael!" he shouted from the door. It was amazing how I was always miraculously right when I was walking out the door.

My mobile was already ringing by the time I reached my flat. The number came up as 'Derren Home'. Good. That meant he was still there and not on his way over. I ignored it and decided to tackle the mountain of mail accumulating on the kitchen table. Amongst the loan and great mortgage offers that were all destined for the shredder, there was a large envelope with my mum's handwriting on the front. I wondered what I could have left behind on my last visit. Upon opening it I realised I hadn't left anything there at all. My mum was obviously suffering from nostalgia as she had sent a picture of me standing outside Santa's grotto with a big smile on my face and a brief note about the how she was looking forward to seeing me at Christmas.

Oh great, the pending onslaught of the festive season is nearly upon us. I thought in my negative state of mind. There was another envelope inside, too. It had a foreign postmark. I gasped and opened it haphazardly. My hands shook as I struggled with the adhesive. It had been stuck together so well I had to pull a knife from the drawer to get it open. I pulled the letter out and threw the envelope to the floor. Before reading the letter I looked to the bottom of the page to make sure it was from him. The letter went over the page. Turning it over, there it was. Four magic words at the end of the letter – 'All my love, Nishantha'. Before even reading the rest I burst into girlish screams and bounced all the way into the living room. I think that took care of "snapping out of it".

"Rachael, what the hell?" Jenny said, coming into the living room wearing her oversized Pooh Corner T-shirt that she used to sleep in if she was ill. She saw the letter and her eyes, now make-up free, widened.

"No fucking way, is that from him? What does it say? Rachael?"

"I don't know! I don't know! I'm too excited to read it!" I sung, still shaking as all the blood rushed to my cheeks.

"Rachael, do you want me to read it?"

"You might have to, my eyes won't stay still!" My eyes darted over the page with a distinct lack of discipline.

"Give it here you big dope."

Jenny snatched the letter in her skinny nail-less hands, screeched a chair out from the kitchen table, sat down, straightened her posture, and cleared her throat.

"Come on, Jenny, you're not addressing the queen, it's just me. What does it say?"

"OK, here we go."

"Dear Rachael…"

"Does it say 'dear'?"

"Yes."

"Dear Rachael..."

"How did he spell Rachael? Did he spell it right? Lots of people get that wrong."

Jenny brought the letter down to her lap and looked at me. "Are you going to let me read this or what?"

"Sorry, go on, go on."

"Right. Dear Rachael, I hope you are settling into life back home better than you had hoped. I know you were looking forward to seeing your friends and family the most so I hope that went well for you. I am sure they missed you and had lots of hugs to give you.

I was sad and happy when you left. Sad that you had gone, and happy that we spent that last night together."
Jenny broke off from the letter and looked up at me again.
"You said you didn't sleep with him?"
"I didn't, not like that anyway. He spent the night with me at Ravi's. What else does he say?" I pulled out a seat opposite her and sat down to calm myself.
"I wanted so much to email you after you left but I managed to wash your email address in my jeans. It is now four pieces of unreadable paper but least it is clean. I am so glad you gave me this address, too. I hope you do not mind, I have had help writing this letter from a backpacker called Ed. There are lots of backpackers here now because it is tourist season. Ed is from England and is on his way to Pinnawela elephant orphanage where he is going to be a volunteer. He is from a place called Manchester but lives near Cornwall at the moment. He has a very different accent to any I have heard before. I think you would like him. He told me to tell you he is a really cool guy.
I know the mail is slow and it may take time before you receive this letter, I just hope you have not forgotten about me by the time it reaches you. I have not forgotten about you.
Now monsoon season is over, we are all swimming in the sea again, I wish you were here so we could finally swim together and I could teach you to dive in…" Jenny broke off again.
"Rach, I can't pronounce this. I think it says Hikk-a-du-wa."
"That's fine. I don't know either."
"Blah, blah, blah… Where am I? Ah, here we go, Hikka-Doodah, where my friend teaches many people this time of year. My mother and father are talking to me but have not forgiven me. Also Johan, baby Johan, as you call him, is quiet if we are all in the same room together. I think he feels torn. Daniel is growing very fast into a handsome boy and Indica and Soma are happy. Indica misses you being around, I can tell. I cannot put into words how much I miss you being here. All I can do is hope this letter reaches you safely. I look forward to hearing from you.
All my love Nishantha. Kiss, kiss, kiss.

P.S. Ed wants me to tell you he thinks what we did was awesome and he wants you to come out here so he can meet you."

Jenny gave me the letter back.

"Jenny, he has written an email address here. Can I?"

"Yes, go on, it's on standby."

"Thank you, Jenny, I love you. Oh, I'm sorry, I'm not being very sympathetic to you, considering..."

"There is no point in us both being miserable. Besides, I want to know if this Ed guy is cute! Ah, is this you?" Jenny asked picking up the photo of me.

"That's me!"

"Did you sit on Santa's lap? I would never let my kid girl sit on Santa's lap. I mean what kind of example is that setting? Sit on a man's lap to ask for presents. That's just asking for your daughter to turn out into a play bunny, or whatever they're called."

"Are you serious?" I asked, gobsmacked.

"Gotcha!" Jenny said, smiling. She knew I had no idea when she was being serious about her extreme beliefs. It was always safer to presume everything she said was serious rather than make the mistake of mocking something that was important to her.

I logged on to Jenny's PC and thought about the laptop and Blackberry I'd turned down from Leon at work. After always being adverse to new technologies that let people keep in constant contact with you, I was starting to see the merit in it now. I stared at the screen that was as blank as my mind. His letter was written weeks ago. What if he had moved on already? I had to be careful not to sound too eager just in case, so I took my time constructing a reply. I then read it through twice and made Jenny read it to make sure it came across how I intended it to. She told me to sign off with just an 'R' to make it sound more personal. She then persuaded me to change 'Dear Nishantha' to 'Dear N'. I reread it one more time to myself before hitting the send button that would sent me straight back in the waiting game. I made a pact with myself to only check my emails once a day. This rule was designed to stop me becoming impatient waiting for a reply. It was while I was breaking my rule on day three that I received a

response. I was at work at the time so I had to sit on my emotions as I read how Nishantha wanted me to come back for a holiday as we'd previously discussed. I had rainy day money saved so the only potential hindrance was work. We were busy and it was not a good career move to take time off in the run-up to Christmas. Annoyingly, the run-up to Christmas these days seemed to start at the beginning of October these days. I looked up at Victor's office door and decided I may as well find out if he'd allow me the time off. Victor's door was open and he was on the phone. He waved me in anyway so I sat in his office planning what I was going to say.
"OK, I'll speak to you later Leon. OK. Thank you. Goodbye," he said, before placing the receiver back down in his usual soft manner. "Ah, Rachael, what can we do for you today? Oh, before I forget, your reports have returned from the editor."
"Oh good. I look forward to getting back something that loosely resembles my work."
Victor ignored me and carried on talking.
"You should know that Dr De Souza is looking to poach one of my team to help with her volunteer recruitment drive. She'll be going all over the country looking for doctors to volunteer in Sri Lanka. I've put you forward to head the drive. The person who goes will end up visiting some of the sites in the field."
"Really?" I said, eyebrows raised. "Does Leon know you have put me forward?"
"I was just talking to him then. He has the final say and will be speaking to you and one other over the next few weeks."
"J.J," I sighed. He was the obstacle in my way over the whole going to Colombo fiasco.
"I neither confirm nor deny. All I can say is that this is a huge opportunity. You will be involved in all aspects of this project, from start to finish."
My eyes lit up at the prospect of spending more time in the field.
"So, how does it work? We want to get private doctors and nurses to give up their time to work abroad for free?"
"They get a small wage."

"So how can you call it volunteer?"

"Because it is enough to eke out a meagre living while they are abroad. Think of it as expenses, if you will. You must keep this to yourself for now, Rachael."

"I will, of course I will. Thank you, Victor. For putting me forward I mean. It means a lot."

"You should be thanking yourself. You work hard and you work well."

"Speaking of working hard, actually, speaking of the opposite of working hard, what are my chances of having some time off?"

"When?"

"As soon as possible."

"You surprise me. After what I have just told you?"

"I have a matter of a personal nature to attend to."

"You know the run-up to Christmas is about to start. You know there is no leave through that period. How long were you thinking?"

"Three weeks, two of which will have to be unpaid, I know."

"Rachael, Leon will not let you go for three weeks at a time, not after you have been out of the office for so long."

"Will you please ask him? You never know."

"I can tell you now it will not be this side of Christmas."

"Then January will do."

"And you do realise that if you are absent during the tour preparations Leon will have to use somebody else?"

"I know."

"It must be something pretty important, Rachael – or someone."

"It is."

"Which?"

"Do I need to specify?"

"No. As aghast as I am, I will do as you have asked. Just tell me, what is his name, this man you met in Sri Lanka?"

"How did you...? It's Nishantha. His name is Nishantha."

"He led you in some of the decisions you made out there, didn't he?"

"Influenced, perhaps, but not led."

"Like wanting to stay?"
"Like wanting to stay."
"Were you there that night, Rachael? When the attacks took place in Kandy?"
I didn't answer, but that was answer enough.
"My goodness. We had a deal."
"I know. And I wanted to tell you, I did."
"But you chose not too because you knew we'd have you sent home?"
"Yes."
"And you wanted to stay for this man?"
"No, not then, not really. I needed to get over what happened to me that night and the only way to do that was to stay there. I wanted to go back to Kandy and, I wanted to see the only person who went through it all with me. Nishantha."
"Sinhalese or Tamil?"
"Sinhalese."
"Who have you told about this in the office?"
"Nobody here knows."
"Good. You need to keep it that way."
"Why?"
"Oh come on, Rachael. You go away on your first trip alone and come back involved with a man. Do you realise how unprofessional that is? Can you imagine what people would think if Jonathon had come back with a Thai or Cambodian girl in tow?"
"That's different?"
"Why?"
"He's a man. People would assume he used her, couldn't keep it in his trousers."
"That's a bit sexist isn't it?"
"But it's true."
"And what if people had said 'but it's true' about all the double standards flying around when you wanted to go to Sri Lanka instead of J.J?"
"OK, Victor. I take your point." We both took a moment to

deflate from the heat of our discussion before Victor added, "Everybody will think he is after a visa from you."
"Yes I know. My parents are convinced that's what all this is about."
"Are you are sure he isn't?"
"Without a doubt."
"Just be careful, Rachael. This is not going to be an easy road to take."
"I don't need easy. I need Nishantha."
"So I shouldn't bother arranging another dinner date with Matthew then?"
"Very funny. Don't even joke!"

Victor and I made up with the aid of a few bad jokes and I left the office unburdened from my secrets. I also realised the catch-22 of my situation. If I worked like Trojan now, without holiday leave, I might end up being able to work again in Sri Lanka. But that was a big maybe and it would be at least two years before that tree bore fruit and I could hardly put Nishantha on ice for that long. Yet if I invested time now in my budding long-term relationship I could end up being an office bod' for the rest of my days. I wanted to put 50 per cent of my all into both but that wasn't going to be enough to achieve both my dreams. So which one was I meant to give up?

Chapter 15

Derren, Derren, Derren, Laura, Derren, Derren, Jacky, Derren, Derren.
I was flitting through recent text messages I had yet to reply to. Laura wanted to know if I fancied a shopping trip as she couldn't remember the last time we'd had one. That's because I value our friendship. Shopping for clothes together has never brought out the best in us. It takes our differences, magnifies them tenfold and makes us antsy with each other unnecessarily. Jacky had texted to see what I was up to and to say it had been a long time since we spoke. I was glad to hear from her and we ended up having a long catch up on the phone. I told her all about Sri Lanka and Nishantha, and she told me all about how quickly her girls were growing up.
Derren had inundated my inbox with pitiful texts begging me to go and see him, just for a drink. I couldn't do that, not this time. I fell for the 'just a drink' request last time when he wanted me back after dumping me for Tanya and it eventually led to us trying again. I had to be steadfast this time around.
I finally sent him a message telling him no. He didn't reply.
By Friday that week Leon had signed off my request for two weeks in January. As soon as Christmas was all done and dusted I would be on a plane and on my way back to Sri Lanka. I knew Leon would give me two weeks if I asked for three, just as I knew he would have only granted one had I asked for two.
Friday also brought with it both a surprise from Nishantha – he called me just for a chat – and the night of the N-Trails gig. When Jenny heard they were playing she made a miraculous recovery from her broken heart and asked if she could come with me. She had seen Nick's photo on the band's website and thought he would make perfect rebound material. I think it was the dreads that sold it. She also spotted Alex and Aiden, two brothers who

wrote songs for N-Trails. I told her I thought they both had girlfriends and that I thought they were pretentious and, if I did, she definitely would. After putting her off Alex and Aiden, I didn't have the heart to tell her that Nick wasn't the best rebound choice either. The old Ben would have been a good choice but Jenny was too late there. He'd changed considerably since meeting Alana. I mentioned Neal but Jenny turned her nose up. He just wasn't her type. Michael was too young and Derren was my ex so it wasn't looking good. Not one to be easily deterred, Jenny came with me anyway, setting her sights firmly on Nick.

While Derren sung, Ben drummed and Nick strummed, the rest of us sat around the table closest to the stage in The Tavern. Pav always made sure that table was left for us when N-Trails played. The atmosphere around the table was strained. Besides the fact that I found it odd integrating Jenny with my friends, everybody knew I'd found Tanya in Derren's bed so I felt uneasy. Luckily, Ben's brother Michael was there. He made such a big effort with Jenny that he made her feel right at home. Tanya and Alana said little to me, despite Neal's attempts to get the conversation going. It took Derren, Ben and Nick playing *All the Small Things* to alter the atmosphere. The pub jumped up and down, singing along with the band, and melting the ice at our table. N-Trails knew how to get a crowd going, it had to be said. They never failed to give me goose bumps with their magnetic energy. I snuck a peek at Tanya while all the attention was on the band. She was looking on at Derren in awe. As I watched her, it dawned on me. Tanya couldn't help who she fell for any more than the rest of us could. I almost felt the weight of responsibility for Derren's happiness shift off of my shoulders and onto hers that night. She was infatuated with him.

The band performed some of their own tracks, written by Alex and Aiden, and they threw in a few covers from Foo Fighters and Metallica's older tracks. When our band member friends came to sit down with us for a break, Jenny and I made our way to the toilet. This was partly to avoid Derren and partly so I could see if

Jenny was OK.

"So how are you doing, Jenny? Are you enjoying it?"

"Oh my giddy aunt, Rachael. I was right! Nick is hot! Love the dreads. You *have* to set us up!"

"Well, they are all coming back to ours for more drinks if you're OK with that?"

"Hell-yeah! Do you think he will like me?"

"Well, there is only one way to find out. Just don't get too upset if he doesn't, there are plenty of men out there."

"Well that's a no then," Jenny said as she reapplied her organic face powder and ran a comb through her long dark hair.

"No, it's not a no, Jen. He's just not a fling... type... guy, that's all."

"That's OK. I just need someone to take my mind of Hardy. A bit of flirting is all I need."

"Listen, I wasn't going to tell you tonight until I heard back from Nishantha, but I can't help myself!"

"No way, you're going back out there aren't you?"

"Yes!" I said excitedly.

"Oh my god! When?"

"I booked my flight this evening for the beginning of January! It's happening, Jenny. I'm going to see him!"

"That's so fantastic, I'm so happy for you!"

Laura walked in just as Jenny was giving me a congratulatory hug.

"Hey what's going on?" she asked. As I was still smiling profusely I decided to tell her, despite wanting to keep it on the low.

"Oh, I thought he was just an email buddy now."

"Not anymore! He called me today too!"

"That's great, Rachael. But are you sure you want to get involved with a… With someone so far away?"

"Laura! You were supportive the whole time you thought nothing could happen, and now something is happening, you're acting like this?"

"I'm just looking out for you, Rachael. I don't want to see you get hurt by him again."

"He didn't hurt me; he washed my email address."

Jenny was playing eye tennis with us from the sidelines. Not a good first impression. I hoped she didn't think Laura and I argued all the time, especially as there was animosity between both Tanya and me and Derren and me.

"OK, whatever Rach. Look I came in here to tell you that Derren is completely blanking Tanya. He has been since you found her at his place."

"So?"

"So, he is doing it because he blames her for losing you and she is really upset. I know what you think of her but imagine how she feels. She really likes him, Rach, and he treats her like crap."

"She was trying to get in his pants when he was still with me! Am I the only one who remembers that?"

"She didn't know you then. And Derren is more to blame for that than her. It takes two to tango you know."

I looked to Jenny, then back to Laura, and then sighed in capitulation.

"Alright, what do you want me to do?"

"Invite her to yours; clear the air, tell Derren to stop ignoring her. He'll listen to you."

"Fine. I'll talk to Derren and she can come to mine, ours."

"Thank you."

"You know, I wish you'd fight my corner sometimes the way you fight hers."

"Well maybe if I didn't hear all your news second-hand I might be able to."

Jenny looked uncomfortable. "I'm going to grab another drink," she said, making a quick exit. The toilets were heaving in the way they usually are at gig intervals.

"This isn't the time or the place for an argument Laura. I'm sorry I haven't been around in quite the same way I was. It's just been a tough time."

"You used to come to me during tough times. It feels like we are drifting apart."

"I know, I know, and I know it's my fault. Look, let's enjoy tonight and let's make a date for some Laura–Rachael time real soon, yeah?"

"Yeah. And thanks for agreeing to talk to Derren," she added before whipping around to walk out of the toilets.

Another set from the band and three pitchers of beer later, Jenny had managed to situate herself next to Nick. Just as she managed to strike up a conversation with him, some guy came along and shook Nick's hand. They got talking and didn't stop until it was time for them to play again.

"Sorry, Jenny. Maybe you'll get the chance to chat back at ours where it's quieter."

"Yeah. Hey, are you going to tell your friends you are going out to see Nishantha? They keep asking me how you've been at home and I don't know what to say."

"I was trying to wait until the Derren saga had calmed down but I can't! I'll tell them back at mine, it's too noisy here."

After their last set in The Tav, I made a concerted effort to clear the air with Derren. I had to if he was coming back to mine and Jen's.

"You all did really well tonight; you sounded amazing."

"Thanks. We haven't played for a while so I think we made the most of it."

"Ah... good. Does this mean we are talking again?"

"We were never not talking."

"Ah... good. Well, it would be nice if you came back to mine tonight, with everyone. Tanya is welcome too, in case she wasn't sure."

Derren nodded and smiled but gave nothing away. This was his standard response when he didn't know what to say. I left it at that. It was a start.

After Pav called time at the bar, in his usual charming way, it was decided the girls would all come back to the flat while the boys helped Pav tidy up. It was more of a mini lock-in for them but they had learnt to phrase it as 'helping to tidy up' so that the girls didn't feel left out. I smiled at a very unsure looking Tanya so that she knew she was welcome to come back as well. Tanya and Alana both smiled back at me and I was glad I'd taken Laura's advice on that one. It was a good call. I had my work cut out trying to convince Jenny to leave the boys alone and come back with us as she was steaming drunk and wanted to stay and "help". I think the flat was so full of memories of her and Hardy that drunken Jenny just wanted to stay out as long as possible. Back at mine, Laura put the music on and poured us all some Black Russian cocktails. Jenny and Alana followed her in a contrived attempt to give Tanya and me a chance to clear the air.

"Rachael, nice pictures," Tanya said to me in a clumsy bid to break the silence. She was looking at the two Winnie the Pooh pictures hanging up on the living room wall. They were simple pencil sketches on a beige background.

"They're Jenny's," I said.

"Oh," she said as the smile disappeared from her face. I hadn't meant to sound rude so I rectified it with an attempt at humour.

"Yeah, if Jenny had it her way, there'd be Pooh all over the flat."

She gave a nervous laugh, which was followed by another awkward silence.

"I am sorry for the other day you know. I didn't want to hide. Derren told me to stay quiet, so what could I do?" Tanya said, starting over. I preferred her more direct approach to the decor flattery.

"That can't have been very nice for you."

Tanya shrugged and lowered her gaze. She had the down-trodden look of a woman who had become a slave to her own emotions.

"So why do you let him treat you like that?" I asked softly in response. I was a fine one to talk!

Tanya shrugged again, hugged her bare arms, and then shrunk into her seat. Sitting there in her little denim skirt, pale knees knocked together, she looked so sad.

"Look, I know it's weird, you and me talking about Derren, but you really need to turn this around Tanya, if you want him to respect you."

"That's easy for you to say. He worships the ground you walk on."

I laughed. "Yeah, now maybe, now it's too late. He wants what he can't have and gets complacent with things he can. I'm telling you, if you make it too easy for him you'll end up unhappy, like I was."

"Maybe."

"Just give it some thought, ay?" I said, giving her arm a friendly squeeze.

"So does...this mean we're cool?" she asked, still looking unsure of herself.

Laura burst into the room right on cue with a very drunk Jenny and a slightly less drunk Alana in tow. I gave Tanya a wink as we accepted the rocket-fuelled cocktails from our lubricated friends. When the boys arrived, Derren took one look at all us girls getting along and that was it, he was on edge. He'd taken the truce between Tanya and me as some sort of alliance against him. The harder I tried to banter with Derren to show I wasn't taking sides, the more patronised he felt. He decided to spend his time talking to Jenny who was trying to get away from him so she could talk to Nick. In her state I thought she would have a better chance by talking to Nick another time so I left her to it and sat on the sofa with Neal and Michael. They both asked me in conversation if I had heard any more from my guy in Sri Lanka. My face lit up and gave me away so I told them. Not my best move considering Derren wasn't yet privy and was full to the brim with vodka.

"Rachael, I would talk to Derren before he finds out from anybody else," Michael said, wrinkling his forehead with genuine concern. Michael looked like a shorter, skinnier, more mainstream version of his brother, Ben. And he was far more sensible – choosing university over the band, a blended step instead of a Mohawk, and he averaged one girl a year instead of one girl a week like his Lothario sibling. "He still thinks that you two might get back together." He added.

"What? No way! What makes him think that?"

"Because you two have always been on and off. He thinks if he is

OK with you going abroad it could work between you. He thinks this guy is just a fantasy and soon you'll realise that."
Neal was cringing, as though he didn't agree with Michael divulging their friend's secrets.
"Oh," I said.
I looked around the room as if I was an invisible observer and caught Nick's eye just as Jenny plonked herself down on the arm of his chair, missed, and hit the floor. Nick helped her up and sat her down before I could move.
"Look, Rach, we're gonna shoot off now," Michael announced, distracting me from wondering if Nick needed rescuing from Jenny or not.
"OK. Are you taking Ben and Ali too?"
"Yep," he said to me, then to Ben who was snogging Alana across the room, "Yo douchebag! Let's bounce."
Ben prized himself away from his girlfriend's lips to retaliate. "Oh sorry, are you missing your milk and cookies before bed?"
Michael rolled his eyes. He was always the butt of Ben's jokes about being more pipe and slippers than party and champers. The trio took off home while I wondered where Tanya was staying. It surprised me to learn she had arranged to stay at Laura's. No wonder Laura was eager for me to invite Tanya back here; I should have known there'd be an agenda. While the remainder of my friends sat chatting in the living room, I headed to the kitchen to start tidying up. A slurry voice from behind me called out as I crushed beer cans in the can-crusher.
"Rach, mate, I don't think he is interested. I think he likes you." It was Jenny. Her thick black eyeliner had smudged and her eyes were glazed from the amount she'd had to drink. This was not her finest moment.
"I don't think so, Jenny."
"Then why does he keep talking about you?"
"How'd you mean?"
"He keeps talking about whether you are going to tell Derren about your up-and-coming trip to see Shinantha, I mean Shisantha. Oh, fuck it, you know who I mean. Anyway, he is

more interested in that than me."
"Jenny, he is worried about his friend, dumb ass! Look, I better go see what's going on."
"Huh, you like him too!"
"No Jenny, I like Nishantha remember, a lot."
"You can never get with Nick you know."
"I wouldn't. He's Derren's friend remember. That would just be... wrong."
"No, no, not because of that. Because his surname is Rivers! If you got married, you would be, like, Rachael Rivers!" Jenny said laughing. "You would sound like a posh slut from a Jackie Collins novel!" Jenny morphed into her posh-slut narrator voice, which, evidently, made her sound more sober than her regular voice.
"Rachael Rivers orders another champagne cocktail at the pool bar on her dead husband's yacht. She dons her gold, Gucci bikini and custom-made Prada heels. The Puerto Rican waiter slips Rivers the eye. They both head below deck where... Alfredo starts to kiss her neck. If only Rivers knew that her bisexual lover - who is secretly in love with the olive skinned waiter - is waiting in the cabin. She is hiding behind the door clasping her weapon of choice, a crystal vase. There's a struggle. Rachael Rivers snatches the vase and hits her lesbian lover over the head. So much blood, she has killed her...
"Oh, so I am a slutty, bisexual, gold-digging, widowed cougar, and a lesbian murderer to boot, am I? Sounds like fun, what happens next? Do I live? Do I get to keep the yacht?"
"The waiter was in love with the woman you just murdered and wants the world to know what you did, so you kill him, too. Rivers lives to see another day but sadly has to pour all her own cocktails now," she added all matter of fact.
"You're actually quite good at this, Jenny. Maybe you should be an erotic mystery writer!"
"Talking of mysteries, you haven't told me what Shinantha's surname is."
"*Nishantha's* surname is Sangrasagra."
"Rachael Sangra...sagra? You should marry him, take his

surname because Rachael Sangra-thingy won't have a yacht or a Puerto Rican waiter."

"Hey, they were the two best bits from your story!"

"Yeah but you, you will have something better. You'll have a loving husband, a really homely home and lots of little cute kids running around. You should go for it Rach, no matter what people say, no matter how hard it is. I mean it." Jenny's drunken point-making was quite funny to watch but she was being so lovely that I daren't laugh. "I really, really mean it," she added, slamming a drunken hand down on my shoulder.

"Well thanks, Jenny. That sounds like a very happy ending, but are you sure I can't keep the yacht?"

"Only if you go and talk to Nick for me? Find out if he likes me? Tell him, tell him I don't usually get this drunk," Jenny said as she staggered sideways then tried to hide it by pretending to dust a crumb off the kitchen worktop.

"Jen, why don't you leave Nick for another day?"

"No, no, no. Go, go, go! And be subtle," *Yeah, I think that ship has sailed,* I thought to myself as I went to find Nick.

Seeking out Nick's company had always been such a no-no in front of Derren that doing so felt wrong. Derren had trained me so well it was hard to break free from the constraints of the past.

"So, you play guitar in a band? Oh my god, that's, like, so totally cool," I said in a fake dumb blonde accent.

"Oh hey, Rach, how be things with you?" Nick asked.

"Yeah, things be good thanks. Any idea how my flatmate got so drunk? She doesn't normally get this bad so it must be down to one of you guys."

"Not me," he said, holding his hands up to protest his innocence.

"I know. She's just split from her long termer. I'm trying to keep an eye on her. Not doing a very good job, am I?"

"Err, not unless she usually slurs her words."

"Don't judge her on tonight. She is a top girl, she really is."

"Wasn't she with that William Harding guy?"

"Yeah. How'd you know Hardy?"

I looked up to see Derren, Laura and Tanya had started a game of

Gin Rummy with my 'I love Spain' cards from Laura. Now there was a card game I could play.
"I met his little brother recently."
"Oh cool, where was that?" Nick screwed his face up while deciding whether to confess to me or not.
"At uni."
"At uni?"
"Yeah. Let's just say you are not the only one who has something they don't want to tell Derren," I frowned at him, not knowing how he knew.
"I overheard you telling Neal and Michael."
"Oh. So go on then, spill. What's your secret?"
"I'm leaving the band to go get my degree in marine conservation, finally. I start in January. Part of the post will see me in Costa Rica, eventually."
"Sweet. Sounds expensive?"
"Yeah, well I bit the bullet and went to the bank of mum and dad."
"Good choice, I hear they have competitive interest rates."
We both laughed.
"You need to tell them, Nick. January is fast approaching."
"Ben knows. He wants me to wait for the right time before breaking it to Derren," Nick said as Derren got up to celebrate a winning hand. "I don't think there's ever a right time with him. How about you?"
"I'll tell him this weekend, if I can get there before everyone else who knows. Looks like we both need to tell him asa."
"As soon as? What's that, the lazy person's version of asap?" Nick asked.
"Yeah you mock me now, but mark my words; one day in years to come they'll drop that needless 'p'!"
"In the way perambulator became pram?"
"Exactly!"
We both laughed and looked up to see Laura and Tanya necking vodka shots. Their forfeit for losing Gin to Derren I presumed.
"OK, I'll do you a deal. If I see 'asa' in print within the next three

years I will buy you a…a hotdog," Nick offered.
"A hotdog? I change the face of our English language forever and I get a hotdog?"
"Well, I might still be a deprived student then. I'm thinking ahead! You can have ketchup too, if it's free."
"Gee thanks. I think we need a clause in our deal. If you happen to be some big shot marine conservation guru saving the last of the world's reefs, I want a Diet Coke, too."
"Conservation guru?"
"Well, it's better than marine conservation-monger! That's what I nearly said, but I heard it in my head first."
"Wow, that's got to be a first!"
"Hey!"
"I'm only joking. You do realise that if you are wrong about this, *you* owe *me* a hotdog right?"
"I won't be," I said confidently.
I looked over at the card players to find three had become two. Laura had disappeared leaving Derren with Tanya. They were talking. I suddenly felt paranoid about what Tanya knew of mine and Nick's secrets from Derren.
"Who did you tell about leaving the band?" I asked Nick shortly.
"Only Ben. Who knows you are going back to see that guy?"
"Neal, Michael, Jenny and Laura. Oh god, I didn't mean to tell so many people before him. What if someone's told Tanya? I wouldn't put it past her to tell Derren."
I walked away from Nick and over to Derren and Tanya.
"Hi guys, is everything alright?"
"I know, Rachael."
"Know what?" I asked, looking about as guilty as Tanya did.
"About you and your corner shop boyfriend. You gave me all that grief about telling the truth, then you go and keep that you're seeing him from me."
"I didn't keep it… Look, can we talk in the hall, in private? And Laura, I think you and Tanya should book a taxi," I said to her as she walked in on the scene. I guessed it was her who told Tanya and it was obviously Tanya who'd told Derren.

"Why, what's happened?" she asked.
"Just book one Laura, please,"
The last thing I needed was Laura getting involved.
"Why did you have to tell him Tanya? You must have known that would be best coming from me?"
"I'm sorry. I didn't know he would care so much," she said, running out the flat in tears. Laura ran after her, frowning at me. Why was I always the bad guy when it came to Tanya?
"Come on, Derren. Let's just sort this out in the hallway or the bedroom or something?"
Derren was about as drunk as Jenny so suggesting we talk at all was a bad idea as ideas go.
Derren said nothing as he as he walked out of the living room and into my bedroom.
"Derren, I should have told you first. You deserved to know first, being an ex and all."
"You can't be serious, Rachael. You're dumping me for a third-world rice-muncher thousands of miles away?"
"I didn't dump you for him? You and me ended way before him. Except, in your head we weren't over, were we?"
Derren ignored my question and instead asked one of his own.
"Come on, Rachael, you can't be serious? This... guy... is in another country. You don't even speak the same language!"
"It's ironic, that, isn't it? English *is* his second language, yet he understands me more than you ever did."
Derren looked hurt. He had the knack of provoking me into bluntly blurting out the raw truth, then making me feel guilty the second I had. He would attack me like a pit bull, and when I responded would have me feeling like I'd just kicked a puppy.
"I can't do this anymore. The way we are, this isn't normal. I didn't like this cycle of perpetual arguing when we were together and I sure as hell don't like it now. I want to be happy Derren, and I want you to be happy too, just, not together."
"Don't do that."
"Do what?"
"Talk like you're better than me."

"Derren, I hate to break it to you, but you go through phases of thinking everyone is better than you. I'm not talking like I'm better than you. This is all in your head."

Derren bounded over to me, making me jump and invading my personal space.

He had me against the wall and was looking me up and down like I was something he'd just scraped off his shoe.

"You do think you're better than me. You always have," he spat. Then, quietly and vindictively he said, "Maybe we should ask a jury."

How could he? How could he bring up what happened to me in court – the worst time of my life – and use it against me? He took a few steps back, seemingly happy with his remark. Nick swung the door open and waltzed in with a frightened looking Jenny behind him.

"That's enough, Derren," Nick ordered, but Derren stayed in my face and began shouting.

"You're a whore! A whore who tried to fuck a doctor, then set him up when he turned you down!"

"Derren, come on dude," Nick said, attempting to calm his enraged friend.

"Yeah. Come on Dezza," Neal added, appearing from nowhere with Laura by his side. Derren stared at me a moment longer with a crazed look in his eyes, then walked up to Nick, pushed him aggressively back into the wall and walked out of the flat.

"Are you alright, Rachael?" Nick and Jenny asked in unison while Neal and Laura followed Derren out of the flat.

"I guess."

"He will regret saying those things tomorrow."

"I know."

"Guys," Laura popped her head back in through the door. "Didn't that brown jacket belong to Nick?"

"Yeah, why?" Nick asked hurriedly, wondering why his jacket was being discussed past tense no doubt.

"Well Derren's just gone off with it. Neal's chasing him down the stairs right now."

"Shit, my keys and wallet are in there. His car keys are in there too."

"What?" I scowled.

"I drove Derren's car back here because I only had one pint at the pub."

"Quick, go!"

We all ran out of the flat to see Derren pulling off, screeching down the road. A very red faced and puffed out Neal came running up to us.

"Tanya just jumped in Derren's car with him."

The cab intended for Laura and Tanya pulled up and it was decided that Neal should go back with Laura while Nick could stay with us because Laura and I could only sleep one each on the couch at our flats. Jenny gave me a sly smile to indicate her delight about our last minute house guest. That's how I knew how annoyed she was with herself when only ten minutes later she found herself wrenching her guts up in the bathroom toilet. Every time I knocked on the door to see if she was alright she told me to go away so eventually I did. Nick made me a cup of regular tea (with caffeine inside it and a bleached outer bag) while I sat on the kitchen worktop reeling from Derren's comments to me and shaking my head at his stupidity at driving off. I held my hands out in front of me, palms down. They were shaking from our argument.

"Sugar?"

"Yes honey? Only joking. No, ta. Just plenty of milk, please."

"OK. Err, should we go and see if she's OK?" Nick asked after we heard a particularly violent retch from beyond the kitchen wall.

"It's not her I'm worried about. I cannot believe he drove."

"Here ya go."

"Ta." I took the tea and placed it down beside me to let it cool.

"I'm sure they will get home OK, with my jacket, keys, wallet..."

"I know. What a jerk. Come on, let's sit in the lounge, it's cold in here."

Nick and I drank our tea while watching late night/early morning

Countdown with the deaf interpreter until we fell asleep. I woke up probably only a few minutes after falling asleep and grabbed a blanket for our guest. Nick stirred as I covered him.

"Night Nick, I'm off to bed. Sleep well. Yell if you need anything."

"Yeah, you sleep well too. Oh, and Rachael?"

"Yeah?"

"Roll on January hey?"

"Roll on January."

Chapter 16

Kandy, Sri Lanka

It was hard to believe I was back in the same country I had been in last July. The quiet, personal air of Kandy had been replaced by a busy tourist-ridden one. The locals no longer stood about idling the time away just as I no longer stood out to them. I was one of many, faceless in a crowd of Westerners. Tourism was indisputably valuable for their economy yet it still saddened me to see the price the locals paid. I witnessed many visitors treating their hosts in a derogatory manner and I had to learn quickly to bite my tongue. It was as though money bought them the right to be disrespectful and I didn't like it.

The new and unimproved atmosphere mixed with the nerves I felt about meeting Nishantha after so many months had given me cold feet. If the feel of the city had changed, what if the feel of Nishantha had too? What if my attraction to him had been magnified in the terrifying situation we'd first met in? I'd read about that, how fear can create attraction. And what if he didn't feel the same towards me? I had flown halfway around the world for the sole purpose of meeting Nishantha and now I was full of doubts. Oddly, I had been excited during the flight over. The nerves only hit me when I had arrived in Kandy to find everything had changed.

Another question to enter my mind was, would we click in the way we had before? The answer was no, not straight away. There was a slight awkwardness between us when we first met. It took time for us to fall back into the rapport we had before. It took time for us to accept the slight changes in each other's appearances. Nishantha had looked uber-buff before and while he still had muscles, he looked a little skinnier with it. His hair had grown a little longer. Mine was a little shorter. Despite near daily emails and intimate phone calls, we'd still been demoted to the status of strangers. Looking back, my doubts had nothing to do with Nishantha and everything to do with the pressure I had put on myself. I thought my meeting with Nishantha had to be like it is in all the films. I thought, in order for it to be real, we had to fling our arms around each other in a dramatic embrace as all those feelings of love and lust overwhelmed us. This, of course, was nonsense. Our meeting may not have been fit for a Hollywood movie but it did highlight another reason why Nishantha was so wonderful. He could see I felt unsure and uncomfortable and his solution was to give me space and time. He took the pressure off and never once asked me why I was so distant. Nor did he make me feel bad about it. He simply put me up in the spare room of his rented Kandy pad and let me find my own way – in my own time. Nishantha was still the same person I'd met before so it wasn't long before I fell head over heels for him again.

By day three I was fighting the urge to kiss him and was left wondering when our first kiss would be. It became all I could think about no matter what we were doing. Shopping in the markets, making breakfast, it didn't matter, I was fantasising our first kiss. It even crept into my mind when he was trying to teach me to meditate. I'd asked him why his mother, his sister and he, were so calm and collected in their ways. He told me they all meditated because it helped them to be clear and calm. He said he would try to teach me, yet when I was meant to be clearing my mind I was imagining his kiss. It finally happened at the most perfect moment I could have wished for. Nishantha and I had gone out again with his friends to *The Ivory*. This time *The Ivory* was filled with tourists and travellers as well as locals. A whole mixed bag of us had formed a large circle on the dance floor as we danced to 80s cheese. Nishantha was on one side and I was on the other which gave me the perfect view of him. It was lovely to watch him singing and dancing, having a good time as I did the same across the dance floor. When the circle broke off we found each other and he put his arms around me while we danced. His touch literally made me giddy as if he had me under a spell. Paul

and Shikandra looked at us and smiled.
Paul asked, "Does this mean you two lovebirds are together?"
"Yes," we chorused. We looked across the dance floor to see Dayani and Vidu looking on at us with sour faces.
Nishantha turned to me. "Do you want to cause a stir?"
I smiled in response even though I had no idea what he had in mind.
Nishantha slipped his hand around the back of my neck and pulled me in for a kiss, the kiss I had so desperately wanted in almost that exact spot all those months before. I could barely believe it was happening. Now there was our belated Hollywood moment, right there. My head spun as the all-encompassing rapture of his kiss took me over. The mini crowd we had drawn clapped and cheered, all except the terrible two that is. After the spontaneity of that night in *The Ivory*, Nishantha and I were inseparable in our lovers' bubble. We had turned into one of those sickeningly happy couples, high on life and hormones. Walking around hand in hand made me burst with pride as people stared at us – the unusual mixed race couple. Whatever anybody thought about us, I could not have cared less. I'd hit the jackpot with Nishantha and I knew it. By the end of the first week I had found my way out of the spare room and into his. It happened the night Nishantha told me he was going to make me a special dinner. I sat waiting at the table he'd made himself, for the surprise meal. The table was a varnished cross section of a wide tree trunk. I do not know which type of tree it was but it made a beautifully crafted table. While I waited for dinner, wondering what it would be, Nishantha came out of the kitchen area with two plates of baked beans on toast. It was not your usual Sri Lankan dish but then neither was Nishantha. He had remembered I'd missed beans on toast the last time I was in Sri Lanka and that is exactly what he made me. He even served the beans on homemade, thick doorstep bread with lots of butter and black pepper. It was definitely one of those 'it's the thought that counts' moments because the beans themselves tasted awful. They were in a dark tomato sauce that, for some reason, was sickeningly sweet. We both left the beans

and ate the toast.

"Rachael, how can you like these baked beans, they are not good at all."

"Actually, they taste a lot different at home, not so sweet. It's just because these are a different brand."

Tears welled up in my eyes as, all of a sudden, I became overwhelmed by the sentiment of his thoughtful gesture. Being cared for so thoughtfully was a new concept to me. I'd been with Derren all my life. Anything nice that he did was usually born from guilt or to butter me up for something.

"What is it, Rachael?"

"Nobody's ever made me beans on toast before," I laughed through my tears as I heard myself speak. "Well, maybe they have, but not like this."

Nishantha looked into my eyes as I looked into his and I knew then we had finally reached that level of intimacy we'd found just before I left in July.

"I am glad you came back, Rachael. I have missed you," Nishantha said, looking at me with those large, deep eyes. I took in his full, perfectly formed lips, his chiselled, square jaw and his dark, curly hair. As I realised how attracted I was to him I began to feel bad for taking so long to tap into my feelings.

"Nishantha, I'm sorry I was so distant when I first came. I've wasted so much of the little time we have."

"No, you have not. You needed that time to find out what it is you wanted. It is OK."

"Were you worried? Did you think I didn't like you anymore?"

He took a moment to consider.

"I hoped you just needed some time but yes, I was worried."

"You didn't show it."

"I did not want to push you away."

"Well, I'm sorry."

"Do not be sorry, Rachael. It did not help that I washed your email address. You must have thought I had forgotten you."

"I did. It was hard, not knowing why you hadn't been in touch. Everyone told me to stop thinking about you, but I couldn't."

"Well, I am glad. Look, Rachael, do you want to go out for food? I have nothing in to make something new for you."
"No, I think I want to go bed."
"Now? It is so early?"
"I know."
"OK. I will go fix your mosquito net."
It was a temporary net that had to be put up each night, like Ravi's only clean and intact.
"Or we could leave it up?"
"I think you should sleep under the net, Rachael."
"So do I. But I was thinking, what if I slept under a different net?"
Nishantha frowned. It took him a moment to catch up with what I was saying.
"Oh."
That was not the reaction I was hoping for and I wanted to retract my words.
"If you're OK with that?" I added quickly.
"But then where would I sleep?" This time I knew he was joshing with me.
"Nishantha!"
"What? I am joking!" Then the momentarily jovial atmosphere turned into an adrenaline rush as he gave me a smouldering look over our uneaten baked beans.
That night, under Nishantha's mosquito net, we finally got to know each other just that little bit better, twice.

"Nishantha, what is it? What are we doing? Are we going somewhere? Tell me!" I asked, holding the bed sheet around my body with one hand and trying to stop him getting out of bed with the other. Nishantha had told me the night before that we were going on an overnight trip, then refused to give me any more information. His midnight revelation gave my mind something to chew on and I couldn't sleep wondering what we'd be doing the following morning.
"I will tell you when I am out of the shower, maybe," Nishantha said, kissing my lips and squeezing my hand before breaking free

from my hold.

Flopping back onto my pillow in defeat, I stared up at the ceiling while listening to the water run in the bathroom. I could hear it run off his body and hit the floor in uneven bursts as I lay in bed contemplating what it would be like to wake up here every day. I only had five full days left at Nishantha's bungalow and despite Nishantha telling me I hadn't wasted our time together, I felt like I had. His bungalow was a small, clean and simply furnished place with just enough character to make it cosy. It backed onto a communal field and park, which was one of the things Nishantha liked most about it. He loved having people knock for him to come out to play cricket if he was in. And during my stay, many did just that. Sometimes we went with them and sometimes we sent them away in favour of being alone together. Nishantha was only renting the place but one day, he told me, he hoped to buy it.

"Hey, Gertie," I said to Nishantha's resident gecko as it snaked into view on the ceiling. I'd failed to notice that the water had stopped running in the bathroom, or that Nishantha was standing in the doorway watching me. Although we'd already had the Gertie conversation, it was still embarrassing having him see me talking to one. His amused smile turned into a half laugh, alerting me to his presence. I sat up again, bed sheet still wrapped around me.

"Tell me now?" I said sweetly, letting the anticipation show on my face to help sway him.

"Nope."

"Oh, come on, you can't make me wait. That's not fair. I might need to prepare!"

"What could you need to prepare? Your day bag? That thing contains everything you would need for any situation. That is why you can-not find anything in it!"

He entered the room and sat on the bed, all glistening and wet from his shower. Droplets of water corkscrewed his helter-skelter curls and ran down onto his chest. Delicious.

He put a hand on my thigh, my skin tingled at his touch but my desire to know where we were going was the greater force at work.

"No, sod off! Go and get dressed," I said folding my arms and feigning a sulk. He smiled in the enjoyment of watching me squirm.

"That will not work on me, Rachael. You are going to have to wait," Nishantha said as he left the bedroom with a pair of jeans slung over his shoulder.

"Jeans? In this heat? Are they for tonight?"

"Rachael, stop trying to figure it out, just... relax."

"I'll give you relax," I muttered under my breath. Once we were both showered and dressed, we sat waiting on his homemade swing-chair outside the front of his bungalow where he still wouldn't tell me what was going on. He told me we were waiting for the van to be delivered that we would be using for our trip. I could barely believe my eyes when an old, rickety heap pulled up outside; it looked like it had just lost a round in *Scrapheap Challenge*. As my eyes bulged in shock–horror at the thought of contending with Kandy's roads in that thing, Nishantha smiled gracefully, pleased his ride was here.

"Here he is!" Nishantha said, jumping up off the swing. "Come and see what you think, Rachael."

I walked over, wondering how to be polite about the heap of crap he affectionately referred to as 'he'.

"It's, err..." I tried to find something positive to say as I slowly made my way around the vehicle, running my fingers along it lightly as I went.

"Well, it...it will get you from A to B right? Hopefully?"

I looked up at Nishantha. He was looking at me with a sidelong smile, like he was waiting for a penny to drop. What had I missed?

"What?" I said, wiping my now dirty fingers on my day bag. "What are you up to, Mr?"

Nishantha looked up at the van's front windscreen.

"Have you said hello to the driver?"

I peered through the windscreen and gasped. Nishantha wasn't referring to his van as a 'he', he was referring to his brother in-

law.
"Indica!" I opened his door for him and he jumped out.
"Sorry, Indica. I couldn't see you through all that dirt!"
"Rachael! Me...old...china!"
"Ha, ha! Wicked! Come here!" We squeezed each other tightly in true affection. "How are you? How is Soma, how is Daniel?"
"We are all very good, Rachael, all very good! It is so good to see you, you come back for your man then?"
"I did, I did. Wow, how long are you in Kandy for?"
"I am staying just today and tonight. Has Nishantha told you? We are having a party!"
I looked at Nishantha who filled me in on the details, finally.
"Tonight we have a party. Tomorrow Indica will go home with a friend while we take our new van on our trip. We were going today but I think this way is much better."
"Will you tell me where we are going now?"
"For this you will have to wait. For now, you two can catch up while I go to class."
"You have to work today?"
"Yes. Will you be OK? I will be back with a few friends this evening. I want every-body to meet you again, this time as my girlfriend."

I had come to associate Indica with sitting on the beach or by a swimming pool. The distinct lack of both threw me and I wasn't sure what we were going to do all day. We decided to make ourselves useful and spent the hottest hours of the day inside, getting the bungalow ready for our party. We chatted and goofed around while Indica showed me how to make some traditional snacks. During the cooler hours, we joined in a friendly game of cricket that had been going on in the field behind the bungalow all day. We had no reservations about joining in because men, women, teens and children were all taking part. Apart from the fact I made for a horrible batsman, it was a fun afternoon. I laughed so much I cried and I ran so much I ached. This simple field gave so much. I loved the sense of community I felt every time I joined in with whoever happened to be using it at the time and I could see why Nishantha picked here to live.

After our cricket match we flaked on the swing chair eating rice and curry that a neighbour had made for the cricketers. I started to miss Nishantha and wondered when he'd be home. My thoughts turned to his parents. They must have missed him. He was their eldest boy.

"How are Johan and Komari?" I asked Indica.

"They are OK."

"Do they know I'm here?"

"No. They have only just started to speak to Nishantha again. Has he not told you this?"

"He told me things were getting better. That's all he said."

"Johan, his brother Johan, was upset by the trouble between them. They are all talking for his sake but Nishantha is far from forgiven."

Later that night Indica and I found our second wind as the party swung into full flow. The arrack disappeared nearly as quickly as the space there was to move. Half the cricket team from earlier had come and the party spilled out into the garden and field. The plain hoppers and fish cutlets Indica and I had prepared earlier were soon overshadowed by dhal curries, tempered potatoes, pineapple and tomato salads and an array of mixed rice dishes I wouldn't know the names of.

Shikandra, Ranil and J.T. were there as well as Paul who, surprisingly, arrived with the pretty receptionist from the institute. Nishantha informed me that Paul and Sharma had been dating in secret. I don't know how much of a secret it could have been – they moved together like swans dancing in a mating ritual, mirroring each other's movements in sync. Cheeky Paul had become chivalrous Paul now that Sharma was by his side and that brought a smile to my face. I tried to play host with Nishantha but the whole night went by so easily there was little for me to do.

Ranil, who had barely ever spoken three words to me in the past, would not stop talking. He told me he thought I was like

Nishantha's Germanic ex, Gisela, at first. The one who broke his heart, but now he could see I was different. I nodded along while secretly wishing he'd stop saying her name. She sounded like a perfect looking model, at least, that was how I was starting to perceive her. After we exhausted his hate for Gisela and his love for poker, Ranil made a comment I didn't quite understand.

"Rachael, it is a shame about Sunil isn't it?"

"Sunil?"

"Yes, the man who was missing. You went to see his family, isn't it?"

"Oh, Irshaad's friend. Yes, I met his wife and children. He disappeared after his son was killed."

"It is so sad that his child found his body, of all people. He drank weed killer. Nishantha has told you this, yes?"

"Err, yes, he has. It is sad," I lied. Nishantha hadn't told me about Sunil.

Nishantha and I revelled in our new found coupledom right up until the last of our guests left. We waved them off from the front door like a couple of smug marrieds.

"Want a smoke?" Nishantha asked as the last of his friends left. Indica had passed out drunk in the spare room so we found ourselves alone again.

"The last time I smoked hash I was on a train headed for Kandy!"

"Well, if you smoke now, tomorrow you can say that the last time you smoke hash was on Nishantha's swing chair, in Kandy."

"When did you last smoke?"

"The last time I smoked was, about ten minutes ago. But, before that, it was a long time ago."

"Oh well I better have some then, just to keep us on the same wavelength."

Nishantha sat on the grass rolling a joint while I sat on the swing hugging my knees.

"So, Rachael. How did you enjoy your day with Indica?"

"It was great! I hadn't realised how much I'd missed him. I was too busy missing you, I guess."

"And to-night?"

"I had a great time. Paul and Sharma make a lovely couple, they are very sweet. And Ranil spoke to me."
"He did? That is surprising to me. He does not speak to new people easily. He is shy and... distrustful."
"He told me how sorry he was to hear about Sunil."
Nishantha looked up at me.
"Oh, Rachael, I was going to tell you. I did not know when but I was going to tell you."
"You don't have to worry about me you know. I can handle the truth. I prefer the truth."
"I know this. You are a strong woman. This is not why I kept it from you. Every time I thought about it, it was not the right time. There were too many moments I did not want to ruin."
"It's OK. Just please be honest with me. I hate lies. I don't want to be around them anymore."
"I can-not promise much, Rachael, but I can promise you that. Now, are you going to light this, or am I?" he said, holding his creation up to me.
"Give it here," I said, snatching the joint.

Half a joint later...

"What was that song called?" Nishantha asked. We were now sitting side by side on the swing chair with my head resting on his chest. The triumphant roll-up rested on the arm of the chair. Neither of us could finish it. Despite the fumes I sometimes inhaled in the flat, I wasn't a smoker, of any substance.
"OK, I'm going to need you to be more specific here," I frowned.
"The song we first danced to together?"
Eric Clapton, Tears In Heaven.
"Err, let me think. Why?"
"I want to hear it. I keep humming it, in my head, yet, do not know what it is called."
"I think it was *Tears In Heaven* by Eric Clapton," I said, as if I'd had to dig a little. Well, I couldn't very well let on just how much I'd thought about that song since he gave it such importance.

"Eric Clapton. I must remember that. You know, I like that name, Eric. Is it a much used name in your country?"
"Well, there's a famous actor called Eric Bana. And a there's a cartoon character called Eric. He used to turn into Banana man when he ate a banana," Nishantha and I sniffed a lazy laugh. "and then there's the little dude with the blue hat in the kids game, *Guess Who?*"
Picturing Eric with the blue hat in *Guess Who?* made me want to laugh out loud but instead I bit my lips together and nestled a little further into Nishantha's chest.
"You know, this is perfect. My friends have all gone home and I get to shut the door on the world with you the other side of it."
I laughed at Nishantha again.
"I hope you've gotten that the wrong way round, otherwise I'll be sleeping on this swing!"
"With you on the other side from the rest of the world, I mean to say. But now I have a picture in my head of you banging on my door." We chuckled uncontrollably together as the medicine kicked in.
"OK, I have to stop laughing. I am so stoned. How are you doing?" Nishantha asked, kissing the top of my head.
"I'm fine," I sighed contently.
"Fine, you always say fine. Fine," Nishantha said as though trying on the word to see how it fit.
"Do I say it that much?"
"Yes. It answers everything yet it tells me nothing. It used to drive me crazy when we first met."
"Well, there you go. An answer for all questions, for a woman should always be shrouded in mystery. How do you say it in Sinhala anyway?"
"Fine? Let me think. Fine. It is 'Varadak neh'."
I fell about laughing. I wanted to say the real reason he didn't use 'fine' was because it took so long to say, not because it was a nondescript word. I could not get my words out for laughing, which made me laugh all the more. By the time I got my sentence out Nishantha and I were laughing so hard that our stomachs

ached and we'd forgotten what we were talking about in the first place. He tried to teach me more of his language and I tried to explain cockney rhyming slang but neither of us could take it seriously so we gave up.

"My flatmate, Jenny, she smokes dope all the time at home. She sometimes gets me to play this question game with her when she's stoned where we ask random and obscure questions of each other. She always ends up telling me it would be more fun had I been stoned too."

"What kind of questions?"

"I don't know, like... What would you do for a million pounds?"

"OK. I have a question."

"What, you want to play?"

"Sure, why not? We are both stoned after all."

"OK. What's your question?"

"That night at the hotel in Kandy, I learn you have many questions about, well, many things. If you could find out the answer to just one of them, what would it be?"

"Ooh, good question. Err, I...I would like to find out the outcome of the world, like, how it will change and eventually how it will end. But I mean I want to know everything: how species will evolve, how long humans will last, what new species will inhabit the earth. I want to know what a map would look like once all the countries have moved even further away from each other, oh, and what the climate will be like."

"Wow. You have a busy mind. I thought you would say something about the universe."

"Is that what you would find out?"

"Yes, I would find out if the universe is infinite, and what other planets are out there that we do not know about. There might even be a planet somewhere, much like earth that has not been built upon and, how do you say..."

"Industrialised? Modernised?"

"Yes, to both. It is interesting. You ask how long humans will be around as if you know we will not be here until the end."

"I think we stand a good chance of killing ourselves off first. In the big scheme of things we haven't been here that long and we are not doing much to sustain our environment. We have stopped trying to survive. I think that is the most destructive force to a species, when it stops trying to survive."

"I have never thought about it that way. You know, I like it when we are alone and we talk this way," Nishantha said, squeezing me closer to him.

"Me too," I said, pulling away so I could look at him. We stared at each other knowingly, the way we did just before our very first kiss. In many ways, this look we shared was the most intimate I had ever been with anybody in my life.

"Right, err, my turn. If you had to come back as an inanimate object what would you be?"

"A what?" he asked, confused by my use of English. I was struggling to tailor my vocabulary.

"An object, a thing that is not living. Like a book or a chair."

"Oh, I will have to think on that. What would you be?"

"I would be a stadium, or a theatre."

"Why?"

"So I could see gigs, comedies and plays every night of the week."

"I would be…a mountain. Mount Everest."

"Why?"

"So I could see what happens to the earth and give you all the answers you wish to have."

"Damn that's a good answer! Why didn't I think of that?"

"I was going to say I would be a paintbrush so I could paint all day, but Mount Everest seemed like the better answer."

"You *should* paint all day. Your paintings are wonderful. When I first saw them I was lost for words, and that's not like me at all."

"Thank you. That is kind of you to say."

"Well it's true. I wish I could paint like that."

"If you lived here, you could come to my classes."

"And I would. OK, go on, it's your turn."

"OK, a question. Let me think. Is there anything you do not like that you wish you did like?"

"Oh, another good one. Jenny would love you! I would have to say... theme park rides."
"Like rollercoaster rides?"
"Yeah, that sort of thing. They look like so much fun but I just can't stomach them. I hate that I'm missing out on a thrill. I actually really do wish I liked them."
"What about you? Is there anything you wished you liked?"
"Baked beans."
"Baked beans?"
"Yes. I keep noticing them now in the movies. People always look like they are really enjoying them. But I did not like them, not at all."
"I can't believe that is the first time you had them! I'll make them for you, one day. If you come to England I will open a tin of Heinz baked beans just for you."
"We have not talked about me coming to see you before."
"No, we haven't. Would you like to?"
"One day, yes, I would love to see how your life is there and see what you do every day."
"I would love you to come over, too. My only worry is that you will find life there materialistic and bland compared to life here. And we spend so much time indoors."
"I understand that it is different. There are good things and bad things about every place. It is easy for you to see all the good points about Sri Lanka and the bad in England because you are a visitor here."
"I guess. I think you would like it where my parents live. People make more time for each other there than where I live."
"People say to me, 'Nishantha, what are you doing falling for this Western girl?' They say, 'You will never leave your home and she will never leave hers'."
"It's like you said. We don't need all the answers right now," I said, sounding more bolshie than intended. Then, with more uncertainty than intended, I asked, "Do we?"

Chapter 17

The trip Nishantha took me on was both surreal and necessary: surreal because it confused my senses no end; necessary because it helped bridge the gap between Nishantha's world and mine.

We headed off in the old, rusty van to an unknown destination at the crack of dawn. I don't know about Nishantha, but the mention of neither of us moving countries last night was at the back of my mind where all good, unresolved issues tended to dwell. Luckily, the state of the van was as the forefront of my mind. Assuming Nishantha was not a member of the AA equivalent, I hoped that wherever we were going, it wasn't far. We followed road signs toward Colombo for a while so I assumed we were going there, or perhaps to Hikkaduwa where he knew a scuba diving instructor. I'd looked it up on my map and it was south of Colombo, so not a bad assumption since we were heading south-west toward the capital. I was surprised and confused when we stopped heading towards Colombo and started following road signs with names I'd never heard of. Only an hour into our journey we pulled up outside Pinnawela Elephant Orphanage.

"Have you ever ridden an elephant?"

"Is that what we're going to do?" I asked excitedly.

"This is the first part of our trip. This is where Ed is volunteering. I told him I'd bring you to come see him."

"Ed from the letter?"

"Yes, Ed from the letter. He say there is a very tiny, baby elephant here at the moment. It is a good time to come," Nishantha said as we slammed the van doors shut before going to look for Ed in the elephant feeding area. Some elephants there were being put to work hauling logs and others were being fed by tourists. The area was large and all outdoors with a few large open shelters. The grounds funnelled in to a road lined with gift and souvenir market stalls on each side. We walked through them and over to the lake: the elephant bathing area. This was where we found Ed. He was showing the tiny, baby elephant to an Irish family with two small, twin girls. The girls were in awe, marvelling at the calf as it played by its mother in the shallows.

"Why is mummy-phlant all chained up?" one of the girls asked. Ed explained that mummy animals can be dangerous because their instinct is to look after their little babies. When the family left, Ed greeted us warmly. He looked like a typical surf dude with his skinny frame and his messy blonde hair and he emanated a laid-back vibe that made even Bob Marley look uptight. As the day drew on I noticed he would occasionally and randomly verbalise hippy-esque affirmations and I thought Jenny would have loved him. He was a bronzed beanpole with a big heart, especially where animals were concerned. We'd caught him at an emotional time because his stint as a volunteer was coming to an end. Behind his smile I could see he was sad he would soon be leaving. His smile looked more like the wall of a dam that could crack at any moment. I empathised with him.

The elephants were mesmerising to watch. I could have spent a week observing them without getting bored. The younger elephants were so mischievous they reminded me of naughty little children. While we watched the herd play in the lake, three young bull elephants made a run for it to the other side – the forbidden side by the look of things. As they ran and their big heads bobbed up and down, one of the Sri Lankan mahouts with very dark skin and a tablecloth sarong stood on a large boulder holding a huge pole. He called out to the escapee bulls and they actually listened! They stopped, turned, and strolled back solemnly with their heads hung low. In the feeding area, an older elephant stood alone and in chains. It was an ancient looking creature with a pinkish tinge to its skin and it was rocking, swaying to and fro, in its solitary spot under the shade of a tree. She had no eyes. It was a very upsetting sight. Ed told me she was the only survivor from her herd. Poachers had killed the rest for their ivory. They had gauged out her eyes – blinding her – and left her on her own so she had been brought here to live out her days. A surge of anger momentarily enraged me.

"People like that deserve a slow and painful death," I muttered inaudibly under my breath. The old, blind cow played on my mind as we fed sugar cane to the adolescent elephants. It was only when we rode a large male, bareback, that I stopped seething over the cruel and senseless acts of the fuckwit poachers. A mahout took us around a designated course on our elephant. Nishantha sat behind me while I sat with my thighs around the elephant's thick neck. While up there I decided I much preferred admiring these magnificent beasts from the ground, especially when the mahout deviated from the tourist track and led us down some rather steep steps. I thought I was going to fly clean over the elephant's head each time his gigantic foot hit the ground on each descending step.

At lunchtime we all sat at the viewpoint cafe/gift shop just chatting and watching the lovely beasts sleep and play. Before we left, Ed let us use his temporary digs to shower off the eau de elephant aroma we'd acquired and we swapped phone numbers. I told him if he ever flew into Gatwick airport he was welcome to crash on my couch. It turned out that is exactly where he was flying into when he went home from Sri Lanka (via Amsterdam) so I gave him Jenny's email address too and made a mental note to tell her about him. I love it when a good plan comes together.

Back in our little van, we headed south on the B279 toward the next part of my surprise. While I took in the sights as they whizzed by out the window, I reflected on my day and decided I had been too hard on my little beat-em-up van and I started warming to him. Henry – for that is what I named him – was reliable, quirky and nobody else had one quite like him. I had no idea where he was taking us to next. All I knew was that we were gaining considerable altitude as we headed up a mountainous terrain. The longer we drove the more my ears popped and the cooler the air became. The lush, deep green valleys and gaping chasms that cascaded down into their very own abyss were like a continuation of the sights I had seen on the train to Kandy, only on a larger scale. As the night drew on I found myself getting chilly. Chilly was not something I had ever been in Sri Lanka before.

"I know you won't tell me where we are going, Nishantha, but can you tell me how long it will be before we get there?"

"Well, we have been driving for just over one hour, so, we have under one more hour to go. Why?" he said, glancing at me while trying to drive. "Are you cold?"

"A little," I said, trying to hug myself warm.

"Look in the bag under your seat."

I felt underneath the seat until my fingers found a thick plastic bag. The bag contained two ribbed, polo neck jumpers, a small one in burgundy and a larger one in cream.

"Jumpers? Where are we going? England?" I mused.

"Yes, actually. That is where we are going."

I frowned, trying to work out our cryptic conversation.

"Mata terinneh neh!" I said, surprising myself as well as Nishantha. "Oh! I do remember some of what you taught me last night. What did I just say?"

"That you do not understand."

"Yes! I thought so!"

"That is good, Rachael. I thought you did not learn anything from our language lesson. I know I did not, with your apples and your pears and your old china plates!"

"We will have you speaking in rhymes before you know it. Anyway, what do you mean, 'We're going to England?'" I asked as we both bumped up and down in the suspension-impaired Henry. The road, and I use the term loosely, was fast becoming an off-road experience.

"Nuwara Eliya."

"No, I don't remember that one."

"Nuwara Eliya is where we are going. It means 'Little England.'"

"Oh. Why is called Little England?"

'Why' was apparent the moment we arrived in Nuwara Eliya. The resemblance of this place to my homeland was uncanny and as a

result, all my senses told me I *was* in England. The tarmac roads were lined with curbs found in any road back home and led onto concrete slab pavements like most streets back home. The pavements, in turn, were lined with trimmed, rectangular privet bushes and behind those were rows of red-bricked terrace houses with the odd scattering of random oak trees where regular grey squirrels dwelled. They scuttled from tree to tree on the soft, dewy grass strewn with acorns and fallen oak leaves. I kept pointing at things and excitingly stating what they were, much like a child who has just learned to speak. *Acorns! Squirrels! Oak trees! Street signs!*
Nishantha must have thought I was bonkers.
It wasn't just my eyes deceiving me in Nuwara Eliya. The song of the sparrows baffled my ears and the cold damp smell confused my olfactory system. The air no longer smelt of the sea or of the Eastern city. It was no longer warm to breathe in as it assailed your nose. It now had a chill to it I could only assimilate with the UK. Perhaps the most deceptive factor in this parallel world was the sky. The sky was no longer infinite and blue, or home to a sun so bright you daren't look up. It was now whitish-grey with no definitive clouds. It was just one greyish whitewash of bleakness and the sun was no longer visible as a separate entity. Although the sun is better known for giving off heat, looking at it actually made you feel colder here. I almost felt claustrophobic under the solid lid of 'white'. While I was pointing at things in disbelief, Nishantha sat himself down on a white and black street-name post, how they used to be at home (and still are in some places.) He just watched me taking it all in as I shivered slightly in my new burgundy polo neck.
"No way, Burrows Road? That's so English!" I said, reading the sign across the road from us. In Sri Lanka I was used to road names such as Sri Dalada Veediya and Sangaraja Mawatha.
"This is so weird, Nishantha. Fuck. I'm sorry, I didn't mean to say fuck, it's just...fuck!"
Articulate, Rachael, articulate.
"Sorry, Nishantha, my senses are screaming at me, telling me I'm

in Surrey! This is *totally* weirding me out!" I tilted my head and gave the smug-looking Nishantha a sidelong glance. "Just like you knew it would!"

He smiled one of those smiles where your whole face takes part whether you meant it to or not.

"I like it when you lose yourself."

"Lose myself?"

"Yes. It is like you are lost in...wonderment. You are happy, with no other care in the world. I would make every day like that for you, if I could."

"Well, you're doing a good job so far!" I laughed in disbelief again. "I have to keep telling myself I'm not in England!"

Once I had recovered from the shock, Nishantha ushered me back into Henry and we bounced up Uda Pussellawa Road to the Grand Hotel. Inside the Elizabethan-style building I indulged in a hot, steamy bath only so that I could wash off all the mosquito spray I'd been coating myself with and smell good for once. I covered myself in my signature scent – Light Blue, like it was the first time I'd been allowed to wear perfume and was yet to learn that less is more. Nishantha made time to find the internet cafe in the hotel so I could give Jenny the heads up on Ed before we carried on with our mini holiday. Quite rightly, she would never agree to a stranger staying without a character reference first. I was going to tell her he may or may not email for a place to crash and that she would definitely really like him. I assured her he was not a psycho; he loved animals etc. To my surprise, there was already an email from Jenny sitting in my inbox asking about Ed. It seemed he had already emailed her. Fast work, Ed. Nice one. I told her to go for it then went with Nishantha to the hotel bar for dinner. Cricket was being aired on all the TV monitors around the bar so Nishantha gave me some lessons in cricket while we ate then we went up to our room because we were both tired after a long day. For the first time ever, Nishantha and I snuggled under a thick downy duvet, trying to keep warm as we slept.

The following day, after a very lazy morning in the hotel room,

Nishantha and I managed to explore a little further than the hotel bar; we walked all the way through it and out into the hotel grounds. The gardens there were immaculately cared for. Light and dark green squares of measured grass chequered the lawns like a giant chess board for as far as the eye could see. Bleached white pathways snaked throughout the landscapes like giant anacondas. Upon closer inspection I saw they were filled with crushed shell, the kind that crunches scrumptiously underfoot. Brightly coloured flowers filled half-moon shaped flower beds and hotel guests played croquet on the lawn while others dined alfresco on the cast iron patio furniture. As we strolled and chatted, a fleeting break in the clouds allowed the sun to shine, warming us as it broke through. It cast light and shadow over the picturesque scenery before us, and the grounds appeared to come alive.

"Would the lady like to take a seat?" Nishantha asked as we reached a little table for two. He pulled a seat out for me in the patio area and gestured for me to sit. The tabletops and the backs of the chairs looked like cast iron doilies, covered with a thick dark green paint.

"Why thank you kind sir."

"The pleasure is all mine."

As Nishantha tucked my chair in, a nearby party of four looked over to us. They appeared to consist of two couples, in their late sixties perhaps. As one of the two ladies called over to us it was clear they were English and it was clear they were upper class.

"Excuse me, waiter, we are ready to order now."

As well-to-do as she acted, I thought her pleated aqua skirt complete with matching aqua costume jewellery was really rather garish.

Nishantha smiled at her and politely advised, "I am sorry madam, I am not a waiter."

"Oh. I am terribly sorry. I thought... Well I saw you seating the lady and..."

"It is OK. Please do not worry."

"So you two... You are, together, are you?"

"Yes, yes we are," Nishantha said, looking at me lovingly.

"Oh, right," the lady said awkwardly, her lower lip sinking into her face. The deep-set wrinkle lines around her mouth from years of smoking accentuated themselves as she stopped smiling and flabby jowls drooped down either side of her mouth. Nishantha sat down opposite me, with his back to the foursome. I had a perfect view of them behind him, and we were all too close for comfort.

"So what would the lady like to eat?" Nishantha asked me. Distracted by the whispering and the 'don't look now's' coming from table behind him, I failed to answer. Nishantha seemed oblivious to the disapproval wafting over from my fellow English citizens.

"Rachael?"

"Sorry, I'll have…"

My ears honed in on keywords from their conversation and I trailed off subject again. The words 'mixed race' and 'disgusting' rang through my ears and rattled my temper. Trying my best to ignore them, I stared at the menu on the table.

"Well, I'll have a cream tea, I think. It seems so very apt," I said, adopting a posh manner for the purpose of our conversation.

"What is a…cream…tea?" he asked, searching for it on his menu.

"It's a very traditional English afternoon tea. They serve tea with milk and white sugar, if you like, and a scone with raisins inside it, with butter, cream and jam on top."

Nishantha read the menu description for himself. "One pot of tea served with two home-made raisin scones… What is a scone? Is it like a cake?"

"Yeah, just not as sweet. It's funny, I never touch them at home but everything about this place is so English I really fancy one now!"

"…With trad-itional Devon-shire clotted cream and preserves.

"What is… preserves?"

"Preserves is a word they use instead of jam when they want to charge you more for it."

"Oh, right. Let us both have a cream tea. I would like to try

something that is traditionally English."
The offending table could not help stealing glances at us with a look of distain about them. We were, to them, the proverbial car crash. Once again I found myself looking over Nishantha's shoulder, straining to hear what they were saying as they huddled in behind their menus to exchange comments.
Nishantha took my hand and leaned in.
"Rachael, you cannot let them get to you."
"You didn't hear what they said. You can't see how they are looking at us," I whispered through gritted teeth. It was bothering me disproportionately because I was extrapolating. The Grand Hotel was so English it was like a test. If I couldn't make it work here, between our two worlds, I would never be able to make it work in the real England. Without knowing it, I had placed an enormous amount of importance on our time there. Another oversight on my part was the importance Nishantha had placed on how I dealt with other people's view of us. He needed to know we were solid in the face of adversity. Our conflicting needs were about to collide.
"I can hear, Rachael. I am choosing to ignore it. It is their problem. It only becomes *our* problem when *you* let it."
I was taken aback at what I perceived to be a direct insult.
"Does it not get to you at all?" I asked, squinting my eyes.
"No. It does not. I am happy, and, I can-not control the rest of the world, or how they think. You do not have to worry about people like them. Not when there are so many good people in your life you could choose to concentrate on."
I bit on the insides of my cheeks and began chipping away at the paint on the curves of the cast iron, doily table.
"You are annoyed," Nishantha said, sitting back in his chair.
"No, I'm not."
"Talk to me."
"The waiter's coming," I said sulkily. Contemplating what Nishantha had just said, I knew he was right. I didn't want them to annoy me so much but they did. It was going to take more than a logical speech from Nishantha to stop them getting to me. As I

watched Nishantha give our order to the real waiter, he looked so adorable I decided I could not let the people behind us ruin our day after all and I made a concerted effort to block them out. As a result of both the unresolved conversation from the night before about willingness to move countries and the poorly received jibes from the table before us, we enjoyed our cream teas, but we did so with an elephant in the room. And by elephant, I do mean the proverbial kind, not the literal – in case there was any confusion.

"You know, these are really good. I am a little sad I have never tasted this before. I have some making up to do."

I smiled at the rate they were disappearing. Nishantha was clearly enjoying this new, delicious discovery. Then came a poor choice of words on his part considering the issue we were trying to skirt around.

"I would move to England just for these."

"So you would, then, consider going to England." Oops, that just slipped out.

"Do you mean going? Or do you mean living?"

"Look," I sighed. "I don't need to know what our future holds, I don't, I just need to know you would consider it so that if I was ever to consider moving here, it would feel fair. Does that sound crazy?"

Nishantha looked down for a moment, as though considering his response then said,

"No, that is not crazy. And, yes, I would consider moving, if that was the only way for us to be together."

"But when I asked you last night, you avoided answering and wanted to go to bed?"

"Because it was late and we had a big day planned."

"Oh." My attention was taken by the table behind Nishantha again as one of the ladies spoke loudly.

"Darling, would you call the waiter over please? They have buttered our rolls. Marjory specifically asked for unbuttered rolls. I do apologise, Marjory. We will get you another one. Bloody foreigners, really, is it that difficult? You heard me say 'no butter', didn't you Geoffrey? I quite remember saying no butter. I

quite remember saying it twice."
I just couldn't help listening to the posh women in the loud suit.
"I heard you, June. You quite clearly stated no butter and the boy nodded as if he understood. Let's get him over here before our soup gets cold," Marjory answered.
"Excuse me!" the man I assumed to be Geoffrey called out to the waiter who was busy clearing another table.
"Excuse me!" Geoffrey tried again, cupping his hands around his mouth.
"Darling, just call him Ravi. They are all called Ravi anyway so you are sure to catch his attention."
They all laughed at the lame joke.
"June, hush!" Marjory reprimanded her friend while nodding over to Nishantha.
"Come on, Nishantha. Let's leave. One more minute of listening to these vile people and I'm going end up seeing my scone again." Nishantha looked absolutely horrified. The posh table looked up at me with the same amount of disgust they had all afternoon.
"I beg your pardon?" the other guy, whose name I didn't catch, said. He bared a laughably mawkish expression on his face.
"How dare you speak to my wife like that? You insolent little girl."
"I wasn't talking to your wife. I was talking to my boyfriend."
"Rachael, let us just go," Nishantha said, looking uncomfortable.
"Yes, I believe you should go before I have you thrown out of here," the man said.
"Oh really. And what gives you the right to do that exactly?"
"Because you are causing a disturbance!"
"I have sat here, biting my lip, trying to ignore your disapproving glances and ignorantly offensive comments all through our afternoon tea. You overhear one fitting comment about your behaviour and feel the need to throw your weight about?"
"Is everything alright here?" a supervisor asked as he appeared from out of the blue. He wore a blue waistcoat, unlike the red waistcoats of the waiters.
June and Marjory both inhaled sharply as though getting ready to

speak but I got there first.

"Everything is fine..."

Nishantha stood and spoke to him in Sinhala while I watched the supervisor glance expressionlessly from them to me.

"My apologies, everything seems to be under control here. Just a misunderstanding I see. Enjoy your afternoon teas ladies and gentlemen," the supervisor said politely as he smiled and bowed slightly, holding his hands neatly behind his back as he made to leave. When he was out of earshot Nishantha announced we were leaving and proceeded to walk in quick, deliberate, strides back towards the hotel. He was ten paces in front of me and I had to run intermittently to keep up.

"Nishantha, wait, please!"

He neither answered nor slowed down.

"Nishantha. Let's forget those people now, please. They were a joke."

"A joke? Such a joke that you had to get involved? You turned into what they believed you to be!"

"What? I was standing up for us! For you and me and the right to be able to sit in a hotel garden, drinking tea without having to put up with snide comments and disapproving stares from morons like that."

"You joined in with those 'morons', Rachael."

I stopped walking, shocked that Nishantha had effectively just called me a moron. He stopped too and strode back to face me, running his fingers through his hair.

"I am not saying you are a moron, Rachael," he stated as if he'd read my mind. "But I do think you were as bad as them. If you had to say something, why not politely ask them to keep their voices down. I do not like how angry you let them make you."

I took a deep breath. "Look, they made me feel inferior and downtrodden. If I didn't stand up for myself back there, I would have come away feeling like a victim."

Nishantha stared at my face as if he was struggling to read me.

"What? What is so hard to understand?"

"The night of the parada. You were so determined to come out of

that without feeling like a victim. And you did it. You were strong. I thought that was who you were."
"Look, let's go inside and talk."
We walked back to our room in silence, but at least we were walking together.
Later, when I'd had time to digest Nishantha's words, I came to see that he was right. If I let everybody who disapproved of us make me angry I would make our lives miserable.

After we had both showered, separately and silently, I tried to apologise. We were both wearing matching white flannel dressing gowns while laying miles apart on the bed.
"Nishantha, I've thought about your words and, you are right," I sighed. "I should have made a joke of it or something. I should have told them your hourly rate is 200 rupees and you come highly recommended."
Nishantha had to think about my comment for a moment before he caught on and smiled.
"Only 200 rupees?"
"OK, maybe 250," we both smiled. "Seriously, though, you are right. I can't act like that every time we come across people like that. I just, I wanted your little taste of England to be perfect."
"It is perfect. They could fill the entire hotel with people like that and it would still be perfect to me. I am not trying to change you, or stifle your passion. I just need to know our happiness does not depend on who we meet that day."
Messaged received and understood.
Later that night, over a dinner of rice and curry, we joked about our first argument as a couple. We even joked about what we'd already had to face together from the very day we met, what with terrorists, pending arranged marriages, disapproving family members, washed out email addresses and the 5455-ish miles of land and sea that separated us. At least we knew we could pull together in the face of adversity.
After a very pleasant couple of days in Little England I was more than happy to get back to little Kandy, or the real Sri Lanka, as I

saw it. I'd missed the heat, the palm trees and the unexplained magic Kandy possessed. Nishantha had to work again upon our return and without Indica around I had to amuse myself. It was my second to last day and I didn't want to go home. I was so much happier here than at home. To take my mind off leaving I read the rest of my book while sunbathing in the garden. I was hoping a cricket match might start in the field behind but nobody turned up. I then looked through some more of Nishantha's paintings, made tea, and broke a cup. After the cup incident, I checked the field again but there was nobody there so I took a stroll through it and all the way out to the other side. Entering unchartered territory I meandered down the part of the main road that led to the old town. The shops here were little huts with corrugated iron roofs, like in the villages, rather than the large modern buildings in the city centre. There were some concrete buildings but these were unkempt and dilapidated. It was the first part of Kandy I hadn't liked. The old town scared me a little, it was so different from the rest of Kandy and I wasn't sure if I'd entered a no-go area so decided to head back home. Only, as I turned, all the side roads looked the same and I managed to get horribly lost as I made my way down all the wrong ones. When I asked passersby for directions they either didn't speak English or they sent me on a wild goose chase, each person sending me in a different direction to the last. As panic began to set in, I finally found the main road I'd been looking for in order to get back to Nishantha's. There was just one problem. Before I could head off I had to cross it. I'd been I had been standing by the roadside for several minutes waiting for a break in the traffic. This part of town may have been rundown but the traffic was still dense and manic. Four lanes of unrelenting traffic sped by hurriedly, aggressively beeping their horns as they went. Nobody stayed in their lane and they all seemed to be trying to overtake each other at the same time. There was no way I was going into that road, not even to tackle it in two parts. As I started to look around for other pedestrians to see how they were tackling the problem, a loud, piercing cry caused me to whip my head round with start. As I looked in the direction of the harrowing noise, I saw it belonged to a dog. He was sitting between two vehicles and had clearly been hit by something. One of his back legs had mutated to point straight up in the air and the other leg hung limply on the ground. The dog seemed to be pleading with the onlookers who were assembling by the side of the road as he dragged himself around in a semi-circle using his front legs. The pitiful high-pitched yelps were heart-rending and impossible to ignore yet ignore them is what everybody did. As he was nearer the other side, I wondered why nobody there was helping. Why were they all just looking on as this poor creature begged them for help? The traffic only slowed a little as vehicles swerved to avoid the dog but nobody thought to stop so the poor thing could be rescued. Then I saw something in the hands of one of the onlookers that made me feel physically sick. It was a black bin liner. They were waiting for it to die.

An overwhelming urge to run out and help the dog myself took over me, but that was quickly offset by the fear of the relentless vehicles speeding by. A few people had gathered on my side of the road to watch the scene so I asked one of them why nobody would help it. The whimpers were tugging on my heartstrings and the little look on its face made me cry. The onlooker ignored me and I lost the fight between reason and impulse and took a step out into the road. The onlooker who had ignored me then reached out and pulled me back without saying a word. I didn't fight him. Instead I stood there, staring on with sad eyes, waiting for the inevitable.

After what felt like an eternity, the front wheel of a motor bike ran over the dog's head, and as the back wheel rolled over it again, the dog ceased crying and his body fell limp. Two men calmly headed out into the traffic with outstretched arms, gesturing for the traffic to stop while a third picked up the carcass up by the hind legs. The dog's head swung lifelessly before its limp body disappeared into the bin liner held open by the one of the men who'd stopped the traffic. Then they all disappeared into a shop. Most of the onlookers walked off and all that was left in the road was a pool of blood from the dog's head. I stared on in disbelief even after the dog had gone.

"If it was that easy to stop the traffic, why did they wait for the dog to die before doing it?" I asked the man who'd pulled me back from the road.

"Kinder, kinder," he said.

"What? How?" I asked, bewildered.

"Kinder, kinder," he repeated. "You need help, to cross?"

"Yes, istuti," I said solemnly.

"Rachael, there are no vet clinics here, not for strays. Only the rich would pay to have their animal cared for," Nishantha told me as he brought another glass of water over to me on the sofa. I'd gotten very dehydrated on my return walk home. The city air was stifling and the shock of the dog taking so long to die while looking so scared and in pain had left me with the shakes. I'd thrown up twice since coming home.

"So why leave it in the road? Why not stop the traffic and kill it humanly?"

"What if it had rabies? Many peoples here die from rabies."

"OK, I get it. It was just so awful to watch, Nishantha. And there was nothing I could do."

"You can-not save everybody or, everything, Rachael. Sometimes you have let go and accept these things, sad as they are." Nishantha tucked a stray curl of my hair behind my ear as he lent down in front of me. I was lying with my head on a pillow from the bedroom.

"In case you hadn't noticed, that's not exactly my strong point."

"I know."

Nishantha stroked my face for a moment before asking, "Rachael, will you promise me something?"

"What?"

"You will never think to run into that road again. I do not care if it me lying there hurt, you just must not do it, OK?"

"It was stupid, and, unless it's you, you have my word."

"Good, because it is dangerous and...mama oyata aadareyi."

"What does that mean?"
"You will have to look it up."
"Oh, I hate it when you do that."
"Ah, but you always remember what I tell you much better when you look it up for yourself."
"True," I sighed. "But now it's time for me to say suba rathriyak. (Good night.) I am sorry I'm feeling ill and... traumatised on our last night together."
"That's OK. Come on, let's go to bed."
The next morning, my last morning, I awoke to Nishantha uttering something in Sinhala to me. The more familiar we got with each other, the more he did this as he stirred awake in the mornings.
"I'm sorry, Rachael, I said that I will go make us some tea." Nishantha got up and walked naked out of the room. Then a moment later, as I was smiling to myself at how lucky I was, he popped his head back around the bedroom door.
"Hey, what happened to my cup?"

Chapter 18

Flights

A flight is a void of guilt free time one can enjoy all to oneself.
Some disagree and see flying as an inconvenient restriction on their time. They see the downside: they cannot carry on ploughing through the pressing issues that must be addressed daily in life in mid-flight. All they can really do is sit in a chair and wait until they reach their destination. But they are missing the upside: they cannot carry on ploughing through the pressing issues that must be addressed daily in life in mid-flight. All they can really do is sit in a chair and wait until they reach their destination.
These people are missing a great opportunity to chill out. You can see the frustration bubbling away in the faces of such people. Smokers are the worst. They are the ones who give out disgruntled sighs at the slightest delay, have jittery hands and feet, chew at the inside of their cheek and generally look like they've been put on death row. I feel sorry for smokers. They have been separated from the very thing they would turn to in a boredom-frustration scenario, such as flying. It must be torture.
I happen to love and cherish my little void of guilt free time away from the responsibilities of life. Whatever problems awaited me in the real world, there was little point worrying about them while sitting – seatbelt fastened – on a plane. The only thing I worry about on a plane is whether I'll make the right dinner choice. I'm always so worried I'll pick the wrong one and get food envy with the person next to me that I actually get quite stressed about this decision and change my mind three times before the stewardesses reach me. The only other decision to make is whether to watch an in-flight movie before or after you take a nap.
I think the things I love most about flying are all the things you can't do. You can't clean dishes, tackle the ironing pile or take

calls from your boss. Hell, if your house was on fire the most you could do, would be to say a little prayer, recline your seat and munch away on the complimentary peanuts.

I half expected to find myself dwelling on how unfair it was that I had to leave Nishantha during my flight, but it was completely the opposite. I knew we would make it work now and I knew I was going to put him before my job if it came to it.

Some of the surrounding passengers squashed mini pillows in the crooks of their necks and pulled eye masks over their eyes to block out the light. As they all tried to get comfortable enough to get some sleep, I eagerly awaited for the scheduled meal to arrive. I looked around me, trying to figure out if anyone else was as eager as I was to get my hands on that tray. A savoury aroma wafted teasingly down the plane to me and I could see the cabin crew handing out the meal trays. So close yet so far. I knew it would probably be a disappointing tasteless meal made up of some sort of aspic coated meat and soggy vegetables but that didn't stop me desperately wanting it to be my turn to be fed. Even if I wasn't hungry, I still eagerly awaiting that compartmented meal tray, just to see what little delights awaited me.

As I waited, my thoughts drifted back to when I had to confess to Nishantha I had broken his cup. We laughed so much that we ached everywhere. He told me he could not believe I had made up the story about the dog and pretended to be sick just so he wouldn't be mad about the cup. Our endless laughter turned into endless lovemaking. What a beautiful way to say goodbye. My head was lost in the clouds, so much so I could have drifted home without the aid of a plane. But on a plane I was and how better to use my time than to learn more Sinhala. I opened my phrasebook while I chomped away on a surprisingly delicious chicken curry. As I flicked through, I remembered I hadn't yet looked up the phrase Nishantha had said to me the day before – mama oyata aadareyi. I'd asked him to write it down for me so that I could look it up. I couldn't find it in my little book so when the Sri Lankan stewardess came back to collect my tray, I asked her.

Very unsure of the pronunciation, it came out almost inaudibly.
"Please say again?" the flawless stewardess asked as she craned her neck to hear me.
"Mama oyata aadareyi, I think."
"Has somebody said this to you?" she asked, beaming a candyfloss pink smile at me.
"Yes, my boyfriend."
She put a hand to her heart as though she herself was touched by the words.
"It means 'I love you'."

Chapter 19

Once I touched down on familiar terra firma, all I could think about was telling Jenny and Laura what a wonderful time I'd had – and that my boyfriend had told me he loved me. So I was over the moon when I found both of them waiting with open arms for me at the front door of our flat. They were wrongly expecting to have to cheer me up and had even made me a moping pack. Needless to say, they were surprised when I burst through the door at 100 miles an hour, ready to retell all the gruesome details of my trip.

The moping pack consisted of a new pair of tartan flannel pyjamas, the chick-flick rom-com, *While You Were Sleeping*, a peel-off face mask and a box of chocolates – Fairtrade of course. To show my appreciation, we all shared a girlie night in anyway but really I just wanted to milk the opportunity to brag about my perfect man. I already knew Jenny had put Ed up for a few nights and I asked her what she thought of him. She didn't say much and I thought that might have been because Laura was there. Their friendship was still in its infant stages after all. The minute Laura left that evening I re-grilled Jenny to get to the juicy bits I knew she was holding back.

"So, Jenny. Still got the hots for Nick?"

"Nick who?" she said, grinning and raising her eyebrows.

"Oh! That can only mean one thing. Come on, spill the tofu. What really happened when you put Ed up?"

"Nothing. I told you," Jenny said, throwing the screwed up foil wrapper from the caramel cup chocolate at me.

"Oh come on, why don't you want me to know? I just spilled my guts out to you about Nishantha!"

"Exactly. Nishantha. You'll tell him everything I say and he will tell Ed and then Ed won't think I'm playing it cool anymore."

"Jenny, I am not going to tell Nishantha anything you don't want

me to. I'm kinda hoping you won't be telling Ed anything I've just told you. Girlie scouts honour?"
"Girlie scouts honour. Now shut up, you dork!"
"Just tell me then!"
A huge smile beamed across Jenny's face as she revealed her 'amazing' weekend with Ed. Once she started talking about him there was no stopping her. She told me they had been emailing every day since he left. I knew they would hit it off but now I had second thoughts in hooking them up together. Hardy left Jenny to go travelling and I just set her up with Ed – the self-confessed nomad.
"Jenny, have you fallen for him or is this just the exciting new beginning enthusiasm shining through?"
"Oh, Rach, he is perfect. He wants me to go and see him in Cornwall as soon as I can get the weekend off!"
"Jenny, he has just stepped off the plane from months of volunteer work with elephants."
"Well, unless he is a sexual deviant who prefers elephant to girls, I don't see the problem?"
"How would that even work? Never mind, actually. Look, I'm just saying, he is a traveller at heart, at the moment. I don't want to see you get hurt."
"I know, I know. I'm not going to stop seeing him just because he may or may not go travelling. We might be bored with each other within a week. Who knows? I don't care. I'm happy now. I'm having fun, like you told me I should be."
"You know what? You're right. Forget what I said. I knew you would get on, within the first five seconds of meeting him, I knew it! And I can hear myself being the annoying killjoy that I so hated when I first told people about Nishantha."
"He has so many stories, Rachael, and he is so laid-back. We went down The Tavern and got wasted and he got me to do something after I never dreamed I would do."
"What did you do?"
"It was the alcohol, Rachael, so don t judge, OK?"
"OK. What?"

"Fuck, promise me you won't ever bring this up again?"
"OK, OK. What did you do?"
"I sampled his shish kebab!"
"Oh, I do hope that isn't a metaphor."
"Rachael! I ate meat. Me! I just don't care about things as much when I'm with him. He takes me out of my world and into some crazy place where everything is fun."
"Did you get up to anything else?"
"No! Well, we kissed, on his last night. We stayed up all night talking and kissing, it was so amazing, Rach! Ooh, you have to find out when you next speak to Nishantha, you know – if Ed has said anything about me, without him knowing that I have asked you, that is!"
"Oh, I see. Now my relationship with Nishantha is useful to you is it?"
"Oh, come on, Rach. Ed told me loads of stuff Nishantha said about you!"
I considered rising above it and not asking what he said, but the devil on my shoulder won out.
"What did he say?" I blurted out through a smile of anticipation.
"Well, he said that it's not like Nishantha spoke about you a lot, but when he did, the things he said and the way he said them, it was obvious he was smitten with you. He said the contented smile on Nishantha's face and faraway gaze made it look like Nishantha went into a secret world of, what word did he use? That was it, a secret world of absolute equanimity. How in touch with his emotions must he be to come out with a phrase like that, huh? Absolute equanimity..." Jenny said, savouring Ed's words as she popped another chocolate into her mouth. I wasn't sure if she was dreaming about Ed or enjoying her strawberry cream. Either way she looked happy.
I smiled at the warmth I felt thinking I made Nishantha happy. Then, with a mouth still full of chocolate, Jenny said,
"I'm dying to meet Nishantha now! Ed only had good things to say about him. I mean, I know you did, too, but you had your rose-tinted glasses on so it didn't really count."

"Cheers! Did he say anything about me?"

"He said you're a lovely chick and that you all had a lot of fun together. He liked it that you never once made him feel like a gooseberry. He also said something weird. He said you and Nishantha were bound by a trauma. When I asked what he meant he said you should be the one to tell me. What did he mean?"

I thought for a minute. I had kept my little secret separate from my life here so well that I honestly didn't know what she was talking about. Then it registered, she was talking about the Tiger attacks.

"Jenny. Nobody can know this. I've kept this from my parents, my friends, from Victor..."

"Tell me, Rachael. What happened?"

"The parade, the one I told you about, the day I met Nishantha. Well, I lied about the date I was there, to everyone. I was there when the shootings occurred."

"What? That was on the news and everything!"

"I know, I know, I'm sorry."

"I don't get it, why would you not want anyone to know you were there?"

"It gets worse. We ran to my guesthouse to get away from the shootings. But my guesthouse was exactly where they were headed."

"Oh my god. Why?"

"They were targeting servicemen. They thought the owner, who is also a policeman, lived at the guesthouse I was in but they were wrong. The owner didn't live or work there. He had a manager running that place while his wife ran another one they owned."

"So what happened?"

"They came into our room."

"The terrorists?"

"Yeah, they went in all the rooms. Nishantha hid. He had to because they were targeting Sinhalese, not foreigners like me. I had more chance of getting out alive if they thought I was alone."

"Shit. I can't believe this. What did you do?"

"There were two of them. They were armed, one with a gun, one with a machete. They were shocked to see me. They looked crazed, not even human."

"Rachael, they could have killed you."

"I thought they were going to. They spoke to me. They wanted to know if I was alone. I was so scared they'd find Nishantha. I was so scared I'd say the wrong thing. But then their accomplices came along and they all left. Those others, who came in at the end, they..."

My words caught in my throat as I tried to tell her about the baby and his mother. The baby's cries replayed in my mind as clearly as if I were back in the room.

"What? They what?"

Tears escaped my eyes. I brushed them away.

"They killed a baby and his mum. I heard him cry, I heard the shots and I heard the silence that followed."

"Jesus Christ! Why didn't you come home?"

"I wanted to stay, I *had* to stay. No one here would have understood. I wanted to see Kandy again, to see life going on after the attack. I wanted to see Nishantha again to talk it through with him. He was the only one who could understand... If I told anyone here, Victor would have brought me back home. I couldn't risk that."

"Rachael, I can't believe this. You seem so calm about it."

"Well, I am. I never thought 'why me?' And I don't feel like a victim. Other people lost a lot more than me that night..."

I trailed off in thought as I realised I would carry the sad death of that infant around with me for the rest of my days. There was no point in bringing that to Jenny's attention. Nothing she could say would make it better. It would only serve to bring her down.

The days that followed my return brought with them many phone calls to and from Nishantha. We were talking whenever we could, racking up hefty phone bills on my mobile and sneaking in calls at work where possible. I used to come in early and stay late in order to speak to him in privacy. We agreed that he must come to England to see me next so we could start to gain perspective on where we would ultimately live together. He knew I would move to anywhere I could feasibly make a living so there was no pressure for him to move to England. My only stipulation was that we didn't move anywhere colder than the UK. I started researching courses that allowed me to teach English to adults as a foreign language. It looked like a plausible way of making money abroad.

Nishantha had to save up to book a flight over to the UK. He refused to let me contribute, which was both admirable and frustrating as I wanted him here sooner rather than later. At work, the opportunity to help promote volunteer work abroad with Dr De Souza had been scraped into the bin like leftovers on a dinner plate. Jonathon Jackson had been chosen while I was on holiday. Victor had warned me about taking holiday during the decision-making process and I had, perhaps short-sightedly, chosen to go anyway.

As I prepared to start my life with Nishantha, wherever that may be, it seemed my friends had started to move on too. Nick was at uni, the band had split and Neal had moved into a rented flat in south London to be closer to work. The other tenant in his flat was moving out so Ben and Alana were considering moving up there, too, to rent with Neal. Derren and Tanya were together but not together, Derren's favourite arrangement. My friends were all beginning to fly the West Sussex nest to do their own thing. I started to spend a lot more time with Laura as our group dwindled. We would meet up at the Tavern like the last little stragglers from our once large group of friends.

On Valentine's Day, Jenny, Laura and I decided to go out together seeing as we had nobody else to share the evening with. We even invited Tanya in case she wasn't seeing Derren but, as it transpired, he had planned to take her out for dinner in London. Laura, Jenny and I had drinks at the flat then went on to a club for a dance and some more drinks. It was meant to be a mad one so we could all have fun and forget being single, dumped or in a long-distance relationship. It was a good recipe so it was a great shame I ruined it. I felt ill from the get-go. Laura and Jenny polished off a bottle of wine each while I was still stuck on my first glass. When our taxis arrived to take us out I assured the girls I would be OK and went with them anyway. The truth was, if I hadn't been the common denominator between Laura and Jenny I would have gone straight to bed. I went out with them and held out until they were so drunk they didn't care if I was there or not. I left them dancing to Wham; they looked happy enough. When I got home, the smell of the Jenny's unlit incense sticks made me feel so sick I moved them to her room and closed the door before curling up in bed.

The next morning I woke up feeling no better at all. Squinty-eyed and half asleep, I toddled into the kitchen for a fresh glass of water. While en route to the kitchen I saw Jenny had crashed on the sofa, still fully clothed and wearing her heels. That's a sure sign of a good night. I poured a glass of water for her too and put it by the sofa. Jenny stirred as I tried to creep away.

"What time is it?" she groaned.

"It's 09.15, sorry I woke you."

"That's OK. Need water."

"Here you go." I handed her the glass.

"Jenny, take it quick, you stink. I think I'm gonna throw up."

The smell of alcohol on Jenny made me retch so I ran to the bathroom sink.

"Well, thanks for the water and the insult, Rach," Jenny said as she stood in the doorway moments later. I was sitting on the floor with my back against the bath.

"I'm sorry, Jenny. You smell of alcohol."

"And that made you feel sick?"

"Looks that way."

The nausea was overbearing. I just wanted it to go away.

"Rachael, is there any chance you could be pregnant?"

"No."

"No? So, you and Nishantha, you're waiting until you are married are you?"

"No, but..."

"Were you careful?"

"I'm on the pill, Jenny. Trust me, I'm not pregnant."
"Did you miss one at all?"
"No!" I was getting really antsy with Jenny. I just needed to sit quietly and be left alone.
"Did you have any sickness or diarrhoea?"
"No! Oh...wait, yes."

I stared at the little white window, waiting for a line to either appear or not appear. Not really believing I could be pregnant, I wasn't overly worried. I just felt rough and wanted to get this over with so I could get some peace, and maybe even some more sleep. Jenny had gone out, even in her state, to pick me up a pregnancy test kit for me. I think in the absence of Hardy she was enjoying the distracting drama of my life. Jenny banged on the door protesting that it must be ready now. It was ready. There was a faint line. I tried to block her out whilst I read the blurb that explained a faint line result but she was insistent and I struggled to take in the small print.
"Err, I think I did it wrong. I'm going to do the other one too."
There were two tests in the pack, a fact I was glad of. I didn't want a faint line. I wanted a definite line or none at all.
"Did it wrong? All you have to do is pee on a stick!" the helpful voice said from behind the door. Ignoring Jenny I peed and waited. Another line appeared, faint also. The information in the leaflet told me it is best to do the test in the morning. It was now the afternoon. I unlocked the bathroom door to let Jenny in. We sat on the floor together in front of the bath.
"Mate, I think this means you are pregnant."
"But I can't be. It takes ages to try for a baby, doesn't it?"
"Plenty of teenage girls at the abortion clinic would beg to differ."
"I can't have a baby, not now, it would ruin everything. I want Nishantha and me to unfold naturally. I don't want him to feel forced into anything. Also, I wouldn't be able to leave my job or move to Sri Lanka, not if I had a young baby to support. I know you have your views on these things but please, please don't lecture me now."

"You sound like you have already decided and you only found out three minutes ago. Besides, I'm not against abortion, Rach, I'm against serial abortionists and girls who have them late on."
"Well, mine will be sooner rather than later so you don't need to worry about that."

I took the next few days off sick because the nausea was both unrelenting and debilitating, and I booked my appointment to have this little problem seen to straight away. It wasn't until the morning I was due to leave for my appointment that I started to have second thoughts. Keeping it had never occurred to me. Telling Nishantha had never occurred to me. I panicked. I had left myself no time to think things through in a balanced manner. Shaking, I picked up the phone and called the one friend I thought would understand the most – Jacky. I felt guilty turning to her as I hadn't kept in regular contact and was only calling because I needed something. Despite this she told me to come straight over. I guess that's what true friendship is.
"Hi, Jacky. Thanks so much for this. I'm sorry," I said as I stood at her door.
"No, no. Not at all, come in. I'm just making the kids' lunches. Come through."
"It's very quiet, are they at their dad's at the moment?"
"Yeah, he'll be dropping them off in half an hour, just to warn you. I don't know how much peace and quiet we will have with them running around. So what pickle have you got yourself into this time?" she said with raised eyebrows.
"Well…" I told her the whole Nishantha saga, so that she could better grasp my predicament. She took the parade events well, understanding instantly that I had to keep quiet about it in order to keep control over my situation. She concluded that I had no moral obligation to tell the authorities because the 'criminals' were dead so it wasn't like they needed my help to catch them.
"And now you don't want an abortion?" Jacky asked as we sat in her living room with a plate of Party Rings. They went down surprisingly well considering everything else made me feel sick.

"Well, this is it. I don't know. And when I allow myself to think about it I panic because I need to know by two o'clock today."
"Why? You can always cancel the appointment, Rachael. I think you have to. You can't go through with it while you are thinking like this. You need to take the pressure off. This is a big decision."
"I guess. I keep daydreaming about little scenarios including Nishantha and me with a big bump," I said, sitting back and replaying the scene in my minds-eye.
"Whoa, that's a contented smile if ever I saw one. I think you want to keep it, you just can't see past the practicalities."
My smile grew.
"No, wait, this is silly. It's just a fantasy. I can't have a baby. I didn't plan it. I never envisaged it would happen this way."
"Let me guess. You wanted the mortgage, the marriage, the annual holiday and the family dog before you thought about having a baby? I'm sorry. Rachael. We all start off with these expectations, but life isn't like that. Do you think I sat down when I was a kid and thought, right, I'll get married have two kids and get divorced by the time I'm thirty?"
"Well, no."
"No. That wasn't my life plan. The way things are now, they're not ideal, but I'm happy. It would be nice to find a man who isn't an arse, but I'm happy."
"But I can't be my usual impetuous self, Jacky. Not about this."
"True, true. You need to weigh it up, and you need to consider if you would be willing to bring a baby up alone."
"What? Why?"
"Your relationship is still new. What if it doesn't work out? What if there is visa trouble? What if he doesn't want it? There are lots of things that could result in you bringing up a baby on your own. You can't just have it adopted because your boyfriend dumps you. Do you know what he would say if he knew?"
"No. I have no idea."
"Right, then. You need to go to the doctor and find out exactly how pregnant you are, then you need to talk to this man of yours.

He needs to know, Rachael. You need to make this decision together, as a couple."

"God, you're right. I need to talk to him. I should have talked to him straight away. What is wrong with me? Why didn't I come to that conclusion before?"

"Just be careful about what motivates your decision. Talk it over with Nishantha. It is the only way you will make a decision you won't regret later on. Hey, from what you've told me, maybe you should be meditating on it," Jacky added to make light of the heavy conversation.

"Yeah, I should be sowing my virtuous karmic seeds and searching for enlightenment."

"What?"

"I don't know; it was in an article I read on meditation."

I watched on in a whole new light as Jacky's two girls burst through the front door and hugged her hello. Seeing she had her hands full, I left her to it and drove home in a daze.

That night I imagined keeping the baby and not only did it begin to feel like the right thing to do, it filled me with excitement. But before I could let myself get carried away any further, I knew I had to talk to Nishantha. I called him later that day with every intention of telling him.

"Rachael, what is wrong?" Nishantha asked, sensing I was distant in mind as well as in mileage. The line was bad. His voice sounded really quiet and far away, like he was sitting under a giant plastic bowl. I needed him to sound close.

"Nothing, I just miss you."

"Well, I have good news for you. I think I will be able to come over in August."

"August, hey?"

"You are not pleased?"

"That's five, six months away."

"It will not always be like this, Rachael. You know, when I miss you, I often think about us living together in a little house somewhere, like the one you described in your snow globe. I imagine us waking up together and I imagine missing you while I

work then seeing you when I come home."
"Sounds lovely."
"I also think about the times we were sitting in the swing chair and imagine us sitting there again, planning little trips together. Do not sound sad, Rachael."
"Nishantha…"
"What is it?"
"Mama oyata aadareyi."
"I love you too, Rachael. We are going to be OK, OK?"
"OK."

I neglected to tell him the news because I now knew what I had to do. I had to go to him. I had to tell him in person.
I borrowed money from Mr Barclaycard because although he charged more interest than the bank of mum and dad, he asked a lot less questions. I booked the next available flight and told Leon I had a personal matter that needed urgent attention. He agreed reluctantly and made me take it as unpaid leave. Victor asked me what was going on and I told him the truth. I went to his house and told him everything. Martha took one look at the state I was in and took herself off to their conservatory with her book of Sudoku. Victor looked shocked at first, then disappointed, but not in me, more, for me.
The doctors estimated I was five weeks pregnant and booked me in for a dating scan, which I would attend upon my return. I told Jenny I was leaving again and she bounced around the room excitedly. She was going away, too, to see Ed in Cornwall. I made her promise not to tell him. She gave me her word.

The flight to Dubai took no time at all because I miraculously slept right through it. I would have felt cheated out of my guilt free flight time if I hadn't felt so sick. And for once in my life, I didn't care for the food tray. Savoury smells of any kind made me want to upchuck. As if to compensate for how quickly time had passed, the wait at Dubai airport took forever. The two-hour wait felt more like ten and there were only so many times you could walk up and down the airport. All the comfortable chairs in the airport were in use and people had taken to lying down on the marble floors as hundreds of strangers walked by their sleeping heads. Still sleepy myself, I was tempted to do the same and if I wasn't pregnant I would have. My mindset had already altered to put this little bunch of cells growing inside me before anything else. Every little decision I made had to pass my foetus friendly checklist first. So instead, I crouched down by a wall and tackled one of the packets of Party Rings I had brought with me.

After I'd finished munching, I started imagining all the different scenarios that could play out with Nishantha when I told him the news. I fantasised about conversations in his house, in the art institute at reception, at Indica's house. In every scenario he scooped me up in his arms and was overwhelmed with happiness. I had to bear in mind that there might not be any happy scooping at all. Pregnancy aside, the memory of Nishantha's touch as he pulled me in close to him and the thought of seeing those big, soulful eyes again filled me with an intensity that made me want to burst. The waiting was driving me insane, especially when my plane was delayed. I'd become one of those people I used to watch, the impatient, stressy kind.

When the flight to Colombo finally jetted off from Dubai airport my fantasy had changed. I was now imagining the look on Nishantha's face when he first saw me. He had no idea I was coming. Again I went through every scenario possible: him doing mundane every day chores and me sneaking up behind him; him at reception with Sharma like the first time I met him. Oh, the possibilities.

The thing I was looking forward to the most was hearing his husky voice whisper into my ear. He could say anything, I didn't care. I tingled at the mere thought of it.

I opted to watch an in-flight movie on this flight because I had to do something to take my mind off Nishantha or the anticipation would exhaust me before I even got there.

Chapter 20

My enthusiasm and energy levels had waned dramatically by the time I reached Colombo and I still had to get to Kandy yet. You can only be euphoric for so long before you start to wilt. As we landed, the captain announced something in Sinhala and Arabic. As he spoke I watched the faces of those around me drop. My best guess was that the weather was crap because the pilot tends to give you useful information like that when thanking you for flying with them. Then a lady burst into tears and then another and then another. They were either really hoping for a sunny day, or that was not the weather forecast they just gave out over the tannoy. The announcement came in English next. They warned that there had been a bomb blast in Colombo so some of the city was inaccessible, due to the damaged area and tighter security measures. They said for more information we should go to the information desks at arrivals. I felt safe in the knowledge that Nishantha was in Kandy and Indica and Johan's houses were out the way of town. Ravi's place was closer but still nowhere near the main spread.
I walked through 'nothing to declare' thinking I do, I do, I do, I do! I do have something to declare! I'm pregnant!
I wanted to walk up to random strangers and tell them why I'd come.
Clothes changed, teeth brushed, hair scrunched, I was ready to get on my way.
"Ayubowan," I said, greeting the driver.
"Ayubowan."
Nama mokadhdha?" the taxi driver said, asking for my name.
"Mage nama Rachael."
"Nama mokadhdha?"
"Feizal! Kohomode?"
"Varadak neh, istuti." I smiled to myself as I told him I was fine.

We pulled up at Indica's and I asked the driver to wait while I knocked at Indica's door.
There was no answer there so I moved a few doors down to Johan and Komari's and just stood there, too scared to knock. I was the reason relations were strained with their first born; I doubt I'd be welcome anymore. Taking a deep breath, I knocked on their front door. There was nobody there either so I asked the taxi driver to take me to the markets where I thought Indica might be working. The taxi driver told me this was not possible and I started to hope the bomb blast was nowhere near Indica's fruit stall. Accepting there was little else I could do in Colombo, I instructed the driver to take me to Kandy. There was no way I was going to contend with trains in my state and after hearing about the bomb blast, I doubted the train station was a viable option anyway.

I slept the two hours it took to get to Kandy and woke up with a start as we pulled up at the institute. It was lunchtime. There was a good chance Nishantha was there or nearby.

Holy shit, this is it.

I was so nervous that my hands shook as I tried to grasp my suitcase handle. In fact, I was *so* nervous I almost wanted to get back in the car and go home. I was about to find out if Nishantha would react to the surprise of seeing me in any of the ways I had imagined on the way here. I made my way clumsily up the steps of the institute and looked around to make sure Nishantha wasn't standing right there watching me, as he was in one of my fantasies on the plane. There was nobody around. Once inside I walked over to reception, my heart thumping with a mixture of excitement and trepidation. There was nobody there either. *Damn.* That wasn't part of any of my imagined scenarios. I wanted to see Sharma's smiling face or Paul's cheeky grin. I think I had imagined they were all miraculously standing there together at the desk the moment I walked in, like my very own welcoming committee. Ditching my bags behind the unmanned desk, I ran up the stairs to the third floor, took the first turning on the left, and stopped at the second room on the right. I peered into the room from behind the closed door. The lights were on and there were two people sitting behind the central platform with their backs to the door. It looked like a guy and a girl. I knocked and entered, all full of energy and smiles. Paul, with the cheeky grin, peered over the platform to see who had entered the room, except this time he wasn't wearing a cheeky grin. He had watery, bloodshot eyes. Sharma looked around too. She had been crying. Her make-up was smeared. I peered behind Nishantha's easel. I knew he wasn't there but it seemed necessary to check. There was a painting on the easel, a beautiful painting. It was the silhouette of a man, a woman, and a child. All three were depicted in Burnt Sienna, as they strolled along the beach. The beach, sea and sky were all masterfully painted in creams and reds that faded into browns. It was different from his usual style but I still knew it was his.

"Where is he?" I asked. My heart beating fast for different reasons now.

They both looked at each other then back at me.

"Where is he?" I demanded, mimicking the tone I'd used the first time I asked. I knew something was wrong. People don't sit and cry here over a chipped nail.

Paul got up and sat me down on the platform. He knelt down in front of me and held my forearms with his hands. A tear from each eye escaped as he prepared to speak.

"Rachael, there has been a bomb blast. In Colombo," he said slowly.

"I know, but Nishantha lives here, in Kandy. He is here, in Kandy, isn't he?" My voice grew desperate and high-pitched. "Tell me he was here, he was here, wasn't he? Tell me!" I shouted.

Sharma turned away from us, unable to watch anymore.

"No, Rachael, he was there. He was...hit."

I breathed in quickly in three short, sharp sobs and grabbed Paul's hands to steady myself.

"Tell me he is OK?" I rasped. Nobody said anything. Then I shouted and made them both jump. "Tell me he is OK?" I held my breath.

"He is in hospital, in Colombo," Paul said. Sharma spoke quickly

and impatiently to Paul in her mother tongue, gesturing to me.
"He is alive! Oh, thank God." I felt a sense of relief but only briefly. An overwhelming impatience took over after that.
"Can you take me to him? Do you drive?"
"Yes," Paul said.
"That is what I tell him. He must drive you to him," Sharma huffed in frustration.
I stood up. "Wait, wait, wait. How do you know all this?"
"Indica call us a few moments ago. It does not look good, Rachael. He may already be... It might already be too late. They said he is dying, Rachael."
"Paul, I don't care what they say. He is alive right now. Just take me to him, please?"
"Paul, just go. Take Nishantha's van, and call Indica on your way," Sharma ordered.
Once we were on our way, Paul pulled out a mobile and tried to call the number Indica had called from. There was no dial tone. He called another number and tried the hospital itself. There was no answer. I tried. No answer. I tried again and again. No answer.
"Rachael, there will be many peoples in that hospital after the bomb blast today. They may not be able to pick up the phone at all. Let us save the battery."
I looked around the van I'd named Henry. It was steeped in happy memories of our weekend away. It felt so wrong being in there with Paul under such different circumstances.
"OK," I took a deep breath and prepared to be brave. "What did Indica say, exactly?"
"I don't know. That Nishantha had been hurt in the bomb blast this morning. That he was at the hospital. And that the doctors say he will not live."
"OK. What are his injuries?"
"I don't know, Rachael."
"What? You must have asked?"
"There was no time, he had to go."
"Why, what was happening?"
"Rachael, I do not know, I am sorry."

"Was it the Tamil Tigers?"
"That is what they say."
"What did they do?"
"It was a suicide bomber."
"What did they blow up?"
"A government building, I think."
"What was Nishantha doing there?" I asked crossly.
"I do not know."
I was becoming unfairly fractious with Paul so I stopped talking for fear of what might come out next. Instead, I glared out of the window, silently cursing every vehicle that got in our way. Paul drove like a maniac on speed, flooring it the whole way. Henry was being put through his paces now and I just hoped he could handle it. Breaking down before getting to Colombo would have probably resulted in me doing something crazy like thumbing a lift.
After gathering my composure, I apologised to Paul for being short with him. He reminded me that he was hurting, too, and we both sat in silence as tears streamed down our faces. Paul drove in silence for a while, gripping the steering wheel tightly and hunching his shoulders forward. I carried on looking out of the window, my body limp and numb. After everything we had been through I did not believe I was going to lose Nishantha now, in this way. We'd had all the bad luck and drama we were due, surely? The thought of losing him was too unbearable to comprehend. As I continued to stare out of the window I caught a glimpse of my distraught reflection. I immediately thought about Nishantha's painting, the one I had seen when I first met him. Thinking back to that day was too emotive so I tried to think of something else, anything else that would not break the damn holding in a whole sea of fraught emotions. I wished there was a radio in the van to distract me. I tried to think of a song, a happy one, one that held no memories and so could not provoke any emotional response.

Nelly the elephant packed her trunk and said goodbye to the circus...

Nelly the Elephant was the song I had to sing on a first aid course while learning CPR. Once the song was done it was time to stop and give mouth to mouth. Why that came into my head I do not know. I prayed that Paul would refrain from talking to me because if he asked me if I was alright I knew I'd break down.
Off she went with a trumpet-y-trump...
When we slowed down we saw two young lovers playfully cavorting by the side of the road. A lump formed in my throat so hard it hurt when I swallowed. I nearly cracked as I thought back to Nishantha and me playing around after the parada.
Trump, trump, trump.
Paul had little choice in taking me to Colombo. He was then snapped at, interrogated and sent to Coventry, yet still he was amazing at the hospital, the way he found out where Nishantha was and where we had to go. The hospital was in chaos and I floated in a useless haze after him as he took charge of the situation. I do not remember much about where we went as we hurried around the clinical corridors of the rabbit warren. Most of the commotion had been in the reception area as people tried to locate their loved ones or find out if they were even there. Eventually, we found ourselves outside a side room occupied by Indica, Soma, Komari, Johan and baby Johan.
Everybody looked at me open-mouthed, while Soma brought her hands to her face in disbelief, or perhaps in relief. I don't know.
"Indica, how is he? How is he?" I broke down and cried as Indica came and put and an arm around me. He spoke to Paul in Sinhala then to me.
"Rachael, what are you doing here? How did…?"
"Tell me he is alright, Indica," I cried. I could barely hold myself up as I begged Indica for some good news.
"Rachael, come outside."
I walked with Indica and we sat in the hallway on the floor.
"Can't you take me to him, please?" My plea had been reduced to an exhausted whisper.
"Rachael, Nishantha was involved in a bomb blast this morning. A bus was blown up outside a government building, by a child

suicide bomber. He has surface injuries and a head injury. They tell us they are now relieving pressure, for his head injury."

"He is in surgery?"

"Yes."

"How long has he been there?" I asked more calmly.

"Just over an hour," Indica said looking at his watch.

We looked at each other, united in grief and both crying.

"I can't lose him, Indica."

"I know, I know. How is it that you are here?"

"I came to surprise him. I came to..." I nearly blurted out my secret but that would have been wrong. Nishantha should know first.

"I just came to surprise him."

"Oh. He has been working through the night and every hour of the day to save for a ticket to see you. He missed you so badly, Rachael. It is amazing that you are here."

"Well, August was too far away. Why was he in that building, Indica?"

"He was not inside, he was just walking by. He was collecting a payment for the furniture we had delivered to the building down the road. He was just walking by when the bus blew up. They say the child was supposed to walk into the government building but I do not know."

"Did you see it happen?"

"No. I was sleeping in the van, just around the corner."

"But his van was in Kandy?"

"No, the delivery van. Nishantha has been delivering furniture to make money."

"Oh."

"I was going to go with him but he tell me to stay and get some sleep. I had been helping him since very early this morning, loading the van in Kandy and delivering furniture from there to here. The explosion woke me and I ran towards it. I tried to reach the building where Nishantha should have been but I could not get by. There was so much dust, I just could not see, I could not breathe. People were screaming and bodies lay on the ground. I tried to help the people who needed it most. The ones laying quiet, but I did not know what to do. So I found a nurse and took her to a body I'd seen, but it was too late. They were dead. The nurse spotted another man laying still not far from the dead man. His face was so badly cut on the side I could see that I only knew it was him by his clothes."

"Nishantha?"

"Yes. The nurse tried to keep him awake but he fell back asleep. She said he must get straight to hospital but then many people needed to go also. We were lucky. That nurse made sure he was one of the first to be taken."

My heart constricted in my chest at the thought of Nishantha laying there, needing help. I should have been there for him. In fact, he shouldn't have been there in the first place.

"I am so glad you were there for him Indica, and the nurse. Did he speak at all?"

"He said nothing I could understand."

"So his injuries?"

"He has no broken bones, just many cuts to his skin. They had to be cleaned but the doctors, they do not worry about the cuts. They worry about his head."

"What is it they are doing now?"

"There is a lady, Dr Olberholze, she tell us they are relieving pressure building in his head. She say we should prepare ourselves for the worst. That is all I know."

"No, the worst will not happen, he is still alive, there is still hope. Maybe I should talk to this doctor, to find out more."

Indica looked up at the door that stood between us and his family. I followed his gaze.

"Johan and Komari. They don't want me here, do they?"

"I do not know. They did not believe you loved their son. Maybe now they will see that you do."

"I do, Indica, I do with all my being. That's why I know he will come through this. We have been through too much for it all to end now. Nishantha and I are meant to be together, he is going to live to tell this tale. He has to."

"Nishantha is one of the strongest men I have met. He will fight. He will."

We sat in silence for a moment while I pictured Nishantha delivering his furniture in Colombo. As I imagined him being pleased he was a few rupees closer to his airline ticket, a mass of guilt turned my stomach.

"Oh, Indica. It's my fault, isn't it? He was only there because he was making money to come to England. If he'd married Somana he would have been somewhere else altogether..."

"Rachael, hush, you cannot think like that. Nishantha lived for himself, he was doing what he felt was right, in his heart..."

"You mean he *lives* for himself, Indica."

"Yes, lives."

I sighed and tried to regain my composure because I was all over the place. One minute I was positive, the next I was inconsolable.

Indica returned to his usual soft tones and gave me a new pearl of wisdom.

"Do you remember how it hurt you that Nishantha blamed himself for taking you back to the Suisse View that night?"

"Yes. I tried everything to get him to see he was wrong."

"Well, it would hurt Nishantha to know you blamed yourself for this. He, too, would try everything to show you that you were wrong."

"I know you are right. I need to see him. I need to see him so badly, Indica." I cried into a tissue as a new ache ripped through me.

"I will go and talk to Soma's parents. I will make sure you can see him when he comes out of surgery."

"Thank you."

While Indica spoke to Johan and Komari I asked a nurse if I could speak to Nishantha's doctor. She took me to a South African lady, Dr Oberholze who informed me that Johan or Komari would have to be present if I wanted news because I wasn't a family member. I hoped Indica had smoothed things over. I was well aware they had the power to keep me out of the loop. I knew they could refuse to let me see him and, after what I had done, who would blame them?

The doctor disappeared and came back with a nurse then we all entered the side room.

"Hello, everyone," I managed to say, my lip trembling.

"Hello, Rachael," Soma said. Johan and Komari looked at me but said nothing. Baby Johan ran over to me and gave me a bear hug. I'm not sure who was comforting who. His mother and father looked on in shock.

"I am so glad you are here, Rachael. My brother, he love you. You make him so happy," baby Johan gabbled quickly as though he was worried he would be hushed. I broke out of our hug so I could look him in the eye.

"And how are you doing? Are you OK?" I said, gently brushing the side of his face with my fingers. He nodded and I explained why the doctor was here.

"We are going to be told some information about your brother from this lovely doctor here," I told him as he looked her up and down. I kept half an eye on his parents. They hadn't thrown me out yet so I carried on.

"Some of those things may be hard to understand and some of them may be sad. Would you like to stay and hear them, or would you like somebody to wait outside with you while she talks to us. Then we can explain it all to you?"

"I want to stay," he said to me, then, to his father, "I want to stay."

Johan nodded yes to his son.

The nurse translated in Sinhala while the doctor spoke to us in a strong Afrikaans accent.

"Now, before we start, I just need to make sure, Johan, Komari, are you happy for this lady and this gentleman to be here?" She was referring to Paul.

There was a delay as the nurse made her translation.

Indica and Soma looked tense as they waited for the answer.

Komari waggled her head. My heart sank as it looked like a "no". Then she smiled as tears streamed down her face and she held her hand out to me.

"Yes," she said. I took her hand and smiled back. Looking into her eyes I could see her pain, and I think she could see mine. Johan said nothing and his face remained unchanged.

"Right then. As you know, Mr Sangrasagra has incurred a severe blow to the back of the head," Dr Oberholze began. "This has caused a haematoma to form; a haematoma is another word we use for a blood clot, ja?"

We all nodded to show we were keeping up so far. I noted she spoke very matter of fact. It was as though she had forgotten she was talking about a real human being. The hospital was in a declared state of emergency so I decided to just be grateful she spoke English.

"The clot is causing pressure on the brain and the surgeon is busy removing this just now. There is also further swelling to the brain that we were monitoring before Mr. Sangrasagra went into surgery. We found that his ICP levels were very high…"

"The what?" I asked. Now there was a new language barrier, that of the medical profession.

"Intracranial pressure. The levels are high. If the swelling increases any further it may be necessary to drill into the skull to relieve the pressure. Do you have any questions?"

Yeah, where's your bedside manner?

"This swelling, could it increase or will it go down?"

"At this stage, I would not like to speculate. All we can do is hope that the brain swelling stabilises. I will come back and find you the minute there is any change."

"Doctor," I started, as Dr Oberholze made to leave. "Is there any chance he could suffer brain damage?"

Dr Oberholze turned to face us all again and looked around the room at the expectant faces.

"If he pulls through the surgery there is a chance he could be left with a certain amount of brain damage, ja. It is impossible to tell at this stage. All I can advise is that you hope for the best, and prepare for the worst. Mr. Sangrasaga…"

"Nishantha," Soma interjected. "His name is Nishantha."

"*Nishantha* is in the best hands, of that I can assure you."

After the doctor and the nurse left us to it, Indica asked Paul to take Soma home so she could pick Daniel up from their neighbour. Johan asked if he would take baby Johan home and look after him at theirs for the night. Paul agreed and baby Johan left without argument. I think the shock and emotion of the day had drained him. Indica persuaded me to go outside with everybody so that he could have a cigarette once they were gone. I didn't want to go anywhere but he managed to convince me now was the best time as we had just had an update and Nishantha was still in surgery. When we got outside I was shocked to see it was growing dark already. The warm night air was a relief from the cold air-conditioned rooms inside the hospital. All my belongings were still in the van so I used the opportunity to pull out a few items of clothes and essentials.

Indica offered me a cigarette but I declined. Before Indica lit up, he looked at me awkwardly.

"Rachael, I am sorry to have to ask you this, but, what will you do if Nishantha has damage to his brain?"

"Indica, you're supposed to be keeping me positive."

"I am not asking for me."

"Oh, I see. Well, you can tell Johan and Komari I am not going anywhere. However Nishantha wakes, he is still the man I love. If it means looking after him myself and taking him back to England, that is what I'll do."

"You do not need to worry about that. He is going to wake up like his old self. I am sorry to have asked, I promised Johan and Komari I would."

"Its fine, Indica, just forget it now."

Indica sat and smoked as we swapped 'typical Nishantha' stories. We talked about puddles and how Indica knew from the very beginning that there was a mutual attraction between his brother-in-law and me. We reminisced over all the times I tried to deny it and we laughed over how I had fooled no one. Being with Indica was comforting, familiar, a connection to Nishantha. Back in the days when Indica was my only link to Nishantha, I would seek him out to lessen my pining. I used to think those times were hell, longing for Nishantha, believing I would never have him. If only I knew then that I would be sitting outside a hospital thinking I'd do anything to go back to those days, when Nishantha was safe and well.

Back in the hospital, Johan and Komari had fallen asleep in their side room while waiting for Nishantha to come out of surgery. Indica and I joined them and before long, he was asleep, too. I got up to turn the overly bright hospital light off. Light from the corridor shone in through the glass above the door, which gave the room a soft glow. Watching them sleep made me feel alone in my pain. Closing my eyes, I pictured Nishantha's fingers caressing my arms. I could almost feel my skin react to his imagined touch. I could feel the kiss of his lips on my neck, the warmth of his breath on my skin. Then as I began to give way to exhaustion, and fall into a dreamlike state, I could even hear him whisper.

Chapter 21

"Rachael, look! It's for you!"
"A puppy? Why are you giving me a puppy?"
"Isn't he beautiful? You have to take care of him now."
"But how will I get him home?"
"You will find a way."
"Why can't you look after him?"
"I have to go now, Rachael. You know that."
"Do you have to go to work?"

"**Hello? Mr** Sangrasagra? Mrs Sangrasagra? Hello! I am so sorry to wake you, but I have some news."
I jumped out of my skin as the steely voice of Dr Oberholze yanked me from my dream. The rest of the room slowly stirred to consciousness. I had been in such a deep sleep that it took me a moment to get up to speed. I had also been dreaming about Nishantha. He was very excited, animatedly so, which is usually uncharacteristic for him. We were by the swing chair in his front garden and he was trying to give me a puppy. It was large and sandy coloured, like a Labrador, and it squirmed in his arms as if eager to get down. Nishantha was struggling to hold it any longer and he wanted me to take it from him.
It was time to switch mindsets. I was not in Nishantha's front garden. I was in a hospital side room with Dr Oberholze. The emptiness of reality pressed down on my chest like a sheet of lead. The translator was with the doctor. She kept her eyes on the doctor's mouth.
"They will be taking Nishantha out of surgery just now. I am pleased to say the blood clot was removed successfully."
"Can we see him?" I asked, trying to stave off the need to retch again. My morning sickness felt strong again due to lack of food. It was worse because my stomach was empty. I wanted to take a

biscuit from my bag to stave off the nausea but it seemed inappropriate to pull out a packet of Party Rings at this time.
"Ja, you can see him when they have moved him. Two at a time, please. It is early days and you must know the swelling in the brain is still a problem."
Johan said something in Sinhala to which the doctor replied, "No, he is still unconscious. We need to keep him that way for the time being while we continue to monitor his ICP levels. He is going to remain on his ventilator, also, for the time being."
"Was there any brain damage?" Indica asked in English.
"There is no way to know the extent of the damage at this stage. By all means, talk to him, hold his hand, let him know you are there, ay? It is possible he may be able to hear you. So who would like to go in first?"
Johan got up and went in with Komari while Indica shrugged at me. I knew they had every right to go in first but it nearly killed me to know I could be in there with him and wasn't. I concentrated on the fact that his operation had been a success and he was out of surgery. Both Indica and I were in better spirits now and we both spoke almost excitedly. He called Soma to tell her and we sat in the hospital canteen eating snacks to pass the time until it was our turn to sit with Nishantha. I ate two oat biscuits from a pack of three to help with my all day morning sickness then started worrying for the baby growing inside me. I was meant to be taking folic acid and eating a balanced diet, yet the only thing I could keep down were biscuits.
When it was finally time for Indica and I to sit with Nishantha, another nurse came to get us. My heart thumped in eager anticipation in my chest as we walked up to his door. Then I saw Johan and Komari's faces. They looked like ghosts. I accelerated from excitement to dread in less than a second and suddenly felt scared at what I was about to see. Indica saw the hollow in their haunted eyes, too so he took my hand and squeezed it tightly as we entered Nishantha's room. Nishantha was in a room of four and each bed had the curtain pulled around it. The nurse pulled back Nishantha's bay curtain and left. He was unconscious and

connected to a ventilator, a ICP monitor, and he had a saturation monitor on his finger to monitor blood oxygen levels. There were tubes exiting his body everywhere. His legs were covered with a white hospital sheet while his chest was left bare due to his raised temperature. Surface cuts flecked the right side of his face, chest and arm as if he had been hit by a small meteor shower. The entire area had been sprayed with yellow and some of the deeper cuts had been dressed with gauze.

"What is this? Why is he yellow?" Indica asked me in a whisper.

"It's iodine. It'll help prevent infection." I said as we stood staring at Nishantha laying in his bed.

"Rachael, you sit here," Indica said as he pulled me over to the seat at Nishantha's left where he looked less scathed. A bandage was wrapped around his now shaven head. With Nishantha's muscular physique, tanned skin and dark eyes, he had always been a picture of health and vitality. Lying helplessly in his hospital bed, he looked like a fallen gladiator. I held his hand tightly and brought it up to my lips.

"Nishantha, it's Rachael. I'm going to be here when you wake up, take as long as you need baby, I'll be here," I spoke into his hand and kissed it lovingly. My tears dripped down onto his skin so I wiped it away. I then kissed his cheek and dabbed his forehead with a damp, tepid cloth. Indica sat there with much the same expression as Nishantha's parents had had. I think the sight of Nishantha was more shocking to them than me because I was used to seeing people hooked up to machines in hospital beds. I used to have to meet my mum at work in A&E so I sort of grew up with it.

As the hours rolled by and the outside world ceased to exist, we all took hour-long shifts sitting with Nishantha and talking to him, breaking only for him to receive medical care. Indica fetched Soma the next evening so she could see her brother. She wept when she saw him for the first time. I had sat and stared at him for so long I completely forgot it would be a shock for her to see him this way. Having to be strong for Soma while she was there probably did me some good. It stopped me indulging in my biggest fears.

I felt bad for poor baby Johan who had been told to stay at home. His parents considered him too young to be sitting at the hospital for any longer than he already had.

While Soma was there we were given some more good news. The Indian doctor who had taken over from Dr Oberholze told us that Nishantha's brain swelling had reduced back to normal levels and now we were just waiting for him to wake up on his own. We all hugged and told Soma she had brought us luck. Indica took me to the hospital canteen to give Nishantha's immediate family some time alone together. It was like old times, him trying to get me to eat something, me feeling sick at the very idea of food, except this time I had to eat, I had no choice. He bought me a sandwich, which I gobbled down while Indica tucked into some rice and curry. Although he seemed OK at this moment, Indica's face looked weighed down and the corners of his mouth slanted downwards. He didn't look much like the Indica I knew and loved at all.

"You still have not talked to his parents, have you?" he asked me.

"I haven't cleared the air if that's what you mean. I was waiting for an appropriate time but there never seems to be one."

"Johan and Komari are coming back with me when I take Soma home. They will sleep at theirs tonight and come back here tomorrow. Komari said you can stay at theirs also... Maybe you could talk with them then?"

"Really? They said I could stay?"

"Yes, it seems they have forgiven you."

A tear welled up in my eye as I realised they had accepted me. That would make Nishantha so happy.

"Maybe we will look back at this one day and think of it as the trauma that brought us all back together," I said to Indica as I stared into space.

"That would be good," Indica said with a brief smile that momentarily defied the weight of gravity. "So are you going to go with Johan and Komari?"

"Nishantha could wake up at any moment. I want to stay here

until he does. I promised him I'd be here. And now I have good news to tell him: his parents have accepted me!"
"Yes, that would make him very happy, for his family and his wife to be close."
"Wife?"
"Well, you are heading that way are you not?"
"What? Has he said something?"
Indica grinned, involuntarily this time.
"Tell me! Tell me, oh please tell me!"
"Why do we always end up with you begging for information on Nishantha?"
"Oh come on, Indica, please."
Indica sat back in his chair. "I can't Rachael. I would be betraying him as he lies up there. It would not be right, in my heart."
I understood that more than he realised. I had kept the pregnancy from him for the same reason.
When another evening drew in, Indica dropped Johan, Komari and Soma back home for the night. He told me he was going to catch a few hours sleep himself before returning later and offered again to take me with them. As much as the idea of a proper wash and a real bed appealed to me, I could not peel myself away and I had no intention of leaving Nishantha alone. The Indian doctor told me the bed next to Nishantha was now free and I could sleep there for a few hours. I wondered about the fate of the person who'd lain there before me but thought better than to ask. The doctor told me I might have to get up at a moment's notice but I still slept soundly knowing I was as close to Nishantha as I could possibly be. I told them to wake me if there was any change in him. I desperately needed that sleep, more than I'd realised.

"Nishantha, how did he get into my snow globe? How can I look after him in there?
Nishantha...?
Nishantha...?"

My dream woke me before anything else did. I was in my

childhood bedroom looking into my snow globe. The little Labrador puppy from my last dream was looking out from inside, his front two paws up on the glass. I was talking to Nishantha as though he was in the room with me but when I turned to see why he hadn't answered, I found I was alone. It may not sound like the worst dream but it left me feeling helpless and abandoned. I woke quickly, feeling distraughtly alone, so I jumped up out of bed to make sure Nishantha was still lying in the bed besides me. He was. Seeing him remedied me but I still felt the need to be close to him so I decided to make the most of my time with him without his family here. As I drew up a chair that had been moved to one side, I noticed his chest had been covered up. Someone had been in to tend to him while I'd been asleep. Before sitting down, I kissed his forehead again and told him I loved him in English and Sinhala. I cried as I held his hand and talked about old times while inside, I willed him to wake up.

While stroking Nishantha's face I knew without question I would never leave him, no matter how he woke up. Putting all negative thoughts aside I thought about him being a daddy to our baby, taking him or her for walks around the field behind the house, then, later, playing cricket with them and the neighbours. It was such a perfect vision it made me desperate for it to come true. Every inch of my body yearned for it.

"Nishantha, you are going to be a dad," I said, tears streaming down my face as I thought of how different this moment was to how I'd imagined it to be on the flight over.

"That is why I'm here. I came to tell you that I'm pregnant with your child. Please wake up Nishantha, I love you so much…" I broke down and held his hand to my face again. I was desperate for him to wake up. To have just the shell of him there was paining me beyond belief. I started thinking back to the times we had spent alone together. I was trying to work out if I had appreciated them enough. I wanted to step back in time to make sure I had. All the things I'd been worrying about then paled into insignificance now. His parents approval, if he would like England, when I was going to see him again, how I would look when I surprised him by showing up unannounced. I felt sick that I had spent so long pondering over such things instead of appreciating what I had.

"You're the most amazing person I have ever known Nishantha, please wake up."

Nothing.

I started reading aloud what I had learnt in Sinhala. If he was awake, I could just imagine him trying to teach me the right pronunciation. The thought of it made me smile. Then I looked at his perfect face and panicked. Why wasn't he waking up? Was I just being impatient? The doctor said he could wake at any moment so long ago.

I rested my head on his hand and closed my eyes. I was tired again. Lack of proper sleep made my head spin but I couldn't let myself fall asleep. I sipped some water and rubbed tiger balm on my temples to try to stay awake.

"Nishantha, do you remember our first dance?" I asked, taking myself back in my mind's eye to my first night in *The Ivory*. Then, looking around to make sure I was alone, I squeezed Nishantha's hand even tighter and sung softly the words from Eric Clapton's *Tears in Heaven*. As I sung through a voice broken with emotion, I saw movement behind Nishantha's closed eyelids. They began to open, slowly. My heart seemed to stop beating in my chest and I sat up straight and accidently nudged the pot of tiger balm on the floor. It landed noisily and rolled out of our bay.

"Nishantha! It's me, Rachael." He continued to look at me then closed his eyes again.

"Come on, it's time to wake up now baby, it's time to wake up."

My heart raced wildly as I waited for him to open his eyes again. I squeezed his hand tightly. After what felt like an eternity, Nishantha's sleepy eyes opened again and he looked right at me, holding his gaze this time.

"Oh, Nishantha. It's going to be OK, you are going to be just fine! I love you so much."

Nishantha squeezed my hand weakly and closed his eyes again.

"Is this yours?" the nurse who had translated before asked as she popped in through the curtain. She put the tiger balm down on the bed. I was glad she was back on shift, it beat having someone here who had no history with us.

"Nurse, he is awake! He opened his eyes, look, watch!" I said excitedly as tears of happiness ad relief graced my cheeks.

The nurse smiled at my elation and watched Nishantha expectantly. Nothing happened as we both watched on in anticipation.

"He did, he opened them. Just give him a moment longer," I said to the nurse. Then to Nishantha, "Come on Nishantha, it's me, Rachael."

Nishantha opened his eyes again.

"See! He is awake! Look!" I said excitedly to the nurse. As I smiled at her I saw her face change to one of shock horror. Whipping my head back around to look at Nishantha I saw his eyes had rolled back in their sockets and his torso had lurched forward rigidly. The monitors went crazy and within seconds a team of doctors had swarmed around him as I stood and watched helpless yet again. I was pulled out towards the door away from the bay.

"What is happening? He woke up. What is happening?" I blurted out to the nurse who had escorted me out.

"No speak, no speak," he said. Apparently he did not speak English.

"Rachael! What is happening?"

"Indica! Thank God you are here! Nishantha just woke up. He looked at me, but then he started fitting, or something. I don't know what's happening. Tell this nurse I want to know what is happening. Tell him!" I was a hysterical mess. "He opened his eyes, Indica. He opened his eyes," I cried as Indica tried to pacify me with a hug. Indica and the nurse exchanged words that to me were just noise.

"He does not know. He say wait for the doctors to come out." Indica said when they had finished talking.

"No, I want to go back in..." Indica and the nurse pulled me back into that dreaded side room as I fought to go back into

Nishantha's room.

"Please. Rachael. He say wait here, let them do their job."

There was no arguing with that.

"So he opened his eyes?" Indica said to me with a calm and positive tone.

"Yes, yes and he, he squeezed my hand, Indica. He squeezed my hand." Indica gave me another hug as I sobbed from the frustration of not knowing what was going on. The wait was long, or so it seemed. Time in hospitals distorts and slows down, I'm sure it does.

The side door opened in entered the Indian doctor.

"What are they doing? What's going on?" I pleaded as I clawed Indica's hand for holding it so tight.

"He may have had a brain haemorrhage. This can happen in this circumstance. He has had a cardiac arrest. We are doing everything we can for him. You must wait here. Perhaps you can call his parents?" he said, directing the last part to Indica.

"I shall call his parents."

"If they can't get a lift or there's not enough room tell them to get a taxi, I'll pay."

When Indica came back I was a broken shell, sitting exactly where I'd just been put. I'd had more than I could take. Indica sat down next to me.

"Has the doctor been back?"

"No," I said despondently.

"Rachael, he will be OK. He has to be."

"I can't lose him, I can't," I whimpered.

"Come here." Indica pulled me into him as he put an arm around my shoulders. I sobbed into his shirt sleeve, letting out all my pain.

"They think he has had a brain haemorrhage, Indica. He was having a heart attack. I don't get it. They said the swelling had gone down."

A few minutes later the Indian doctor walked into the room and closed the door. Indica and I stood up and clasped hands tightly for support. The doctor said something to Indica, in Sinhala I guess, although he was Indian.

Indica replied in English so as not to discount me.

"His parents, sister and brother, they are on their way," Indica said.

The doctor wore a sorry expression on his face.

I knew what was coming. My body turned cold and numb in preparation and my red, tear stained face screwed up as more tears fell onto my cheeks.

"I am very sorry. Nishantha suffered a massive brain haemorrhage as we thought. He also had a cardiac arrest. We tried to restart his heart. I'm afraid we could not revive him."

The room whirled until I didn't know which way was up. Unable to accept the news, I pulled out of Indica's grip.

"No, no, he can't be dead, I don't believe it, he can't be…"

My legs buckled under the weight of his words and I fell to the ground. Shaking, I held my stomach, it pained as if I'd been punched there. My entire body rejected his words, refusing to accept them as truth. As I sobbed the words no, no, no, no, over and over, Indica tried to put his arms around me.

"Get off me. Don't touch me," I screamed. Grief stricken and unable to deal with truth that Nishantha had died, I couldn't bear for him to touch me. It was as though even my skin could feel the pain. I pushed him away with conviction. So desperate I was to have Nishantha's arms around me, anybody else's only highlighted the fact that that would never happen again. I cried hysterically and dug my nails into my arms until the skin broke. Indica prized my arms apart and forced me to look at him as he wiped tears away from his bloodshot eyes.

He looked broken and in pain too so this time I put my arms around him as we both cried over our loss. Consumed by grief and unable to comprehend Nishantha was dead I was inconsolable.

When we were allowed to sit with Nishantha's body, I decided to do so on my own. I walked in slowly, sat down on the chair and gently held his hand. It still felt warm. His face looked so peaceful. It was as though he would stir if I just whispered into his ear. All the tubes had been taken away and the machines had been switched off, yet even as I sat with him, I still didn't believe he was gone. I could still feel him here. I was so sure he was going to open his eyes and look at me as he did just a little while before, back when he was going to wake up and we were going to be a family. But I had to accept the truth. When Nishantha closed his eyes that day, he closed them forever.

Three Years Later

DABDA: denial, anger, bargaining, depression, acceptance. What a wonderfully clinical acronym for the grieving process. What a shame it ends there. They should add an "S" on the end and make is DABDAS. It could stand for sadness, sorrow, self-pity, scars, because you are left with all these things once you have come out the other side.
Personally, I spent a lot of time hanging around the first D and then the last D before I completed the process. For the days that followed after Nishantha's death, I was a wreck. I wanted to smoke and drink and I didn't want to eat. But the life growing inside my belly didn't permit me the luxury to self destruct so I made myself eat even though full from grief.
Apart from the obvious sense of grief and loss that comes from losing a loved one, I also carried around a cutting sense of anguish about Nishantha not knowing he was going to be a father. Why didn't I tell him when he opened his eyes? I tore myself apart over not making the most of those few moments. I'd thought they were the beginning of so many more, not the end. I was even angry with the nurse who gave me back my tiger balm. If she hadn't have interrupted, I might have had the chance to tell him.
Jenny watched me suffer that fact for two weeks before finally confessing that she had told Ed I was pregnant, despite her promise not to. In turn, Ed had told Nishantha, despite his promise not to. Ed thought Nishantha needed a 'heads up' so he could gather his thoughts before I got there. He didn't tell him when I would be going because he didn't want to ruin all the surprises. Jenny was so afraid of my reaction that she made my mum and Ed come over to our flat so they could be there when she told me. So Nishantha did know he was going to be a father and, according to Ed, Nishantha had reacted by saying, 'I do not know what to say, yet I can-not stop smiling.' I cried tears of happiness when Jenny

made her confession and the three worried looking faces before me breathed a collective sigh of relief.

As the layer of anguish disappeared I found I was carrying around with me a lot of hate, bitterness and guilt. Hate for the terrorists indiscriminate killing of such a good man, bitterness at the untimely and unjust death of such a good man and guilt for being part of the reason he was there in the first place. I know Indica was right, that Nishantha was living his life how he wanted, but there were times when that failed to ease the pain. My mum and step-dad told me you can't play the 'what if' game because who is to say he wouldn't have come to his end sooner if he hadn't met me. As they held my hand and gave me their advice I silently thought maybe they were right. Maybe Nishantha might have met his end with the terrorists at the Tooth Temple parada if I hadn't been there. And I know he would have tried to help that baby at the Suisse View if he hadn't been so worried about me. Logically, I know the "what if" game is pointless. Unfortunately, logic and grief do not always have much to do with each other. Upon leaving Sri Lanka, Soma told me she me she was happy I had given her brother the chance to know love. Her words gave me more strength than all the other help I was given put together. I promised Soma and Indica I would be back to see them. However, I am yet to deliver on my word. I still find the concept of Sri Lanka without Nishantha too painful to think about. Another source of comfort to me was a challenge I set myself – a charity climb up Mount Everest. As I trained and raised money it was as though I was working toward being close to Nishantha again for that is where he said he wanted his soul to rest when his time came. I'm not sure how healthy that thought process was now but my friends and family supported the idea because it gave me something worthwhile to strive toward instead of giving way to depression. They all knew the only reason I wanted to do it was because I was trying to hang on to Nishantha in any way I could. Logically I knew Nishantha hadn't become a mountain but, again, logic and grief do not go hand in hand. Sometimes we find comfort in the strangest of places and mine was a little way up that mountain.

Completing the climb gave me a massive and unexpected sense of achievement, partly because my baby boy was only thirteen months old when I completed it and partly because it was hard work, it pushed me both mentally and physically. I don't care what anyone says, I could feel his presence on that climb. Most of the other climbers I met there had also been driven by the loss of somebody close. We were all united by this sad common denominator and, of course, the challenge we faced together on our climb. When I reached base camp back at the bottom of the mountain, I really felt strongly that I had honoured Nishantha's memory.

I decided to bring the baby up at my parent's place in Ulverston. Leon made it easy for me to leave work by turning the charity into an overpriced, moneymaking volunteer work scheme where people pay to work as a volunteer abroad. It is now a profit-making business and Leon is a very rich man. He paid me off, giving just over what my maternity entitlement would have been. He kept Victor on. Victor wasn't happy with the change but he was too worried he wouldn't find another job at his age.

Although I had moved away, I found an unlikely friend in Derren. I think the birth and death in my life made him realise that there are bigger things out there than him, or maybe he just finally grew into his skin. We all find our way in our own time. Jacky, Laura and Jenny all dote on my little boy when they visit or when I go back down to West Sussex. Jacky's advice about making sure I was prepared to raise a baby on my own had turned out to be good advice, but she was genuinely upset that it had turned out the way it had for me. I named my baby boy Eric. Eric was the only name Nishantha had talked about and I wanted a name other boys his age were unlikely to have, so Eric it was. I plan to tell Eric he was named after Eric Clapton when he is a little older. And I will tell him why. Laura says she is glad our first song wasn't by Percy Sledge because naming a baby Percy would be plain wrong.

Tears in Heaven still takes me right back to my first dance with Nishantha and brings tears to my eyes that I wipe away discretely so Eric doesn't see his mummy crying. But I can't protect Eric from everything. The Tiger attacks in Sri Lanka may have ceased for now but terrorism has become a worry on a global scale. Nishantha died for being Sinhalese; it now seems it is a crime to be Western. This is the world I have to bring my son up in. Nishantha would be heartbroken to know how terrorism has so sadly swept the modern world.

I hope every day that Eric grows up to have some of his father's attributes, other than his looks, that is. Eric has tanned skin and huge dark eyes like his father. His hair is curly and dark. I struggle not to give into his every whim when he looks up at me with those huge, familiar eyes. I think he has cottoned on to this. He is a curious boy, full of energy and into everything. He also displays patience, even at his young age. Sometimes, when Eric's little face is gazing out the window, lost in a daydream, I can see a glimmer of Nishantha shining through. I like to think of Eric as the puppy in my dream and I like to think Nishantha died assured I would take care of the symbolic puppy, our son.

Two weeks ago I left Eric with my mum to spend the weekend at Laura's place. My mum thought a weekend away would do me some good. While there I went out to do some clothes shopping and pick us up a sandwich and a latte so we could have a lazy lunch at Laura's. She was sleeping off a hangover from indulging in too much wine the night before. It was then I bumped into Nick Rivers. I barely recognized him when I saw him in Starbucks. I was standing in the queue, skilfully balancing my shopping bags on my knee while trying to tell the man on the end of my mobile, no, I do not want to purchase card protection for my cards and, no, I am not interested in your survey, thank you very much, when Nick tapped me on the shoulder. He had lost his long dreadlocks and now had a dusty blonde, almost shaven head. He had the weathered, deep golden tan of a man who spent all his time outside in the sun. When he greeted me with a friendly enthusiasm I thought, who is this nut? Then I realised who it was and we sat and drank the coffees I'd ordered for Laura and I. He told me he had finished his degree in marine biology and is now living in Costa Rica looking after turtles and studying reef environments. We arranged to meet up the following day, with Laura too, for it was her I'd come to see, and I was surprised to see there might be something between us after all. He knows I am not quite ready to enter a new relationship but he has invited Eric and me to stay with him in Costa Rica all the same. He told me I have to come; I owe him a hotdog.

Today is the third anniversary of Nishantha's death. I am sitting alone on the cool sand waiting for the sun to rise over the English shore. I find myself contemplating how I never used to believe in fate. I thought fate was a word overused by romantics. Watching my little boy splat his way through all the puddles on the beach while my mum looks after him, I can categorically say I was wrong. Fate plays a part in everybody's life.

Watching the sunrise always reminds me of sitting on the beach in Colombo with Nishantha. As I wait for the sun to rise today, I steal this rare, quiet moment to myself to scribble a few thoughts down to Nishantha.

So will I be purchasing a Spanish phrase book any time soon? I can't say for sure. If I can learn to let go of the past, there is a chance I may. After all, this is only one chapter in my life's story – at least, that is how Nishantha would want me to see it.

All I do know for sure is that fate brought Nishantha and me together, if only briefly, and fate gave us our child before he died. Losing Nishantha broke me, but having known him in the first place gave me the tools I needed to put myself back together. No matter how painful it is proving to be to say goodbye to him, I believe very much that we were meant to be.

It was all *meant to be.*

A few scribbled thoughts

Dear N,

The first birds make their morning call,
The first rays of sunlight touch down upon all.
Slowly the waters reach out to dry sand,
The lapping tide caresses new land.
I close my eyes to imagine you here
Sharing this moment, feeling you near.
A rainbow of emotion fills me inside
But trapped in this prism the colours soon die.
Eyes still shut tightly I go back in time,
When I had you there, your hand in mine.
Unbearably my heart still aches for you,
Then I open my eyes. The sky has turned blue.
The sun warms my body like the love I used to know
And I breathe out deeply, letting you go.

Love Always, R

Coming Soon...

The 5ᵗʰ Agenda

Alana, Kevin, Jada and Nicole all have their own wants, needs and agendas, but with one person's happiness depending on another's demise, who will prevail and at what cost? With misery, heartache, and a life hanging in the balance, is all this chaos really down to our four? Or is it down to somebody else entirely, somebody with their own, hidden, agenda?

PROLOGUE

Present Day

Alana: Brisbane, Australia

Mending Jason's vase had been sitting on Alana's to do list for weeks, right between hand washing her Lipsy top and defrosting the freezer. Today was the day she could finally cross it off, done. The length of time it had been outstanding seemed directly proportionate to the satisfaction felt when penning a line through the middle of those words, 'Jason's vase'. The broken lip of Jason's hideous cerulean blue vase looked as good as new, almost, Alana thought as she held the pieces fast to allow the glue to append. It wasn't long before she found herself smiling at the incident that caused the breakage at her 30ᵗʰ birthday party a few months back. The details were hazy; too many Black Russians kind of hazy, but she knew it involved a broom handle, a blindfold and copious amounts of neat vodka. Partaking in a game of limbo always seems like a good idea at the time, though, not so much after the fact. Jason had had accused Alana of breaking the damned thing on purpose because she'd made no secret of hating the garish, oversized vase from the day she moved in with him. The breakage had been an honest, drunken accident. And now that it was fixed, Alana hoped Jason would forgive her and refrain from telling their friends she'd done it subconsciously on purpose – whatever that meant.

While holding the pieces together, Alana was jolted back to the present by three slow, deliberate knocks at the door. *Who knocks at the door like that?* she mused as she made her way across the cream tiled floor to the large oak front door.

"Just coming!" Alana motioned to put the vase down on the hallway table then decided it was more important to keep the join steady.

"Err, I'm really sorry, my hands are full, the door is unlocked though, if you want to push it open?"

The door began to open, slowly.

"I can't let go of this vase you see...."

As the door opened further Alana looked up and right into the eyes of her visitor.

"Oh my..."

The vase fell and smashed into a thousand cerulean shards as Alana's hands flew up to her mouth in disbelief. Slightly different yet intrinsically familiar, the face that greeted her evoked the same reaction it always had, instantly stirring her at the core.

"Kevin?" she whispered as though she'd seen a ghost.

"Larni."

Network of Novels

Factually, all the novels in the 'network of novels' will be in sync, with main characters from one story cropping up as sub characters in another, and sub characters from one story coming into their own in the next. The beauty of this framework is that once you have invested in a character, you never know where you will see them again or what you might learn about them next. While you continue to build layers of knowledge and understanding, you will also find each story to be fresh and unique and with new characters to get to know throughout.

Acknowledgements

Firstly, I would like to thank all the inspirational people who made my time in Sri Lanka so poignant and memorable.
Secondly, thanks to Jules for coming travelling with me at the drop of a hat, and for being so chilled about everything we encountered.
And thirdly, a big thanks to Chris for all his support, technical and otherwise.